a small bite out of Eternity

~

THE

SQUARE

MIRACLES

~

Matthew
Kambic

For more information:
chalkhillpublishing@gmail.com

"*A small bite out of Eternity* plunges a loving young couple into the vast spiritual currents churning behind their cozy world. Cosmic forces, unholy designs and cosmology-rattling miracles unfold in this fast-paced tale woven with humor, wonder and dread. Every turn of the page promises a new surprise in the company of characters drawn with warmth and humanity – even the monsters. Nothing and no one is left unchanged on this riveting journey, including the reader."

Matt Kennedy ~ Veteran Pittsburgh journalist
'Last Voyage of the S.S. Panglossian'

*

"Somewhere between enchanting and gripping, *a small bite out of Eternity* explores ancient beliefs through a contemporary lens. I found it hard to put down, and the ending was unexpected but deeply satisfying."

Lynne Wilkins ~ Musician, singer-songwriter and writer
'When the West Wind Blows'

*

"A page-turning theological adventure, filled with wisdom, humor, and imagination, as lives are turned upside down by metaphysical happenings in a neighborhood park. Beautifully structured, insightful and thrilling, readers are left pondering its provocative implications."

Dyana Wells ~ Author, artist, teacher
'Anchors in the Open Sea' trilogy

*

"An exquisitely crafted story that takes readers on a rollercoaster ride of faith and faithlessness. Matt Kambic delivers a magical, madcap, deeply thought-provoking story that keeps readers guessing if love and humankind's noblest impulses can survive this supreme test. A gratifying tale that is sure to uplift – even those who doubt the impossible."

Ken Gormley ~ President of Duquesne University
and **New York Times** *bestselling author*
'The Heiress of Pittsburgh'

*

"Kambic has penned a tale of enchantment and faith, a love story of sorts to the neighborhood and natural environment he once inhabited. In a narrative that blends a page-turning plot with deep explorations of religion and family, liberally spiced with hints of Hogwartian-styled creatures and the comedic, life-affirming hijinks of *A Midsummer Night's Dream*, *a small bite out of Eternity* offers the reader something new and much needed: a big bite outside of our worried world."

Benjamin Wecht ~ Author, educator, musician
'Cause of Death and Grave Secrets'

This book is dedicated to my oldest brother,
Robert T. Kambic
living a monk's life with
quiet conviction and prayerful faith

About the Park

Frick Park is the largest municipal park in Pittsburgh, Pennsylvania, United States, covering almost 640 acres. The eastern park boundary is Nine Mile Run stream, a formerly heavily polluted watercourse which was restored between 2003 and 2006. Record rainfall and wind damage, contributing to erosion and landslides, was also repaired. The Park has sports facilities, a popular dog run area, and an iconic playground, to go with miles of woodland paths, a recently built environmental center, bike trails and picnic shelters. Shakespeare plays are staged annually in the Park, along with foot races, festivals, and other community events.

Frick Park
Pittsburgh, Pennsylvania

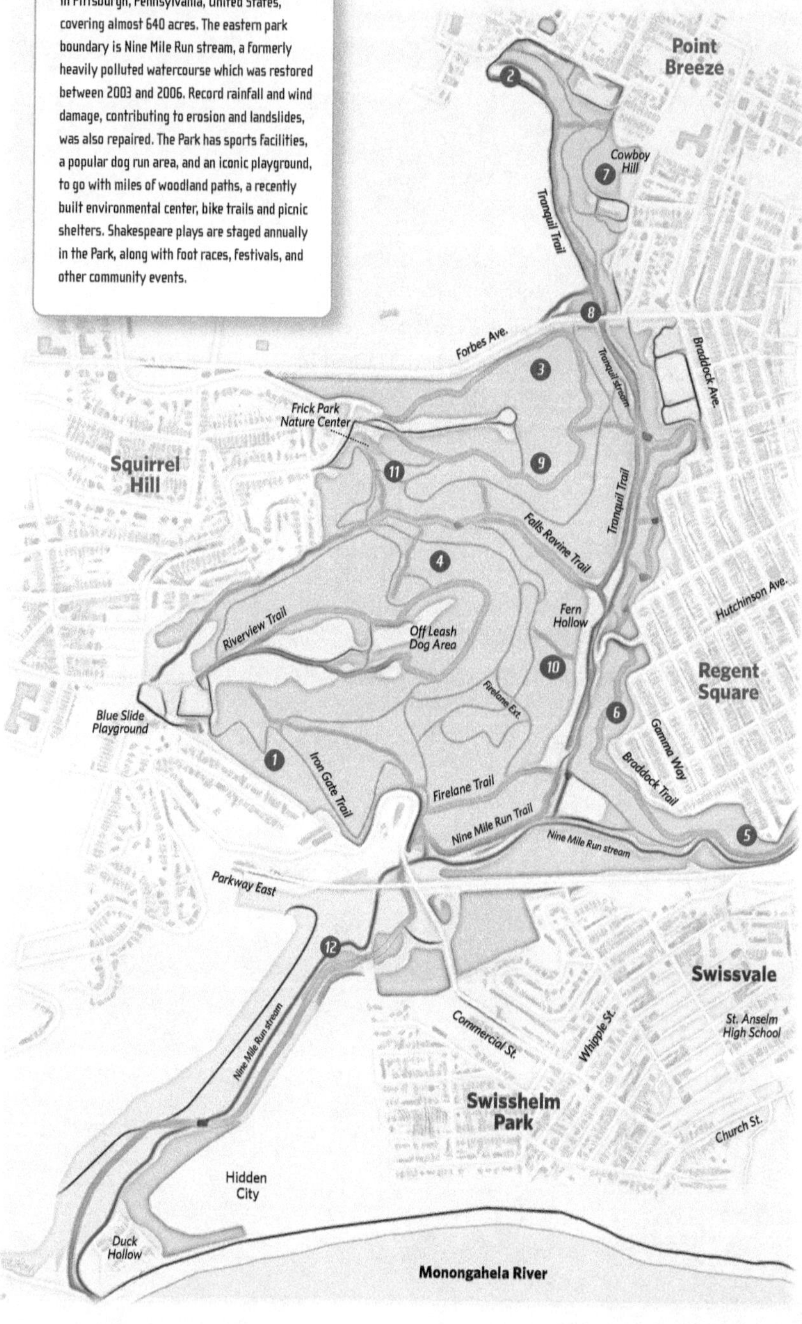

a small bite out of Eternity ~
THE SQUARE MIRACLES

…based on a story many consider to be true…

FRICK PARK, LOCATED in Pittsburgh, Pennsylvania, is an oasis of trees and meadows, quietly-flowing streams, and verdant grassy knolls. Measuring some 640 acres, much of it set in a deep, flattened dell between forested hills rising green up its flanks, it's almost preternaturally hidden from the busy urban neighborhoods of Swisshelm Park, Regent Square and Squirrel Hill that surround it above.

In 2004, record rainfall deluged the Pittsburgh area, with Hurricane Ivan contributing to the city's second highest annual precipitation. On September 17th of that year, six inches of water pelted the region in one day. This single-day record still stands. Besieged by the power of the elements, Frick Park's trails, waterways, and woodlands were dramatically reconfigured. Landforms that had stood for centuries, and longer, were separated from their histories; hillsides slipped away, existing streams were dammed or sunken, and new earth surfaced in both the oft-trod areas and the hidden nooks and crannies of the Park. Nature, with its rejuvenating hand, was pushing up fresh growth, seeding these ruined tracts and transforming broken ground into vigorous plenty. In some areas, where daylight and water had been diverted for untold ages, the sun's long-exiled beams met virgin soil, as generations of cached spring water trickled over newly-emerged stones.

One particular setting, a meandering way up a small hill, past thickets and around a newly-sculpted sandstone overhang, opened into a rounded glade. Tempered with lush grass, and girdled with small white flowers, it appeared as if a gardener might have been at work here, gently orchestrating this arrangement. It was new ground, yet very old ground, resurfacing to the sunbeams and rainfalls it had known eons ago. Along with spry dandelions and a smattering of poison ivy, a small tree had come through the center of the circle, unfurling tender young branches.

A few years later, the tree, slight but sturdy, bloomed with blossoms, and buds, forecasting its fruit.

Now, it was the first day of October.

ONE

'Is there a God?'

'Hell, yeah,' said Abel Green.

Abel didn't utter profanities. *Hell* he could use on a technicality, a destination as much as a swear word. In this instance it carried a certain fitting ring. Something to help nudge his wife's existential deliberations.

Abel and Emma Green were husband and wife, she a biology teacher employed by St. Anselm High School, he a media designer at Carnegie Mellon University. Abel was 27, Emma 28, both born and raised in the area and both relatively content with their station in life. They worked at maintaining a compatible union, broken by the occasional snits and small animosities that plague any human relationship.

Overall, if surveyed, they'd agree they were 'in good shape', 'looking forward to starting a family', 'interested in the news of the day but not driven to distraction by the world's unstable condition', and 'very pleased they lived in Regent Square.' Their red brick and shale-roofed home was a modest two-story dwelling on Gamma Way, one of the tucked-in and sycamore-lined alleyways behind the main thoroughfares of Regent Square. Only a few of the houses had *alley* as opposed to *street* addresses in Regent Square. They were pleased theirs was one of them.

As with many couples, the Greens shared a more specific enjoyment of certain mutual activities. Long walks into Frick Park was one of these, as they were doing at the moment.

'Regardless of what you think and believe, or what anyone thinks and believes, including the Pope,' said Emma Green, 'there might not be a god. Or God, with a capital G.'

It was Saturday. They had woken, peered outside at the orange leaves playing in the dawn's genial light, postponed the morning's domestic tasks, dressed, and left the house. A short detour to the 61B Cafe for hot coffee, then back across a few blocks, trees swaying in welcome, to one of the paths leading down into Fern Hollow. Soon they were strolling under a lovely autumn canopy.

'Check out the beech. Check out the bark.'

Abel reached to run his hand up and down the smooth grey bole of the beech's trunk. They were like pillars carved of granite, and up they went, spreading out, scintillating the air with their finely-wrought, elliptical leaves.

'Of course there's a God. Who made this stuff?'

Emma stooped to find a sassafras shoot. She spied one and lifted it from the soft soil. She broke the root stem back against itself and held it to her face. 'Put your nose on this.'

Abel leaned in for a sniff. 'There's God again. Why would a random universe create a sassafrassian fragrance of such sublimity just for the heck of it. Ask yourself. Seriously.'

'I'm not saying you're wrong. I'm just sayin'.' She smiled at him.

Emma was a slim, handsome woman, Abel observed. Her wavy, pliant red hair and curiously lidded eyes complemented each other. She looked sleepy much of the time. Her eyes were a feint, though. She could go from sedate to amped in a blink of those lids, when set off by certain irksome topics.

He felt he could read her better than she could read herself. He knew it was a questionable concept but held it close, in case it was true. It was the kind of logic that followed when he considered what a 'man's man' might think. He wasn't sure exactly what a 'man's man' was or did, but figured it had to do with things men did uniquely smarter, or better, than women. Otherwise what was the point of categorizing it by gender. But when it came to parsing that concept into the very logic he was hoping to emulate, a more intuitive notion advanced: that women were better at almost everything.

He admired the heart of women. The female disposition anchored in peace and nurturing. They spoke better, they looked better, they perceived things better, they hugged better. Of course not all of them and not all the time. Even Emma had a sarcastic streak. But, to his thinking, females were born with original selflessness. They cared and attended across boundaries that big husky alpha males had no idea even existed. Emma brought this message home whenever he found himself kicking at the morons who held different political views, or rooted for the wrong football team, or cut him off on the highway.

He envied her female heart. He even envied her theological doubt. It was easy for him to buy the whole package of a loving, fair, mostly easy-going God up there – big grey beard and all – who'd welcome them into the friendly skies upon their earthly decamping. His cradle-Catholic upbringing by warm-hearted, good-intentioned, church-going, second-generation immigrant parents was a foundation of faith that kept on providing, even though he practiced less and seldom found time to pray. At times, his wife's half-hearted agnosticism eroded this solidity. At other times, it seemed dangerous, even stupid. And rarely but markedly, all too rational. Emma refused to lend her tack-sharp mind and snarky disposition to the possibility that life on Earth was not all there was. Her doubt glowed healthy. Full of wit. Trendy, even. Maybe she simply wasn't dealing with the Big Questions.

She wasn't saying he was wrong…*'just sayin'.* There she was, standing there, his lovely wife.

'You're just sayin'. You won't be thinking that on your deathbed, will you?' he said.

'I'll say "please let me in wherever cool stuff is happening." I don't want to be bored for eternity.'

Abel looked around, up into the forested ceiling, at the leafy quilt hovering in quiet motion above them. There was a wonderful palette of muted hues to enjoy. They wandered down a few more wooden steps and reached Fern Hollow, where a field of lustrous, green turf unfolded into the distance between the ridges of hemlocks, oaks, maples, and beech. Under the wooded banks were growths of trillium, wild strawberry, cinquefoil, and meadow garlic.

'These groves have fresh shoots. You see them?' He pointed at a few areas that were incongruously greening up. 'There, and there. And up there. It's autumn, when everything should be winding down and retiring before the snow shows up.'

'October's gone green.'

'Only the first of October, of course. Your birthday.'

'I thought you forgot.'

'Unlikely.'

'Ha. You forgot last year.'

'You remembered that I forgot. Not fair,' said Abel.

'It's love and it's war, honey. All's fair.' Emma raised her eyebrows in some sort of pretend wink.

Far away, someone whistled at a barking dog. They left the narrow, open flats of Fern Hollow and turned to saunter up Falls Ravine trail. Usually the trail was busy with Saturday morning walkers; today they were remarkably alone. The warm light, suffused by the multi-colored leaves, cast plaintive, quiet shade over the path and their faces and bodies.

She stretched her arm out over the soil, waving at the dirt.

'Imagine the plants that were cast in shadow all day every day before the big storm hit. Imagine being the dirt, the seeds, waking up one day and there's Mr. Sol. Finally saying hello. And having their first shower.'

'Look up there,' said Abel.

He gestured at a pool of light, flickering – almost pulsating – a way up the bank. It was like a reflection off a surface they couldn't quite discern, behind a hidden fold of land. They looked at each other, and began a short, tricky clamber towards the spot. The ground was thick with brambles and climbers, some apparently still growing with late season vigor, others desiccating as summer wound down, both still a barrier to easy walking.

They heard water, a steady trickle over small stones, then noted what appeared to be outflow from a small spring – maybe newly surfaced since the landscape had been reshaped. The park's waters were considered unsafe (absolutely don't ingest, probably best not to walk through or let your kids play in) due to the urban areas surrounding it. Recent years had shown it was recovering – holding its own – as air, soil and water contaminates all poised patiently for more opportunities to invade. Plastic bottles, junk food wrappers, and discarded beer cans were markers that never quite disappeared. A fresh source of potable water would be a good sign.

Abel stooped to splash fingers in the runnel. 'This might be safe to drink.'

'Don't drink it.'

'Bet it's good.'

'Bet you'll get sick.'

Abel tickled the water a bit more, then rose to continue their hike.

'Where'd it go?' said Emma.

For a moment or two, they lost track of the reflection. It continued to fade in and out, teasingly. Finally, after a too-breathless scramble for what they considered their strapping young state of fitness, they rounded a bend and reached their destination.

Stalks of slender grass blanketed the small dell. White flowers hung their heads in a curiously symmetrical circle around a small apple tree, growing sturdily and with graceful, upthrust branches. Belying its obvious youth, three ripe red apples hung from its branches.

'Hmmm,' murmured Abel. 'This is novel.'

'Strange,' said Emma. 'Hey. Poison ivy. Don't step in it.' Strands of the ivy intermingled with dandelions and other plants not far from the base of the tree. 'Anyway, not that mysterious,' she said. 'Apple trees do grow in Pennsylvania.'

Abel looked up to fathom how the sunlight might be producing the unusual illumination they stood beneath. Several tall conifers were swaying in the understory, opening and closing, permitting the sunlight and then blocking it. Like a soft focus filter, the light that shone in was diffuse and ethereal.

'*Ethereal* – a good word for this,' he said.

'Not sure if this was, maybe, intentionally planted here? Or somebody tossed an apple core up from the trail and the seeds rooted,' she said.

'Be a pretty good toss,' said Abel. He stood on his heels to try to see Falls Ravine, but the hillside folds blocked his view, just as it had blocked theirs from below. 'What kind of apple, you think?'

'Can't tell. Not a crabapple. Should be good to eat.'

Emma steadied one of the branches with her hand, then pulled off one of the apples. She looked at her husband. 'You want a bite?'

'You temptress. Just warned me not to drink the water. Now asking me to chomp down on an unidentified hanging object.'

'Say *apple tree*. A-P-P-L-E. Spell it along with me.'

'Ha ha ha.'

'Pretend I'm Eve. We're in the Garden of Eden. You're Adam.'

'So take your clothes off.'

'Ha ha ha.' Emma looked again at Abel, raised an eyebrow, and set her front teeth into the red skin of the fruit.

The fruit's skin cracked, loudly, as she bit through. She chewed, then swallowed.

'Good.'

She handed the apple to Abel. He bit.

'Very tasty.' A thin trail of juice ran from his mouth, which he wiped away.

'Let's take one of these back to the house and see if we can ID it,' she said. 'I want to know its genus. Probably going to be hard to nail. Nothing really distinctive, shape or color. You have your phone? We can take a photo and reference the leaves and bark.'

'Didn't bring it, according to our mutually-agreed and wise policy of disowning the world and all its bad news when we come down here.'

They shared the rest of the apple, Abel finishing it with a last noisy *chomp*. He turned and flung the core into the bushes above.

'Don't…!'

'What?'

'We should have kept the core,' she said.

'Why?'

'I don't know.'

'Maybe another tree shall sprout. Or Frick's ants will have a welcome feast.'

'Hmmmm,' she said.

'Hmmm?'

'Hmmmm.'

'*What?*' he implored.

'I'm worried for it. Worried for the tree. I want it to grow. And be safe.'

'This is off the beaten path and the only reason we saw it was the glow.' He looked up. The sun and treetops had conspired to cease their work spotlighting the dell. 'Which is gone.' He put his hands behind his head and cracked his neck. 'Why would any one mess with an apple tree?'

'Well. This is like a little garden, right. But there's no one to garden it. Protect it from disease, bugs, rodents, deer – in fact, why haven't the deer and birds chewed this thing up?'

'Don't know. They don't find everything. Do they get poison ivy? Maybe it scares them off.'

'Birds find everything. Worms, too. Squirrels, chipmunks. And worst of all, people.'

Abel knelt to look closely at the two remaining apples, hanging innocently from this small, innocent-looking tree.

'We're sure this was an apple, right?'

'It was – they are – apples,' said Emma.

He took an extra deep breath and reached out to touch the tree's slender trunk.

'So maybe no one else from the animal or human kingdom has stumbled on this hidden orchard with its lone apple tree. Why are you and I beckoned here to see that it is only us who, who…' Abel faltered, unable to say what he meant. Something was out of kilter.

'Not sure we should have chomped this fruit so fast.'

'You okay?' Emma asked.

'Yes. But…'

'But what?'

He walked in a circle around the tree.

'Why are we talking about this tree this way?' he said.

'We're protective of the ecosystem. We care about this park. This is nature. This is growth, and food, and maybe just the joy of stumbling over something grown from dirt and water and air and tastes delicious. Why wouldn't we want to nurture it?'

Emma moved over to kiss him, lightly. He wrapped his arms over her shoulders.

'Because,' he said, 'there's a zillion apple trees growing around these parts, including one we can plunder by walking out our back gate.' He thought he noticed her hands, straddling his neck, were starting to tremble.

'Abel…' Emma pulled away, ran fingers across her brow, lowered her sleepy eyelids, and fainted.

*

She had slumped softly into the middle of the poison ivy. Abel lifted her up, brushed her off, and sat her on a nearby ledge of sandstone.

'Emma. You fainted.'

'I think I did.'

'You Ok?'

'I don't know. I don't usually faint, do I?'

'No. And you landed in the poison ivy. I'm sure it's on me too now. Let's get home and find the pink stuff you put on this, before it spreads. You Ok to walk?'

'It's calamine lotion. It won't stop the reaction. Just helps with the itching.'

He scratched at his wrist. She stretched out her arm. He pulled her up. They took careful steps, down and away from the unsettlingly peculiar dell. They reached Falls Ravine trail and looked back up to where they had come from. It was almost invisible without the orienting glimmer that had led them there. Now it was time to get home and ransack their medicine cabinet for something to stop an eruption from the poison ivy.

TWO

'So what do we think, here?'

Emma lay on their red couch, near a large window that looked out across Gamma Way, where Frick Park's venerable white-trunked sycamores were set like guardians on the crest above Fern Hollow. The sycamore stand carried down the hill; one could peruse both their brawny roots and their leaf-mantled crowns. On the wide sill, two cats, Seren and Dippity, reclined as a single furred entity, occasionally stretching to indicate they were two, and breathing.

Emma pointed at them. 'Cats.'

Abel sat across the room, black-rimmed glasses helping him focus on the book, *Northeastern USA Fruit Trees*. Looks like a studious academic, thought Emma.

'I'm not sure.' He scratched his wrist again, the only spot where the poison ivy had apparently invaded his epidermis. 'Darn this stuff. It better not spread.'

'I think we goofed, eating the apple. I don't feel like I need a doctor, though. I need a psychologist.' said Emma.

'Or a priest.'

'A priest?' Emma lifted herself up by one arm, and brushed back her hair with the other. 'I'm worried about some psychosomatic effect it might be causing. Like I've just gulped down a mug of ethanol. Also *doesn't* feel like that.'

'If we're sick from food poisoning we need to get tested. Get to the hospital. You fainted up there.'

'Don't we have any doctor friends we can consult? I feel like a fool,' said Emma. 'Why did you say *priest*?'

'Because something's going on.'

'What do you think this is?'

'I don't know.' Abel exhaled, forcefully, as if trying to purge his body from whatever had happened to them down in the park. 'I don't feel like anything is life-threatening. That we die. Have our minds been trespassed? Feeling very very very *off*.'

'Same here,' said Emma. 'We'd better check in with somebody besides Google. And get a sample off that tree. One of those two remaining apples.'

'You think we should head back?'

'You don't think so.'

'You stay here. I'll get the apples,' Abel said.

Emma shook her head. 'Better to go together. I don't like being alone after fainting. I feel Ok now, but still. And I don't like you wandering down into the park alone, either, at least right now, with all this stuff…ethereal stuff, as you noted, manifesting.'

'Manifesting is a big word. So Ok.'

She smiled. 'It's late afternoon, no more sun in Falls Ravine, all in shadow. Not sure we'd find it.'

'Only a hundred feet up the hillside. If we can't find it we're either stupid or… exceptionally stupid.'

Emma sat up straight and stared at the cats. 'Mobile sculpture that you feed and for which you maintain a litter box,' she murmured. The two cats shuffled their furry selves into a new aspect. She gathered herself to stand, adding a fretful sigh.

'Ok, this shouldn't take long. Let's get the sample and get back here and maybe I'll call Sheila, she's a nurse, and we'll see what she thinks. We're not having trouble breathing, we don't have heart palpitations, we're not hallucinating…'

Abel walked over to lock their windows.

'I don't know. We're *different.*'

*   *   *

They dressed for the chill that the October afternoon was dipping towards. Unnerved, they re-entered their favorite haunt, a place that had gifted them with numinous bounty in their years adjacent to it. Where they could count on nature's sublime handouts: the healthy exercising through their walks, the happenstance meetings with acquaintances, the abundance of animal and plant life. Frick Park was a reservoir for spirit, mind and body.

Now, though, it seemed altered, like a threatening chess move had just been discharged, and they were suddenly pawns. At the same time, their fears and suspicions felt ludicrous. Up and down. Down and up. They could identify no precedent for their current state. Other than what was, now wasn't. The skies darkened as they dropped into the hollow, with autumn's earlier sunsets eroding summer's daylight.

'There must be rain coming in. I didn't see it in the forecast, did you?' asked Abel.

She shook her head. 'Didn't. Dark much sooner than last weekend. Did you bring a flashlight?'

'No. We'll never find it. Should go home. Gonna get soaked.'

A flash of curious, greenish lightning heralded a coming weather front.

'And I'm going to get poison ivy. Let's get the heck out of here,' said Emma.

*   *   *

Up above Falls Ravine trail, busy in the night's darkness, a grey squirrel sniffed around in search of nuts and seeds to hoard for the coming winter. The squirrel's Frick Park diet was steady, if a bit dull. Then lo and behold, it found an apple core. Not to be saved, this dainty. The core was gone, chewed and swallowed, in almost no time at all.

*　　*　　*

Home again, Abel and Emma were sharing a bottle of sparkling Sauvignon Blanc. 'Alright now. Be open. Your mind is suffused with the knowledge of good and evil,' said Abel.

'Already possess that. I teach at a Catholic high school.'

'The Garden of Eden. The Apple Tree of Knowledge. You were tempted, and I bit.' They smiled, and clinked their glasses together, letting the wine flavor the moment. He poked her in the ribs. 'Those extra ribs are Adam's, you know.'

She raised her glass again. 'Nothing but excess weight to haul around.'

'Ha. *Touché,*' he said. 'So tomorrow we go down and take pictures and see if everything looks the same,' he said. '*Feels* the same, I mean.'

'We wear boots and tuck in socks for the poison ivy and bring back the other two apples and, what else can we do? Do we bring anybody?'

'Not yet, not just yet.' Abel looked at her. 'Were we called up there to that spot?'

'That's insane.'

'I know. Just had to ask.' He swallowed another mouthful of the wine. 'You feeling the *thing*. Maybe we're just feeling the Sauvignon.'

'It's like, uhmm. What's it like? Anything familiar?'

'How about, ummm, a movie that catches you by the throat? Book so good you want to be inside it. Sermon that up-ends your soul. That's my first lousy attempt to describe this. They all sound dumb. And wrong.'

'This seems less like a reaction, more like insight. You don't get insights from food. From drugs, maybe. Were the apples spiked?'

'You're the biologist. Is it possible some ingredient, some weird chemistry, was brought up through the soil, with the water, into the apple?'

'Not likely,' said Emma. 'Anyway, drugs and chemistry may impart enlightenment or some sort of doorway to new perception, but they aren't usually off-loading *new* information. New facts, that is. Not hallucinogenic fictions that seem like facts but prove not to be. Is that the right word for what we feel, or think, is occurring?'

'I'll take a leap and you can tell me how stupid this sounds. We're getting fed from our conscious and subconscious memories, our lives' past sensory input, from birth to now, opening lockers in our mental storehouse, if you will. What else?' Abel scratched at the back of his head.

He looked at her. 'We seem to be able to substantiate that these insights are legitimate – ratifiable. That's ridiculous. Completely.'

'We're confused. It's Ok.' She bit at the tip of her thumb. 'Let's step back. Stop trying to be scientific or logical. What are we *feeling*?'

'Like someone drilled a hole in the top of my head and has been pouring upgrades in through a funnel. Like my IQ has ticked over. Like I might understand those math problems that always stumped me. Or like there's a spigot opened in my synapses that was locked off, now unblocked. Insights rolling in free of charge, no work, no effort to attain them.'

'Still seems like the effect from drugs,' Emma said. 'You *sound* the same. I mean, your voice and manner of speaking sound the way you sounded before you bit the apple. But I agree. I feel like the parameters of what I can know have expanded. Like there's unprecedented material at hand. Knowledge percolating inside my head, like bubbles, dispersing synaptically, containing data, that I was either exposed to…or my apple-tainted brain is now running background algorithms on everything I've ever glimpsed – ever taken in – from books, teachers, experience, TV, about anything and everything, from how to care for infants to quantum mechanics to the friggin' Bible.'

'Don't say *friggin'* Bible, wife. Please.'

He stood up and looked out the window. Rows of streetlights glimmered in the brooding darkness.

'It's more than that: more than some IQ jump. As if we can *use* information now in new ways. Calculate. Connect things. See past old constraints.'

'Let's experiment. Get proof of concept,' said Emma.

'That's good. We can start with some subject that's confounded us.'

'Math for you.'

'Cooking for you.' Abel turned away from the window to smile at her. 'Kidding. Then again, if you *can* tap into a newfound culinary expertise, who would I be to complain.' He took another swig of wine, emptying his glass. 'Or maybe we wait til we're off this alcohol. Since we sound like we are off our rockers.'

He picked up the empty wine bottle and headed towards the kitchen and the glass recycling bin. On the way, he reached to tousle Emma's hair. 'And lest we forget, Happy Birthday…'

*　　*　　*

The squirrel was convulsing; retching and twitching, scattering the rotting leaves and stirring the night's other active creatures into vigilance. Something in the apple core didn't agree with it. Finally, the squirrel lay still, unconscious, its animal breaths a solemn rasp. In the next few hours of the night, its fur transmuted from light grey to Black.

THREE

SUNDAY MORNING. GIDEON Moss had another day away from the school he loathed. The school where he was Principal: St. Anselm Catholic High School. He'd have thanked God, but there was no God in sight to thank. So he thanked himself for being clever enough to stick with it, even as it pained him to front up as a believer. The nuns who taught there pretended not to see through his ruse. But the lay teachers were cool, and the times were lenient.

Moss was middle-aged, but didn't hold with any mid-life crisis tropes. Much of his adult existence had been a steady reign of low-profile suffering, wasted calendar days, and indistinct horizons where hope was methodically punctured. He weighed slightly more than he'd have liked, but his skinny legs compensated for his puffed belly. His hair was thick and black, no grey at all, and he thought his face was passably agreeable. But it was all a hoax, or farce, in the end. His particular journey had been throttled before he had half an idea of what life was supposed to be, could be, for him. That woman. That party. *That* was *that*.

Outside, it was overcast, as he preferred. Sunny mornings and blue skies reminded him that there was some form of beauty and joy waxing in the world. He couldn't reach it. It had been locked away when he'd *depersonalized* many decades ago.

Depersonalization – along with its doppelganger twin, *derealization* – were odd, incurable, often un-diagnosable psychological conditions that both stymied the professional ranks of would-be curers and appeared more and more frequently across every demographic. He'd 'caught it' as a young adult, just nineteen, after an evening of enjoying a single, high-quality joint of marijuana. *'One toke over the line, sweet Jesus…'* the song sang. He wasn't a regular imbiber, didn't do drugs, wasn't some hip cat. A beer once in a while, a joint or two now and then. Stayed far away from anything wilder. Cocaine, mushrooms, LSD, no way.

It was the summer between high school and college. Those fabulous months when the fonk of high school washes off your skin and the promise of your future gleams off the fenders of cool cars and beckons from the smile of every girl. Girls who were transitioning into a new edition he was pleased to acknowledge: *women.*

He was at a party, and it was rockin'. The room was filled with pretty people. Instrumental jazz rose in a bassy beat from under the floorboards, sent up from another party one floor below. The woman sat down next to him on the beat-up couch. She elbowed him, then handed him the joint. 'Thanks.' Open-mouthed, she ran her hands up the front of her neck, as if preparing her body for some next big adventure. He pulled in several good hits from the joint, then handed it back to her. 'Thanks.' She lowered her head and stared at him. 'You want something else. Something *good?*' He shook his anesthetized head. She dared him, moved her eyes around as if she was probing his face for a weakness, '…try this, this little yellow pill, you'll fly like a yellow birdie…' 'Don't want to fly like a yellow birdie,' he'd said. He could see (the more he'd smoked the more obvious it was) she wanted him, as the marijuana took their story into wondrous places.

She got up, went into the kitchen, and *he* never came back.

Morning arrived as a wan, other-worldly rejig of what had been reality. Some experiential exoskeleton had fastened itself tightly, like a strait-jacketed cloak, to his faculties.

Hard to this day to describe in language that even came close to making people understand, but he tried. Like a milky glass wall had been put up between his past way of experiencing the world and this new, awful, twilight-zone present. And then, also, and almost worse, a slowly-grasped but immutable realization that the doorway, any doorway, back into that former life and that specific, Gideon Moss way of experiencing existence, was locked away. Gone. Forever.

The *derealized* Moss (once he stumbled on the professional diagnosis years later he felt *derealized* fit his condition more accurately than *depersonalized*) looked, sounded, and even acted remarkably similar to the 'before derealization' Moss. Friends, family, future companions, and the mother of his only child, Ray (or 'Razor' as he was known), would empathize as best they could with his plight. But never understand it. *I wish I had cancer* he thought at one juncture. At least people would get it. Can't say that out loud, though.

The negative aspects of his condition were numerous and often evolved into worse. One near the top was the inability to feel any joy at past joyful instances. Present and future joys were non-starters. But his memories with his family, growing up, with his small successes in school, in sports, with females, and other youthful recollections; why couldn't he recall those, and find some light in this house of horror? No. The memories, as clear as ever, were devoid of the sentiments they used to evoke. Now worse, because he *knew* what these memories used to convey. *Heartstrings*, society troped it. His, unstrung.

So this particular grey-cloud weekend morning was one more soft parade into anhedonia; another emotionless, soulless, crawl into another soulless day. A single critical acknowledgment kept him going: if he gave up, if he *died*, there was no chance of anything. He'd either be – if there was no God – voided out, or – if there was a God, a *decent* God – standing trial for the funk he was in and the various indulgences he'd plied looking for anything worth anything.

The amusing part, and it made him smile grimly, was how he'd managed to become principal of a Catholic high school. He got his degree from St. Francis University, a Franciscan-run college in Loretto, PA, its campus situated in the mountains an hour or so east of Pittsburgh. The wooded school grounds could pass for an American Hogwarts. Stonework, water courses, fir trees, walking paths, shaded co-ed dormitories. Freshman year, he'd joined a fraternity. Hazing, drinking, studying, field hockey. What should have been at least passably enjoyable, was not. The specter of derealization never lifted. The universe, a sick joke.

He made enough frat-brother acquaintances and did well enough academically despite the killing fields in his heart and head. Completed a B.S. in political science. One of his graduating frat brothers headed into the seminary. Ended up as a parish priest in Swissvale and contacted Moss when the high school needed a new history teacher. Moss's political science credential would suffice – standard Catholic Diocese policy. Many of the teaching Sisters of Charity did not have degrees. In the end, he got the job, and became principal when Sr. Marie passed away suddenly at 48.

He blew out a harsh breath.

'Gotta get up.'

He brushed his teeth, spat into the sink, watched it drain. He washed and dressed with no urgency, then wandered past the closed door where Razor should still be sleeping. Unless his teen-age son had stayed the night elsewhere. He was a good kid. Gideon loved him. Or at least, staged his life as a parent to represent the love and care he knew a child should have. Even if his own life was ultimately a bust, there was no reason to shovel the truth onto Razor. He'd find out.

So this morning… what was a good way to waste it? Stretch his legs, get away from the kid for a while, try not to think about thinking.

Frick Park was a fairly long walk, down Commercial Street, then off to the right under the great concrete Parkway East bridge. A car had plummeted from the overpass a few months ago, crushing the driver when it hit bottom and reminding everyone how far the drop was. Maybe he'd find the spot where they'd dragged the wreck away. See if there was blood on any of the gravel.

He called out to his son. 'I'm heading down to the park. Back in a couple hours.'

'Yeah, Ok…' came the mumbled reply.

Moss proceeded down along the concrete sidewalk that abutted Commercial Street. The sidewalk ended abruptly near the bridge. There was no sign of the wreck. No sign of life. No sign of death.

He crossed the road to the park perimeter. Below him, large cement culverts channeled rainwater, mixed with whatever urban sewage had spilled into it, away from the park, down between the slag dumps, and into the Monongahela River.

But Frick Park was, as usual, a showcase – autumnal glory gamboling from tree to tree, the canopy a living work of art daubed in every classic fall hue. He hated it, as a matter of course. He ducked past the Nine Mile Run trail entrance sign and strode forward, already despairing that the woods might provide an inkling of something for his empty heart. He headed for the familiar Falls Ravine trail, but changed his mind. There was another path that ran up the slope and carried on above Falls Ravine. Firelane Extension, it was called. From there, you could look down and spy other walkers and amuse your wounded psyche with fictions about who they were and how sorry *their* lives probably were.

*　*　*

Abel and Emma Green woke up, stirring in the cool air that wafted through their bedroom window screen. It was Sunday morning. Abel pulled the alarm clock closer to his eyes and squinted. 'Guess I'm missing Mass again. Your fault,' he said.

'Ha.'

'I'll say a prayer in lieu of attending. Dear God, make my wife want to go to Mass with me as I am lazy and do not wish to rise on Sunday mornings.'

'Sounds really sincere.'

'God's Ok with it.'

'She told you, huh.'

'*He*, remember. He.' Abel gently poked her in the back. 'Ok, maybe She. How about 'It', with a capital 'I'?'

'That could work.' Emma rolled to stretch against him. 'You dream?'

'No.'

'I thought I dreamt something. Green colored fire, or something. It's gone.'

'Come here.'

'I'm getting up.'

'Just a hug,' he pleaded.

She moved towards him. They tucked in, pulled themselves close, wrapped legs over legs and sent arms and hands in pursuit of favorite places. 'We should get down into the park, lover,' said Emma. Abel applied one last squeeze and rolled over to sit up.

'And so we shall,' he said. He looked at his wrist. 'Hey, did I give you poison ivy?'

'Don't think so.'

'Good. Now get up, you wily temptress…'

Emma reached to slap at her husband, who escaped and headed for the shower.

The day was overcast, with short squalls of light rain splattering against the windows. They had coffee 'in', the walk to the cafe abandoned due to laziness and the weather. She engineered a carefully-brewed espresso roast. His, drizzled into a cardboard cup, a pod-coffee-brew.

'Let's take a bag for the apples,' he said.

'Two apples. Don't need no bag.'

'Wear a poncho.'

'I'll take my umbrella,' said Emma. 'You can wear your ripped poncho. The one that makes you look like a denizen from the house of doom.'

'You're goofy.'

'You're a misogynistic mystic.'

'That. Makes little sense.'

'Since when did sense matter. We're married. That's the end of the story.'

'That's the beginning!' said Abel, wearing a sly grin.

'Hmmm. Let's get out the door before some agent from the dark side finds our tree and plunders it.'

Emma loved her husband. That said, there was some reserve in her she could never quite identify. People called them "soulmates". No such animal. He was a trustworthy partner, would make a good father, had no hair on his chest. She couldn't articulate what she didn't like.

Now they were sharing something that felt both a binding link and a disturbing, potential rupture. She thought, contrary to last night, they were avoiding a discussion of the strange notions and cognitive riffs that were playing around in their cerebellums. What in God's name – a god she wasn't sure existed – was happening? And how would they explain it to a trusted friend or family member without sounding gonzo.

She looked down, noted, again, her hand quivering, and slapped it.

*   *   *

Gideon Moss's eyes were downcast as he trod up the trail. He passed a few other Sunday morning walkers. Too many. Didn't want conversation, or fake-happy hellos.

He changed direction to follow another trail option, a seldom-used, unsigned side trail off Firelane Extension. Used by mountain bikers when less muddy, it should be empty today, with the showers. Now it rained harder. He was getting wet. His walking shoes were supposed to handle slick surfaces, but the treads had worn smooth. He slipped, and toppled, and then (couldn't believe it even as it happened) he, Mr. Gideon Moss, the Principal of Saint Anselm High School, 53 years old, and not usually a muddy wreck when out in public, rolled headfirst over a short, slippery slope, and landed with a pathetic *thrump* in the middle of a patch of ivy.

'Christ. I should just end it all now…'

He sat up. Wiped the dirt and dreck from his face. Moved his hand to steady himself. Saw his hand was smack in the middle of poison ivy. Rose on his wet knees. Held his face up to the rainfall. Felt his sock getting damp. Noticed one of his shoes was no longer on his foot. There was his shoe. Against a small apple tree, where two red apples hung ingloriously.

'This is what I get for taking in bliss-fucked nature.'

He pulled at one of the apples, which resisted his efforts to free it from the tree. He twisted the stem til it gave way. Stared at the apple for a moment, then took a large bite.

*   *   *

Abel and Emma ran under the trees and sheltered as the cloudburst rained down.

'This is kind of ridiculous,' said Abel.

'Just wet, husband. Water won't kill you, unless you're planning to drown.'

'I should have worn that poncho you made fun of.'

'I should have brought that umbrella.'

They noted other hikers jogging towards the Fern Hollow lower parking lot, and heard cars being started.

'We got the place to ourselves again. Let's find the tree,' said Emma.

Not quite drenched, they retraced their steps from yesterday.

'Up there? Yes, up there,' said Emma.

'You sure?'

'Course not.'

'Then let's go.'

*   *   *

Moss had fainted, and was slowly coming to, when he heard voices.

'I'm going to burn down the Frick Nature Center,' he said aloud.

Two people came around the bend into the hidden, water-logged glade where he lay slumped, muddy and pathetic.

'Gideon!'

It was one of the teachers from his high school. What was her name… Green. Emma Green.

'Gideon. Are you hurt?' she asked, leaning over him, reaching a hand out to help.

'I'm wet…lost my shoe. I'm Ok.' As he struggled to stand up, his foot nudged the half-eaten apple down the incline. Abel stopped it with his boot.

'It's me – Emma. Are you sure…'

'Yeah, Emma. Thanks. I'm just a mess. Nothing broken. Fell down from the trail above –' Moss twisted his head and pointed up the hill. Furrows from his plummet scored the slope. A roll of thunder rumbled somewhere off to the west.

'You bite the apple?' asked Abel, who picked up the fruit and gave it a little shake. Moss said nothing. He wasn't sure he'd bitten it. His mind was fogged, and he was embarrassed and wanted no part of the Greens.

'Can you help me… *ahh*…find my other shoe. I'm going home. Need a shower.'

'Sure,' said Emma. 'You've met Abel, I think, my husband.'

'Some faculty reception, I'm sure, yes,' said Moss.

'Here's your shoe,' said Abel, handing him the mud-caked footwear. Moss took it and slid it over his slimed sock, then stood.

'I was wondering if you bit the apple?' asked Abel, again.

'What the hell, man?'

The rain was picking up again. Emma stepped in front of her husband. 'Sorry, Gideon, sorry,' said Emma. 'You sure we can't help you? You can walk up to our place – it's closer than yours I think. We can drive you home.'

'Nah. No. I'll follow you down to the main trail. Sure as hell won't climb back up there.' He gestured with his thumb over his shoulder.

'Sure,' said Emma. The three of them began working their way cautiously back down to Falls Ravine. They reached the trail just as a sonic crack of thunder split the air. They all cowered.

'I'm heading back to Commercial Street. See you in school tomorrow,' shouted Moss. He trotted away, sodden and spattered, holding his jacket over his already soaked head.

BOOM..*!* Another bolt lit up the sky and split their ears.

'Let's boogie, Emma,' said Abel. They raced across Fern Hollow and mounted the wooden staircase towards Gamma Way.

BOOM.*!*

*   *   *

'Did you notice?' asked Emma. They had reached the safe haven of their side-porch, where the roof overhang blocked the rain. The watery deluge continued, blitzed with flashes of the vaguely green-hued lighting, and now slashing winds.

'I know. The third apple's gone. Let's get inside.'

The entered through their side door, and quickly closed it.

'God that is a fine storm,' said Emma. They removed their water-logged jackets and soggy shoes. Emma shook her head, showering Abel's face with water from her hair.

'Do that again and there'll be trouble,' he said. She did. Her grabbed her by the waist, pulled her in. They kissed. 'I suggest you get out of those wet clothes and into something more comfortable.'

'More comfortable for whom: you or moi?'

'You'll catch cold.'

BOOM*!*

FOUR

In the kitchen, Emma put a kettle of water on the gas burner, and rummaged through their large collection of teas.

'What is it about tea, at a time like this, that makes some kind of strange sense,' said Abel.

'You want coffee? Plug in your pod-maker 2000.'

'Tea, tea, tea. With ginger, lemon, and honey…and honey…'

She threw him a big fake grin. 'I get it. You can shut up.'

They sat together on their wide couch and sipped the hot brew. Moss's half-chewed apple sat on a plate in the middle of the glass coffee table.

'He bit the apple. He bit *this* apple,' said Abel.

'Wonder if he's feeling it.'

'He said something, just before he saw us. Did you hear it?'

'About the Nature Center. I'm going to *blank* the Frick Nature Center.'

'Whatever he said, can't blame him if he got the same dose we're dealing with,' said Abel.

'What *are* we dealing with?' asked Emma. 'Where do we go with this?'

'I think…first, I think we need to do something about the tree itself.

It's exposed – you said it. Anyone can get up there and do whatever to it.'

'And there's the other apple, the third apple, missing.'

'Possibly eaten,' said Abel. He ran a hand over his cheek. 'Should we level with Moss? Start a *Bite* club?'

'Not yet. We don't know what we're into. No point widening the conspiracy. Could all be fantasy.' Emma bowed her head and rubbed her hands over her face.

She looked up, a cold stare. 'Are we sure something else isn't happening here? Schizophrenia. Alien abduction. Twin simultaneous brain tumors. You and I cannot take this on as truth – your intimation that we're receiving a gift from your so-called heaven. I'll be enrolling at Western Psych if we keep down this path.'

Abel stretched and stood up. 'I wish I had a clue.'

'I don't know about you, but I'm going to see a doctor. And a psychologist, if I can find one.'

'I'm going to talk to Father Jack.'

*   *   *

The rain changed to a light drizzle. Abel opened his umbrella, stepped off the porch, and headed to Braddock Ave., a main thoroughfare that bisected the local neighborhoods. It was busy, as usual, with fume-y buses, oversized SUV's, and walkers not wanting to waste their weekends because of the rain. He wasn't at all sure about visiting Father Jack, unbidden and unannounced, but needed to escape the house and shake his head a bit. The whole thing was dreamily pathetic.

His wise, science-savvy wife was not wrong in her suggestion they may have somehow been chemically-induced, in a manner which led to far-fetched mental ramblings. The problem, he believed – and she seemed to feel this also – was that in their hearts they were suspecting it could all be real. Really real; as in the tree was The Tree and the apples were The Apples. Thus he wanted to broach, in a general, non-self-incriminating way, to Father Jack, that some spiritual affair was afoot not only in their vicinity, but *inside them!* Good God. A 'yes' to all of it opened the gateway to more than he could imagine, desire, or contemplate. The flip side was that it was the Holy Grail ~ a 'real-time-real-life' confirmation that God (or Something Awfully Big) actually existed, a definitive elixir for human faith, the blessing of blessings.

Walking towards St. Anselm Church and being in proximity to Father Jack was a way to alleviate this combination of dread and being struck dumb. He looked up. Grey clouds promenaded past, wholly unconcerned. A reminder. *All shall be well and all shall be well and all manner of thing shall be well.*

*   *   *

Emma felt ill. Possibly needed to throw up. Opened a window and let the fresh, rain-washed air soothe into their living room. Seren rose, stretched, and nosed silently out onto the porch. Dippity scoffed with a yawn and went back to his slumber.

Could this really be some metaphysical event. Happening just over the hill, and possibly inside their digestive tracks? No, please, really. She buried her head deep into the corner of their couch.

*   *   *

Gideon Moss hobbled into the foyer of their home and kicked off his wet shoes.

'That you?' came a voice from upstairs.

'Yes.'

He moved to the kitchen and sat, heavily. The clock over the stove read 12:02. He harnessed a breath to yell. 'Get up, Razor. It's past noon. We need to get groceries, and you need to finish raking. The leaves are getting into those basement window wells. We don't need that wood to rot.'

'*Tiiiired…*' came a moan.

'Well, get up anyway.'

There were shuffling noises from the second floor, and, eventually, the sound of the bathroom door shutting.

Moss had no idea what to do next. His head seemed to be tugging his thoughts in a weird direction. And he again mouthed out loud the phrase he'd said at the tree. 'I'm going to burn down the Frick Nature Center.' He stood up and wandered to the kitchen sink, where he splashed his face with cold water. At least he wasn't, so far, itching with poison ivy symptoms.

Razor bounced down the stairs and into the kitchen. He grabbed a milk carton from the fridge, pulled a box of cereal from the shelf, and sat down across from his father. He filled a bowl and stuffed a sloppy spoonful of Chocolate Crunchies into his mouth. Then looked up. 'What the heck happened to you?'

'I fell. In the mud. Slipped in the rain on the stupid muddy trail. And of course some teacher from the school had to show up and see me wallowing in slop.'

'Good for you, pops. That'll keep you humble, eh? What were you mumbling about The Frick Nature Center?'

'I didn't mumble about the Frick Nature Center.'

'Sounded like it. I'm going to *blankety-blank* the Nature Center. Are you planning to volunteer up there? What's the gig?'

'Nothing. Do the dishes. I'm going to take a shower. Then we'll go up to Giant Eagle and get some food.'

*   *   *

The Black Squirrel scoured the path ahead with keen eyes.

It held the apple – the last one that had hung on the tree – in its teeth by the stem, careful to avoid breaking the skin. A full, ripe apple, it weighed more than the Squirrel should be able to manage: some newly enhanced strength provided. The Squirrel had taken it while the human lay nearby, unconscious; a fateful moment as this apple had been the tree's last fruit.

Had the human stirred, there might have been an encounter. The animal might have had to bite the human. Biting the human would have satisfied a strange non-instinctive urge.

The Black Squirrel fidgeted, wheeling its head and field of vision in manic bursts, keeping an eye out for intruders who might try to steal the fruit. It darted from the darker underbrush to the next darker underbrush, slowly making its way west, up the hillside, in the general direction of the wooden structure that would have to burn to release the apple's generative properties.

*　　*　　*

'So, Father Jack, why does the original Apple Tree from the original Garden Of Eden decide to show up now, in our own Frick Park?' Abel could hear himself asking this question, and imagine Father Jack's amused, humoring eyes. He walked down McClure, passing the rectory twice. The morning Masses were all done, so there wouldn't be parishioners swarming out to question his curious behavior. He struggled to bring himself to the point where he could at least knock on the rectory door. One more deep breath. He crossed the street, proceeded to the rectory entrance, and rang the bell.

A young lady opened the door, and smiled. 'Hello.'

'Is Father Jack in?'

'Sunday afternoon he golfs with his pals. A couple Protestant ministers.'

'Ahh. Doing the Lord's work beating those heretics.' An interior grimace at his attempt at humor rose like bile in his throat.

'Father Jerome might be upstairs. I can see if he's napping.'

'Ahh…no. That's alright. I wanted to see Jack.'

'Shall I tell him who stopped?'

'No, thanks. I'll phone and set something up. Yeah. Thanks again.'

'Ok. Have a peaceful afternoon.' She smiled and gently closed the door.

FIVE

LARS PATTON WAS St. Anselm High School's second best science academic. (Some senior dude named Norman Armstrong was 'first best'; nerd-athlete, class president, a busy fellow and a busy body. Lars couldn't wait to see Armstrong don the cap and gown and get the heck out of his scholastic way.) The school maintained a jaundiced eye concerning Lars' penchant for home-based experiments with semi-illicit, volatile reactives (known about 'through channels'). That said, the faculty largely recognized young Mr. Patton was gifted. They provided as much leeway as they could, balancing his scientific fervor with the need to keep him from accidentally blowing up the school.

He lived in Regent Square, and on a given night, you might find him down in Fern Hollow testing another custom mixture of combustible solids. Several decent-sized divots in the flat grass area used for youth soccer were markers for both failed and successful studies in these oh-so-diverting disciplines.

Monday mornings were generally *jacked* (as he put it). School. Just not his thing. A school bus flat tire wouldn't hurt. *How about it, Monday?*

He was a sophomore. As he admitted, most of the teachers (many of them nuns) weren't half bad, but as with many high schools of the Catholic persuasion, St. Anselm lacked the funding and thus facilities to outfit a decent science lab. Sr. Saint Basil, despite her age, was a wise-cracking good chemistry teacher. (Barb Castonnovi suspected Sister Basil was around 75, but no one was really sure since she, as with the others in her order, wore the traditional Sisters of Charity habit that, except for their faces, disguised most of their physical attributes.) She made up for the glum, pathetically ill-equipped 'science classroom' with her withering social commentary and spikes of outrage at the hems some of the girls dared to retro-raise on their uniform skirts. Her science was sound. She liked Einstein but thought Hawking was over-rated.

Lars' home basement lab was the better place to think big, and wide, and boldly go where students his age had not gone before, nor were supposed to. Before heading out to catch the bus, he often took a short minute to open the basement door, switch on the lights, and take in the mess of his *H*eadquarters for *U*niversal e*X*ploration (HUX). Chemicals, tubes, Bunsen burners, a small kiln, scrap metals, tools of every ilk, oily rags, spray paint caps junked up with screws, batteries, and other paraphernalia; all accumulated precisely for the kind of chaos he preferred as he dabbled.

His parents had even installed an overhead exhaust fan, ostensibly so he and they and his sister Astrid wouldn't perish from unidentifiable fumes emanating from the HUX depths. His Dad had passed away three years ago, suddenly, an accident at work where he was a machinist. The family had plugged along, untethered from whatever a normal life in a friendly middle-class neighborhood entailed, clutching at ways to heal. Time fooled them into thinking things were better. Eventually, they fooled time and things *were* better. Dad would have wanted them to thrive. With his father gone, his mom was his biggest patron. Maybe she didn't care as much any more about life and death. She smoked cigarettes, which he thought bold.

'Go catch the bus, Lars. I'm not driving you up,' his mother stated.

'I'm gone.'

On the bus, he got out one of many small colored notebooks he used to keep track of the various sectors of exploration HUX was investigating. The green notebook, in which he wrote with a green pen, probed biology, including local manifestations of anything he found compelling, and especially, anything out of the ordinary. In Regent Square, out of the ordinary was ordinarily someone seeing the big snapping turtle that supposedly lived over by the cemetery, across Forbes Ave. Or the weird purple spotted-wing lantern fly bugs that had invaded the Northeastern USA, and were climbing trees in Frick Park, to the horror of environmentalists and the delight of those who appreciated cool aesthetics in their invasive species.

But here was the thing.

Something was going on down in Fern Hollow.

He'd been down there over the weekend with one of his co-conspirators, Dixon, and *ordinary* had sustained a notable crack. There were blossoms forming on some of the smaller undergrowth, despite it being October. Weird but not cataclysmic. Most curious, though, was immediately after he'd caught a brief look at a squirrel. A *black* squirrel. The species was known, a mutation spawned when the Eastern Gray squirrel and the Fox squirrel mated. Concealment and thermoregulation were advantages of the dark coloring.

Here was the thing – this particular creature had done something to him. The fleeting glimpse had made him feel something like light-headed, sort of, but more like *weird*-headed. It was just a squirrel. Not a specter. Why'd it feel so creepazoid? In Celtic folklore, black squirrels were associated with magic, occult knowledge, and the otherworld. Creepazoid.

He mused out the bus window as they headed down McClure. Students grappled with their backpacks and books preparing to exit the vehicle. 'Probably something in that enchilada I had from Taco Bell,' he said out loud. The bus stopped in front of the school. A girl in the seat across stood up, shook her head at him, and exited.

*　　*　　*

Emma had called in 'un-well' on Monday morning. She didn't want to face a classroom full of teenagers, didn't want to cross paths with Gideon Moss, and didn't want to do anything, really, except hold a cat. Both were reluctant to go with the program: Seren and Dippity had launched themselves out the side door after breakfast. Abel had bicycled off to the Carnegie Mellon campus.

Their night in bed together had not been restful, punctuated at 3:00 a.m.-ish by a car alarm going off somewhere down the alley.

'I'll try to get home early,' Abel had yawned. 'We'll draw up possibles. On paper.'

She thought that made sense, if nothing else did. She grabbed a couple blank sheets from their printer, sat on the couch, and jotted down some thoughts.

> *~ is this <u>the</u> Tree*
> *~ why would we even think this?*
> *~ should not have eaten apple*
> *~ talk to Moss?*
> *~ apple dissection*
> *~ hope apple contains jive thing that explains everything…!*

She stared at her list and spoke out loud.

'See doctor. See psychologist.'

She rolled on her back and stared at the ceiling.

'Not a priest.'

*   *   *

Despite the lack of sleep and curious events at hand, Abel found his concentration at work keen enough. He poured himself into the day's website revisions. Worked on two new departmental logos. Had a short lunch of a single hard pretzel from the vending machine and a jumbo latte from the university cafe *Entropy*. After lunch, he sat outside on a bench where he could enjoy the campus trees in their lovely autumn decay and watch the students, faculty and staff wander past – most of their heads bowed fervently as they attended to the Church of the Holy Phone.

He got back to his workstation office around 1:30 pm, and remembered that he had told Emma he'd get back early. Now he was inclined to stay until 4:00, and keep his mind off the apples and the tree. The *Apples* and *The Tree*. He restarted his Mac to flush the PRAM (good tech policy now and again) and there it was, sitting in the middle of his 33" display monitor: the Apple logo with the bite taken out of it. *Now God's using product-placement.*

He laughed to himself, stretched in his chair, and logged off. Then grabbed his jacket and headed to the bus stop on Forbes Ave. A large crowd was already jostling for the next 61B Port Authority Bus. He'd walk, and get home in forty minutes. More head-clearing time. He took a moment to turn off his phone.

Up a long, tree-lined incline, the neighborhood of Squirrel Hill was reached; an intersection of eclectic shops and eateries, featuring its colorful melange of don't-get-in-my-way humans, to go with the usual jammed up, clamorous traffic. He hurried past the businesses, casting a quick eye at the Dunkin' Donuts and Starbucks *(nah not today dang)* and headed onto Shady Avenue, which led towards Beechwood Boulevard, where he realized he was doing his usual route, which meant proceeding down into Frick Park and onto Falls Ravine trail into Fern Hollow and climb up to Regent Square and Gamma Way and Emma.

Did he really want to stroll past… the apple tree?

He shook his head, undecided.

Crossing Beechwood was always a tad tricky. *Should he walk past the tree?* A distinguished breed of Squirrel Hill motorists seemed to think they were racing LeMans, and liked to rev their ego-stroking engines coming around the big, blind bends. *Should he walk past the tree?* The road was wide and tree-lined, so visibility of incoming and length of crossing time had to be computed in order to protect one's existence. It was clear of vehicles as far as he could see, and hear, so when the silently-whirring Tesla appeared doing 45 mph, he got the end-of-life flash no one wants to get: *this car is going to hit me.*

*   *   *

Emma felt the cell phone vibrate. She was in a bed, in the hospital. To be more precise, in the hallway of a hospital. She had fainted again. Fortuitously, her neighbor Sheila Merrick had come over bearing a neighborly platter of warm, buttery, blueberry muffins, knocked a few times, then peeked through the living room window and seen Emma on the floor. She'd raced back to grab the Greens' spare house key (they'd exchanged keys for just such an emergency), got inside, roused Emma, and driven her to the emergency room.

Emma put the phone to her ear. It was Abel, sounding dazed: 'Emma! I'm in the hospital, honey. But I'm Ok...'

'You what?'

'A Tesla almost ran me down, but I jumped, and it missed. Hit my head on something – tree root I think. On Beechwood.'

'Honey honey honey...'

'I was walking home early,' he said. 'Got distracted.'

'Sheila's been trying to call you –'

'Ahh sorry. I turned my phone off. Wanted not to think –'

'I fainted again,' said Emma.

'*What?* You Ok?' His voice came up an octave.

'Don't know. Sheila brought me to Shadyside Hospital,' she said.

'We're in the same hospital. God.'

Emma laughed out loud.

'Can't believe this. Any of this,' he said. 'Is Sheila there. To talk to?'

'She stepped out. Honestly, I feel Ok, health wise. Or if not Ok, then *normally* not Ok. That make sense?'

'You're a basket-case otherwise?'

'Not quite that far.'

'Ok, listen,' he said. 'I have one more concussion test to do, then I'm released. What ward are you in? This is ridiculous, you know.'

'Seems to be, Mr. Green.'

'I'll come over to your room and we can share a platter of hospital cafeteria food.'

'What could be better,' said Emma. 'I'm not in a room yet. Crowded here. They're working through us newbies to see who should be admitted, so they line us up on gurneys in the halls til they can check us in or out. It's not bad, except for seeing some nurse rush down the hall looking like she's in a desperate hurry.'

'Ask not for whom the bell tolls, it tolls for thee.'

'The Tesla ding obviously didn't affect your wit.'

'Ha ha.'

She could picture him smiling into the phone. 'I'll be at your hallway door shortly, Madam Green.'

*　　*　　*

Gideon Moss got through Monday by sequestering himself in his school office and scattering important looking documents around his desk, a thin but practical disguise for those who felt compelled to check on his status and whereabouts. He spent much of his first hour there clutching his hand in a fist. Watching his knuckles stretch to a point where he believed his skin might split. After a point, he looked up 'epidermis' on Wiki.

"...the outer epithelial layer of the external integument of the animal body that is derived from the embryonic epiblast specifically: the outer nonsensitive and nonvascular layer of the skin of a vertebrate that overlies the dermis..."

And so. Here was the problem. He had procured more or less this same definition in his head, prior to looking it up online. This, despite having no background in biology or medicine or related. There was something...

wrong. Or, maybe. Maybe what…? Had something gone *right?*

He had to go back and find the Tree. With the capitalized '*T*'.

He abruptly remembered he had a bible, a Gideon's Bible, lifted from a motel somewhere in his travels. Saved as kind of an Americana Route 66-esque memorabilia. Something in there he should read up on. Hocus pocus about Eve and Adam, and that tree and that infamous apple bite.

*   *   *

'You look pale,' said Abel. He found a stool and slid it next to his wife's gurney.

She held out a limp-wristed hand. 'I feel fine. If I'm pale, it's because it's hard to get a decent snack. Sheila ran off to get me something a while ago. Must have been waylaid by some hot young intern.'

He took her hand and stroked it. 'I'm worried for you. Bearing false innuendo about your neighbors.' They smiled at each other.

'How's your head, you dummy?' Emma asked.

'Big time headache. But no Tesla logo embedded in my chest. I was lucky. Not even a bandage. Just a royal knock.'

She pulled her hand back. '*Abel…* you could have been killed'

'I know. Scary. I looked both ways, honest. I'm fine. No damage. Maybe slight damage to ego.' He leaned in and kissed her.

Sheila strode up carrying a coffee and small wrapped sandwich. Someone who appeared to be a physician was at her side.

'Hey Sheila,' said Abel, standing, reaching out to shake her hand. 'Thanks for the rescue!'

Sheila shook his hand. 'She scared me. I saw her lying on your rug. Can you believe both cats were sleeping up against her – those devils. This is Dr. Haskley. I work with him in Obstetrics.'

'How are you feeling, Ms. Green?'

Emma turned her face towards the wall. Then back towards Abel, smiling again. 'I'm pregnant, right?'

The doctor nodded.

Abel's eyebrows went straight up. He leaned over to stare closely into his wife's face. 'I'm not sure what to say. How about…I love you?'

She blinked. 'That'll do for starters.'

Abel lifted his head to speak to the ceiling. 'Jesus H. Christ, with all due respect.' Sheila leaned over to offer him a quick neighborly hug.

'I'm happy to see you in my private practice, Ms. Green. We can schedule that for this week. When you're feeling up to it. Let Sheila know and she'll pass the word to me. Based on these initial tests, even though brief and basic, I'd say your fainting was due to your pregnancy.' He lifted his hand with a quick wave and headed off down the hall.

Emma turned to Sheila, incapable of hiding a grin. 'I'm eating for two, right, so I'm thinking you guys should head to the cafeteria for some additional chow. For me and this new kid and both of you.'

She reached to take the sandwich from Sheila and unwrapped it. Sheila handed the coffee to Abel, who slurped out a sip.

'Abel, your head. I heard about the accident. How you feeling?' asked Sheila.

'Shell-shocked. Not from the Tesla. From this woman.'

'You stay here and I'll get more munchables. Anything special you want?'

'Yes. A white table-cloth, champagne glasses, and candles. Honestly, another cup of coffee – big one please – is all I can handle right now. Get something for yourself. And bill me, please!'

'Don't go away,' said Sheila. She turned and headed off.

Emma let the sandwich rest on her stomach. She raised both hands and presented them to Abel. He kissed each one. 'You see a wheelchair anywhere? I'd like to get the heck off this bed. Crumbs'll be everywhere. Now that we know I'm not fading, but merely gestating.'

SIX

LARS FOUND DIXON near the back entrance of the High School, which was situated somewhat awkwardly near the sheltered portico of the Sisters of Charity convent. Students often saw the nuns quietly tending the grounds' gardens, or in rockers on their shaded porch. Many of the nuns retired there, cared for by their young wards.

'Dix!'

'What's up, dude?'

'Don't call me dude.'

'Dude,' said Dixon.

'Ok, here's the thing. You know when we saw that black squirrel yesterday.'

'Yup.'

'It spooked me.'

'Get outta town. How is one *spooked?*'

Lars laughed. Dixon's conservatively-disposed parents did not permit him to swear or curse in any way under any circumstances. At least in front of them. He drummed up a plethora of wacked-out alternative exclamations to stay in tune.

'It was weird. Did you feel anything?' asked Lars.

'Dude. Not sure what you mean by *feel*.'

'You feel creepy, or dragged by some metaphysical inertia, maybe across some trans-dimensional flux point?'

'Oh sure, dude. *That* I felt.'

'Ok. Just want to check. I have no idea what it was. Or even how to classify it, as a human reaction. Part biological, part emotional, and part spiritual.'

'Part spiritual. That's kind of cool,' said Dixon.

'Yeah. I'm going back down to scrounge around and see if I can locate that little bastard. Maybe Thursday after school. Still some daylight. Anyway, let's get to the bus stop before Charlie the Uncaring whisks off without us.'

'He's a gold-shuckin' son of a mother,' said Dixon. 'I can't go Thursday after school. Chess Club.'

*　　*　　*

The Black Squirrel could see the roof of the Nature Center. The structure was old, weather-beaten, and conveniently flammable in all the right ways. A unique feature of the architecture was the way its three levels stepped down to follow the contour of the slope, which fell away into the forested areas below. Large windows enabled visitors to study the exhibits in a wash of daylight and enjoy the view of the natural world tucked up just outside the panes, while protected from rain, cold, or snow. October often brought the first harsher weather. Winter would show up before the new year.

The Black Squirrel pondered where best to position the apple. It must be hidden from humans: that was primary. It should be up high on the structure, where the flames underneath could incinerate the apple's components and elevate them in the rising heat, the better to spread throughout the park. The Black Squirrel, gifted with its new capacities, knew these things instinctively. It also 'knew' that one of the humans would participate in the upcoming happenings. One of the humans, the one who had fallen and taken the bite. The one who would light the match.

*   *   *

With the School's Out bell still faintly echoing in his head, Razor Moss walked towards Whipple Street, and home. His father, being the principal, seldom got home before 5 o'clock, leaving a nice interval for Razor to decompress. He looked forward to opening the fridge, remembering there was a container of sliced carrots and hummus waiting. He'd grab the carrots, grab the hummus, grab a seat, and grab a book.

Today he was finishing *Measure for Measure*, one of the Bard's 'dark comedies'. More escapist fare he saved for after any pending homework, before he fell asleep. He was the odd kid who eschewed the mad explosion of technology. The expensive cell phones, the goofy social media sites, the wasted hours his friends were spending on computer games. His great reverence for Shakespeare solidified his dream of a career in drama and the theater. St. Anselm had no drama department, nor was it inclined to 'release' him for stage plays put on by the nearby public schools. Even though his own father was the principal. *What do you do with that?*

He was good at letting things that bothered him drift left or right, up or down. His drama aspirations moved into some holding area. With this particular passion, though, the holding area protested. *He that will have a cake out of the wheat must tarry the grinding.* Troilus and Cressida.

He unlocked the front door and swung his backpack onto a hook in the hallway.

'Razor. Come in here.'

His father was home. Bummer.

'What are you doing here?'

'Come in here, I want to talk.'

Razor squeezed his eyes shut and spread his fingers wide. Then walked into the kitchen, where his father sat nursing rye in a tall glass.

'Why are you home early?' asked Razor. He pulled open the fridge and stared at the contents.

'Can you sit down?'

'I'm hungry.'

'Sit down.'

Razor twisted his neck to supply his father with a 'what gives' look, grabbed a Milky Way bar, and dropped into the chair across from Gideon. 'Are you Ok? What is this?'

'Something's happened and I don't know what to do with it.'

'Something's happened? Do you want to see a doctor?' Razor unwrapped the bar and chomped into it.

'I'm going to need your help, anyway.'

'So you're not sick. You didn't get fired, or something?'

Gideon smirked. He lifted the glass, stared through it, and swallowed the drink's remainder. 'No, son, I have my job and my physical health. You'll be fed and housed until you move out into the great big messed-up world and find your own ghettos.'

'That's encouraging. Aren't you the principal of a Catholic school, pop? Must be something in your contract against being a doom sayer.'

'Listen Razor. You don't, and won't ever, understand what I've been through. I wouldn't wish it on my worst enemy. I just want your help with a small task. Can you manage that?'

Razor pulled away from the table to stretch his arms over his head. His dad was out of sorts. Majorly. His dad could float between 'sorts', for sure. This was fairly exceptional.

'Ok. What?'

'I found a tree down in the park. An apple tree. A small, single tree – no one will miss it. I want to go back there, dig it up and replant it here, in our backyard.'

'Don't think we're supposed to dig up trees in Frick Park.'

'Listen, it's young and not even our height. It's unprotected there and near some muddy slip areas and not much sun, anyway. We're probably saving it if we pull it out.'

'So you want to go up with a shovel and a bucket and we just mosey back here while passers-by nod approvingly?'

'I was thinking you can get that kid from school, that science guru, Lars, to help us. Make sure we get all the roots up, the tiny ones that are like hairs, and make sure we get the right garden mix for fertilizing. He's a biology whiz-kid and that expertise would be good. I don't want our neighbors in on this. Really don't want anybody but you and I and that kid, if you can talk him into shutting up. I'll pay him.'

Razor stood up and retrieved a Snickers bar from the fridge. 'I don't know what to say, Dad.'

'Just do it. Don't ask all about everything. For once, don't argue me into pain. Just listen and obey, if you have at least one obey left in you.' Gideon rose from the table. 'I want to do this on Thursday. Really early. Pre-dawn. Talk to that Lars kid. I'll take Thursday off. There'll be that many less people in the park.' He shuffled off and headed up the steps to the second floor. 'Just do it.'

Razor wished there was someone he could call. It felt like every time he and his dad were moving towards a more adult recognition of each other, this stranger showed up. A pretty good dad was hiding somewhere in the man.

*　　*　　*

The roof of the Nature Center was the place where the Black Squirrel would deposit the apple. The building would be vacated before evening. The Black Squirrel waited, impatiently. It listened to the *tic-tic-tic* of a few katydids in the twilight. Leaves rustling over roots. The sunlight finally faded over the western hills. In the ensuing darkness, clenching the apple stem tightly in its sharp teeth, the Squirrel scaled the wooden walls and reached the roof. Weather-beaten shingles covered the building, many split or cracked, though intact enough to keep the elements at bay. The Squirrel moved furtively across to the stone chimney, with its metal joists and bolted cross-bracing. Under one of the trusses was a small alcove, protected against wind and rain, and indented into a bowl-like recess. The Squirrel ran its eyes over the scene. This decision was critical. No human must find the apple before the Nature Center was consumed in flames.

The alcove would serve. Carefully, it lowered the apple and watched it roll into the hidden hollow. It came to a gentle stop, under the shadows. For a moment, a red gleam shone like fresh blood against the darkness. The Squirrel was reminded of the urge to bite something, somebody. It glanced around again, then turned to climb down from the roof. Its next assignation would be almost as important as this last.

*   *   *

Tuesday. Emma, feeling better but hardly normal, returned to the high school to teach. She managed to avoid crossing paths with Gideon Moss. After work, accompanied by Abel, she visited Dr. Stewart Haskley at his Shadyside offices. She had decided her 'instant' pregnancy was probably responsible for her psychological funk. She and Abel decided that digging into the apple's strange inducements would be put on hold for a while: *she was having a baby*. Abel, thank goodness itself, had understood, and hadn't pursued more endlessly perplexing discussions about the apple and its fallout. At least for the moment. They carefully held off relating any Garden of Eden narrative to Haskley: it was enough he knew they'd eaten fruit growing on a Frick Park tree.

After a few introductory niceties, the doctor suggested a general program for Emma's pregnancy, including staggered visits throughout the next nine months. 'We'll do the first ultrasound around 13 weeks from today.'

Emma studied the sonogram monitor slung over the room's bed, balanced on an elongated, mobile arm. She studied the dials, switches, saw the probe and the curled cable attached to it.

'Doctor Haskley,' said Emma. 'Do you mind if I had one today? Like, now?'

Abel screwed up his face. 'Emma?' He glanced at the doctor with the same look.

'Would you mind?' She asked again.

'It's really not necessary or appropriate. And this first consultation is free.'

'Please.'

'Honestly, Ms. Green…'

Abel leaned forward on his chair. 'We'll pay for the ultrasound, Doctor. Just see what it shows,' he said. Emma reached to squeeze his hand.

The nurse, Carmen, came in from the outer office and assisted in the minor prep. Gowned, in the bed, Emma had the gel applied to her flat stomach. Dr. Haskley sat down on a stool next to her, switched on the equipment and placed the probe near her navel. 'Can you switch on the screen, please, Carmen.' He began to run the transducer probe in gentle circles over her skin.

All four of them stared as the black and white monitor flickered awake, revealing three small human-like forms wriggling ever-so-gently.

'This cannot be,' said Dr. Haskley. He tapped the display once or twice. Hoping it would resolve to 'blank', thought Emma. She had already guessed. The babies inside her were not only growing at an unusual rate: there were three.

'You must have been pregnant from several weeks prior.'

'I was not.'

'This cannot be.'

'Looks like…' said Abel.

'Undiscovered country. Putting it mildly.'

'What should we do, Doc? What should Emma do? Is this an emergency?'

'It's not a medical emergency, now, that's indicated. It's just not normal physiology. It can't really be. Medically, it's…' His voice faded off.

Emma reached over to flick off the ultrasound and pulled the robe down over her bare belly. 'We'll go, Doc. I can come back in a week and we can see where we are.'

'Yes,' said Dr. Haskley. 'Don't touch the equipment, please.'

'So three, did I see that right?' said Abel.

'You did,' said Emma and Dr. Haskley simultaneously.

'Thank you,' said Abel. 'I'll be stopping at a drug store on the way home, if anyone needs anything. Must be something for shell-shock.'

Smiles. Emma dressed, and the Greens departed.

Haskley tapped at the ultrasound display as if to jiggle it into compliance. He and Carmen stared at each other.

'What do you think, Carmen?' he asked.

'Did you record the session?'

'No. Usually when a woman is pregnant for 48 hours or so you don't get imagery of three small kids bobbing around.'

'We see her again in a week.'

'Yes. Get ready.'

*   *   *

'What do you think?' asked Abel.

Emma and Abel sat in opposite corners of their living room, both studying Emma's torso. Emma took a deep breath and said nothing. Her hand maneuvered inside a large bag of dried fruit.

Abel leaned back, hands squeezing his neck. 'I think… I think… is this our friendly neighborhood apple again?'

Emma pursed her lips. 'Don't know,' she said.

'Well, we wanted to start a family. Didn't think we'd get a full set in one go.' He smiled. 'I'm happy and scared and whatevered.'

Emma popped another handful of apricots and raisins into her open mouth. 'At least it's not a virgin birth,' she said.

Abel recalled their love-making the night of the storm. After their apple-fest. Shook his head.

'We're going to have to see some specialists. Very soon,' he said.

'Let's wait one week, and then see Haskley, and then he can advise. Obviously, we want healthy babies. Somehow, I'm not worried, though. For better or worse; it's the influence, and intuition, from the bite. We need a private label for it.'

'*Seedy?*'

'I like that. Our *seedy* brains are not working normally. Ok. *Seedy*. I am somehow clear of concern for the health of these three kids' – she paused to tap her belly – 'due to my *seedy* state.' She held the fruit bits bag up to her throat and poured in the remaining pieces. 'I'll take the apple, the apple Moss chewed on, *ick*, to the school lab tomorrow. I'll get Lars Patton, our science wizard, into the lab with me for some simple bio tests. Cut it in half. I'll see who else we can get to look at it.'

'MIT, Stanford, the Vatican. They'll be lining up for a piece of the action.'

'Get me food.'

*　　*　　*

As the lunch bell was blaring over the loudspeakers, Razor Moss caught Lars Patton at his locker in the second floor hallway. He stepped closer and raised his voice.

'Lars. You got a second?'

'Moss. Am I in trouble with your dad?'

'Nah. He wants me to ask if you can help with something.'

'Like what?'

'You have lunch? We can eat out by the gym.'

The two students moved out into the crisp air and found some seating on the gymnasium's tiered concrete abutments.

'Listen. My dad's got this crazed idea to dig up a tree in Frick Park. He wants you there to make sure we don't kill the roots or do something else that might damage it. Wants it carried back up to Whipple and replanted in our yard.'

Lars bit into his peanut butter and pickle toast sandwich, and raised a single eyebrow. 'Doesn't sound kosher. Like these pickles.' *Crunch.*

'I think it's a major mistake that might get him fired. And us in trouble with – whomever – legal entities. Or maybe no one will care. Who knows? I'm here to ask you to come with us and help me convince him that he will kill the tree if we dig it up. He says he'll pay you.'

'I want no part of it. Sorry.'

'You sure?' Razor asked. He pulled a sandwich wedge from inside his brown lunch bag. 'Ok, ok.' He unwrapped the food and took a small bite. 'Thought you'd say that. Don't blame you. Had to let him know I asked. Call me if you change your mind. We're in the school directory. He's taking tomorrow off. We're going down before sunrise.'

'What's with the tree? Why's he want it?'

'I can't tell. If he does this, and I can't figure out why the heck he wants to do it, like, legitimately, I'll talk to somebody. Maybe my Mom.'

'Tell your dad I don't know enough about trees and transplanting anyway. I'm interested in the natural world, and love the park, and am guessing maybe your dad just wants a piece of that place closer, to enjoy, maybe, out his back window.'

'No. All completely wrong, Lars.'

'What kind of tree is it?'

'Apple tree.'

'How much was he going to pay me?'

'I forgot to ask him. Would it make any difference?'

'Cool million might.'

'Ha. Remember where he's Principal.' Razor took another bite, stood, and walked back inside the school.

Lars nibbled at the last bit of peanut butter stuck in his teeth. *A friggin' apple tree.* The crime of the century and he was in on it. Plus, he noted with some relish, he could integrate this extraordinary occasion with the fact that biology teacher Ms. Green only this morning had requested his assistance in the science lab to dissect a half-chewed chunk of apple.

What the heck?

Ms. Green had stopped him after their morning class and asked if he would skip his study hall to assist her with a half-hour review of some fruit she'd procured. A somewhat unusual request; but of course he was keen to stay in the good graces of one of his teachers. They wouldn't find out much – this was a high school lab after all. A diocesan high school lab, in fact, which meant only rudimentary implements considering the kind of deep-dive results Ms. Green appeared to be after. They looked through the microscope, just to note any weird visual contrasts from what a 'normal' three-day old half-bitten piece of fruit should look like. No evidence of non-apple particulate. Nothing that appeared out of the ordinary, as closely as they could magnify it. Weirdly, the lab *did* have an only slightly-dated, handheld mass spectrometer. The apple's constitution gave up no secrets. Ms. Green carved a small bit of the fruit and asked Lars to set up a culture that might indicate abnormalities. Whatever the heck they were hoping to witness she was reluctant to provide meaningful background as to why they were doing these tests. She only said 'My husband and I were curious about this particular strain. We've talked about an orchard someday. Something that would grow easily and fruit well in our Regent Square backyard is really what we're going for right now.'

Lars noted that Ms. Green was stretching hard to avoid telling an outright falsehood. He decided the mysterious alignment of the Moss and Green apple stories was succulent. He'd call Razor Moss and join their curious expedition. It was simply too fruity to miss.

SEVEN

ABEL WAS AT work, his mind buzzing, maxed out with the happenings of the last few days. I may wake up from all this and Emma and I will re-start with our lovely stroll under the autumn leaves of Frick Park, he thought. But no – he wouldn't trade the dream at this juncture. He was point man on a modern day miracle-in-the-making. An actual miracle. Way above what the Church would need to canonize somebody. St. Abel. St. Emma. St. Gideon. All fresh from the neighborhood Garden. Was it actually *the* Garden? Frick Park. Did they need to call archaeologists in on this? Didn't Cain kill Abel somewhere back then? Catholics seemed, generally, to be not nearly as Bible-savvy as the denominations that followed on from Rome. He'd need to get his dusty copy off the shelf and read up. While continuing to do his CMU work, and assisting his wife through a pregnancy and delivery that was already jumping off any charts as far as standard. Good God. That's what he needed most – *Good God*. He needed to pray his head off. Tonight. Kneel down after Emma's asleep. Pray your head off.

Truth to tell, there were actually two active miracles-in-the-making. First, there was his awareness of the bloom of his mental acuity, running like freshwater into a drought, these great currents of awareness, knowledge, insights, this awe-full gift from the miracle apple. He and Emma had to catch themselves to avoid stumbling as their transformed minds filtered this new cache of thoughts and manner of thinking through their resident human physiologies. Again – it felt logically impossible even as it resonated as 'real.' Real. What did *real* mean? Secondly, her pregnancy. Alarmingly, yet somehow not as much as it should be, she was apparently growing these embryos at some unprecedented speed. They needed to get to specialists. How would they pay for all this? She'd need to quit her teaching job. Good God.

Ok. Calm down a minute. They were paying him to be a media designer, not a road-warrior monk.

He looked at his monitor and realized the whole time he'd been musing, he'd been tapping his fingers against the keyboard as a kind of accompanying mantra, in TextEdit, the rudimentary typing app on every Mac. In a narrow window adjacent to the brochure he was designing for the upcoming University Family Weekend, there were words he had typed:

fiat lux

In the deeps of time, before the gardens of humankind flourished in the good earth, the Creation Decrees were not locked in finality. Even as the laws of physics were honed and polished to the last calculation in readiness for the beginning of time, so the life that was to come on earth was generated, studied, and prepared. All would be wrought for the highest purpose: to be companion to humankind.

It was the time of the Great Crucible, when all of living nature was demonstrated before watchful and knowing eyes. Those of the animal and plant kingdoms that passed the test would become part of the world, and grow or decline within its history. Those that were deemed wrong, for whatever reason, proving in their behaviors that they were unfit for a world of fragile women and men and their children, were removed from history. Their destiny was oblivion, a fate unchangeable once invoked.

In service to the Great Crucible, areas of the Earth were selected where newly-formed species could interact and complete accelerated life cycles. These areas, the Manifests, were monitored and graded by the Sub-creators. The Manifests were spread about the Earth; some set in deserts, some in polar ice, some in verdant forest. A special one in the Garden.

And for each Manifest a Selector was given, who ensured that The Will was done in the task of forming the Earth, and indeed the Universe. And closest to The Will was the Prime Selector, whose charge was to oversee the Selectors, a duty both grave and of cardinal importance. For unto the Selectors fell the task of eliminating those life forms that would not be passed on to Earth. Unto some of these forms, awareness had been given, and extinction brought fear. But The Will placated those fears with a grace of forgetfulness.

Yet as the Crucible was nearing its completion, one of the Selectors blanched: for it deemed that some of these forms selected for extinction should not disappear. They were formidable in form and shape and bearing and worthy to be included in the Earth's book of life, it judged.

Abel jumped up from his workstation and looked around, mouth hanging open. Did somebody notice this, anybody see it manifesting on his screen while he sat there? Was he cracking up? One of his co-workers yawned.

He took another look at the screen. Maybe this was something accidentally downloaded from a *Dungeons and Dragons* site. Some pop-up that got through the University's VPN. Should he call IT? He pulled some hair from his scalp and held it up to look at. *I'm going bald.* Maybe, ahh, some co-worker was playing a gag on him. They knew he liked Tolkien.

He saved the file as *Banshee* – a title that popped into his head, recalled from Boy Scout days – and dragged it to his personal folder, then e-mailed it to his home account. His fingers twitched at the thought of sending it to Emma. Not yet. *Oh Good God.* All he could think. Took a deep breath and began a search in the university photo archives for some campus event stock. He'd better get some work done before he sprouted wings and was raptured off.

*　　*　　*

Gideon Moss, son Razor, and Lars Patton were heading down Commercial Street in the predawn mist. The air was warm, for October, and soggy. Lars cached how cool it was to play hooky from school while accompanied by the Principal. He'd informed his mom he had to get to school *uber-early* to correct something on the apple culture he'd begun for Ms. Green. A good excuse – almost true. Well, not almost true, but related to some wide-ranging near-truth thing in that it dealt in the trending subject of apples. *Ha!* Conscience absolved.

They all carried backpacks with tools and flashlights, which Gideon had directed to be kept turned off until absolutely necessary. Lars toted a black plastic bucket he hoped would be wide and deep enough for this crazy tree heist.

'I can't see where I'm walking,' said Razor.

'Follow me. Don't talk,' said Gideon.

'We can talk, Dad. Nobody's dumb enough to roll out of bed at 5:00 a.m. on a Thursday morning and walk in wet woods.'

'I don't mind not talking,' said Lars.

They intended to complete their task before morning's rush hour crowded the road with cars and witnesses. A solitary car motored past, the brief dash of headlights helping to guide the walkers. They trudged onward, eventually crossing Commercial Street, and trundled into the park under the slimy, dewy leaves.

'How far is this thing?' asked Razor.

'Ten minutes. Firelane trail we want, next.' He paused. 'No, no, we'll go to Falls Ravine and up from there. Firelane Extension is where I slipped. Too steep in the dark.'

They proceeded along the fringe of Fern Hollow, in the deeper darkness its wet overhang of trees provided. A lone car was parked in the small lot provided for weekend picnickers and sports teams. Gideon stopped.

'One of you sneak over and make sure that car's empty.'

'Yes, sir, sir.' Razor saluted, bent over, crept over to peek in the driver's side window, then padded back. 'No humans unless midgets.'

Gideon moved past the car, and they followed him to the trail head. He pivoted left, then flicked on his flashlight, keeping a flat hand against the beam. 'We're close. Come on.' Lars couldn't see much, but remembered they were near where he'd seen that weird squirrel with the black fur. He tugged at his ear, wondering why he'd agree to join this foray. He couldn't beg off now. The forest creaked and seemed almost to snuffle, like it was breathing. Leaves rustled under some movement across them, a scuttling. Far off, an owl hooted. This would be fun, if it only wasn't.

They walked a few more minutes up Falls Ravine trail, then Gideon stopped again. He shone his light to the left, and stepped off the trail to follow the beam. After a few minutes of scrambling and soft cursing, they found the tree.

Gideon, breathing in shallow gasps, knelt down and ran his fingers along the trunk. 'Look at it...'

Razor, flashlight in hand, followed him down.

'Dad, you feelin' Ok –'

Gideon turned, and slapped Razor across his mouth.

'– *ouuuch!*'

Razor lurched back, shoving his father's hand away.

'Do that again and I'm outta here,' he snapped, training the flashlight's beam into Gideon's face.

Gideon blinked, hid his eyes, and fell back on the dank earth. He pulled his hand up and stared at it. 'Poison ivy,' he said, brushing himself off. 'Get the shovel.'

Lars watched it all play out. Razor seriously ticked. The big reveal was coming: Razor and Lars were going to thwart Gideon's ill-considered tree burglary. This would be painful to witness. He felt bad for both of them. Bad for himself. Wished he was still in his bed.

Razor stood and aimed his flashlight beam at the fragile-looking tree.

'This tree will die if we move it,' said Razor. 'Ask Lars.'

'Bring me the shovel,' said Gideon.

'Lars, tell him.'

Lars organized whatever reluctant courage he could muster. A noncommittal balance between helping Razor and not getting expelled was a good way through. Just then, an animal, some creature, a large dark squirrel, raced up his pant leg, hung from his jacket sleeve, found the flesh of his neck, and sank its teeth in.

'Whoa…! – that *did not* feel good.'

He collapsed, hand against his neck, saw the dark blood smeared on his fingers. A noisy scramble, leaves tossed about, a flashlight beam strobing branches above.

'Bastard took off…!'

Razor yelling. Razor stooping to check on him. Razor probing the bite with his fingers.

'Ahh, can you move that beam, Ray. Going blind…'

Gideon knelt beside them. 'You Ok, Lars?'

'Need a bandage. Not much blood. Didn't hit your jugular,' said Razor. 'Thank God.'

'Felt deep. Sharp. Whew…' Lars sat up. He was feeling…strangely *fine*. 'We can use the bucket. Tree's not that big. Let's dig.'

'He's Ok,' said Gideon.

Razor stood up and stood back. 'How the hell do you know if he's Ok,' He knelt next to Lars. 'Lars. Should get you to the ER. Gonna need a rabies shot.'

'Nah, I'm Ok.' He felt at his neck. There was prickly pain. Bleeding had stopped. 'Let's dig the tree out.'

Razor put a hand on his shoulder. 'Lars. We'll kill it. If we dig it up. Remember? Tell my dad.'

'Should be good. Get it out of here and up to Whipple. Down here anyone could stumble on it, and steal it, right Mr. Moss?'

Gideon seemed to understand immediately what had occurred. Razor was out in the cold. Razor's an *accessory*.

'Lars….' Razor's last plea melted into silence. Stumbling in the darkness, he moved to the rear of the alcove. He stared, arms folded, as Lars and Gideon carefully dug up the tree, placed it carefully in the bucket, and covered the hole with dead leaves.

'Let's go,' said Gideon.

They worked their way back down the hill, and reached the Hollow.

'Let's go, Razor,' said Gideon, walking away with the bucket and tree in hand.

'I'll head up to my house, other way,' mumbled Lars. He called after Moss. 'See you in school, Moss.' Gideon waved a hand over his head without looking back.

Razor leaned in, his mouth to Lars' ear. 'Get that bite checked, Lars. You let me down big time.'

'You do your thing.' Lars watched as Razor headed away in the damp dark. 'I'm good.'

He was alone. Freshly bitten. The shadowy woods took on unsettling hues and quiet murmurs hissed softly from the recesses. The night air hung suspended, mixing with other hidden currents. An eerie brew was bubbling in the trees and around the park and he took a deep breath. It felt strangely corrupted. Felt, strangely, satisfyingly *good*.

*   *   *

It was a grey morning. Since her birthday, Emma hadn't seen the sun.

Abel had been unwilling to tell Emma about the magical screen apparition when he got home from work the night before. They'd spent a relatively quiet evening; Emma cooked them up a brilliant Moroccan stew (something she'd never before managed to her satisfaction) which they promptly devoured. Abel dug out *The New York Times Sunday Edition* and romped through the puzzles, including math-based exercises. She told him about the non-event of her and Lars' look at the apple sample. They'd avoided addressing the 800 lb. incorporeal gorilla roaming freely inside the gates of their previously mundane lives.

Now, they woke to a sullen morning as pregnant as Emma.

'I'll call in work for a half-day,' said Abel. 'We should talk.'

'Don't tell them I'm expecting.' She moved his hand to her belly. They felt movement. 'Tell them we're both under the weather,' she said.

He got up and went to the hall for his phone.

'Hello, Roman… Sorry to wake you.'

He looked over at Emma, nodding.

'Yup, yeah. Just for the morning. Wife feeling a little woozy, too. I should be good, though, if I take something. I'll come in around noon.' Abel wrapped up the call and returned to their bedroom.

'What about you? You have to teach.'

'First class at 10:00 today. It's only 7:00. Let's go make coffee and talk.'

Seren and Dippity appeared in the kitchen rubbing the nearest human ankles. Emma fed them in the foyer at the top of the basement steps. 'Meow,' she said. They paid her no attention, crunching their Friskies. Abel brewed his wife a 'real' coffee, using her espresso coffee-making *thang* (as he called it), while his own drink hummed into existence inside his instant pod machine.

'Here's your expresso.'

'*ES*-presso.'

'S. Yes. And *S-presto!* There's mine done.'

They sat at the kitchen table, under the pale light from two small windows.

'Well. Somehow our babies are growing at a miraculous rate,' he said. 'Are we worried?'

She nodded. 'I said I wasn't. Now that feels like a lie.'

'Hey, we're taking it as comes. Being yanked every which way is our new normal.'

She nodded again.

'I keep badgering Sheila for more names, more doctors and people in the field. Says the Vazyovichs might have connections, too: Dan and Betsy. She's checking. She's a blessing.'

Emma reached over to touch Abel's arm. 'But right now, I want a week without outsiders, you know. Just you and me and these three.' She patted at her belly. 'And we reserve the Genesis talk for only a few, selected souls, right?'

'Agree completely,' said Abel. He crossed his arms and tipped his chair backwards. 'You're good at Web-digging. Any basis in science or medicine? Any clues at all? Other than our Garden of Eden rewards card?'

'Two negatives, but they aren't apparent until after babies are born. Acromegaly. Gigantism. Hate those words. Both cause unnatural excessive growth from a hormone that's not performing to spec.'

'Doesn't sound like this,' he said.

'No.'

'Any precedent, anywhere, historically, for a mother to have full-term babies at less than nine months?' he asked.

'Babies born before 28 weeks have a low survival rate. Complications almost guaranteed.'

Abel tucked a hand under each armpit. 'We need good news.'

Emma took a careful sip of her still steaming coffee and looked down at a note she scribbled. 'Found this last night. Curtis Zy-Keith Means – what a name – apparently born at 21 weeks and survived.'

'Five months and a bit. Wonder how he's doing.'

Abel grabbed his phone and keyed in search terms. 'Here's another. Ellyannah Lopez born at 20 weeks, weighed less than a pound and about the size of a can of soda. Now weighs 12 pounds. Alive and apparently thriving.'

'Yes. I read about her. That's better,' she said. 'I'll keep looking.'

'Listen. I want to talk to Father Jack. You Ok with that?'

'You went there Sunday, remember? Told you I'm Ok with it. Just don't make it sound like we're one hundred percent onboard.'

'Onboard?'

'With the idea that we have eaten, you know, from the, you know, actual garden. *Return of the Tree, Episode IV.*'

'He'll like that one. Once wore a stormtrooper outfit to the parish festival,' said Abel.

'A good egg. This may scramble him.'

'It scrambled us.'

'True,' she said. 'What about Moss? Seems mostly normal at school; roaming around like a bad tempered dog. He bit the friggin' apple. Isn't he feeling anything?'

'I still don't want to approach him. Just don't want to.'

'That's good with me. He's never been a good listener; never felt like a soul I had common ground with.'

'We may now. But still no,' said Abel.

'Apple number three. Somewhere. Don't know what we can do but we have to remember it exists. Or existed.'

'Apple number three. Stored.' Abel pointed to his forehead and carried his coffee cup to the sink. 'Another thing. I couldn't tell you last night.'

'Should I lie down?'

'Actually, yes, let's retire to the living room.'

They went, Abel bringing his laptop. Emma reclined on the couch, her feet up on the armrest, and was identified as a warmed cushion by the cats, who jumped up to join her. Abel opened the laptop and sat on the floor next to his wife.

'I'm lying down. Two cats protect me.' Abel held the screen up so Emma could study it. *'Fiat lux.* Who wrote this? You wrote this?' she said.

'I typed it. Can't say I wrote it.'

Emma read it carefully, then closed the laptop.

'I was thinking about all our *seedy* stuff, at work. Looking at everything but my screen, I guess tapping away with my fingers on the keyboard with nervous energy. Looked down and there it all was.'

'So now we're getting stuff from the other side, directly.'

She covered her face with her hands, sobbing. Abel chased the cats off her belly and maneuvered in behind her, to cradle her in his arms.

*　　*　　*

Razor had left for school, without a goodbye for his dad. Gideon was glad. The kid was not helping. But Lars Patton, *that* kid, and that weird squirrel, and that bite... that was something.

Rumor at the school was that Lars knew about explosives, tinkered with C4 even, down in his home-based lab. Tomorrow he'd corral him in the Principal's office for a private session disguised as a reprimanding. There, they could plot the best way to torch the Nature Center.

Though thoughts were coming in through a diffuse gauze, he understood that the apple had given him unusual abilities and dark insights. He understood the squirrel might be complicit. And that the tree might wield more power. Power that might be accessed for diverging moralities. A sense was also growing in him that he was a player in a wider, deeper, far more consequential disturbance in the making. That his actions – moving the tree, lighting the fire – would bring about some metamorphosis long held back.

He looked up for a moment, teeth set in an unholy grin. Then he went to their small backyard shed and gathered the garden tools he'd need. He dug the hole carefully and set the tree in it, adding water and fertilizer that Lars had recommended. It was a simple undertaking, really. He hadn't been sure why he'd even included Lars in this escapade – it was making more sense now. As if he was successfully following a pre-scripted set of directives that became logical after the fact. His mind felt tethered to something unknowable in its totality but significant in its immediate rush. One perception, though, he *was* able to lock on, and he clutched it as hidden gold; that eating more of the tree's fruit might be the key to un-doing the derealization that stubbornly refused to budge.

Where was his goddamned Gideons International Bible, anyway?

*   *   *

Dixon found Lars in the science lab, bent over and poking at an experiment he and Ms. Green had set up. A note was scrawled and taped above it. 'Touch this and you will be sorry :)' The happy emoji took the sting out, but it was still a bit weird.

'Lars, you nutball. What's this supposed to be?'

'I'm helping Green drag the truth from this apple.'

'Looks like a guilty apple. Actually looks more like apple sauce.'

'This is just a bit of it. She's sending the rest to some U.S. agricultural institution for a full-on, high-level, don't mess with us or we'll arrest you kind of look-see.'

'Dude,' said Dixon.

'See my neck. That nasty squirrel bit me this morning. The black one.'

'You went down the park this morning? Dude.'

'Think its venom's in my blood and feeding me incense and peppermint dreams.'

'Dude. You serious. What about rabies?'

'My mom rinsed it out and put some antibiotics on it. Said it didn't look bad.'

'On your neck! Dude. You will die until dead.'

'Don't call me dude. Hey, Dix, I gotta get this data to Missus Green, so if you would be so kind as to make like a tree and leaf.'

'Dude,' said Dixon, and walked away, shaking his head.

*   *   *

Gideon Moss sent a note via a hall monitor to Lars' homeroom that he should report to the principal's office immediately. The boy showed up, eagerly shaking Gideon's hand after the closed door had given them privacy.

'Moss, you are the man.'

'Lars. Firstly, thanks for the help this a.m. You look tired. Did you wash out that bite?'

'Don't even feel it.'

'Should get you to the ER for a rabies shot. Can your mom drive you?'

'Don't need it. The squirrel wasn't rabid.'

Moss's eyes narrowed. 'Listen, Patton. You need to reconsider the way you're talking and acting. Don't call me Moss. Be your normal self while you're at school. And home, for that matter.'

'I can easily do that, Mossy-man,' smiled Lars. 'Just kidding. I can chill it back down. You're right, my pals and teachers and mom will be comparing notes and come to some wrong conclusion and our activities might be curtailed. What do you need?'

'You know how to blow things up, right? You can mix up solid-fuel fire-starters?'

'Of course.'

'And disguise them?'

'Of course.'

'Don't want legal trouble or me fired or you expelled.'

'Nope.'

'Go home and prepare enough material to start a good fire, able to ignite a wood structure. Make sure it will burn fast and hot. By the time the Fire Department shows up I want it to be a done deal. Creosote all over the wood so that'll help.'

'I shouldn't ask where or why, should I?'

'Not yet. Can you have the stuff ready by this weekend?'

'No, because I have to order some supplies from the dark web, to make what you're asking. Probably closer to the end of the month.'

Moss rubbed at his chin. 'Ok, if that's the fastest we can do. Nothing in our lab here that would substitute?'

'Are you kidding?'

'Ok. Now this meeting was officially a reprimand, so no one gets talking. What do you want to be reprimanded for? Won't go on your permanent record. Just a verbal warning, the Sisters will be told.'

'I'll just spread the word you're a real dufus and I didn't do anything wrong.'

'That won't work.' He thought for a moment. 'You borrowed something from the science lab, intending to return it. Can't do that with school property.'

'That's dumb. Never happened.'

'Come on, Lars.'

'This will work – *you're a dufus!*'

'Ahh. Yes. So you have taken pains to slur me on the sly, outside of other teachers' hearing, and you were caught. By me. I think we can spin that enough to fit this office visit.'

Lars stood up and slow-walked out of the office.

'Thank you, Mr. Principal. I promise to do better, in my daily habits, my bearing, my interactions, my fruitless escapades, ad nauseam, ad infinitum, amen…'

EIGHT

FATHER JACK RECEIVED a text that a parishioner was hoping to meet with him this evening for a short talk. These talks were seldom short, though, and he had just rented the *Passion of the Christ* DVD. Mel Gibson was coarse with his story, but his fervor was undeniable. He has also rented *The Incredibles*, and was mulling which to watch first. But the parishioners fed his soul like nothing else. To be surrounded by every iteration of faith, doubt, tradition, modern love, old age fears, disparate stories from desperate souls, heart-warming reconciliations and pitiless unravelings. Who needed fiction when life fed you this.

He agreed to meet the person, Mr. Abel Green. He retained a slightly selfish wish it wouldn't be marital troubles, believing that he might have heard them all, and that his answers were beginning to feel like tropes.

A half hour later, the rectory door chimed, and Fr. Jack opened it.

'Mr. Green?'

'Yes, hello, Father.'

'Come on in.' They retired to a small antechamber off the front lobby. Like many Catholic rectories, it was embellished with statues, paintings, Jesus, Mary, Joseph, and flowers on small oak tables. They sat in the plush-bottomed, stiff-backed chairs.

'Who's that guy?' asked Abel, pointing to a painting of a bearded, pious looking gent.

'Obi-Wan. Surely you know him,' said Fr. Jack. He smiled. 'That's St. Anselm, Father of the Church. Our patron saint.'

'Oh God, sorry,' said Abel. 'And sorry I said "oh God".'

'We say it a fair amount around here. What's on your mind?'

Abel blew out a deep exhale.

'We tackle just about everything, Abel. There's confession if you prefer.'

'No. Ok. If you can keep this confidential, for now. This is not a confession.'

Fr. Jack rose, and gracefully pulled the antechamber's door shut. He sat back down. 'Sorry, I usually do that first. Go on.'

'My wife and I – you may know her, she teaches here, Emma Green – we are experiencing some kind of…' His voice wavered. 'My wife Emma and I are trying to figure out if we are dealing with something. Possibly, something, super…natural?'

'Sounds reasonable.'

'It does?'

'You're discussing this with a priest. If there is no supernatural, we are in the wrong business.'

'Ok, there's that. Religion, the church, tradition, Mass. I'm talking about real-life supernatural experiences.'

'Visions?'

'More than visions. We're experiencing, some sort of – how can I put this –' Abel wrung his hands.

'Tell me how this started. Does that help?'

'That's the crux, Father.'

'Ok. Crux me.' He smiled again.

'Last weekend we took a walk down into Frick Park. We found this hidden nook up one of the hillsides, with a young apple tree, growing there, three ripe apples hanging off it. A little unusual, maybe, to find down there, in the park. But not exceptionally odd, by any means. Three apples. Emma pulled one off the tree. So of course she took a bite and I took a bite.'

Abel paused to smile at the priest. 'Maybe you can guess where this is heading.' His smile retreated. 'From that moment, from the moment we both finished off that apple, we are being hit with one crazy impossible after another.'

Fr. Jack listened expressionless. The story was as familiar as it was sacrosanct. Preemptive doubt jumped in to stake a claim. It was almost silly, the suggestion that this apple was akin to *that* apple. But something in Abel's voice kindled a curious hope, to accompany the priest's doubt. His heart picked up a few beats per second.

Abel looked around him. 'Can I get a glass of water?'

Fr. Jack went out and returned with two glasses. His, also a clear liquid, filled with gin. Abel took a gulp of water.

'Go on,' said Fr. Jack.

'Well, I'm coming to you because we're experiencing a kind of influx of, well, miraculous happenings across the board, Father. From expansion of knowledge to insights we are given, to my wife suddenly becoming pregnant with triplets and possibly these babies are already growing like wild weeds inside her.'

Abel gulped down the rest of his water. He pointed to Fr. Jack's glass.

'That's gin.'

Fr. Jack raised his glass in a toast, and took a sip. 'It is, it is.'

Perceptive indeed.

'Can I get some?' asked Abel.

Fr. Jack set his gin down on a small end table.

'Tell me how your beliefs are taking all this,' he said.

'Beliefs?'

'You are a guy who comes to Mass now and then – think I've seen you there. You believe in a Christian God. Your wife does, I assume. Do these experiences match up in some genuine way, to what you believe?'

'I'll be honest, Father. This is so far out of my league with what faith is. Faith is believing what you can't know, right? It's the opposite of certainty. I was happy with my understanding that God is present in the world through the Church, and people, and the cool things the Universe keeps throwing in our faces. What do you do when something real takes the place of faith?'

'I suppose the Apostles had the same dilemma.'

Fr. Jack leaned back and placed one leg across the other, hoping to relax them both a bit. 'Apologies for disguising this gin. Sometimes helps me find the spirit when my dulled aspirations can't quite bridge the gap. Seemed like a good moment for it.'

'So what do we do?'

Fr. Jack stroked his chin in the best Saint-Anselm-father-of-the-church-wisdom-extolling manner he could manage. He was definitely out of *his* league, even while he was simultaneously precisely in it.

'We should set up a time for a more extensive kind of session. Maybe your wife could join us?'

'She's not an active believer. She's not an atheist. She's a good lady. She wouldn't want to discuss it with you, but she said she didn't mind if I did.'

'And here you are. I'll confess to you I am not the best candidate for scriptural comprehension. But everyone knows Genesis. If you're re-living the Garden of Eden experience note-for-note and you ate this apple without being tempted to do so, then the apple's benefits should come without the Original Sin. I'm painting with a wide brush, here, Mr. Green, keep in mind.'

'That's your department, Father.' Abel ran his hands over his face. 'There's something else that might help you. Help us get what's occurring. I am somehow writing up material which seems to provide background, for all this, *from the other side.*'

'The other side...' Fr. Jack felt his hackles coming uncorked, rather suddenly. 'The authors of the Bible were given material, long after Christ walked the earth, in some cases, and scribed that into divine *revelation*. Are you suggesting your material has the legitimacy of Holy Scripture?'

He caught himself.

Getting a bit testy here, he was.

'I better go now, Father. Pray for us,' said Abel.

'I will. I'll keep everything confidential. I want to contemplate what you've given, so freely, and with humility.'

'Not humility, believe me, Father. I am freaked out and wish this was not happening to my wife and me and not sure if it was wiser to see you or go to Western Psych and see a shrink.'

Fr. Jack had one last smile to proffer.

'Leave your number. We should talk again soon.'

*   *   *

Emma was out walking and saw, a couple blocks distant, Abel drive past on his way home.

How can this be?

She felt lost and found. Or found and lost. No legitimate purveyor of reality would buy into the premise that the Garden of Eden had reappeared in time and space, somewhat inconsiderately in their backyard park. In this gross reenactment, she was now 'Eve'. Her husband – now receiving wireless revelation throughout his transcendental fingertips – was 'Adam'.

Where was god? Or God? She began to doubt her doubts. Was this whole spectral shenanigan for real?

One of the most troubling parts, besides her atypical pregnancy, was she didn't know who to confide in. She and her husband shared a healthy bond of trust, and they both understood that self-diagnosis and too-willing ratification of the apple's effect and possible origin was confounding their judgment. But he believed. With that capital 'B'. Did she know any mystics?

Up ahead was one of the neighborhood's well-loved book boxes. Sturdy and well-stocked they stood, fixed on posts about every third block of Regent Square. Each had an aesthetic: some with windowed, latch-able white doors, others dark and voluminous, with magazines, hardcover and softcover titles practically falling out the front, a few painted like they'd tripped in from Woodstock, swirly, over-colored and fabulous. Emma's mind blanked – that lovely kind of moment when she forgot everything but her appreciation of reading. This box on LaClair Street usually had at least one fetch-worthy paperback. She peered inside and (of course) there it had to be: a small Jerusalem Bible. *Nova Vulgata* popped into her head. Oh, please.

She pulled the book off the shelf and strode to a bench at the edges of Frick Park. Her phone woke with two *dings*. Texts from Abel.

'You - not home'

'Home soon - walking'

Genesis told the story of Adam and Eve and the serpent. She didn't recall snakes in Frick Park, other than garter snakes, which she watched slither in harmless reverie across grasses and under rocks. There was one in their own garden that they had named Marty. Ultimately and unfortunately, Marty didn't fare well up against Seren and Dippity. Abel had yelled at the cats and sent the snake soaring for a last flight over his woodsy home.

So the idea, in the Bible, seemed to be for the first two humans who ever existed (a pretty big deal in itself) to enjoy the Garden, but don't eat from the one tree. Tree, that is, with a capital 'T'. Pretty good deal, overall. But if you *did* bite the apple, you'd get some extra special superpowers. Such that, you would be like God. And also attain the knowledge of good and evil. And your mate you can bring along and he gets these powers also. So spake the snake. And Eve, who to be fair, didn't seem to have a huge amount of time to take in everything this would mean, must have just thought *the hell with it*, or maybe *the heck with it*, or *can't be totally wrong* because God wouldn't let it be so. It was not a set-up, but potentially catastrophic considering it would lead to every person born after them arriving bundled with Original Sin (though that notion maybe wasn't communicated thoroughly in those fairly overwrought moments.)

Millions, billions, of Christians have known this story as truth. Some biblical scholars give a little leeway and describe it as a narrative that delivers truth inside a framework of parable. What it had to do with how you lived out your faith, Emma wasn't sure, and didn't think it was time to review that aspect. She closed the book, got up, and walked back to Gamma Way.

*   *   *

At the end of the school day, Father Jack was called from the rectory to the High School to help welcome the new religion teacher, Sister Melanie Ignatius. Ignatius had arrived after a lengthy period living and serving with the Poor Clares, a reclusive order whose more traditional habit she still wore. Somewhere in her young forties, she was rumored, with admiration, to have maintained lengthy periods of silence.

He reached the comfortable waiting room outside the Principal's office, where leather chairs served both school visitors and put upon students. Apparently, Gideon Moss was indisposed; part of the reason Fr. Jack had been called. They were joined by the disciplinarian, Major Bruno (Jack was tickled Bruno happened to have that wonderfully capo-ish sounding name), Sister Jane Antioch, the Assistant Principal, and the secretary, Pauline Schneikert.

Sr. Ignatius rose to greet him.

'Father Jack.'

'Sister. Welcome to St. Anselm.'

'Thank you. I prayed for a return to a more sharing kind of practice and am grateful to be here.'

'I think you'll enjoy the parish, and school. The kids are all over the map, of course. Most of them end up Ok.' He couldn't help adding a grin, and wondered if it made him look sarcastic.

'A pinch of sarcasm, Father?' She smiled, disarming him.

'Teaching religion to them is easy. Teaching right and wrong…'

'I'm eager to plow those fields, Father,' she said. Her expression reset and she took a moment to look directly at those present. 'I understand Mr. Moss does not use his position to expound and enrich the students in the precepts of the faith as much as might be useful for them.'

This was a loaded item, up front. It was true, though, and perhaps the Bishop or some Diocesan people were getting reports to this effect. They had all gotten used to Moss's ways. A detailed manager who was professional and polite, Moss's biggest plus was some magic gift for raising money. One wondered how his often dour countenance worked so well in this realm. (Jack theorized that Moss's St. Francis University frat brother connections, Phi Kappa Theta boys who'd succeeded in the business world, would be part of it. 'Give, Expecting Nothing Thereof' was their motto.)

'We're happy with his efforts, Sister,' said Sr. Antioch. 'He's a solemn man at times, but has never flagged in supporting our school's mission.'

'And what is the school's mission?' asked Sr. Ignatius.

Sr. Antioch blushed slightly.

'To whip these rapscallions into the saintliest saints ever canonized,' said Bruno.

Jack wagged a finger at him. 'Pay no attention to Bruno. He's happy when he's happy. When the kids get him roiled, his sense of humor devolves.'

'You nailed me,' said Bruno, smiling. They all laughed, quietly. A few more introductory matters were explained, then the meeting ended, with warm regards extended by all. In the hall, Fr. Jack asked Sr. Ignatius to wait behind for a moment.

'Don't be long,' said Sr. Antioch. 'The convent's beef stew is exceptional. We have it every Friday except during Lent. Best way to savor fish for six weeks running is to have it as seldom as possible.' She waved over her veiled head and bustled off.

Jack and Ignatius spoke in a small alcove near the school's back exit, now empty. 'I'd like to discuss a matter with you that concerns one of our parishioners,' he said. 'Happy to meet at a table in the school library.'

'You mean so we don't have rumors starting about Father and Sister meeting in private. Is that really the state of the world?'

'I don't know if it is or isn't. I don't want to be secretive. I want to be discreet. Partly because this particular concern is something that is both deeply spiritual and slightly unnerving.'

'Unnerving?'

'Yes.' He looked around, noting no one was within earshot. 'Listen, I apologize. This is a discourteous way to welcome you. Why don't you go get some of that stew and we'll talk.'

'Thank you.' She turned and left through the back doors of the high school.

He wondered if he'd been hasty. Abel Green had asked for confidentiality. Father Jack's idea was to delve into a general, broad-brush type discussion, that wouldn't reveal the specifics of what the Greens were encountering. He needed an objective, spiritual ear to help divine the Divine.

NINE

EMMA RETURNED TO Dr. Haskley. The babies were healthy and growing. He'd asked the Greens about bringing specialists in, and they'd agreed. Several physicians rotated in and out over the next month. By early November, all of them could only offer their professional astonishment and ask to be included in updates. So far, all of them had been willing not to bill for services. If they were called in again, they requested compensation.

The 'apple' aspect of the Greens' medical journey drifted into the background, for which Emma was especially grateful. The doctors, including Haskley, were dealing with biology, not theology. Whatever she and Abel thought, felt, or were moved to consider as far as some impossible metaphysical component, it should not be part of their medical prognosis. Her would-be offspring had enough to do, after all – prepping for birth!

Sheila Merrick and another set of friends in the neighborhood, Dan and Betsy Vazyovich (known as Mr. and Mrs. Vaz), were mounting a local campaign to get the Greens both medical advisement and babysitting support. Emma had informed her seventy-seven year old mother Etta that Emma was 'with several childs' (Etta had cracked up laughing) and warned her to pack suitcases.

*

Abel had not had more episodes of *fiat lux* testaments sent through his fingertips to his screen (even after some attempts to repeat the feat), and so began to think it *had* been some kind of hack. He had not had time to re-schedule with Fr. Jack, overwhelmed with doctor visits, baby room ideas, mad work stuff, and what was left over. He did continue adding to what he now termed the *Banshee Patrol* document, which he tried to keep as up-to-date as possible. He would add in the *fiat lux* 'revelation' material when and if it showed up. All quite mad.

*

Father Jack had been unable to arrange more meetings with either Abel Green or Sr. Ignatius, mostly due to busy schedules. Sr. Ignatius had a full slate of new duties, and needed to familiarize herself with the school building, the faculty, the students, and the convent. She was still a Poor Clare, housed with Sisters of Charity. Charity was required from all parties.

*

Gideon Moss's apple tree was alive, but not looking robust going into the upcoming winter. He wondered if he should put it in a big pot and bring it indoors. He was getting impatient for Lars to let him know when they could do their next excursion into Frick Park.

*   *   *

There was a box outside the door, shipped by DHL. Lars Patton had received his special order of chemistry. He carried it down to the HUX labs and eagerly cracked it open. Everything looked good. He and Moss Man could get busy with the mission royale. But did he still want to be part of this? Moss had revealed the 'master plan' in a furtive note passed to Lars at school. It surely cooked and it surely reeked. Lars couldn't digest why he was heck-bent on helping Moss incinerate the Frick Nature Center. While his other half froze in resistance. He was now inside the story of Mr. Hyde and – *who was the other guy? The doctor? – Jeckel, Reckle?*

He supposed Moss was not going to take no for an answer at this point. Maybe he'd check in with Razor. Razor had been avoiding him at school. No wonder. Even Dixon was staying away. Things could get supremely messed-up, that was obvious. But things could also could become extremely historic, and vault him into some unique operating hemispheres. Many are called but few are chosen. Many are cold but few are frozen.

He yelled up to his mom. 'No dinner, Ma. I'm going to work up some big incendiaries.'

'Don't singe your eyebrows,' she called back.

*   *   *

The Black Squirrel was dying.

Whatever ingredients had been part of the apple, they were in the final stages of transforming the internal organs of the animal. Biting the human was worth anything that followed, but it had come at a price. Now it wished to survive to witness the flames from the building that would send the fertilizing chemistry aloft over the Garden, carrying it to the seeds – the *boneseeds* – buried in the deeps of time, to be restored and spawned into an unsuspecting world. The Squirrel has assisted with this consecrated mission as best it comprehended. With its new self-awareness, it understood that death awaited, containing mystery and, possibly, resurrection. It wasn't enough. The Squirrel needed assurance.

It twisted its head from side to side, suddenly fearful. Its kin in these woods never knew this existential terror. They were born, ate, hunted food, mated, raised young, and passed on. The Black Squirrel ingested the most bitter of truths. Time tore away the veneer of mindless being.

It would die.

*   *   *

Razor was out, away from the house. He'd been absent more often since the thievery in the park.

AND THE LORD GOD PLANTED A GARDEN IN EDEN, IN THE EAST...

Gideon Moss held the highlighter above the pages of his now well-attended bible. He was running his yellow-green over lines from Genesis. 'Frick Park. Who could have imagined.'

AND OUT OF THE GROUND THE LORD GOD MADE TO SPRING UP EVERY TREE THAT IS PLEASANT TO THE SIGHT AND GOOD FOR FOOD. THE TREE OF LIFE WAS IN THE MIDST OF THE GARDEN, AND THE TREE OF THE KNOWLEDGE OF GOOD AND EVIL.

So which tree? Two trees? Which tree did Adam and Eve eat the apple from? Were there apples on both?

A RIVER FLOWED OUT OF EDEN TO WATER THE GARDEN, AND THERE IT DIVIDED AND BECAME FOUR RIVERS.

Monongahela, Allegheny, Ohio, and the hidden fourth river that flows under downtown Pittsburgh. It obviously fit.

AND THE LORD GOD COMMANDED THE MAN, SAYING, "YOU MAY SURELY EAT OF EVERY TREE OF THE GARDEN BUT OF THE TREE OF THE KNOWLEDGE OF GOOD AND EVIL YOU SHALL NOT EAT, FOR IN THE DAY THAT YOU EAT OF IT YOU SHALL SURELY DIE."

So I'd be innocent. I saw a tree, picked the fruit, and had no commandment to avoid doing so.

NOW THE SERPENT SAID TO THE WOMAN, "DID GOD ACTUALLY SAY, 'YOU SHALL NOT EAT OF ANY TREE IN THE GARDEN?'"

AND THE WOMAN SAID TO THE SERPENT, "WE MAY EAT OF THE FRUIT OF THE TREES IN THE GARDEN, BUT GOD SAID, 'YOU SHALL NOT EAT OF THE FRUIT OF THE TREE THAT IS IN THE MIDST OF THE GARDEN, NEITHER SHALL YOU TOUCH IT, LEST YOU DIE.'"

BUT THE SERPENT SAID TO THE WOMAN, "YOU WILL NOT SURELY DIE."

Are we talking eternal life, here. *Oh man....* must figure out which tree was in Frick Park.

"FOR GOD KNOWS THAT WHEN YOU EAT OF IT YOUR EYES WILL BE OPENED, AND YOU WILL BE LIKE GOD, KNOWING GOOD AND EVIL."

Knowing good and evil is one thing. Eternal life is the game-winner. *The* Game-Winner of game-winners. Is knowledge of good and evil straight up knowledge? Confusing. *Need an advisor.* The new religion teacher nun? Ignatius? Crazy idea?

SO WHEN THE WOMAN SAW THAT THE TREE WAS GOOD FOR FOOD, AND THAT IT WAS A DELIGHT TO THE EYES, AND THAT THE TREE WAS TO BE DESIRED TO MAKE ONE WISE, SHE TOOK OF ITS FRUIT AND ATE, AND SHE ALSO GAVE SOME TO HER HUSBAND WHO WAS WITH HER, AND HE ATE.

The tree 'makes one wise'. I've been gifted wisdom, obvious. Which tree did I eat from? Is there another growing there? If I can get more apples growing in backyard – *what the hell*. Monetize wisdom. From the Source of Sources.

THE LORD GOD CALLED TO THE MAN AND SAID TO HIM, "HAVE YOU EATEN OF THE TREE OF WHICH I COMMANDED YOU NOT TO EAT?" THE MAN SAID, "THE WOMAN WHOM YOU GAVE TO BE WITH ME, SHE GAVE ME FRUIT OF THE TREE, AND I ATE."

THEN THE LORD GOD SAID TO THE WOMAN, "WHAT IS THIS THAT YOU HAVE DONE?" THE WOMAN SAID, "THE SERPENT DECEIVED ME, AND I ATE."

Not pertinent. I was not tempted. A Frick Park snake didn't hiss about any deal, any arrangement. Got the apple and its goodies for free.

TO THE WOMAN HE SAID, "I WILL SURELY MULTIPLY YOUR PAIN IN CHILDBEARING; IN PAIN YOU SHALL BRING FORTH CHILDREN. YOUR DESIRE SHALL BE FOR YOUR HUSBAND, AND HE SHALL RULE OVER YOU."

Oh, the feminists must love this *rule over you* bit.

AND TO ADAM HE SAID, "BECAUSE YOU HAVE LISTENED TO THE VOICE OF YOUR WIFE AND HAVE EATEN OF THE TREE, CURSED IS THE GROUND BECAUSE OF YOU; IN PAIN YOU SHALL EAT OF IT ALL THE DAYS OF YOUR LIFE; THORNS AND THISTLES IT SHALL BRING FORTH FOR YOU. BY THE SWEAT OF YOUR FACE YOU SHALL EAT BREAD, TILL YOU RETURN TO THE GROUND, FOR OUT OF IT YOU WERE TAKEN; FOR YOU ARE DUST, AND TO DUST YOU SHALL RETURN."

Merciful God, not so much…

Moss briefly studied his forearms. Assured there were no thorns appearing there, he re-read the text and noted the thorns would not appear on him, but probably where he planted crops. Better. He dusted each forearm and continued highlighting.

THEN THE LORD GOD SAID, "BEHOLD, THE MAN HAS BECOME LIKE ONE OF US IN KNOWING GOOD AND EVIL. NOW, LEST HE REACH OUT HIS HAND AND TAKE ALSO OF THE TREE OF LIFE AND EAT, AND LIVE FOREVER –" THEREFORE THE LORD GOD SENT HIM OUT FROM THE GARDEN OF EDEN TO WORK THE GROUND FROM WHICH HE WAS TAKEN.

Ok. Based on this, I've eaten from tree #1 – *Tree of Knowledge of Good and Evil*. Includes general knowledge. Other tree – #2, is *Tree of Eternal Life*. Gotta get back down to the park. Soon. That other tree…

Note – God addressing someone off-stage here '…THE MAN HAS BECOME LIKE ONE OF <u>US</u> IN KNOWING GOOD AND EVIL…'

Who are '<u>us</u>' – Angels, Trinity? Got to be major players.

HE DROVE OUT THE MAN, AND AT THE EAST OF THE GARDEN OF EDEN HE PLACED THE CHERUBIM AND A FLAMING SWORD THAT TURNED EVERY WAY TO GUARD THE WAY TO THE TREE OF LIFE.

This is a corker. *Cherubim and flaming sword*. Maybe torching the Nature Center will represent the new age flaming sword. Need a Cherubim to complete the narrative.

Moss put the marker down and leaned back in his chair. He needed spiritual advisement. Tomorrow, he'd see what Sr. Ignatius thought about a tryst with her new Principal. Moss threw his head back and snorted. 'Just kidding, God. Not a tryst. I know good and evil, now, remember?'

He picked up his phone and began a text to Lars Patton. They were overdue for a visit to the park.

*　　*　　*

Riley Cardle had a nose for news. It was her editors who didn't get it. If you want numbers, you need click-bait. Sensation. Empty reads that led to the ads, and held the viewers, both in print and digital media.

She was what was left of the pool of 'beat' reporters for the *Pittsburgh Post-Press*. Had fought her female way through the male-choked legions and made a small name for herself with some early 'legitimate' investigative pieces. One had been long-listed (a value-short category if ever there was one) for a Scripps Howards Foundation journalism award. How ironic, she thought, considering the manner in which more and more reporting aimed for subscription numbers vs. objectivity.

She sniffed around a variety of places for enticing leads. One came from Shadyside Hospital last week. A records-maintainer who had noted a number of high-profile specialists attending to an unusual medical situation. She didn't think it'd be earth-shaking, but you never knew til you poked around these benign-appearing spots where, surprisingly often, monetizable narratives could be lurking. A bit more snooping and she discovered the name of the family: Green. From there, it was fairly easy to get their address and basic facts. A mosey over to their neighborhood and a stroll past their house always served. Painted in a *feel* for the scenario that words on a screen could never.

She lived a few miles away, in Point Breeze. A walk across Frick Park would get her to Regent Square. The weather was quite chilly. Looked like it could even snow. She pulled on some warm clothing and headed out into the bracing November air. She'd need to be back before dark, just to be on the safe side.

*   *   *

Lars had assembled a goodly amount of incendiary elements. He prided himself on neat components, well-labeled. Sure, it was evidence, but most of it should blow up or burn in the conflagration. He'd even remembered a timer, so they could safely get away before the mushroom cloud appeared over the Frick Park Nature Center.

Moss had texted him: *Meet in Fern Hollow at 8:00 p.m.*

His Mom was reading, book in one hand and cigarette in the other. He informed her that he was heading down into the park to blow some stuff up. She nudged her reading glasses up, sprinkled some of her cigarette ashes in the tray, and nodded.

It was dark and cold. Snow was falling, the first of the season. If it got deep, their footprints would show up quite clearly. He threw away the concern and trudged down the hill, wearing a backpack stuffed with a fine array of reactives.

The shadowy form of Moss appeared near the locked restrooms.

'Lars.'

'Moss Man*!*'

'*Shhhh.* Keep in down, Lars.'

They turned and headed up Falls Ravine, agreeing they would veer off the maintained trails soon and make their way via a more direct and conveniently more hidden route. The wind picked up and the snowflakes fell bigger. Serene, a quieted wonderland, the moment waxing benevolent, considering their mission. Lars was glad no people would be anywhere near the place they were about to roast. The Nature Center had some while ago been closed up for the season and the park should be largely deserted. He began to hum a marching song.

The wind through the barren branches and soft, dampened crunching of their footfalls on the dead leaves muffled his song. He ceased when the silhouette of the Nature Center loomed rather suddenly out from the white of flakes and dark of sky.

*   *   *

Cardle had stayed much later than planned, scoping out Gamma Way and stopping for a meal at D's Hot Dogz. There was nothing exceptionally telling about the Greens' home, nor about the vicinity. But she knew it would provide fodder for the story opening, if nothing else. She'd also noted the Regent Square Theater was showcasing a local filmmaker's low-budget (the filmmaker had called it 'no budget') science fiction flick, *The Weapon*. She could go to a screening, write up a review and make some cash on the side.

She finished her Chicago Dog, delicious, and the last french fry. The restaurant window was being battered with flakes.

'I'm stupid. Now it's snowing. Buses will be late if they even show up,' she thought. Walking back through the dark woods of an urban park was not the wisest decision. But there was an element of drama and risk that could make it semi-compelling. She laced up her walking shoes and pulled a tossle cap out of her pocket.

Don't mess with me, night.

Out onto Braddock Avenue, left on Hutchinson, forward march.

*   *   *

The Black Squirrel knew its time was rapidly winding down. It had crawled in pain back up towards the Nature Center. Now climbed in anguish back up the wall. Slunk to small space. Saw apple gleam. Settled. Weak now. Will be consumed. Carried up as fuel, and potency. Worthy ending. It breathed a quiet last breath, and closed its eyes.

*   *   *

On the lower side of the Nature Center, facing into the park, the roof might be accessed where the corner shingles fell close to the walkway that led around the building. Lars and Moss had no ladder; this would have to do. Moss hoisted Lars up where he was able to grasp part of the gutter, which miraculously did not bend. He caught his toe in one of the horizontal slat beams and pulled himself up to the roof. The snow made it slippery, but the angle was not severe. Moss lifted the backpack and Lars pulled that up.

Though it was cold and night had fallen, and he was relatively concealed on the back roof, Lars felt exposed. More snow blew in, and visibility dropped dramatically. A minor blizzard was at hand. He crawled up the slant and reached the flattened center of the roof, where the stone chimney rose. In a small recess near it was a dead squirrel, resting beside an apple. A black squirrel. *The* Black Squirrel! *Holy mother…* Ok, this story just got double-weird. And I'm in the middle of it. *Go slow, Lars, go easy.* And what in the hell, *another apple.* The apple tempted. Lars wanted a bite, heard Dixon's incantations. *Death most instant.*

He took a breath and laid his backpack against the chimney. It was easy to set up the explosives and timer. He pushed the minute hand around to fifteen. They should be able to get a safe distance away and watch. Good the snow, now falling thick and blowing wild, would wipe out their tracks. That's better. He ventured that a *bwha ha ha* kind of villainous sniggering would nicely accent the scene as he slid down to the roof corner, dropped his pack into Moss's hands, and jumped off.

'Factum Perfectus, Maestro Moss,' he grinned. Moss returned a principal-ed look which only made Lars grin more. They moved away, in a different direction from where they'd arrived, doubling back in short loops to disguise their boot prints.

*   *   *

Cardle found herself humming. Was that an echo? Nah. She stopped, and stepped more cautiously down towards Fern Hollow. Falls Ravine would take her into Squirrel Hill, probably safer than the shorter but more isolated paths under the Forbes Bridge that headed directly into Point Breeze. *Where the Wild Things Are,* she thought.

A beautiful, arching light lit the sky on the hillside above her, followed in a split second by a soft crack. Cardle, already freezing, froze. Did a drone just crash into Frick Park?

The wind gusted along with her reporter's instincts. She began to gallop up the trail, in the direction of the Nature Center. Out of breath almost instantly, she slowed down and took out her phone. She started the video to capture the sheen of orange glow from what was obviously some kind of fire, above where she was, up near the top, maybe a Squirrel Hill mansion. Gas explosion, probably. Amber snowflakes raced in swirls overhead. A curious green cast now bloomed. Another deep breath and she hurried up the hill.

TEN

THE INITIAL EXPLOSION, engineered to fine specification by Lars, blew an opening downward through the roof. As planned, a container of flammable liquid dropped through the hole, shedding its membrane and splashing fire throughout the Nature Center's main exhibit room. In seconds the building had combusted into a furious blaze. The apple and the body of the Black Squirrel fell into the inferno, their unfused chemistries rising in the flames and heat. The poorly-maintained sprinklers opened for a moment before their nozzles melted shut. Small flashes of green perforated the scene.

Moss stared at the accomplishment, his eyebrows flush with reflected flames.

'Your eyebrows, gone green,' said Lars. 'A sight to remember.'

They watched the fiery tongues blazing through the roof, morphing from orange-yellow-red into markedly unusual hues. The chimney tilted, lurched, then crumbled, collapsing into the burning. Moss basked in the satisfaction of executing the task. Something significant would come of this and he the catalyst.

They'd hurried down over the east side of the terraced Nature Center area. The snow looked to be blanketing their steps. A faint illumination was cocooned in many of the blowing flakes. The snow whirled and twirled through the empty tree branches. Some of them flared incandescent and arrowed downward, chased by gusts into the snowbanks.

'We need to get away,' said Moss, reluctant to leave the spectacle he'd fomented. He looked at Lars. 'The fire trucks will be here soon.'

There was a flash – flakes suddenly hissing in front of their faces. Moss ducked, heard a *sizzling*, looked up to see Lars' head erupt in green-yellow fire. The boy screamed and plunged his face into the snow, his scalp sheathed in flashes and sparks. He writhed, gasping in agony, mane smoldering, as Moss shoveled snow over his head.

'Lars – *Lars!*' Moss patted out the last sparks.

Lars rolled over, staring, puzzlement and awe in his eyes. 'Doesn't hurt too bad –' He groaned, sat up, patting at the top of his head. '...*ahhh*... it does hurt.' He bent over and rocked, cupping his hands against his skull as a shield against further infliction.

'Your hair is gone,' said Moss.

'God, you kidding me –' He looked at Moss. 'I am toast.'

Moss helped him stand. 'Listen, we have to get out of here.'

'So toast,' said Lars.

He tugged his hood over his scalped pate, grimacing.

Moss took Lars' arm and led him down and around the hillside, away from the Nature Center. A fair distance beyond the conflagration, they sat and caught breath.

'What do you need? Need the hospital?'

'I'll go home and ask mom to take a look.'

'What'll you tell her?'

'She's seen me burn up with my bombs and stuff. She'll be glad when I'm home. It's late and this snowstorm.'

'You sure? Don't want to see a doctor'?

'No, nah, gotta move. Home.'

'Bit by a squirrel. Torched by a snowflake. You have stamina, Patton,' said Moss. He took another measured look around. They had to get out of the park as quickly and discreetly as possible. 'If you're good to move…'

Lars grimaced, nodded, and stood. 'This sucks.'

They moved down into the darkness, along the North Clayton trails above Forbes Ave., opposite the way they'd come. At some point they'd cut across Forbes and into the Homewood Cemetery. They'd then split up: Lars heading back towards Braddock Ave. while Moss traversed Squirrel Hill and returned via connecting trails to Commercial Street. A very long detour but safest way to disappear as the police and fire brigade deployed.

*   *   *

The apple was consumed and its robust ingredients – its animating chemistry – carried aloft, assisted by heat and fumes and wind and snow. The Squirrel's carcass was a green torch, fueling the proceedings as a propellant. Currents of air lifted the material and sent it north, east, and south, where in the deep recesses of the park, the carefully positioned *boneseeds* would welcome its stirring prompts. But all in due time, all in due time.

*   *   *

Cardle shook herself into attention and realized she had yet to call 911. Surely someone across Beechwood Boulevard would have heard or seen? But maybe not with the wind blasting from the west and the snow cloaking the night skies and noises. Then she heard the sirens.

She'd almost topped out to a point where she could get good video and watch unhindered. But staying here, too close to this burning edifice, would not be safe; the sparks might ignite the woods where she stood. She continued up and around, through the blizzard, surprisingly powerful for November.

There were tracks here! Two sets of footsteps just disappearing in the blow. She took a careful moment to photograph them, then stepped back to try to provide their orientation to the Nature Center.

89

*　　*　　*

The Nature Center burned. By the time the fire trucks had been able to get near enough, forced to detour around twin stone guard houses that had long stood at the north park entrance, the building was no more. Red-hot beams toppled into the raging middle, a giant campfire fluorescing its kaleidoscope of striking hues out through the wintry trunks of silhouetted trees.

The apple's chemistry proceeded as a searching sentience, drifting down to every corner of the Garden, a small store of heated energy assisting as it burrowed through the protective veneer of frozen white.

It would find them.

Each one.

Thirteen.

*　　*　　*

'What is going on?' asked Emma, waking on the couch from a too-short nap, a book on her lap, to snaps of wind and sirens in the distance.

Abel rose to open the window. The curtains jumped wildly and flakes drifted through. 'What a nasty night for firemen to head out. *Really* snowing.'

'Women. Fire men and fire *women*.'

'God, Emma,' said Abel. 'Someone might be in trouble. Forget your semantics, just for a moment.' He closed the window with an extra vigorous shudder. Emma wrinkled her lips and picked up her book.

*　　*　　*

Cardle watched the vain efforts of the multiple Engine Houses who showed up, running their tonnage of trucks over the manicured lawns near the Nature Center. By now the water was freezing and they pulled back the hoses. Smoke drifted and snow fell and a curious acid green smoldered where one of the appreciated and iconic jewels of the community had been.

Though it had been built half a century ago and had needed renovation, in its heyday it had served young and old in good stead. It was now completely gone, and the people that had known it would wake to a severe shock.

The embers wound down to a gloom of smoke. Flashlight beams gamboled and truck engines restarted. Cardle made her way out of the woods' shadows and into a circle of police who were assembling barricades. A few short comments would add to her tale. That completed, she headed for home, shaken and exhausted, carrying the quiet secret of the snowbound foot prints. Too early to declare that. She'd see where the story headed and play her investigative reporter hand when the time was right.

*   *   *

Razor heard his father come in. Gideon was wet from the snow and almost limping.

'Where the heck were you? I heard sirens.'

'Out. What do you care?'

'Dad. Get out of those clothes. You'll get sick. Where were you?'

Gideon got himself to the basement steps and hung his jacket, hat and gloves over the railing.

'I went for a walk, over street. Can you make me a tea?'

Razor set the pot on the burner. Prepared a cup and saucer. His dad liked 'plain brown' Lipton, with a bit of lemon. The kettle hissed as Gideon pulled off his snow-crusted boots.

'Dad. It's cold. Stupid to go out and freeze for no reason.'

Gideon looked at his son with hollowed eyes.

'Make sure it's hot.'

*   *   *

The news of the Nature Center's ruin spread as rapidly as the flames had the night before. Emma learned about it before heading off to school. Their park, their Frick Park haven and comfort station and getaway from all the rest was becoming an epicenter of the opposite. Arson was a candidate, but with the aged wood frame, obsolete wiring and creosote seal all contributors, so was an accidental spark.

She needed to talk to Moss today about a leave of absence. She was peeved at her husband for not putting out the recycling. She was tired and hungry. The day was shaping and not up.

Lars Patton was absent. Disappointing, as she wanted him to suggest some further examination regimes they might use on the apple. She'd looked into some other sources that could probe into this mystery, using science, not theology. Their sample would need refrigeration at least, freeze-drying even better. For now, the faculty lunchroom would have to suffice. Aluminum foil wrapped and with her name taped to it, the 'magic' apple (as she now preferred to call it), resided next to Sr. Angelica's convent-made plum pudding.

It turned out Gideon Moss had taken the day off. Getting to be a regular thing with him these days. If he's 'magic apple cognizant', she thought, he might be doing anything. Studying online for a doctorate. Joining Wicca. Trending in web circles as an influencer. Where was her own head, anyway, conjuring up such bizarre red herrings?

She checked in with Pauline Schneikert, who provided access to a cache of Leave of Absence applications. The Diocese could be pretty generous about pregnancy leaves. Emma wasn't ready to disclose the news to the wider community yet, and her expanding belly would announce things regardless. She felt her face go slack, suddenly remembering. Moss, he'd mumbled something, when they found him up near the Tree that day. About the Nature Center.

*　　*　　*

Lars was in his room, with a green Grinch hat on his head. All of his hair was gone, in a tidy operation that must have found some compatible combustibles in his follicles. Because it had burned like a flash fire, his skin was hardly wounded. Even his eyebrows were spared. His mom, rarely emotive about his shenanigans, actually laughed when she brought him in out of the cold the night before. His sister Astrid considered her brother both a genius and an idiot. 'You're doomed,' she said, when he shared his new look with them. She then marched upstairs to read her Jane Austen Zombie Retcon.

*　　*　　*

Abel's workload at CMU had expanded, and he'd found it easier and easier to accomplish the tasks. *Accelerated everything*, was how he termed it. Missing was useful progress with Fr. Jack, plus a weird void opening between him and Emma that had no form other than its reserved actuality. His professional work done for the moment, he sat at his keyboard, worrying for their future. And looking down, at last, there it was. More *fiat lux*. (He penciled a quick note, clarifying that no conscious attempt to receive this stuff worked. He had to be distracted and it had to be unintentional. Surely this would be more and more impossible.)

fiat lux two

This Selector was named Bazle. Bazle sought council with the Sub-creator Arrimaus. Bazle asked: "Why should these created and cherished forms, wrought judiciously and with appropriate attention to feature, be sent into darkness? The world is wide, the time of humankind will be an unmeasured epoch. We have not set up a place for idleness and unbridled plenty. We are commissioned to make a place for humankind where free will can drive its destiny. In this place there will be suffering, and decay, set against beauty and joy. And death as the last gateway. Will we make humans soft, and deliver them from all but the simplest threats, and engender in them a love for convenience, and waste, and all that is bland?"

Arrimaus heard him: "I don't disagree with you, Bazle. I too have sought for a world that is more challenging, breathing with the fire and ice that will forge humans into beings that can stand before The Will unflinching, for they will have borne their own Crucible in life on earth. But The Will is Mercy, and seeks a middle ground that is weighted with blue skies, white clouds, glowing sunsets, and clean wind. Or more than a middle ground, maybe."

Bazle said, "It is a glorious creation, and full of mystery even for us. But I would make it even more glorious. Remember our own Crucible!"

"It is not for us to change, Bazle. We cannot petition against this."

Abel copied the text into the Banshee Patrol folder, encrypted it, and e-mailed the file to his home. The *fiat lux* feed contained potent-sounding revelations; some entity on the 'other side' describing all sorts of bizarre notions. No mention of apples or what happens to people who bite into them. Was the tree part of this *Crucible?* Did it access some gate to the present and just pop up through the ground? Is *The Will* supposed to be God?

Dumbfounding, gut-funking; equal parts. Abel thought the language was way too medieval and was silently grateful his was not the pen, but the medium. But it could all be fake. This was only the second delivery. Something about it made him feel like gagging.

*   *   *

More snow had fallen throughout the day, lying several inches deep across the park, and banking up in drifts over the hollows. It provided a thermal buffer for the wind-borne chemistries that now moved inside the Earth, tunneling to their targets. Each boneseed welcomed its generative counterpart, reacting as an ovum might in a fertilizing spring.

Thirteen there were, all stirring. After an eternity, the *nereBegats* would be raised.

ELEVEN

'I'M NOT GOING to school with a green head.' Lars called down to his mother. He stood at the top of the stairs, a pillow over his face.

'Can't understand you, Lars. Sounds like you have a mouth full of oatmeal. Come down here,' said his Mom.

'Get me a wig. Can you find a wig? Even a Halloween wig.'

His mother moved to the bottom of the stairs where she could survey the situation. 'I don't know what you did, son, but this is surely the winner. If you won't go in you'll have to wait til tomorrow. I'll get down to the Waterfront and buy something. Your classmates aren't about to let you wear it for long, you realize.'

'I don't give a fig.' Lars turned around, fell face down on his bed, and wished he was. Not dead. He didn't wish he was dead. But. What the *hell* did that god-forsaken black squirrel do to him, anyway.

*   *   *

Fr. Jack had called, and with his spirited articulation, convinced Abel to share his story with Sister Ignatius. Jack extolled Ignatius' expertise in theology, and the manner in which she was anchored in the Church; both its traditions and in the more progressive practicalities espoused by the current

Pope. Abel agreed readily; the story – his and Emma's mind-scrambling transmogrification from happy Regent Squarers to metaphysically tortured and sanity-suspecting humans – had reached some apogee. Even with his new *seedy* brain, he felt removed from a direction that looked viable. Ignite the Ignatius fuse and *fiat lux* indeed.

They met at Biddle's Escape, a lovely, beat-up, colorfully-festooned cafe and eatery ensconced at the edge of Regent Square's less-posh environs. It was crowded and loud, which would usefully mask their conversation. Abel noted that Sister's Poor Clare habit didn't stand out from the proceedings, mixed as they were with every sort of personage and fashion.

'Thanks, Father, and Sister. Appreciate your time and really feeling needy, to be honest.'

Ignatius shot a marginal glance at Fr. Jack. 'I believe if it's counseling you seek, there are credentialed professionals that could serve.'

Fr. Jack leaned forward as their hot chocolates and tea were brought to the table. 'Sister. It's not your usual scenario. And if I'm honest, we're not the individuals Abel needs to see. But he can start with us. Hear him out, if you will.'

Ignatius raised her tea, blew on it, and held it forth as a spare conditional toast.

'Abel, probably best if you tell this. Not sure I'm even caught up,' said Jack.

'Yes. Sister, if you can shed your preconceived notions about miracles, and... and God... and everything else, we can move forward a bit quicker,' said Abel, in as earnest a tone as he could manage, his mind and heart spilling past the unsustainable stoppers he'd attempted to install.

Ignatius took a small sip of her Earl Grey, and nodded. At this slight recognition, Abel felt tears welling.

'My wife, Emma, and I, stumbled on an apple tree – October first this was – down in Frick Park. Not far from here.'

'I know it, a bit,' said Ignatius.

'A young tree, three apples on it. Pulled an apple off the tree. We both bit the apple. Came home feeling strange. Like our IQs had jumped, and we were getting a feed of insights, into everything, every aspect of life. Absolutely crazy. Thought we might have been drugged. Didn't know what to think. But one far out possibility kept jumping the queue. Insistently, for me, especially. That this tree, *these very apples,* were duplicates, or offspring, of the Garden of Eden's.'

Ignatius nodded.

'Emma is expecting. Triplets. They're growing at a speed that is not normal. But they're healthy; we've been seeing medical specialists and, other than the rapid development, all appears well.'

Abel took a moment to rub his palms together. It had all come out like a dam broken. Felt wonderful to get it off his chest and share.

'I feel isolated. Afraid. Afraid it's true. Afraid it's not.'

He looked directly at Ignatius. 'Haven't even mentioned I'm getting backstory from heaven.'

'Backstory?' asked Ignatius.

'Text on my computer, typed by me, as if I'm typing in tongues and the Mac translates it into post-modern Old Testament. And Sister, I am happy to be rebuked, excommunicated, canonized, whatever. Just need some graspable realities to hang on, right now.'

'Realities,' said Ignatius. 'There's an overburdened word.'

Then her face began a transfiguration.

She seemed to be mulling over some spiritual coordinates, pursing and unpursing her lips at possibilities unconsidered, stirring her out of her becalmed center. Some light, or some grace, took hold. From a mild, only half-hidden glower, through an expression of reluctant acquisition, to an affirming visage of acceptance.

She reached into a deep pocket and lifted up a pair of rosaries. After briefly kneading the bead that announces the First Mystery, she set the rosary gently on the table.

'I've not noted a false note in your words, Mr. Green. Much as I think I would have preferred to hear – those notes. Some voice, perhaps my own form of *backstory*, is telling me to listen. To what you have to say.'

'Call me Abel, please.'

'Abel. It takes courage to relate what you have. And that also feeds this realization – that you wouldn't concoct a tale such as this just for attention. Or other reason. So I am listening. Continue.'

'I have nothing left. I'm here to listen to whatever you can suggest.'

'Do you know if anyone else had access to the tree? Do you think others might have partaken?'

'It's possible. I'm reluctant to say. Til we figure out what any of this means, you know, Sister,' said Abel. 'But, yes, there was more than one apple on that tree.'

Ignatius took another sip of her tea. 'Is there any sort of assessment, Father Jack, you know of, that Mother Church provides for in this kind of situation? We would want to protect the privacy of the Greens, along with pursuing ecclesiastical resolution, or at least providing spiritual sanctuary as it unfolds.'

'Spiritual sanctuary. What do you mean?' asked Jack.

'I mean a place where the story can reveal itself with trust in God and the people enduring it. How can the Church best achieve this?'

'We'll need higher ups. The Bishop to start. More specifically-studied religious, who cover this kind of ground. Rome, in the end.'

'Part of me says no, to that, instinctively. We may have a circus, with the opportunities for excess. I also know it's reasonable to pursue this as you suggest.'

Abel stretched his hands to grasp the edges of the table. 'You believe all this?'

'It… you and the story… are rich with that intangible that makes faith brighter and life exponential. You, Father?'

Father Jack brought his hand to his mouth, to help him voice the words.

'My doubt feels like a sieve and my belief alternates between nightmare and blessedness.'

Pushing the rosaries back into the folds of her habit, Ignatius turned to Abel and reached out for his hand. He held it out and she clasped it. 'Let us go to the Bishop and request this: Your Excellency, we wish an audience with the head of the Dicastery for the Causes of Saints.'

Did this nun just wink at him?

She pulled her hand back. 'Father; rather than work up through the ranks, we'll shoot for the top dogs, so to speak.'

'I'm all in,' said Jack. 'I'll check with Bishop Garner tomorrow.'

'Good,' said Ignatius, swallowing a last slug of tea. 'I have faith this will be a worthy mission, Abel. I'm not sure why. When in doubt, trust your habits.' With that, she stood.

'Abel,' said Jack, reaching out his hand in farewell. Father and Sister left together. Abel sat for a moment longer. The metaphysical cat was out of the temporal bag.

*   *   *

Boneseed first was engineered to erupt in the briefest time, in part to test the efficacy of the method. It curled open under the ground, and pulled sustenance from particulate in both its make up and the surrounding elements. It would be a simple creature, though one that had been denied in *The Crucible*. There were reasons it had not been allowed as part of creation. These would become evident, soon.

*   *   *

Bishop Garner wanted no part of the scenario Father Jack presented. Miracles involved – *miracles*. Not a parishioner who *thought* they *might* be experiencing holy visions, or holy some such. And pregnancy, with all its physiological permutations, was also not a valid reason to rush to Rome for consultation. Garner was not mean-spirited, thought Jack. The Bishop could not be expected to be graced with the kind of bridge Ignatius and he were given in Abel's presence. The tactile verity of a breathing human relating it bolstered Abel's story. Jack would have to see what Sr. Ignatius thought they might do next, and he was hopeful.

*　　*　　*

'Abel, we have to get back to the tree. Get the tree protected.'

'You're not heading out in this weather, lady-with-childs.' Abel brought a blanket to set over Emma's knees.

'That's covered with cat hair. Get the mohair one out of the closet.'

Abel bowed, got the blue-green mohair blanket and spread it over Emma.

'Thank you. Do you think we should dig it up?'

'We might kill it. Maybe we'll leave it alone for the winter. It's tucked up in that hiding place. Not many hikers roaming in the cold. That work for you?'

'Yes. I guess.' She sighed, and pulled the mohair up to her chin. 'We have to do something. It's all stuck.'

'I know. Seems like it. Not sure how to feel, really. We ate an apple, got a supercharge. Still eat and sleep and shower and go to work to make money to pay our bills. Fr. Jack and the new nun, Ignatius, are plotting some spiritual expertise we can tap. May take a while as they are wrangling for someone from the Vatican –'

'The *Vatican?* Seriously?'

'Yes the Vatican. And we have doctors wondering what's going on with our triplets. And still no real clue what's happening. It's all stuck, as you say. If you have suggestions I'm willing.'

She took a deep breath.

'Look, Emma; no one has any real idea what we're going through with this *seedy* stuff. Let's just act as normal as we can. I'm hoping the *fiat lux* gets lucid and gives us a useful mission statement. Our job will be to concentrate on bringing these three new souls into the world.'

'Abel, thank you. It's something to hang on to.'

*   *   *

Winter's winds roared through Frick Park, and, after the new year, used Christmas trees were gathered for a bonfire. The Iron Gate trail was an isolated path, running from its start near Squirrel Hill's blue slide playground, down into one of the deepest ravines in the park. *Boneseed first* was growing. Now only a last crust of ice barred its route into the daylight.

*   *   *

More obstetricians, neonatologists, and other medical experts had joined in during the Greens' office visits to Haskley, or weighed in remotely, all intrigued and mystified in turn. It was tiring for Abel and Emma, and frustrating. They didn't expect answers but felt like lab rats.

Emma liked and trusted Dr. Haskley, and so she asked him: 'What do you think, Doctor? In all honesty. If this was your wife or daughter and their pregnancy, what would you advise?'

'You should be hospitalized,' he said.

Emma was grateful for the idea, that she be sequestered away while her 'dashing' pregnancy evolved to full term, however frantically that might unfold. But she didn't want a hospital.

'We don't really know what to make of your situation, Emma,' said the doctor. 'Only that considering the unusual aspects surrounding this, and keeping in mind you and the babies' best case for a healthy delivery, we think it's necessary. You need to be monitored and need to have robust exigency services near at hand.' He looked at Abel, then back at Emma. 'What would you say to that?'

'I'd say, never say *exigency* to a pregnant mother,' she grinned. 'Abel and I will discuss it, alone, please, for a moment.'

'Sure.' Haskley stepped out of his office and closed the door.

Abel sat down next to her. 'You know how our seedy heads are working overtime? Mine came up with an idea.'

She looked at him from under her lids.

'What about the convent?' He paused. 'Ok, listen, before you melt down; there's medical care onsite. It's close to home. Sr. Ignatius is onboard with our story. I think she's already thinking the same. Point being we have a convenient place to hide you in relatively plain sight, safe, and close to Regent Square.'

'Prick.'

'Prick??'

'Don't be so smug when you're correct.'

'Prick?'

'Not apologizing – just forget it. And call Sister Iggy.'

'Iggy?'

'I'm not about to roll out with that nunnish name – not even her real name, right – every time we mention her.'

Abel sat down and ruffled his own hair. 'Honey. Dear. Please watch your vocalizing. If you're going into a convent you can't bandy your verbal bonbons around the nuns. They'll be helping you. Don't blame me if they exorcise you.'

She started to sniffle again, caught herself. 'I know. I know.' She pulled her head up straight and reached for his shoulder. 'Get the doc back here. We'll see what he thinks.'

*   *   *

Razor Moss felt his Dad had calmed down somewhat. Maybe he was on tranquilizers. One missing wrinkle bothered him, though. Circled around in his head but he couldn't pin it. He finally remembered. And wished he hadn't. It was his father's words after the fall-in-the-mud excursion into Frick Park. *'I'm going to* blank *the Nature Center.'*

Now the Center was gone. He'd tried sharing the outlines of the story with his mother. She'd sympathized, but steered clear of offering to mentor him about his father. There was a chasm there and she would not be re-crossing it.

He had to do something, to alleviate the guilt he felt for his father, and for himself, now a sort of accessory to a crime.

*   *   *

Riley Cardle had prepared a lengthy feature on the Frick Nature Center fire, a calamity that had excised a much-loved facility from the surrounding community. She'd contributed to the original news story the morning after, but knew there was more to stir into this confection. Burnishing the facts with some heady exaggeration and the hinting of arson had earned her more column space and the promise of robust numbers online. Her exclusive 'I was there that night' account was going to press.

'In November, fire struck the Frick Park Nature Center, sending an historic, venerable, long-cherished if woefully maintained icon of its surrounding communities up in a blaze of curiously greenish vapor. What really happened that night? Our story begins with some ominous reflections by Park Environmentalist Lydia Woods...'

She had also gotten an additional clue or two about the Greens, and their unusual situation. Optimism, for more money and better exposure, was on the horizon. There was one galling problem: as the 'Nature Center' edition of the paper was being printed, a new source of info had appeared out of thin air.

She stood outside the newsstand, puffing in the crisp, February air, and opened the paper to her feature. Large before and after photographs from the site revealed the destruction. A smaller photo showed the footprints she'd seen. She'd gone to the police, finally, with her evidence. They were both pleased and perturbed. She claimed she thought they were her own footsteps, til 'it hit her', that the boot sole imprints were not hers and she realized two other people had made the tracks. 'Why'd you take a photo?'

she was asked. 'I was taking photos of everything, trying to avoid being scalded.' The officers said they'd be talking to her at more length. 'Read my story,' she said. Arson was indeed the lede.

A man, or older teen, had called her on the phone, early this morning.

'You're a reporter, right?'

'Yes.'

'You saw the fire, were there that night?'

'Yes. Who is this?'

'It was arson. Almost positive. Just so you know.'

'You know who did it?'

'Yes.'

'And?'

'Have to hang up.' He did.

Alas for timing. Maybe another feature. Meanwhile, she would work on her other story; there was a nurse named Carmen who had treated the Green lady and her unusual gestation.

Carmen Walker. She would check her out on LinkedIn.

*　　*　　*

Gideon Moss wondered if he could last another term at St. Anselm.

Derealization, ever-present, lurked, a stolid reminder his apple-gift was not redeeming him. His recent activities, distracting in a sick way, now seemed empty. The Tree was alive, but struggling; he could discern that. What was he supposed to do? Just hang around waiting for more dubious inspiration to perform cryptic tasks?

Razor, he suspected, had guessed that Gideon was complicit in the Nature Center catastrophe. Maybe not the prime mover, but a main player. Razor – smart, sharp. *He won't give my name to the police. My son.*

He'd better not.

Catholic High School. Nuns, their habits overflowing with good intentions. First day back, he was surprised he didn't cause a metaphysical chain reaction, just walking past Sr. Antioch. There was no recognition, from within, or from others, that he'd been blessed or cursed in some unique, powerful, and enduring manner. His added cognitive function was not as accessible as it first seemed to be. He guessed his derealization was once again, as with everything else, disrupting and reducing this apple-bestowed gift.

There was Sister Melanie Ignatius, walking down the hall towards him.

'Good morning, Sister.'

'Good morning, Gideon.'

'May I have a word?'

'Here?'

'Maybe, how about out on the benches, the convent gardens?'

'Cold.'

'Just ten minutes,' he said.

They exited the back door of the school and strolled to the rear of the convent, where a small garden was maintained, its flowers and vegetables under a blanket of snow. Moss brushed the dry snow from the wood bench, and they sat.

Ignatius crossed her arms against the chill. 'Is it something with my teaching, Gideon?'

'No, no…' He leaned forward and stared at his feet.

'I'm feeling very, ahh, spiritually challenged.' He looked up to catch whatever sympathetic expressions his attending nun might emote. None forthcoming so far. 'So I wanted to see, to ask, if we could take a part of our school schedules, not to interfere, and you are busy, maybe once a week, spend an hour, half hour, do you think?' He felt like a student again, in her presence. It was somehow comforting.

'We can.'

He raised his eyebrows as high as possible, and smirked – all he could manage as an affirmation. 'Good. Let me know some times when you're free to talk.'

'Busy, as you know, but we'll make time.' She closed her eyes in synch with a small bow. 'Now, shall we get back inside? It's very cold.'

*   *   *

The Sisters of Charity welcomed Ms. Emma Green to their convent. The elderly, warm Mother Superior, Sister Ana, had agreed to the arrangement, leaving the logistics to Ignatius. Emma was provided with a small studio apartment, usually reserved for the Sisters' relatives or visiting clergy, nestled in the sedate convent basement. It had several slotted windows, fixed above ground level, that looked toward the garden, making it diffuse with soft, withdrawn light. Directly above was the infirmary.

Ignatius had agreed with the Greens that the Eden-Apple 'ingredient' of their situation would be on a need-to-know basis, contained, for everyone's sake. Some of the nuns, graced with a sisterly-kind-of-sixth-sense, seemed to guess, Emma would swear. Well, maybe not *swear.*

Dr. Haskley had advised the convent medical staff of the situation, and they'd hustled in Charity fashion to make good on all his requests. Abel was in moderate shock. Gamma Way suddenly empty. But it made sense. The circle of their seedy-ness, and needy-ness, for better or worse, grew like Emma's belly.

*   *   *

Ignatius, navigating multiple labors with grace and energy, worked through channels with the Poor Clares, and succeeded in getting word to Rome that they would welcome and appreciate and, really, required, in-person consulting to deliberate on these remarkable proceedings. Sr. Loyola Pancratius was being sent over to confer, as a start. Father Jack suggested Ignatius offload some of her responsibilities. She asked him, only, to pray.

*

Sister Ignatius was scheduled to pick-up Sister Pancratius from the Pittsburgh International Airport at noon. It was Saturday, the weather stubbornly refusing to show signs of warming. With the tumult of the Greens' situation, her teaching role, and tasks as part of the Convent's daily duty roster, she'd been unable to catch up with Gideon Moss. Was he able to accompany her to the airport? They could talk en route.

Sister appreciated the chance to get away from her labors, worthy and rewarding though they were. She'd noted and even pitied Moss's general sense of estrangement, though she'd only known him since her arrival last term. In the convent's general-use station wagon they headed out. The Parkway West was less busy with the weekend's traffic. Ignatius slotted a Gregorian Chant CD into the car stereo. The monks' voices rose quietly underneath the highway's thrum.

'What is it…you wanted to discuss?'

'I'm struggling, Sister. It's, I think, a realization I have no bridge, any more, to the spiritual.'

'God doesn't ask or require an invitation to rejoin the scrum.'

'Scrum?'

'Your separation is a choice you make. There's no re-entry form or qualification. Only mercy and welcome.'

'Ok, so I know that. I get that. But I – I'm facing some deeper, uhh, more consequential situations. And I can pray, sure, and maybe get some inklings of whatever it is God dispenses. I'm looking for clarity.'

'Clarity, as in, specific actions you can take that are spiritually enabled? Might we say… heaven sent?'

Sister glanced to see if Moss warmed at all to her mild humor. Reacting to something in his presence, she swallowed.

She gestured towards the road ahead.

'Look at that BMW passing everybody. Doing ninety. At least.' Moss saw her tap fingers on the steering wheel. 'God never tells us what to do. God doesn't rearrange synapses. I don't know that *technical* miracles exist, if that's what you're expecting: things that break the fundamental physics God's given us.'

'Maybe I have some news for you, Sister.'

'I've been witness to events some would term miraculous. I see them as part and parcel of the miracle of this Universe, created for open-ended discovery and humanity's benefit. If God dropped down in front of you and stated "*I am I*", would you react with the free will to say "prove it", or be overwhelmed with the brute fact?'

'That's a question for a Sunday talk show. I need direction. Not confession. Not absolution,' he said.

'I'm happy to offer what I know from my own life.'

Ignatius began to flex her shoulders. Muscles there cramping. *What was this about?*

Gideon clasped the seatbelt in front of his heart.

'The other side is here.'

Sr. Ignatius looked over at him.

'Really, Gideon. A bit dramatic.'

She pointed out the window. 'Look. The State Police nabbed that BMW. Some prayers get quick answers.'

She put her foot down, gently, on the gas, accelerating a bit, thinking she'd prefer not to spend this kind of isolated communion with Mr. Moss.

*   *   *

Emma Green had three babies, delivered on consecutive days in late February. All three babies were full-term at five and a half months, healthy in every measurable diagnostic. Emma was also fine, resting and sleeping. The lengthy, first-of-its-kind three days long triplets delivery, to go with the unprecedented nature of the entire pregnancy, was unrivaled in recorded medical history.

*   *   *

Out in the park, where the first blossoms heralded the unending newness of another spring, *boneseed first* was rooting at tendrils in the earth.

It had an unusual capacity, one the world had never suffered to witness. It could melt water.

TWELVE

THREE GIRLS, ALL beautiful.

Abel was sobbing, the Sisters beaming, Emma smiling, the babies crying. Dr. Haskley had served as attendant obstetrician – fending off several nuns who'd insisted on close quarters. Ignatius had been curiously absent, though she'd put so much energy into the arrangements, most surmised she just needed space.

In keeping with the phenomenon of the babies' 'pioneering' parturiency, each one had waited, spaced over a 25 hour period, before following their sister into the world. Other than that, and the startling full-term weights and excellent marks on newborn well-being (considering their five and a half month period as in utero triplets) the births were as normal as they could be. A small blood sample from each girl's heel was collected and sent for testing. No genetic disorders surfaced. The normalcy of the results stood out as the abnormality. *Caroline Dragon* arrived first. *Rebecca Miller* second. *Margaret Boyd* third. February 27th, 28th, and 29th were marked as their birth dates.

Their middle names honored a wish by Emma's Croatian mother Etta Zenovick. Triplet brothers Dragon, Miller and Boyd Zenovich were Croatian nationals living near Zagreb during the start of WWII. In some unexplained fashion, the three brothers had sacrificed themselves to save their baby sister, Etta, who had then pleaded with *her* only daughter, Emma, to commemorate the three brothers if she had children.

When Emma had suggested this to Abel, a week ago, he suggested she swallow a pharmaceutical. He posited that naming the girls – especially these girls – after uncles, males, was not in keeping with their 'slightly' unusual situation. Emma argued the uncle's names be the middle names, at least. Disagreement was not advisable at this time.

As one reporter had seen fit to snoop her way into their private lives, Abel and Emma decided they'd agree to be interviewed by her, a Ms. Riley Cardle. This, they thought, would allow all the wild truths to be wrapped up in one tidy, publicly-released package. Then the conspiracies-theorists could flood the media in such as way that the whole thing would wax ludicrous, roar through its moment, and disappear, to everyone's disparate satisfactions.

'What a clever plan,' said Father Jack. 'Wish I'd have thought of that.' He christened each child on March 19, secretly celebrating his own birthday. By then, the babies had each doubled its birth weight. Dragon and Miller, in front of their parents' astonished eyes, and several adoring and astonished Sisters of Charity, were rolling from their backs to their bellies.

Father had broken with Catholic tradition, convention, and regulation, and decided that the original Dragon, Miller and Boyd would serve as Godparents to the child named after each of them. If these long-deceased Croatian fellows were not up in Heaven studying the goings-on below, bound by flesh and blood as participants therein, what was the point of anything he was doing.

*   *   *

Abel was back at his desk, its surface festooned with flowers, boxes of candy, and a 'value-size' bag of disposable diapers. His co-workers had all congratulated him, even as he noted their whispers at the suddenness of his fatherhood and oddity of the 'birth date spread'.

He idly rested his fingers at his keyboard, as digital photos of the three Green sisters, his beautiful daughters, floated en masse on his screensaver. Just look at them.

And then, there it was.

fiat lux three

Boneseed fifth

Banedaggers are both insectazoid and crablike, flattened and low-strung, dark mottled reddish black in color. They move with unusual speed. Sharp, serrated stingers extend from both sides of their plated, oval shape. Six legs sprout from under the thorax and abdomen. Contained in the first sting is a swelling venom that enters a victim's bloodstream. The second, subsequent sting launches powerful antidotes into the victim, removing the toxins of the primary sting. Thus, in the instance of an attack, a banedagger must be contained and brought to the victim for a life-saving second sting.

Boneseed seventh

The weaselmander was

The *fiat* stopped mid-sentence. *Fiat lux* was having technical problems. A good omen. *Not.*

He saved and closed the text, then leaned back in his chair and looked around the office. His co-workers were productive (when not messing with their phones) and made his life easier with their attendant normalcy, as the stress levels mounted in his alternate universe. His own enhanced abilities allowed him to nail assigned tasks rapidly and effectively. That blessing remained a constant through the unrelenting current of unrealities that attended everything in his and Emma's lives since October One.

This *fiat* was not Old Testament styled ruminations on the genesis of their recent experiences. It was more like a quick start guide to abject terror. It appeared to explain in all-too-outlandish detail one of the incoming denizens from the *Great Crucible*, referenced in the first one. *Banedaggers* sounded like cast-offs from a direct-to-video sci-fi movie.

He elected to finish the day by working on the Annual Spring Carnival promotions. It felt important to nullify the assault on his psyche this *fiat lux* had triggered.

*   *   *

Lars Patton felt like a discharged battery. He was given time off from school; a 'special dispensation' handed out by the usually recalcitrant Principal, Mr. Gideon Moss. His mother appeared to take it all calmly, though she upped her smoking, and purchased a box of Phillies Cheroots. Lars made a mental note to acquire the cool box when his mom had smoked the cheroots.

He was given homework assignments, largely ignored. More interesting was his hair, now a remarkable shade of green, including new hair that had grown in. He looked like a Grade A freak, to go with some mysterious mental transmutation continuing within him, via the Nature Center's green chemistry bomb, all kickstarted by the chomp on his neck by that now black-as-ash rodent.

Skipping steps on the way down from his bedroom to the HUX basement land, he hailed his mother. 'Mornin', Ma..!' A glance at the kitchen: she was there washing dishes, with her back to him, wisps of smoke trailing up with each puff.

'Go get 'em, tiger,' she said.

The sample of his short fuzzy hair was easy to pluck. He put it under his microscope and opened his eyes.

*   *   *

Sister Ignatius had not meant to miss the Greens' birth celebrations. Sister Pancratius, from the Vatican, had asked to meet away from the convent, at the Bishop's Residence. Asked to recuse himself from the discussion, Bishop Garner was more than pleased to do so. Father Jack Murray, Sister Melanie Ignatius, and Sister Loyola Pancratius were sworn in by the Bishop, who then congenially stepped out, closing the large wooden doors behind him. Jack felt as though he was in a Conclave, for a moment, in Rome. Sister Pancratius, though petite in size, and suffering a slight crook in the neck, was sharp as a blade. She had what sounded like an Austrian accent.

'You've called Rome and here I am.'

Before her, on the large oak table, was documentation from the Greens' case. Pancratius, wearing thick wire-rim spectacles that hid her eyes, organized the material to her liking and slid small packets in front of Jack and Ignatius. Jack was amazed at how much she'd accrued. Ignatius must have been burning the midnight incense organizing it, not to mention playing host to this small, wiry Sister, come to hear their particulars and – Jack suspected – not given to suffer fools. Even fools for Christ.

Pancratius paused to take a sip from the Deer Park Spring Water, smacking her lips as she set the bottle down. 'I'd anticipated the water from Pennsylvania's springs would be good. I love mountain spring water. You taste the minerals.' She took another sip. 'I'm here not necessarily to confirm a miracle. I'm hear to consider what we have and make recommendations,' she said. 'Let's start with you, Jack, the preliminary contact.'

Jack proffered all he knew, and some he suspected, while Pancratius penned notes. He went over the pregnancy and birth of the three babies.

'Tell me about the tree. The apple tree,' said Pancratius, directing her gaze at Sr. Ignatius.

'We don't know much. None of us has gone down to find it. At least none of us from the parish, and nor have the Greens, I believe, since they came upon it,' said Ignatius. 'We don't want a false Fatima induced here. In fact, its location has not been related; just the general area of Frick Park.'

'I think that's good,' said Pancratius. 'If this turns out to be legitimate, and its cause forwarded in the Church, it won't be possible to stem the multitudes from visiting. It might be better to transplant the tree.' She paused and looked at them. 'God knows.'

'A way forward here, Sister,' said Jack 'is to advocate for a single, incisive interview with the Greens. They have experienced a rush of emotional and psychological changes, immediately after consuming the apple. It might be chemistry. Might be some other less common but explainable influence. The husband has accrued content, somehow, through his computer, a feed of metaphysical backstory to what's been occurring. And the babies, of course, as you no doubt have been informed, are developing at record-breaking speed. Fortunately healthy, mentally and physically.' Jack continued as he could, refusing to over-embellish as much as to thin the realities into concoction.

'That's not much, Father,' said Pancratius. 'There's nothing miraculous in this composition. Conjecture. Possibilities. Has someone been cured of disease? Has a cup levitated off a table? The story of Eden resurrected has smitten both of you in its easy compatibility with Genesis.'

'Text appearing on a screen by itself is fairly remarkable,' Ignatius said. She leaned back in her chair, as Jack leaned forward.

'You didn't come all the way from Rome to tell us this,' he said.

Pancratius took a long swig of her Deer Park. 'No; the Church does not turn away from events that harken our mission. To find God, to see God, to know God. Not just from venerated writings and the tradition of ceremony. Not just from the love and charity of other humans. We are not blind. We are discerning.'

'So what shall it be?' said Ignatius.

'Read the information I've supplied, from material Sister Ignatius has dutifully organized, in the packets in front of you. Then prepare. I will recommend we send representatives from the three major faiths, Christian, Islam, and Judaism.'

Jack opened his arms in supplication. He hoped it depicted a 'welcome', though what he was feeling felt more like a pleased shock.

'We will arrange for this meeting to take place at the Sisters of Charity Motherhouse, at Seton Hill. We'll plan for high summer – the 4th of July

American holiday. A way to divert attention, should that be useful. It's a bit further along in the calendar but there's some logistics to facilitate, as you can imagine.' She paused 'Would Mr. Green provide us with the *fiat lux* material?'

'Maybe, possibly – I'll ask,' said Jack.

'Forward that when you get it. Be sure it's encrypted. This 4h of July summit will be coded as *Fireworks*. Your three guests will be known as the *Three Wise Guys*.'

Jack had an inopportune recall of Moe, Larry and Curly in white robes. They all paused to take some breaths and gulp down some water.

'You taste the magnesium, potassium, and sodium?' asked Pancratius. 'I use to lead a choir at a small parish. In Vienna. Some of the boys made it to the Vienna Boys Choir. I had them drink mineral water to keep their vocal cords in tip-top order.' She rose, stooped over the table and began shuffling her documents into order. 'Can you get me an Uber to the airport?'

*　　*　　*

Boneseed first was the leopard pillbox slug. Rising out of the earth made soft and muddy from the melting snow, it crawled with slow intent across this fresh universe. Its dulled consciousness knew only random generalities about existence. The Makors had imbued it with the base survival and reproductive instincts of the majority of creatures already living on the Earth. It was new, and hunted for food. Food was plants. Elimination was unusual: the leopard pillbox slug digested and, through a unique series of intestinal plumbing, transformed its excretions into a catalyst that would *melt water.* The process separated the water's hydrogen molecules from its oxygen molecules; here was a non-flora species able to enact a kind of photolysis. A shift in one of nature's fundamental life-providing cycles had entered the equations of the world.

*　　*　　*

'Earth to Emma, earth to Emma, come in.' Abel was holding and rocking Miller, watching his wife try to sleep while nursing the other two girls.

She looked up at him with her sleepy eyes. 'Hello.'

'How ya doin', lover?' he said.

'Kinda tired. You mind taking these three to Kennywood for the afternoon?' She smiled through her droopy lids.

'They're growing like weeds.'

'They are weeds. Where's our lawn-keepers...' Abel reached to tickle the bare bottom of her exposed foot.

'My mom was over, at last. She gushed,' said Emma.

'And why not?' said Abel. 'She come in with Charlie?'

'Yes. They're at a hotel in Monroeville, for now. Didn't want to bust up your Gamma Way bachelor pad.'

'That's well-mannered. She stickin' around?'

'Yes. Wants to know our plans, our schemes, what we're feeding them, what schools they'll go to. And when they'll be baptized.'

'You tell her we got Jack to do a stealth baptism?' said Abel.

'No way. You can tell her that.'

He stooped next to the bed and stroked his wife's hair. 'You still Ok with the reporter?'

'Today?'

'Yup.'

'Why not. Soon?'

'Yup. She's here, waiting,' said Abel.

'And we're giving her the whole scoop, minus the top secret stuff we agreed on,' asked Emma.

'Yup. I've written down everything.' He held up a piece of paper. 'All on this sheet I'm giving her, so she won't go too far astray.'

'Ha! We shall see.' Emma rose from her bed, set the squirming babies in their oversize crib, and smoothed out her clothing. Abel set Miller down between her sisters.

'Where, exactly?' asked Emma.

'We go up to the chapel and meet the reporter there. Riley Cardle from the *Post-Press*. The Sisters – several Sisters, Sisters of Charity – are eager to get time with the three Green sisters. Free on-site babysitting, mother!'

Several nuns bustled in to take over the nursery. Abel and Emma climbed the short stairs. Mother Superior Ana greeted them outside the chapel door, which she swung open. She held a finger vertically against her mouth. 'Keep things quiet and respectful. I've asked the same of Ms. Cardle.'

'Of course, Sister,' nodded Abel.

Shafts of light daubed the quiet. A small alcoved altar was covered with heavy crimson cloth. Riley Cardle sat in a pew near the rear.

'Ms. Cardle,' said Abel. 'I'm Abel Green, this is Emma.'

Cardle rose to shake their hands. 'Thank you so much for this opportunity. I'm eager to tell your story and share it.'

'We thought, by keeping it to a single reporter, you, we'd curtail some of the conjecture that'll be flying around out there,' said Emma.

'It surely will. Congratulations on your triplets. You guys must be beat.'

'We are. But the Sisters of Charity here are true to their namesake,' said Abel. 'Here's a note for you: names, birth weights, some backstory on us,' said Abel, handing the paper to Cardle. The Greens sat down in the pew behind her.

'I'd like to record this on my phone – '

'No', said Emma.

'Ahh…Ok. Sorry.' Cardle placed the phone back in her bag, pressing the 'record' button as she did.

'And very, very, very, very specifically,' said Emma, 'we do not want you to print where we are living, raising these children. Either here or if and when we return home.'

Cardle nodded. 'What people will be most interested in is your accelerated pregnancy. Ok if I call you Emma?' Emma nodded. 'Emma, five and a half months, babies and mother in good health. Can you tell me what this all means as far as medical science?'

'Not really.'

'Your doctors must be – incredulous.'

'Our doctor, Stewart Haskley, has been a wonderful physician throughout. He never assumed, remained very thorough, and simply acted and reacted as any good doctor would, as our case unfolded.'

'But this is an unprecedented medical event, according to any accessible records.'

'Our children did not just pop out of thin air. They grew and developed more rapidly than most, but every fetus develops uniquely.'

'I'm sorry; it sounds like you're dumbing down something that's close to miraculous,' said Cardle.

'You're jazzing up a medical event that's occurred, so is no longer unprecedented,' said Abel. 'We're hoping for less emphasis on hyperbole. Put the facts in your story and let the readers amp up their own hyperbole. Please.'

Cardle took a deep breath and ran some fingers over her lips. 'May I get a photo of the triplets?'

Emma shook her head 'No'.

'Why don't you both just relate to me what you can. I'm grateful for this interview. Remember that the community and the region will enjoy your story and want to know.'

'And tomorrow they'll all forget it,' smiled Abel.

'There is one aspect I can't resist asking about. I hope you won't think I'm being too forward,' said Cardle. 'The babies are healthy and we understand growing… growing –'

'They're growing, yes,' said Emma. 'Ms. Cardle. I'm exhausted and will get back to my children. Use the material we've provided on that sheet. Odds are you won't find a Sister here willing to corrupt her vows with some insider scoop.'

Emma rose from the pew and marched out of the chapel.

'Ms. Cardle – Riley, is it,' said Abel. 'There's not really a story here, despite what you may have gleaned from your various sources. We're a local family, blessed with three healthy kids, who broke some long-standing records in their hurry to join us. All we ask is you don't make fact into fiction.' He rose, reached for her hand to shake it, and stood back to allow her to leave first.

*   *   *

Over the next months, the three Green Sisters flourished in exceptional ways. Abel and Emma, with Ignatius' concurrence and blessing, kept the children at the Charity convent. Dr. Haskley monitored their progress. He told the Greens plainly he was both amazed and frightened. Their accelerated physical advance remained healthy across all markers. The unsaid reckoning behind it meant they would not live long.

He arrived with Carmen, his assistant, on a warming April morning, looking a smidgen more relaxed than usual. The girls were wandering about their play area; the entire studio apartment a jumble of color and somewhat-controlled mayhem. Abel sat amongst them, delivering items for their review.

'I have hopeful news,' he said. 'And I brought Carmen along to share it. She's been a great help keeping track of interested practitioners and also fending some of them off, thank you, Carmen! And she wanted to see the babies.'

'Adorable!' said Carmen. She shook her head, then opened a notebook to read. 'The girls are tracking at roughly 30 weeks as far as developmental metrics; this at 8 weeks from birth. Except for talking and walking, and –' she turned to note the girls '– they seem to be on the brink of both. The better news is that the tests we took Monday indicate a reduction in the speed of their development. Slight, but measurable.'

Dr. Haskley lifted Boyd from her perch, settled against a pillow on the floor, the soon-to-be-toddler running numbers on an abacus. 'The slow down is minimal,' he said, 'but, of course, so welcome.' Boyd reached for the doctor's chin, which Haskley bent to provide.

Emma let out a hopeful sigh. 'Thank you, doctor, Carmen. You hear that, young ladies?' Miller, Boyd and Dragon made no move to acknowledge their mother's inquiry.

'We'll raise them here, as long as the Sisters are Ok with this,' said Abel. 'A hard thing, not bringing them home.'

'Maybe you can, Abel,' said Haskley. 'Let's talk about it more. No need to assume the neighborhood environment will harm them, in the longest run. The park's your backyard, your house fairly hidden away, from Braddock Avenue; you have good, supportive neighbors. And these good Sisters…' he waved his hand about him '…who we all know will be impossible to keep away.'

'I'd love that,' said Abel.

*   *   *

Boneseed second emerged in March. It did not survive. Its truncated corpse was decaying not far from the Point Breeze cemetery near the northern border of Frick Park.

Boneseed third formed in an egg. On the thirteenth of April, it hatched in a hollow on the flanks of Clayton Hill, not far from the Forbes Ave. roadway. The hatchling was able to move from its broken shell to a nook, set above ground, formed from a spread of a dead maple's main branches. The sun was up and shining in the sky. The batbird managed a beginner's meek but pleasant call.

It was Easter morning.

*   *   *

Lars needed equipment from the dark web. And money to order it. Moss had promised him cash for his part in that *event-which-shall-not-*

be-named-you-bozo that he'd never collected. Contact with Moss became necessary. Bummer.

*   *   *

Gideon Moss plied his Gideon's Bible and versed himself in the passages. He'd pursued Sister Ignatius, coerced her, despite her evident reluctance, to continue meeting. Their conversations had given him – if not hope – a distracting sense of movement to somewhere better. Perhaps. Different, at least. He couldn't articulate it. With no direction other than the thread of her slowly-revealed philosophies, he had few options. And he couldn't quite bring himself to mention the apple. There was something else, occurring, when in her company. Something he couldn't see himself admitting, even as desperate as he felt. He'd begun to *like* her. The woman.

*   *   *

'Can you ask your dad to fork over the money he promised?'

Lars was on the phone with Razor Moss. Razor sounded sad.

'I can ask,' said Razor.

'Don't know about school, going back, yet. Need some hair dye that'll stick,' said Lars, adding a chuckle for effect.

'I heard you were not well,' said Razor.

'Yeah, well... Ok, let me know what he says. And if you can drop the cash off at my house. Hutchinson Ave., 444.'

'I'll let you know. I'll text,' said Razor.

'Thanks. See you.'

Razor didn't even ask about why he needed hair dye. Lars found himself in need of a confessor. Astrid mostly laughed at him. His mother, well... at times it felt like her cigarette and cigar smoke was starting to spool out of her like stitch-work coming unseamed. He needed to make sure she was Ok. In addition, he now had a formal delinquency to contain, tree larceny (ha!) and arson (bad), and regret, frothing up in his conscience. The Black Squirrel spell must be wearing off.

*   *   *

Emma was in crisis. The children, the daughters, were amazing. Despite the medical extravaganza, of burst records and their unguessable future, she knew she and Abel had been blessed. The nuns had been a 24/7 blanket of care, in every possible manner, and then some. They always respected her privacy, but seemed to have a miraculous knack for being at the apartment door when she needed assistance, which was often.

Abel came daily, often before and always after work. She could see he was maxed out, but also that he was feeling marvelous in so many ways it was giving her nausea. A contrary reaction, that. This thing brewing in her could no longer be waylaid. She knew about postpartum depression. She knew the science. Here it was, at triple strength. And the postpartum, she realized in the middle of the night, was a veneer of something more insidious and, she would have thought, impossible. She wanted out.

She wanted a separation, from her husband and from her children and from her new-found glimpse into faith. All of these tore at her ability to know contentment and the umbilical cord to her true nature. The cries of the babies, the coos hinting at their flowering sentience, the murmurs of metaphysical mirth, the loving oversight of her husband and the bustling nuns. It made her a cripple. Uncomfortable in the self she had cast over her twenty-nine years in the kiln.

Abel was coming soon. She looked at the ceiling, looked at her sleeping girls, looked at the windows, where buds were sneaking out on the waving tips of crocuses. If she didn't acknowledge the sludge of her state, it would get worse.

He tapped gently, opened the door, entered, and, with a smile at his wife, tiptoed to the cradles to gaze at Miller, Boyd and Dragon. The three Green sisters. She stood and came over and put a hand at the back of his neck.

'That's cold. You need a hot water bottle?' he said, turning to kiss her.

She offered a slight grin. 'Let's get the sisters. Let's go up for a walk in the garden.'

'It's more like a three foot patch of flowers.' He put his head around the corner into the hallway. Sister Alison smiled, gave him a thumbs-up, and waited for the couple to exit.

They put on jackets against the spring's mix of cool wind and warming sun.

'Let's walk around the block,' she said. They headed down Church Street, towards the railroad overpass.

'You doing Ok, honey? I miss you and the cats hate me,' he said.

'Tell them to "cat up". Is that the phrase – *man up?*'

'Yes. Every man's man knows it. Like a pledge; you are offered a sturdy, high alcohol drink, in the company of strangers, in the quiet of a railroad station, running scared…'

'You Simon or Garfunkel?'

'Anyway, sorry, you *man-up* and drink it. Then fall down on your stupidity.'

She took his hand, under a large white oak tree that hovered in front of the funeral parlor that had closed some years ago. Like others, this parlor had sprouted near the parish, when it was burgeoning with Catholic families, Catholic births and Catholic deaths. Now these – businesses after all – were closing, as the Catholic population trended with the rest of the world, and slowed their birthrates. He knew to sit, with her, on the cold cement.

'What's the matter, Emma?'

'I can't get it to come out. Use your seedy mind and extract.'

'My seedy mind is barely functioning as a normal mind. Metaphysicals are moody fabrications. You know.'

'I need to leave you, and leave the children.'

Abel looked at her, then away, then back, his face the kind of blank she hated. 'This doesn't fit well with the story.'

She began to cry, in great heaving sobs. He leaned to put an arm around her.

'Listen,' he said. 'Everything is completely off from what we thought was normal. From where we were, on September 30th.' He looked down and ran his free hand in a circle. 'Remember the Tilt-a-Whirl, at Kennywood?' She nodded. He handed her a Kleenex. 'You spin and you push your body in some direction to make it go slower or faster, and depending on the other cars and where in the track you are, your push makes a difference, or sometimes does the exact opposite. Of your intentions.'

Her face was in her lap and her hands were on her knees. 'Stupid.'

'Ok, maybe. Sorry.' He brushed the hair from her slumped back, watched it fall over her slumped shoulders. 'Whatever you're thinking or feeling, you gotta have room to let it run free. There are things at work beyond our reach, for one thing, and secondly, and most of all, because I want you to find a safe place to regroup and key in to what you can take and know and hold.' He paused. 'Sounds like an Dale Carnegie speech, don't it?' Now he was tearing up.

She reached for his hand and squeezed it.

'What do you want to do?' he asked.

She kept her face buried. 'You take the kids and go to Gamma Way.'

'What do you do?'

'I stay. Here.'

'And become a Sister of Charity. Sister Mary Agnostic?'

She nodded, and kicked him in the shin.

'Let's walk around the block and get back before the Sisters lose their zeal for watching over three prodigies.'

They stood up and walked the rest of the way in silence. Of course, she knew, Abel's heart had been dismantled. Here, she wished she could pray for him.

THIRTEEN

Abel pulled open the refrigerator door, eyed the fodder, then closed it. *I'm bringing those kids home.*

He called Emma's mother, Etta. She responded with every warmth he'd expected, til he'd mentioned Emma's 'plan'. There was a good minute of silence, in which Abel could hear her resolve channeling. Finally: 'She's a good girl.' That was enough for Abel. Etta would go with the needs of the moment and not try to figure out the trajectory of her daughter. Abel had no wish to drop through yet another emotional trapdoor, and was grateful Emma's mother could set aside her trepidation for a higher cause.

Etta had had her 'long-term' bags packed, apparently, anticipating some form of grand-mothering adventure. Triplets, after all! Her male companion, Charlie, was fine with heading back to Lancaster to organize his own senior bachelor pad. As long as Etta didn't stay away so long that he 'dropped dead' before she returned.

Abel went into their study and perused it. Cribs will fit here. The way those ladies are growing, three beds upstairs, soon. I'll take the third floor garret and Etta can have our bedroom. Have to buy food. Toys, Diaper service. Babysitting help. Some of those nuns, maybe. Call Sheila, check with Dan and Betsy. They're retired and might jump into the breech.

He knelt down and folded his hands.

'God. I've just about lost the ability to say anything. There's a lot of important things going on in the world, all over the world, people in need with major crises on their hands. So I'll keep this short. Help Emma find her way. Watch over the three babies. Figure out what you want to do about all the apple tree stuff, and send me a note so I don't have to guess.'

*　　*　　*

Razor got another text from Lars asking him if Gideon was going to pay him. Razor had avoided asking. He texted back to say he'd find out, right away. His father was out back, sitting on a dilapidated wooden bench, beside their crumbling brick barbecue grill, studying his tree. He held one of the red bricks, turned over and over in his hands. Razor walked over to him.

'Lars Patton is asking about that money you promised him.'

'No blossoms. This tree is not healthy. Can Lars help us with this?'

'He's not a botanist. Are you going to pay him or not?'

'Yes, yes. Take a $50 out of my wallet. Give it to him in school.'

'He's not in school. He's out for the term.'

'Take it to his house. Ask him about the tree, what we should do...'

Razor went inside the house. The whole thing was a mess. He needed to free his conscience of the bleak truth he was hiding: that his dad, and probably Lars, had been the arsonists who burned down the Frick building. He walked back outside.

'Dad. You need to – get to a police station – and confess.'

Gideon looked up, for a moment his eyes sorrowful.

'Is that what you figure, Razor. I'll lose my job, go to court. Then jail. Lars expelled. You ready for all that?' He stood. 'I'm not unwilling to confess. There's a reason this was done. There's something else, something more to do, if I can see it. I need more time.'

'There's a *reason*,' said Razor. 'Hey, yeah, like – they'll build a fancy new Environmental Center, now that the old one is burnt down. You did the community a service. Is that your idea?'

Razor smirked. He thrust his arm across, in front of Gideon's face, to grip the tree's trunk. He jerked it out of the ground, roots dangling, and hurled it into the bushy weeds at the edge of their yard.

Gideon gathered himself, stood up, and threw his shoulder into his son's sternum. Razor toppled and fell backwards, his head cracking on the bricks beside the bench. He slumped, unconscious.

Gideon reached down to feel the back of Razor's head. There was blood. 'You brought this on yourself.'

*　　*　　*

Ignatius spread the word that Gideon's son Ray – Razor – had suffered a fall at home. Gideon asked for privacy. Razor was in a coma at Shadyside Hospital. Gideon would be away from work and was reportedly, understandably, in shock.

*　　*　　*

Lars found an envelope in the mailbox containing $513 in cash. Gideon was generous. Something treacherous this way comes, though. His high school Principal, more and more, was exuding a kind of mob-boss aura. And now Razor was in a coma.

Don't want to know how that came about.

This was way too messy for Lars, the humble high school genius-type-kid. Lars blew out a deep breath. *Ok.* He had to move his head out of that space and get busy.

He needed a chemical-tracker of some sort. The exotic chemistry in his green hair was idiosyncratic. Some sort of compound combining two or three elements that usually didn't like each other's company. He wanted to see how it reacted to some additional proddings. And, this the bigger deal, he wanted to see if he could wrangle up some technical instrumentation, like a metal-detector you use at the beach, that would 'beep' if the trace was identified. Once invented, he'd go into the park and nose around to see if this weird chemistry was manifesting in the park, after the fire. Since it obviously got spread by the flames and wind and snow, and had colored his hair green, via a biochemically-startling and robust single flake, it could be playing havoc with any number of organic mechanisms.

*　　*　　*

Abel had one last thing he wanted to complete before the triplets came to Gamma Way. Something he and Emma had both wanted to do but had never managed since last October. Go see the Tree.

He rose early on a fresh May Day Saturday and headed into the park, now splashed with spring sunshine and showing off to many walkers, with their dogs, frisbees, radios, and good spirits. He'd walk a discreet, roundabout way to the apple alcove, hoping to discourage attention and avoid acquaintances.

What if it was fruiting? The Tree. Good God, *one more time.*

Down under the Frick Park ceiling felt strange; both familiar and not - the snow long gone and a wide range of greens strutting its stuff. He fought to summarize the headlines in his life. Wife… *living in convent.* Three new daughters… *growing faster than they should.* Husband and wife bearing a qualitatively-unmeasurable additive wrought from an apple bitten last fall. Brains parsing vast library of previously unavailable or newly-rendered content. Insights into daily life and cosmic outliers. All of it drenched in spiritual immediacy and their standing awareness of their own personal moral and mortal inefficiencies.

Story replete with other 'apple-biter' (behaviorally-suspect high school principal), missing apple, and helpful supporting cast of nuns, priest, neighbors, mother-in-law, and medical personnel. Side show of Frick Park Nature Center's suspicious fire and possible knowledge of who is to blame, lacking inertia to follow-up with authorities. Son of suspect in a coma; an accident?

And last but hardly least, the *fiat lux*. Free occasional backstory and front story on the ongoing miracles of Regent Square. It was small wonder Abel was able *(ha!)* to keep his head just above water. He needed Emma to bounce things off – she the wise mirror and steady voice. She the caustic and sharp against the dulled and fogged. She the lovely lover, and now, lost as mother. The missing. The missed.

He found that he had traced his steps, without thinking, up to the hidden alcove. There were the little white flowers, in a circle, and the poison ivy. The Tree was gone.

*　　*　　*

The Black Squirrel bite and Green Snowflake zap had indeed steroided Lars' brain. He was sketching a diagram for a sensing device that would flag the chemical compound registered in his hair. He didn't know how long this engineering acumen would last, and so hurried his work in the HUX lab to complete it. Gideon's blood money had funded the venture. Though he'd still have to use material from his resident archive of goods.

'Come and eat, Lars.' His mom calling from upstairs.

'Throw down some chips, please*!*'

The best potato chips were made near Lancaster, PA, in Pennsylvania Dutch Country, Martin's Kettle-Cook'd. He occasionally spotted them at the Swissvale Giant Eagle and demanded his mother buy at least four bags.

His mom carried a bag halfway down and Lars placed it in a wire basket he'd fixed above his work space. Opened the bag, reached in for a single chip and set it in his mouth. *Cruunch.*

So what would he call this green snowflake finder thang? Flake-Finder. Fonk-Finder. X-Detector. X-Tector. Yup, *X-Tector* would do.

So... hand-held, lithium powered. He'd need it to have robust range. No way he could traipse through 600 acres of park and locate every trace. He guessed that the green snow's activating substance was contained within the park, and that many of the flakes had fallen on unsuitable soil, or chemically-disassembled after a week or so. Most that might have floated up into the nearby neighborhoods would have landed on house roofs or roadways, or landed on snow that would be salted or shoveled and melt away to be drained into the sewers. Of course, there may have been strays. There always were in horror stories. But this wasn't a horror story. Was it?

Another chip. *Cruuunchh.*

If his tech could cover a one hundred yard circumference circle, he could sweep the whole park in about a week. That'd be cool. Maybe Dixon could be recruited. He lifted one more Martin's chip from the bag and remembered Razor. *That* side of his conscience was not doing well at all.

*   *   *

Abel stumbled inside. He splashed water on his stricken face. The apple tree had been uprooted and – stolen?

Why. Where. Who could he turn to ask? Who should he tell?

Seren and Dippity studied him balefully. Etta's coming. Girls this week. I can work from home for a month. Roman would Ok that. Tree was stolen. Someone. Had to be Gideon. Gideon pulled it out and either killed it, since his brain is as scrambled as ours, or is hoarding it, to find a way to exploit it. Monetize it. *Eat our apples and get a super-boost. Feel and think younger. Know stuff you never imagined existed. Kick butt in every stratum of life.* God, you gotta show up soon and stop monkeying around.

He found he'd opened his laptop and had been tapping at the keys. There it was.

fiat lux four

Thirteen boneseeds will be introduced, through the fruit of the Tree of Knowledge. Planted there when the Garden of Eden was at the end of its time in the Great Crucible. Placed without the permission of the Prime Selector, who answers only to The Will. Designed to be reborn once the flames and fumes from the tree emanate out into the Garden's resurrected spaces. These thirteen boneseeds are the voided who were hidden, and saved, and unvoided, and buried in the great deeps. Their future depended on uncertain factors. That the landscapes would un-hide them, and give the Tree's powers a chance to seek and seed them. Certain Makors and Throwers, in league with the Selector Bazle, had schemed to see their designs become part of Earth's history, understood their own culpability, and that their boneseeds, spawning into humankind's time, could transform that time, bringing thirteen unknowable energies, physical anomalies, and existence-undermining elements into play. Elements that had been rejected as unfit. And would now erupt.

The boneseeds are as follows

The feed ceased.

For Christ's sake, *literally.*

Whoever was sending this had their own technical problems. You'd think they'd have the best IT staff. Really.

Or maybe it had all come from the appled-blessings inside him and he was merely transcribing it as it skewered its way through his muddled, mystified mind out through his fingers and onto the screen.

'I'll feed you guys,' he said out loud, leaning over in the direction of the two whiskered, unconcerned cat faces.

FOURTEEN

RILEY CARDLE HAD been down with some kind of flu. She'd kept herself busy, writing from her bed or couch. The Greens' interview had been published *(Triplets Arrive in Style for Local Family)*, so thin on substance it practically dissolved after reading. She knew there was much more there, that would take time and some luck to ferret forward.

Something about the Nature Center story and Greens' story, some weird channeling, seemed to be angling the two narratives towards each other. As far as new leads, or information, both had gone dry; most of the Frick fire details had been done in her first report, as hard news. Her current material largely covered a planned Nature Center rebuild. But she still had that phone call and those footprints. The Greens' piece, some sort of follow-up to the short interview, was not a print-worthy feature yet in her mind. Listening to the illicit recording she'd made at the convent, she had to wonder why this medical miracle wasn't breaking bigger as local or even national news. Where was the *Mayo Clinic*, *The Lancet*, the *Cleveland Clinic?* She knew that representatives from some of those organizations had visited the Greens during the pregnancy.

Carmen Walker from Haskley's office had provided some provocative medical news flashes. By themselves, though, they just felt like more disposable reads in the mass hash of trendy nothings today's news feeds pitched the world. She wanted her readers to catch the deeply-drawn importance of what Riley Cardle, journalist, discovered. These babies had been born way ahead of schedule. But they were healthy and cared for and she couldn't see an angle that didn't sound like the *National Enquirer*. Unless she went whole hog and suggested they were freaks of nature.

No, she couldn't. A venture into that sordid place, regardless of money, was a one-way ticket out of legitimacy.

Walker had reminded her not to use content that could reveal Walker as a source. She wanted to keep her job; had just felt the situation was so wildly unusual that it should be out in the open. She'd felt Haskley was hesitant, and thus unable to make sure they were not missing something. Something that might endanger the mother or babies: that Haskley's respect for the Greens' privacy had eclipsed his professional willingness to pursue every avenue of prenatal expertise.

Cardle felt Walker was wrong and, frankly, disingenuous.

The story of the Greens' journey couldn't be a tight-rope walk. If the Green sisters' physical acceleration went public, with its accompanying, fairly shocking detail, neither she nor Walker could claim some high-handed, noble position. They'd have to live with their role, as individuals whose unconvincing excuses for spotlighting a family crisis were as poor as their hope for a dollop of renown was strong.

And again, was there a way to bring the fire into this thing? Frick Park. Regent Square. Three babies. This would take some work. She pulled her covers up around her.

A blackbird flew past the window, cawing like a lost crow.

*   *   *

Ignatius wasn't sure how to comfort Gideon Moss, who had been traumatized by his son's accident, when he was already flailing in a spiritual wasteland. He'd related his experience of derealization, which she had been only vaguely familiar with. A degree of everyday torment that no human should have to bear, from what Moss described. After her slight rebuke in the car, the day they'd traveled together to the airport, he never clarified exactly what he'd meant by his remark that *the other side is here*.

He'd hinted less directly of some recent experience he'd gone through that had wrenched him, moved him, to take some desperate action against his state. He'd only admit it was part of the main – that his emptiness was from multiple factors. He was looking for some truth to cling to. He wanted faith without believing, she thought.

She decided, despite her trepidation about meeting with him, to give him more of her time, if he was comfortable with that. She could be an ear for him in a more personal forum. It might do no good; but mercy and charity demanded it. And Ignatius demanded it, of herself.

She'd texted to ask if he'd like to walk through Frick Park. She could take tomorrow morning off from school and meet him at the Hutchinson Street entrance. There'd be nature's quiet peace around them, and evidence of spring's annual insistent renewal, a positive harbinger, regardless of the world's travails. 'Yes' he'd texted back almost immediately.

She walked up to Regent Square the following morning. It was clear and pleasant, with a thin overcast and no wind. Moss was there, pacing with his head down. He turned to see her and what looked like a smile broke against his sallow countenance. The smile faded as she got near, and she wondered if it had even happened.

'Hello, Gideon. How is your son?'

'He's in intensive care. Don't know how long. His mother is at the hospital, all day, every day.'

'I'm so sorry.'

'I visit him and just stroke his forehead.'

'I pray for his healing. Please let us know what we can share with the faculty and students.'

'I will.'

'There's a Mass for him next week. I'll text you if you care to attend.'

'Thank you, Sister Ignatius.'

'Shall we walk?' she said.

They turned and headed down into the park. Moss seemed to know where he wanted to go; Ignatius followed his lead, in silence. She wanted to offer him something, and searched for the words. They reached Fern Hollow and headed up the Falls Ravine trail. Other than an elderly man, with his two small dogs on leashes, there were no other people in sight.

At some point, not far from the trail's start, Moss stopped. He looked up the slope to the left.

'Are you Ok with some hiking off the trail?' he asked.

'Will we step on new growth? I don't want to squash anything.'

Without replying, Moss turned and began to walk up the hill. Ignatius followed. They reached a small, out of the way alcove. A ring of white flowers grew in a patch of poison ivy. Moss appeared to ignore the ivy, and stepped to the back hillside, which he leaned against, upright.

'Poison ivy here, Gideon. Do be careful.' She gingerly moved to the hillside wall, and leaned back herself, a few feet away from the man.

'It is a lovely little alcove. A little garden.' She lowered herself to get a better look at the new growth gathered about her feet. 'This is cinquefoil, I think,' she said, pulling up a vibrant yellow bloom. 'God won't mind if I steal one.' She stood.

Moss sighed.

'Gideon, you have so much on your plate. You have a lot more inside you that you won't say.'

He looked at her, with hopeless hope in his eyes.

'As far as your son, we can pray. His life is not ours to divine, though. Prayers don't do what doctors do. I'm not trying to be pessimistic here. I think it's important to be realistic. And doctors may do what prayers elicit.'

She found herself talking to fill the silence emanating from Moss. She began to fear that she couldn't read him at all on this day. As if she was now with a complete stranger in an out-of-the-way area of a fairly deserted urban park.

'I can't relate as a psychologist, or lead you to God or some other salvation. It's yours to explore. I guess I would say if you can begin to seek with a humble heart and an openness to – maybe small graces – you may find some direction.'

'So God has a plan for me…'

Ahhh. Now *there* was something Ignatius could begin to volley. She recognized this particular flash point might shove his son's plight, derealization, and spiritual lethargy into the back row. Calm. Down. Sister.

'There is no plan,' said Ignatius. 'If God had these trillions of plans for every moment in every human's life – let's start with Genesis. Did God *plan* for Eve to be tempted?'

'You tell me.'

'God knows. If that's the first plan, it didn't work out very well.'

'So there's no God in any plan, in any free will choice?' said Moss. 'We're on our own, to grope our way along with an occasional dash of grace, or hope, or answered, or unanswered prayers. Sister, how do you rationalize your membership in the vast union of so-called believers?' He halted, and chafed, his voice reaching for sincere. 'I'm toying with evidence that the Garden of Eden may be where you and I are standing. That, then, everything in the Bible may be a fact. All true!'

He slid down the back wall, slumping onto the ground, holding a hand over his face. 'You see why I'm a lost cause.'

Ignatius bowed her head. The cross hanging around her neck weighted her. Her words wouldn't resolve, up against this man's inner emptiness, emotional confusion, maligned reasoning, and caustic aura. She'd been cornered into the kind of place she dreaded. Where she'd have to trust her faith to save her, and that this faith, in this moment, could not guarantee her physical well-being.

She also understood, as a profound underpinning to the moment at hand, that this was where the Greens must have happened upon the Tree. That she might indeed have her feet upon Holy Ground. And that Moss's fateful 'experience' took place here. He too, possibly, had tasted the Fruit. It was too easy to mouth the word *God:* and never seemed more appropriate.

Fainting was not an option. She recited the fastest prayer ever, that she might prevail to say something that might unite reason with empathy and bring – whatever it would bring.

'Is this spot where you were given this, this new *awareness,* where you realized you needed to find God. Find God again. Or find God for the first time?'

She moved slightly closer to Moss and flattened her hands against the warm earth behind her. 'Tell me how the Garden of Eden is here.'

He looked up at her, eyes bloodshot, with what might have been tears, or could have been allergies, or a weird metaphysical affliction reserved for just such an occasion. She really felt like running away. He reached his hand up to grasp hers. She let him take her hand, a gesture of human warmth and connection. He raised himself and leaned in, brought his face towards hers, whispered the most unlikely sentiment, as unexpected as if St. Peter has waltzed in to join the chat.

'I want to make love to you…'

With that he consummated the distance to her mouth and kissed her, fully, on her virginal, wine red lips.

*   *   *

'Emma, what do we do?' he said. His voice, on the phone, Emma noted, was a melding of pain and need. She'd seldom heard that timbre since their seedy beginnings. For whatever reason, it did not scare her. She'd been sitting on the floor of the convent studio apartment watching three young creatures stride into their inscrutable futures. News about a missing tree was really no great shakes, at this juncture.

'Man up, man. Not the end of the world.'

'Who has it?'

'Not our job to figure out every corner of this madness, is it?' she said.

'How are the girls?'

'Beautiful. Starting to gab. All of them walking.'

'Good God,' said Abel.

'I guess.'

She heard him sigh loudly, into the mouthpiece of the telephone. She slumped back against the side of the bed.

'I'm not asking you to come home to stay. Can you just come with the babies, this afternoon?' he asked.

'Etta's there, right?'

'She's here. Drove to Trader Joe's to stock up. The Tree is somewhere, ripped up or dead or somebody who knows what it can do has it.'

'Ask her to use the basement freezer if she needs it. Forget the Tree for now. What's the point of running yourself like this? Look at me: I jumped ship. You'll end up the same way.' Her own voice took on apprehensive shades. 'I'll come with the kids. You know I love these girls, Abel. I want to be around, as myself, to see them grow. You're the you I depend on. Forget the Trees, and the seedy *fiats* and just *be* – til I'm also – just able to be.'

'I love you, then,' he said.

'I love you.' She was in tears, again.

They paused in a short, shared, comforting silence.

'What time are you getting here? I'm as ready as can be. Etta will be back in a half hour.'

'We're packed. Three Sisters are coming along to get us situated. Betsy and Sheila will show up once we give the word.'

'See if you can loot some altar wine on your way out.'

'I will.'

*　　*　　*

In a flush of mercy, Sr. Ignatius pulled Gideon into a tight embrace.

This vice-like hug served a higher calling, as she knew; he could not maneuver his face back to hers. Her veil also protected her. He seemed shocked, then, for an instant pleased, then irritated he could not repeat what he had accomplished.

She carefully moved her head so her mouth was near his ear.

'This was a mistake, Gideon. If you ever try it again, I will disappear and not be found. You will lose your employment and possibly go to prison. So please.'

She cautiously lessened the powerful pressure her muscles had found, drew back her arms, and moved away from him to a space across the alcove.

'I'm going to walk back to the convent, alone. Please wait a few minutes before you leave this spot.'

He stared at her. 'I'm not sorry. You're a woman.'

'I'm a nun. Who has made inviolable vows. You need a different kind of support that I cannot and will not provide.' With that, she turned and, with as fast a gait as practical, got away from the alcove, reached the main trail, and hurried across Fern Hollow, where she'd climb the wooden stairs and reach the relative safety of the Regent Square streets.

She did not look back, as he called out.

'You're a woman. A man can desire a woman, no matter what she wears or thinks is so goddamned important…'

*   *   *

Riley Cardle watched from above, in her own small alcove nestled near the Firelane Extension trail.

Feeling much better, she'd gone to the park to get some fresh air. Brought plastic to sit on, a notepad, and drifting ideas of how to mount her current stories. It was not a special location; she wanted places away from the walking paths, not camouflaged but not out in the open, where she could sit, write, hear some birds, think some thoughts. When she'd heard animated voices, her beat-savvy reporter self had reflexively hunched over into a crouch. She moved quietly to where she could see the people through a tangle of japanese stiltgrass. And watched.

A nun. A middle-aged man. Some conversation. A sudden kiss. A tight, reciprocated embrace. Oh brother. Oh Sister.

*   *   *

Ignatius reached the edge of the park, could see the streets and the way back through the neighborhood, to the haven of the convent.

Moss was nowhere to be seen, or heard, behind her. No temptation in this matter. A murmur of self-regard washed over her, realizing how efficiently and, in her way, empathetically, she had foiled the specter of transgression. There was never any doubt, of course. She tasted the pride – she was human, and stumbled over a root with her foot, her other foot thumping into a rock. Her big toe smarted, quite loudly.

'Ahh *shhhh…*'

No cursing, Sister.

In this mix of slight pain and slight triumph, she remembered her 'slight' problem. There was an apple, wrapped in tin foil, in the High School faculty lounge, in the refrigerator, with a note signed by Emma Green taped to it.

'Do Not Touch! Property of M. Green, Biology. Thanks!'

*   *   *

Three Green sisters, flanked by three Charity nuns and Emma Green, arrived at 222 Gamma Way. Emma rolled down the van window as Sr. Antioch cut the engine and pulled up the hand brake. Sheila Merrick and Betsy Vazyovich sat on the front steps, host-ambassadors. Dan Vazyovich sat on the porch swing, fiddling around with chords on his six string banjo. Abel and Etta near the curb, sitting on a slope of lawn.

'This grass! My rear is wet, Abel.'

Etta stood up and brushed at her bottom. Abel laughed and stood up, as the Sisters each carried a Green child from the open van door. Abel took Dragon, Etta took Miller, and Emma took Boyd. There was a general, joyful commotion. Emma knew that her friends had been told about her soon-to-be-medium term absence. But the banjo rang, the babies cooed and wrestled, and the entourage managed its way up the stairs and in the front door. Seren and Dippity had long since bolted for safe haven. Abel handed Dragon off to Sheila, Betsy reached for Boyd, and Emma and Abel pulled each other into a firm squeeze. Both had tears in their eyes; Emma could feel her mouth stir from awful frown to sweet beam. She'd imagined this day, back before all the seedy-ness had entered their universe. It felt wonderful, even if it was to be momentary, to drink the nectar that flowed. And so they did.

FIFTEEN

LARS PATTON WAS down to his last bag of Martin's. And getting nowhere, slow. He was not the techie he imagined himself to be. Or else the Green-Zap-Black-Rat gift was so unpredictable in its potency that he had no predictable way to predict if he could succeed. It ticked him off.

He needed to call Dixon. And every time he thought of Dixon, he thought of Razor. In a god-awful *coma*. And then he thought of Gideon Moss. As icing on the ruined cake, he'd get a glance at himself reflected in a window and almost throw up. Green.

One step at a time. Slow down. Astrid called from the top of the basement steps. 'Hey, brother green. Dixon is here to see you.'

Oh man. Dude. *Friend.* Lars dashed up the stairwell and through the living room, where a pall of cigar smoke drifted in front of his mother. Dixon was out on the front lawn. A three-speed Raleigh bicycle rested against the sidewalk.

'Dixon*!*'

'Hey Lars. How you shakin'?'

'Dude. I am a piece of work as unworkable as an unworkable piece of work can work.'

'Sounds like you all over, pinhead. See my new bike? Used but classy.

Can I put it on the porch so hard-case Regent Square blue-bloods don't burgle it?'

Dixon entered the house. Astrid took a moment to review him, watching from the top of the stairs. He waved hullo at Mrs. Patton, who blew out a welcoming smoke ring in his direction. Lars and Dixon loped down the basement steps to HUX headquarters.

'Rabies bite turned your head emerald green,' said Dixon.

'You finally showed. I might have been a corpse already for all you cared.'

'You'd really turn green then.' Dixon took a moment to peruse the basement. They'd spent good hours together here. Mostly Lars burning something and Dixon eating something, but enjoyable.

Dixon grabbed the Martin's bag from its basket and poured the last crumbs down his gullet. 'Wanted to see if you're still breathin'. When you coming back? To school?'

'Probably September. My real hair better grow in.'

'Come to school with green hair, monkey man. No one will care.'

'Can't.

'Why?'

'Because.'

'Good reason.' Dixon crumpled the chip bag and tossed it in the wastebasket.

'I'm not right, Dixon.'

'Ok. I don't want to know, anyway. You staying busy down here?' Dixon picked up a rudimentary-looking object Lars had been attempting to manufacture. A piece fell off. 'Sorry.'

'It's a thing I'm trying to build. Ok. Remember the Nature Center fire?'

'You went AWOL the day after.'

'Anyway. The fire sent something out into the park. Some weird chemistry. I'm trying to build a machine that'll find that chemical, where it may have rooted.'

'Rooted?'

'Yeah. Like, this is my redemptive task for my temporary insanity.'

'How'd you know there was a chemical fog floating into the park?' asked Dixon.

'It's how my hair went green. I was over on Lancaster, poaching for that squirrel. Snow came down and fizzed me proper.'

'So snowflakes zapped your cranium?'

'Told you the park was going creepazoid.'

'Totally bogus, man. Think up a new story.'

'It's true,' pleaded Lars.

'Like why aren't there a hundred people running around with green heads? And critters. Your black squirrel might be camo by now.'

'I know, I know. Forget it, Dix.'

'Lars, you're a smart dude. Trusting you didn't do anything super-fonked.'

'Pretty fonked.' Lars sat down at his work bench. 'Squirrel bite fucked me up, dude.'

'Do not say the 'F' word, dude! My mom always knows. *Geeze.*'

'Flock. Fig. Flog. Frig.'

'Man, I told you to get checked. If that bite messed with your head, you should be checked by doctors. Don't you want to get checked? No, you wanna die.'

Lars blew out a long breath, and drew folded hands up under his chin. 'I'm in kinda deep.' He looked at the floor.

'Anything I can do, dude. Let me know. I won't do it but I'll know it.' Dixon reached over and shoved Lars in the shoulder.

'Listen. Get checked, Ok? It's kinda stupid to die with that cool hair you got going. Barb Castonnovi is going to drool.'

'You're hallucinating. *You* should get checked.'

'I'm outta here. Say bye to Astrid for me.'

Dixon bound up the stairs and hustled his way out. Lars was glad he'd showed. In his current state of mind, any exchange with his old pal was healthy. It was back to the drawing board, though, for his X-Tector. He Googled 'detect chemicals at a distance'. One of the top hits was for the *'Thermo Scientific MarqMetrix Proximal BallProbe Sampling Optic.'*

Good name. He'd have to rob a bank to even look at the schematics.

*　　*　　*

Life at 222 Gamma Way turned out to be surprisingly reasonable. Abel sat watching the three girls, each now walking and saying basic phrases, fraternizing with each other, and being wonderfully kid-silly. Nuns were around daily, along with neighbors who rotated in and out, with help and more. He began to call his side door the 'food door', for how often neighbors Nikita or Delmar would knock, holding up a plate of russian-styled salmon, KFC, or more bottles of baby food. 'No more baby food, Nikita. Thank you *sooo* much,' said Abel. 'These ladies are wolfing down whole foods. They're weeds.'

They were weeds. Haskley's recent pronouncement about them slowing down was a false positive. Every month they advanced, developmentally, based on all those infamous standards charts, by an equivalent of around twelve months. By May they were indicating three years maturation. If anything, they'd accelerated. Abel could only imagine the medical records accruing. Of course it was ridiculous. And of course they all worried. The doctors ceased predicting. Of course, thought Abel. There's not much he could do but love and father them. With what was left over, he would mother them.

Riley Cardle's interview had been published, and read, largely tame, and mostly forgotten, though there was some very slight 'newsy' intimation that the girls would need to be institutionalized. Even Abel understood that as a frightening possible, though he was irked Cardle had even suggested it. He made a note to get in touch with her and suggest she stay the heck, permanently, out of their lives.

Emma and he had, thankfully, stayed in touch, though she never appeared at the front door. Which he thought was pitiable, pitiful, and heart-breaking, in equal measure.

The situation at the high school was muddled. Emma on a leave of absence. Ignatius curiously less available. The Principal, Gideon Moss, back but, according to the 'charity grapevine' (an excellent source of family-rated gossip), morose and reclusive. Abel began to cultivate the idea that he and Moss should have a summit. The man probably bit the Apple, and may have had some part in the Nature Center fire. But he and Moss had something in common, something very uncommon, and might help, or at least console, each other during the astonishing times they'd found themselves in.

'Daddy. We watch TV?'

Dragon, his two and a half-month old daughter, had laid her small hand gently on his knee.

'We don't have a TV, honey. Who told you about TV?'

Dragon lifted a magazine and held it in front of Abel's eyes. The front cover photo showed a family gathered around, eyes bright with attention, the big screen shouting its Disney logo. The mailer had arrived with the daily boatload of kiddie-oriented sale pitches. The Greens had three kids, so the sales were potentially-thriced. How nice.

Dragon put the magazine on the floor and wandered over to watch Miller and Boyd stacking Lego blocks. Abel let us head fall back against the pillow behind, and closed his weary eyes. 'Going to contact Moss. Get a morning away.'

*   *   *

Abel was able to make a short run into CMU to clear his remote-work status with his boss Roman. His stint at home was approved; the university had an idea about the nature of the situation with his three new daughters, some of it from Cardle's article in the *Post-Press*. They also recognized the speed, quality, and efficiency of Abel's ability to meet and exceed his job assignments. Abel knew they were a *seedy* enhancement, had no idea how long it would endure, and went with the mad predicaments of the present as best he could.

He checked in with his perpetually congratulatory co-workers and they discussed work flow and how much he could take on. 'A lot', he'd said. He spent a bit of time at his computer, copying over material and resources he'd want to access from home.

'How you holding up?' asked Adam, the office go-to guy for good-natured collaboration and a mellow kind of need to make sure everyone was more or less distraughtless.

'Crazy.'

'I can't imagine.'

'Kids are good.'

'How's Emma holding up? She must be a busy mom.'

'Uber-busy.' Abel whistled softly, his fingers tapping away.

'Well. Let us know whatever way we can help. Charlie and Sarah are trying to pick up slack; but apparently you are managing to pick up theirs! So rock on, brother. Bring those kiddos around here someday so we can drive Roman mad.'

'He'd love 'em, anyway. A softie at heart,' said Abel.

'True,' said Adam. 'I'll leave you to it.'

And there it was…

fiat lux five

NereBegats they are called – the spawn of the thirteen boneseeds. All are parthenogenesis-enabled. They can reproduce without mating and without fertilization from exterior functionaries. Perceive that nereBegats are not intrinsically evil. They were wrought with care and deep affection. The Makors and Throwers engineered each work. The Selectors reviewed them.

Here the thirteen, to be awakened in the resurrected Eden:

LEOPARD PILLBOX SLUG - *secretes a catalyst that disassembles water.*

KLATCH - *unknown form.*

BATBIRD - *disruptive radar emissions.*

GIANT CLOUD TARDIGRADE - *emits gaseous bloom - toxic cloud.*

BANEDAGGER - *venom then antidote in successive stings.*

FRUIT OF THE LIFE - *prolongs human life.*

WEASELMANDER - *no natural enemies - lifespan over 500 years.*

SNAPPER MANTRA - *causes major eardrum damage.*

UPJAW-DROPJAW - *upper jaw at one end and lower jaw at other.*

BLACK ROSE - *oxides food into radioactive carbon dioxide.*

WHEELBONE - *perfect circle - unverifiable constitution and nature.*

SILVERMARE - *horse-like with metallic chrome hide.*

NERE-X - *unknown form.*

The *fiat lux* technical problems were solved, for the moment, anyway. Abel tucked the new file away, send a copy home, and slumped back in his chair.

'You get some news?' asked Adam.

'Nah. Yeah. Another message from God. Keeps pestering me.'

'Nice to have that resource.' Adam smiled.

Abel smiled back, then rose from his seat. 'I'll see you guys in a month or two,' he said. His co-workers showered him with 'good lucks' and 'call us' and 'bring those urchins in here' and left him with a vision of jollyness and warmth. There was a normalcy existing, still, that he couldn't touch right now but was grateful had not dissolved.

Somewhere in the murk of his stupefaction, he began to wonder if he should better disguise the *fiat lux* material. He could incorporate it inside a pretend fantasy novel. Maybe call it *Bite* - or something. The novel could become a depository for these heaven-sent intelligence briefings. He'd have a pretext if any one stumbled on it. Of all the things in this mad adventure that made him feel like he was losing his grip - and they were legion - the *fiat* arrivals were near the top. Sure, the girls were a miracle. He and Emma's enhanced aptitudes were a grace. But direct, written communication from *upstairs?* That shook him. A fantasy novel, where he could hide it all.

Forget it. Their current circumstances were already convoluted and confusing and what did it matter if people knew he'd brought his own tidy biblical ruminations into the world.

Old Testament. New Testament. Now Testament.

Maybe his faith *was* lacking.

If only they could do a little time jump and return to October 1st. Not take that walk in the park. Not eat that apple. Revisit that day. When the ground opened and eternity came rolling on out.

*   *   *

Emma's life had slipped out of its container and run expediently off, also. The only vaguely-approvable decision of her last few months was the one to separate from her newborns (rapidly becoming oldborns) and husband and Regent Square. Physically, emotionally, spiritually, it was the only way she could see to survive. How expedient of her.

She had been bound by nature's tenets – its physics, its verifiability, its steadiness, its reality. With all of that tossed under the apple cart, her own mind was demanding answers she could not begin to calculate; this even with her newly-acquired seedy wisdom. Maybe God threw in caveats if you didn't believe. *Sorry - that's Believe with a capital 'B', right?*

To have a fair chance at equilibrium, a getaway was imperative. Indeed, it was essential. Crying all day – at her abandonment of family, crass willingness to flee, and utterly disastrous reckoning she'd even been able to do it – was how she spent much of her conscious time.

She requested a meeting with Ignatius, who came in the evening. The studio had been cleared of baby-toddler stuff. Emma knew she was taking up space the nuns could use for their own purposes. And what did the Sisters think of her actions? Mortal sin should have been short-listed, though the nuns, other than Mother Superior, had not shown any kind of disdain; of course it could easily have been hidden under the shadows of their habits. But no – they never failed to ask cheerfully about Margaret, Rebecca, and Caroline, who Emma had to remember were Boyd, Miller and Dragon. The Croatian names seem to be stickier.

Ignatius knocked softly.

'Come in.'

'Hello Emma.'

'Sister. How are you?'

'Busy. School is out for the summer soon. I confess I need a vacation as much as the students.'

Emma folded her arms against her chest and bowed her head. The Sisters were an inspiration and blessing; an agnostic-filtered example of robust spirituality that only made her feel worse.

'I'm taking up space here I don't need.'

Ignatius nodded, took a seat in one of the soft chairs. 'Tell me what you're thinking.'

'Well. I will leave. Not back to Abel. I can't do that.' Ignatius hid whatever thoughts this evoked and remained quiet. 'I'll tell you what I'd like to do, if possible. You tell me if it is,' said Emma. More quiet. 'The Charity Motherhouse at Seton Hill. I'd like to go to your Motherhouse, and study in the novitiate.'

'You wish to become a nun. A religious?'

'I need an anchor to hold onto. I'm like a version of Mary, Sister – a human who has been targeted by the powers-that-be, the off-screen ones, the Bible-based cast and crew – who insists, to herself, despite all indications to the contrary, that this cannot be. And if I don't crack the puzzle, if I can't endure to a viable, livable, logical answer… then *I* may crack.'

Ignatius shifted in her seat. This nun had expended so much energy helping the Greens. Emma felt her entreaty provided a kind of hand-off that Ignatius would go for. Get the mad Green woman out of the convent, out of the neighborhood, away from those amazing girls. Maybe even lock her up out there, under guard in the Motherhouse tower. Bread and water.

'I see that might make sense,' said Ignatius, carefully nodding her head.

'You do?'

'In some ways. Your capacity to learn is on fire, though your battle to find out where your science and faith might meet is undermining your way. At the Motherhouse, as a novitiate-in-training, you'd be under a singular regime, and have every opening and advantage of those women who are exploring likewise.'

'Yes,' said Emma.

'The Charity Motherhouse is not mine. I'm a Poor Clare. Of course we both know the generosity of the Charity Sisters. I can contact them for you.'

'Thank you, Ignatius.'

'You cannot take vows to become a nun. Unless your marriage were annulled,' said Ignatius.

'I don't want an annulment. I want my brain and soul to get it together.'

'Ok. I'll confer. Have you spoken with Abel, about this?'

'No.'

Ignatius nodded in a fashion that communicated the opposite. 'Why don't you talk to him, and I'll talk to the Motherhouse.'

SIXTEEN

IT WAS A pretty June morning. Abel had arranged for all-day kid-sitting. Dan and Betsy had become de facto supplementary grandparents, with Etta administering the show from her perch as a direct relative. The three girls. showing advanced astuteness along with more typical toddler behavior, were a good match for their adult supervisors. There was pretty much all-day astonishment for all accompanying parties.

Abel had contacted Gideon Moss, partially as a gesture of concern, but more as an opportunity to parse the apple narrative. He hadn't, of course, heard Moss confess to biting the apple on that October morning; but the evidence was so obvious that he hoped Moss would come clean. They'd both benefit. The Nature Center fire was, ironically, on the back-burner.

Emma had sent him a hand-written letter – his hands shook opening it – indicating that she was moving to the Sisters of Charity Motherhouse at Seton Hill. Abel knew of it, located on a semi-rural college campus about an hour east of Pittsburgh. He'd breathed loudly in relief: she wasn't asking for any kind of formal separation. She wanted to be surrounded by Sisters and study the theology that she and Abel were now caught inside. Her brain and heart held long-consolidated logic that constantly thudded up against the faith-fabricated story they were living. It was a scourge that needed her full attention, for a while yet. She loved him (still) and loved the children (always) and wished things were not as they were. And she signed it 'love, Emma'.

Abel didn't know much himself, at this point, about what was moving the pieces in their universe. The *fiat lux* material at times struck him as completely ludicrous. Boneseeds – *come on*. And incomplete deliveries. If Heaven's IT crews couldn't get their cloud operations to work flawlessly after an eternity of fine-tuning, what hope was there for Admin saving souls? Besides, the material never locked in on the 'apple tree' content, specifically enough, nor did it explain how their children might be affected by the seedy implants they might have inherited.

To top it all off, it was only a matter of time before that Cardle reporter, or some other, broke the story of their wunderkind-freak children in a widely-disseminated, privacy-crushing release. Cardle's short interview would not hold off the wolves. Maybe the world deserved to know. He didn't know. So how about Moss? How was he faring? He'd gotten Moss's school e-mail from Emma and written him.

Gideon,

Emma's husband here. We're both hoping for the best for your son. I know you've taken some time from work. I'm wondering if you'd want to sit down over a coffee and talk.

Let me know. Yours, Abel Green

Moss had written back later that day.

Abel, let me know when and where. G.

They'd agreed to meet at a cafe in Squirrel Hill called Commonplace Coffee, on Forbes Ave. It was one of the few places in Pittsburgh that knew how to make a proper 'flat white', a drink he'd learn to enjoy from a co-worker who'd been to New Zealand. Abel promised himself he'd get down there someday to visit Middle-Earth, where attractions from the movie trilogy dotted the landscape. And if Emma didn't want to go, he'd take

Miller, Boyd, and Dragon!

Gideon Moss had found them a corner table. It was crowded, but private, with the chatter of voices and sound of espressos brewing.

'Mr. Green,' said Moss.

'Gideon. Thanks for coming. We haven't seen each other since that day in Frick Park.'

Moss deferred responding, stood up. 'I can order. What do you want?'

'Ask for a flat white.'

'Flat white?'

'New Zealand coffee mash-up. Really just a latte with extra foamy milk. I like the name.' Abel noted that Moss appeared to stall at the complexity of ordering something he didn't know. Abel rose from his seat. 'Hey, I'll get it. What do you want?'

'Just black coffee.'

Abel placed the order and waited while it was brewed. He glanced over once to see Moss staring out at the Squirrel Hill sidewalk. He brought the two drinks back, glad to set them down.

'Hot.' He blew on his fingers.

'If the coffee's not hot, the cafe should go out of business,' said Moss. He took a sip.

'Just want to say that Ray is in our thoughts and prayers.'

Moss took another sip. 'Does your wife pray?'

'Not much.'

'I don't pray at all. Useless.'

'Definitely a personal thing. I don't write it off, though. Something's running this show.'

'Running this show?'

'The Universe, etc.'

Moss lowered his face for a soft laugh. He took another sip of his black. 'Listen, Green, I know why you're here. I know what you're hoping to discuss. I want to talk about it, because it's radically intrusive, and I'm guessing you are finding it the same.'

'Yes. I agree with that.' Abel teased the foam off the top of his drink. 'Good stuff.' He put his cup down. 'I think we do need to get one thing established. Did you bite the apple?'

'Yes.'

'Chewed and swallowed?'

'Yes – for God's sake. What do you think – you saw it sitting on the ground with several bites out of it, next to me.'

'Ok, listen, don't get bent out of shape. If you did bite it, you know it messes with your constitution, all the way from A to Z. If we're going to find some common ground, some useful ground, then maybe consider a more congenial style, here.' Abel leaned back and carefully slurped at the foam of his flat white.

'I'm not here to play games, Green. I've got a sick kid and, frankly, an unwell mind. What are you proposing we do with our common experience?'

'Well. Maybe for starters, just share what we think it is. Share how it made us feel, And share what makes sense going forward.'

'That's for starters.' Moss shifted in his chair. 'Did you ever fall for a woman you couldn't get?'

What the heck was this? Maybe the apple had done different kinds of wacked out things to Moss. Guide the dialog back to the reason they were meeting.

'Sure. We all know that story.' said Abel. 'Not my charge right now, to take that on with you, Gideon.' He paused to study Moss's face, see if his expression might open to useful communication. 'If you bit the apple, well – did it affect you?'

'Did it affect you?' asked Moss.

'Yes. Both Emma and I had an almost immediate reaction. As if someone had needled a mental steroid into our heads. We were blitzed, really. Intellectually, emotionally, spiritually.'

'Blitzed is a good word for it,' said Moss. He exhaled and rubbed at his forehead with both palms. 'Pretty much I've been smacked with a cudgel. Try running a Catholic high school with freshly injected rotten apple juice.'

'Hey, I'm not blaming either of us. I'm looking for some answers, or maybe at least some ways of dealing with this, that you've stumbled on.' Abel took a long, deliberate mouthful of his flat white. 'Or we can just retreat, here. Circle back when there's some middle to divvy up.'

Moss looked like a man unwilling to open the shutters on his plight. In a way, Abel pitied him; he seemed more and more isolated, had a son in a coma, and was on extended leave from the contact and distraction his work at the school might provide.

'Look, Gideon. It's not the end, here. Stay in touch, call me, let me know if you want to *core* this thing.' Abel offered a quiet smile to go with his quiet joke. 'I'm going to head back and rescue the babysitters.' He stood to go.

Moss looked up. 'How are those girls?'

'Pretty much as overwhelming and impossible and beautiful as you know children are from having your own kid. Times three.' For the first time, he thought Moss whispered a smile, even though his own son, Razor, was in a hospital, in a coma.

He looked at Abel. 'Maybe we can meet again and get somewhere.'

Abel nodded. Moss stood up, turned, and left, without looking back.

*　　*　　*

When Abel got home, two babysitters were snoozing on the couch and one against a chair on the floor. The three Green sisters were huddled together, all lying on their bellies, legs akimbo, crayons scattered about them, scrawling words on paper. He walked over and knelt, placing his hands on Miller and Boyd's shoulders, and looked. Words.

Banshee Patrol is a good.
There be light. Be light.
Mom a Seton Hill, noyt Seton Hall.

*   *   *

Lars gave up. He was unable to move the needle on his X-Tector efforts. The Frick Park green flake chemicals would remain a mysterious additive. Unless they did their 'loud green painting' (like his hair) kind of action down in the hollow, that he'd miraculously be able to spot in the weeds.

He was too tired to think about it, and his own conscience was serving more and more as a whack-a-mole adventure. He helped steal the tree. Whack! *It was just a tree.* He helped burn down the Nature Center. Whack! *It was old and flammable and a new one will be better.* He was practically a felon and certainly a liar. Whack! *So was everybody.* His skill at keeping painful truths pummeled into submission under the mallet was wearing very thin. Summer had, fortunately, arrived. He could miss another three months of stupid school and figure out a viable way to navigate this confustication also known as his life.

*   *   *

Emma arrived at the convent grounds with one suitcase. She managed a thin smile, noting that the Sisters of Charity Motherhouse she was 'joining' was located in Greensburg, Pennsylvania.

She hoped to strip her life down and figure out if it was figurable-out. Knowing how readily she'd been able to abandon her family assured her that this action had become a necessity. Her seedy-activated ancillary gifts were propelling her mind and body; but her essence, her basic self, was still inside, stumbling for a center that would stick.

Emma saw a man, middle-aged, and aged further in the lines of his face, with a long black mane spilling down off his shoulders, hair she found distracting and beautiful, an odd beginning to her new station at Seton Hill. Seton Hall's Mother Superior, Sister Jill Happe, was of Native American heritage. So it was that her brother, a theoretical physicist, had been permitted temporary lodging while he recovered from an undetermined ailment. His name was Grey Cloud Roaringman and it was he Emma saw.

*   *   *

Riley Cardle now had a bevy of speculative material but still didn't know how to combine the three very-loosely affiliated kernels into one shame-filled whole. She refused to believe they weren't connected. Every instinct in her reporter's soul said so. It was a grand riddle that she knew had special potential: sin always made good headlines.

*   *   *

Ignatius was grateful the students were on their summer break. She wanted no part of Moss, even as she was able to find heart to pity him. She, herself, object of a man's attraction? She threw her head back and laughed. Not that that in itself was a bad thing. She recognized she was considered a good-looking woman. It was simply not a thing since she'd made her vows, happily, and assuredly, to devote her life to God and prayer. The decision to re-enter a more public space and the interactions thereof by way of her teaching commission, was in response to her own solicitation to the Lord to use her, in any manner He might deem useful. Because, Ignatius believed, the forces in the world that were advancing against belief were legion.

Tell me how, she'd asked, kneeling before a few lit candles. The answer came from discussions with a Poor Clare associate Sister at their Santa Clara, Ohio, convent, who shared Ignatius' vocation to move the world forward, to God, or backward, to God; this despite their order's avowed solitude and place at the edges of society. Mother Superior had seen their fervor, recognized the age of the world for what it was, and blessed each sister with the freedom to find that arena where each could help stem the tide of godlessness. 'My prayer is not for results, but for pathways, that might lead souls to awareness,' she would say to them. 'God must do the rest.'

Sister Ignatius took it as a bolt from the blue – *direct wire from heaven.* She could relate her own passion for God by teaching. By teaching religion in a Catholic School. A high school would be the best proving ground.

The younger children had their parents' beliefs conferred into them, mostly for good, where there was Faith. In high school, the kids took a stance against simple acceptance of the rote. Everything was up for grabs. There was, first of all, sex, informing every spectrum of their lives. Males and females, blooming in the last years of grade school, were now fourteen and fifteen. Across, in the next desk, was a body refined into a wonderful shape. Along with sex came the need for affirmation, through appearance, by disguising defects, trying to make friends, avoid bullies, finding a workable personality. And then, maybe, doing the school work. All of this countered by whatever home life and family upbringing they'd known.

Their teenage minds, their ability to grasp what was happening in these experiences, weren't up to the task. Society and culture readily jumped in with empty-vessel constructs about conquests, and popularity, and fashion, and coolness, and cliques, and all the rest. In the middle of this combat theater, dropping a leaflet for religion was a tremendous challenge. Sister Ignatius felt the fire of the need, and knew she'd be able to stake a claim. It was never her intent to delude the kids, or discourage their odysseys into adulthood with some lecturing or high-brow-holy steerage they'd laugh at the moment they exited her classroom. She wanted to power into the hard things, retrofit their wings by attaching the Universe-created-by-a-good-God concept to their mantras.

And so she had begun. And then the Green surprise and the Moss razzia had been dropped in her Poor Clare lap. She laughed again. It was all good. If she wasn't a nun, she'd say *damned* good. God had a sense of humor, right?

Alas that His sense of humor had snuck in a bad joke. The apple piece, however much of it was present in the school fridge, beckoned. She knew why, and it felt legitimate. If this apple had graced the Green family with a direct conduit to their Holy Father (not the one in Rome, the one above); if this apple was a descendant of Eden's apple; if this apple constituted a spiritual rebirth incomparable to anything in modern times...

Her thoughts hung in the air. There was no sin in looking. There should not be a sin in tasting. She had not been countermanded as Eve had been to avoid this taste. It was the dark echo in her scruples that came up like an acid reflux of the soul.

She had a loose plan to visit the 'specimen'. The Faculty lounge was locked for the summer, as was the school. It might be safer to retrieve this item. Secure it. She wasn't sure. She made a note to make a note, resisting the urge to chase it down immediately. Something about the Moss episode gave it more urgency.

Pray. She would find a way.

Propitiously, she had a pending responsibility which required her attention: facilitating a summit meeting between three eminent theology authorities of three major religions and three much younger heads of the Green family. It was apparent from her communiques with Abel, that Miller, Boyd, and Dragon (as they were now commonly referred to) were communicating more and more articulately. And the July 4th summit, coded as *Fireworks* with the *Three Wise Guys*, was just around the bend.

She'd received the information packet from Sr. Pancratius. The three clerics were Cardinal Ethan Mirangue from Rome, Imam El-Muhammad from Mecca, and Chief Rabbi Ben Winkel from Jerusalem. They were traveling together out of Paris, where they could get a direct flight to Pittsburgh International Airport, and would arrive at Seton Hill in one week's time. Sister Pancratius would accompany them.

Before her renegade thoughts about the specimen in the fridge, Ignatius had been able to avoid, for many reasons, judging the ramifications of The Garden of Eden and the Apple Tree of the Knowledge resurfacing in Frick Park. The most fundamental, to her, was that this incident could never replace the communicated message of Faith supplied by the Church, regardless of its origins. She just could not see that God would allow this. If God did allow it, she'd try to be a supportive player. There was a pang of joy in the realization that three heads of three major religions would spend time together on this mission. That in itself was a very good thing. Ecumenical, right there.

All this she thought about, en route to Seton Hill, to arrange for the *Fireworks* summit. She would also talk with Emma, and get her perspective on everything, and, especially, her permission to allow the children to be interviewed by the Wise Guys.

*   *   *

Moss left the hospital, walking at a clip. He didn't want to meet Razor's mother, who'd be coming soon, again, as she spent long vigils at her son's hospital bedside. Razor was soon to be transferred to a separate facility, Remediation of Pennsylvania, where comatose patients could be cared for as they healed, and, hopefully, one day, awoke. It was east of Pittsburgh, in Greensburg. He'd have to drive for an hour to see the boy. It'd be a good excuse to miss some visits.

Razor had ripped out the Tree, thrown it into the weeds. Almost like blasphemy. Gideon had struck, instinctively. Razor had brought this action on. In his effectively cauterized lucid moments, rarer by the hour, Gideon Moss had hints inside his derealized, apple-cored head that he was making a pathetic excuse for pathetic behavior, but he could override that easily with self-pity, and so he did. As far as he was concerned, his ex-wife could sit at the bedside and stare at an unresponsive body all she wanted. Moss had his own problems.

He felt his already squashed-up mess of a world shrinking fast. The nun he'd kissed. That held all sorts of ruin. The fire at the Nature Center. Lars was an unreliable collaborator who might suddenly find his conscience. The Tree, he brought inside, trailing mud and weeds, and replanted in a large bucket in Razor's bedroom. It was alive, barely.

He began to wonder where he could turn. His re-wired brain was a panic – providing a bounty of considerations and directions and alignments and prospects for salvation to go with warranties of doom. He squeezed his eyes shut and nearly slammed a knee into his car door.

Need somewhere to go.

Take something. Kick something. *Make something stop.*

SEVENTEEN

Boneseed fourth emerged in May, a giant cloud tardigrade. It grew rapidly, consuming nearby greens. In a few weeks, its waddling locomotion was accompanied by a bloom of debilitating gas, which enveloped it and drifted off in soft plumes behind it. The plumes were colorful, and drew some insects, which fled, sick and some dying, not long after entering its cloud.

Boneseed fifth was spawned in June. The banedaggers were fearsome looking from inception, a cross between a thick-bodied centipede and a scorpion. Black and crimson, its two sets of stingers contained both venom and antidote. The initial sting contained fatal poison, a second sting contained its antidote. Its creator had deemed this function as appropriate to co-exist with humankind. It had been rightfully rejected. Now it was here.

*   *   *

Abel was working hard to co-ordinate the *Fireworks* summit planning with his always helpful neighbors, and Ignatius and Emma. The girls would be attending, and Pancratius was recommending they get time alone with the Wise Guys.

He'd not been supplied with additional *fiat lux* material (praying for a 'quick-start' guide had not worked). His *Banshee Patrol* journaling, however, was at least consolidating and condensing the story in front of them. He'd decided not to share the *fiat* releases with the Wise Guy contingent. There was too much, in too wide a circle, going on. Let's see what this summit brings. He thought for a moment of inviting Gideon Moss. That had its own issues, and he decided against it. A simplified *go there, do it,* and come out the other side was his intention.

'Girls. Hey.' He'd stepped out into their modest backyard, where the four-years-progressed-in-maturity prodigies had engineered a three hole mini-golf course.

'Dad, look at our course!' said Dragon. 'Miller made it up. One hole in the center. Three places where you hit it from*!'*

Dragon and Boyd were smoothing out the grass on three tee areas the young ladies had concocted. They'd also dug up an old putter and whiffle-type golf ball.

'Dad,' said Miller. 'You gotta play!' Boyd took a wack and dropped a hole in one across their uncut grass.

'Total luck!' shouted Dragon. 'Do that again!' Boyd retrieved the ball but could not duplicate her feat.

'We charge a dollar to play. Forget that lemonade stand kowabunga!' said Boyd. They all laughed.

This is not unlike the movie where the kids have glowing eyes and bend the minds of the adults who don't listen to them, thought Abel. *Village of the*…don't even think it. He sent up another prayer. At this point, he was running a significant tab with God.

'Cool, girls. Really. I'll dig up some money and play later.'

'We'll give you the family discount,' said Miller. They all tittered again, in unison.

'Dad, we have nicknames,' said Boyd.

'Hit me,' said Abel.

'Dragon the Tamer. Miller the Destroyer. Boyd the Subduer,' she said.

'Pretty cool. Any meaning hiding behind those?'

'Not really. Maybe,' said Dragon. 'Working on that.'

'We're reading the *Banshee Patrol*, Dad,' said Miller. 'That Ok?'

'Did I print it? Did I leave it out? Can you guys read that well?'

They all nodded.

'It's cool. The apple tree. All the stuff. Our names. It's cool,' said Boyd.

Abel sat down on the back porch steps and waved his hands around in the air. '*Ai yi yi*, as my mom used to say. Come over here and sit on the grass for a minute.' The three Green sisters did.

'You guys,' he said. He looked into their beautiful faces and amazing eyes and understood readily that their capacity and awareness was on the threshold of surpassing his own, in just about every category he could imagine. He wished he could faint. Or levitate. Or do something that might impress them.

They sat, pleasant but not over-accommodating expressions on their brows, waiting patiently for their fallen father to speak.

'Ok. You're all very smart. And perceptive. You seem to get what's going on. So I won't enrich your current standing because I think you might still be able to be kids for a while. That blessing is one of the greatest of all. One of the few I might give you.'

They smiled a bit more legibly here.

'On July 4th, next week, we're driving up to Seton Hill, where the Charity Sisters have what's called their Motherhouse. Many nuns there, your mother's there, Sr. Ignatius will join us.'

'Sounds cool,' said Boyd.

'We wanna see Mom!' shouted Miller. They looked at each other with wider grins.

'We'll see Mom. We can bring her some Taco Bell –'

'Taco Bell…!' they cried in unison. 'I want the refried beans, Dad,' said Dragon. 'Remember you said it was a good substitute for that soft baby food in jars? You said it would put hair on our bellies.'

'God, you remember that stuff? You're not supposed to recall every wacky thing a parent mumbles to his babies!'

They looked at each other knowingly. It sent a unique warm chill down the back of Abel's neck.

'Should you say *"God"* like that? Out of context?' asked Boyd.

'No, I shouldn't. Add that to your ledger of parental failures. I'm afraid there's going to be many.'

'*Nahhh,* Dad,' bellowed Miller. They all looked at him with suppliant eyes; eyes bestowing evidence that their renown as 'windows to the soul' was an immutable truth in the case of the Three Green Sisters.

'Anyway, you'll be meeting three gentlemen, each representing one of the Earth's major religions.' Abel figured by now his girls might already know the major theologies. They had tons of books around their house, on every sort of subject. He'd have to double-check there wasn't some loose tech lying about where they could get online. He also mused that Etta was probably espousing her colorful world views to both the girls, directly (e.g. *'they have their dirty crust'* in relation to bureaucrats), and also to Dan and Betsy and Sheila, spiced accordingly and covering politics, cooking, and the stupidity of shopping channels, which the girls of course would eagerly overhear.

'Catholic, which will stand in for Christian, we hope in a fair manner. Judea, Jewish. And Islamic, Islam. Three gentlemen who want to hear our story. They'll talk to Mom and me and you and Sister Ignatius.'

'No ladies?' asked Dragon.

'No ladies,' said Abel. He wouldn't tackle that at the moment. 'So, really, nothing to prepare. Just wanted to let you know. I'll go find a dollar so I can get busy here beating your scores on this course.'

*   *   *

Father Jack had asked to be recused from the *Fireworks* summit. He was finding, perhaps like Bishop Garner, this Green episode was like walking through rose bushes in a t-shirt and shorts, trying to enjoy the sights and fragrance while your skin was shredding, your red blood over the red roses. He did have a stray idea about the ongoing developments, which he tucked carefully away.

*   *   *

Lars' mom had somehow found out that Moss was taking his son to Greensburg for extended medical care. That neighborhood grapevine again, a reliable source for community scuttlebutt. As soon as he found out, Lars wanted to visit Razor. Lars had his learners permit, but his mom refused to let him drive that far. Maybe he could dig up a ride; she wasn't going to drive him there.

His Black-Squirrel-ness not yet completely erased, he thought of a plan. A combination of *bad* things to result in maybe some *good* things.

He'd helped burn down the Nature Center. More than helped, for cripe's sake, he'd made the bomb and lit the thing. If he could locate the green chemistry he'd assisted in disseminating into Frick Park; those green flakes that might do something disagreeable in that warm bed of fertile nature – that'd be a percentage of good. He *felt* that, as much as *knew* that, all seasoned with the squirrel-dust. Though his X-Tectoring had stalled, he intended to double-down trying to build it. *Bad thing. Good thing.*

Here was the trickier bit: could he come clean with his part in the fire? Get a reporter in on the story. Implicate Mr. Moss. Plead guilty. And ask the reporter for a ride to see Razor, where he could offload his confession. Since Razor was Gideon's kid, the reporter might buy into that.

Visiting Razor was definitely a good thing. *Bad thing. Good thing.*

With his tweaked conscience, and squirreled-psyche, and split-personality decision-making, things were the opposite of clear. He suspected his better side was evolving forward, though, in spite of the penalties it would incur: facing justice, and his mom and sister knowing what he'd done. Maybe he'd wear a mask when he met the reporter. *Ha.* Not even funny.

* * *

Riley Cardle had not succeeded in merging the tales in front of her. Something needed to break the logjam, or she'd lose all three stories. Her phone buzzed.

'Hello.'

'Hello. Is this Ms. Cardle, the reporter?'

'It is. Who's calling?'

'Hi. I'm a kid. From Regent Square. I can let you know, my ID, and everything, and I will, I mean I know you can't write a story and use some deep background crap and say outlandish things for your readers, from somebody you can't even name. I can let you know. I can tell you.'

'Do go on.'

'I have a weird request.'

'I'm listening.'

'It's weird.'

'Yup.'

'Ok. If you'll drive me to and back from Greensburg, I'll give you some inside scoop on the Nature Center fire.'

'You called me a while back. Sounded different. Was that you?'

'No,' said Lars, guessing Razor had come close to spilling the beans. Maybe he had. 'What did he say? Did he say anything about anything?'

'I'm interested in hearing what *you* have to say. A lift to Greensburg is not a good idea. You sound underage.'

'I'm sixteen.'

'As I said.'

'Well, you can't have anything unless you agree to that. You have my number, now, in your phone. You can contact me if you want.'

'Ok, wait, wait. I might be able to manage this. I need your parents' permission. And, really, your name.'

The phone went silent, and Cardle thought the kid had hung up. 'Hello. You there?' She heard a plaintive sigh.

'I'm Lars Patton. Please don't use my name or look me up. *Please. Please.*'

'I don't promise that kind of stuff, Lars. I'm a reporter, not a guidance counselor. Where do you go to school?'

'St. Anselm.'

'Ok. Listen. Get me some kind of permission from your parents or guardians. Written. Send it to me at the newspaper; the *Post-Press*. I'll have it notarized. Then we can take this a step further. Or, or, you can just tell me everything now, over the phone.'

'I'll send you the letter. Ok, thanks, bye.' He hung up.

This was good, thought Cardle. Maybe the Gordian knot just got frayed.

*   *   *

Lars took care to properly imitate his mom's handwriting.

Pittsburgh Post-Press

Dear Ms. Cardle

This letter confirms you have my permission to drive my son, Lars Patton, on a day trip to Greensburg PA, to visit a friend who is in medical care. The trip should start by 10:00 am on a weekend morning and Lars should be home before 3:00 pm.

You can reach me at 412-242-5652.

Sincerely,

Mrs. M. Patton

He walked it to the mailbox, then headed to Giant Eagle Pharmacy to see if he could find some hair dye that might disguise his alien head. He'd dug up a random phone number and hoped the reporter wouldn't call his mom. What a mess.

*   *   *

Her room at the Motherhouse was small. But it looked out over a quiet forest of trees, which ran in serpentine elegance across low hillsides, as far as she could see. The clouds were happy to complement the scene, soft cotton in the near airs, stratus winging in the high winds. What looked like a fox snooped in rushes near the slope close against a stone bridge. A nun was there, looking, stirring the stillness with her own profound hush.

Over Emma's bed was a crucifix. One more of those religious tokens that had stalled her own ability to believe. Why would this god have to wander down from heaven and get nailed to a cross to forgive sins, including the original sins of kids who weren't old enough to walk, let alone swear? Why didn't this god just announce that you should treat others as you'd like to be treated, and leave out all the rigmarole and indecipherable Biblical texts which would be interpreted in as many ways as there were humans on the Earth.

What did these young women, these Sisters-to-be, find in the idea of a celibate, meager, constrained existence that couldn't be achieved as comfortably and usefully as a life out with the people who needed them? She of course knew the Sisters did endless works or mercy and charity. But. Was this in order to get a ticket to heaven? And what was heaven supposed to be anyway. Did you sing to the god, and smile at your fellow angels, and shake your head now and then for those down below who didn't make the grade? And on what precisely, was the grade made? If you lived a good life, but committed a mortal sin just on your deathbed, were you a metaphysical goner? Or the reverse. Did you sin merrily through 80 years, then authentically repent, and gain the pearly gates. You got the best of both worlds.

She did, sincerely, want to know.

Her seedy self had a myriad of new insights from the Bite. Perhaps the most compelling was the apprehension that her next actions could not be long delayed. This crux: of biting the apple, and delivering these babies, these fresh souls, and separating from them and her husband, were all actions she'd never have countenanced before the Bite. *Seedy. Needy. Pleady.* There was no way forward without a profound remedy, an elixir fit-for-purpose, a clarity. Prayer would serve, here. *A prayer to be able to pray.* Maybe that was a place to start.

* * *

Lars and Cardle agreed June 30 would be their expedition date. She'd pick him up in front of the Regent Square Theater. They could hop onto the Parkway East and head to Greensburg, with plenty of time to talk. Cardle guessed the letter from Lars was a forgery. But it was too good an opportunity to miss. This was something, she felt, akin to the first small cracks in a dam. A trickle seeping out from the rich intrigue that'd accumulated, seeking to spill out from behind. So delicious, she was happy to mix metaphors to accommodate it.

* * *

'Dad, we want to add stuff to the *Banshee Patrol* document? That Ok?'

Miller was standing before her father, who had fallen asleep on the porch swing. Abel rubbed his eyes open. A cardinal fluttered past, bright red against the green maple tree leaves out front. He sat up.

'Hey, Miller. They call you Rebecca ever?' asked Abel.

'Sometimes. When Dragon's complaining about something she uses our first names.'

'Mom does that to me,' he said. 'I thought I secured *Banshee.*'

'We already read that one, remember? The one you printed.'

'What age level are you and your sisters digesting these days, as far as language?'

'We learn fast. Language is pretty easy. Everybody's talkin' at you. To you. And radio and internet.'

'You've been on the web? I'm going straight to – that place that begins with a capital 'H'.

'No you're not,' said Miller. 'It's all good, Dad. We just want to add stuff and correct stuff in *Banshee*.'

'How'd you get on the web?'

'Just logged on. No password on your laptop. And you never said not to. We logged in as 'guests.''

'Ok, geeze…' Abel stood up and looked down the length of Gamma Way, rubbing his forehead. 'Use a different name. For your version.'

'*Aww, Dad…* we like the name! We're starting a band, and calling it *The Banshee Patrol*. I'm learning the banjo, thanks to old Dan. Boyd will be on bass, Dragon on the mouth harp.'

'Are you kidding me?'

'Nooo…! It's good for the soul. Old time music, some bluegrass, some folky stuff.'

He could hear Boyd out back belting out a verse. '…*bring out ol' Dan's records…!*'

Abel ran his hand through his hair and laughed out loud. 'Ok. Make a copy of the file. Call it *Banshee Patrol*. I'll rename my version. I'll add *Dad Version*, or something.'

'We'll rename your version *Dad's Banshee Ark*.' Miller hopped back through the front door, her voice trailing, 'Thanks, Dad!'

Abel bent over and stared at his stocking feet. His socks were striped, bright orange and blue, like something Dr. Seuss would put on his Cats. 'Where…who put these on my feet? Those girls are nuts. Emma should see this.'

He opened the screen door and ambled in, feeling less and less in any kind of control and more and more at the mercy of whatever-in-heaven-or-elsewhere was occurring in front of his only-semi-able-to-believe eyes.

His three girls were fussing with his laptop, chattering in a combined voice about what they were going to compose. He heard a single ominous note that punctured the merry ambiance of the moment. It was Dragon's voice: '…because we don't know how long we'll live…'

*　　*　　*

It was nearly July in Pennsylvania. The days were hot but not stifling. The Charity Motherhouse was the sanctuary Emma had hoped for. She found the initial studies interesting, and gave them as much attention as she could manage. There were diversions in her head that couldn't be banished, though. The upcoming *Fireworks* summit would once again land her directly in the seedy places. She'd see her husband and kids. Maybe wouldn't recognize the girls, based on what Abel was telling her in his e-mails.

The bell rang for afternoon vespers. After that came the evening supper. Grey Cloud Roaringman took his meals with the Sisters. After Grace was said by Mother Superior, the assembly sat at long tables, where the food was served in large bowls to be passed around. Emma preferred her new solitude, but the only way to eat was this way. The nourishment reminded her of trips to the Amish country; simple fare that provided good sustenance without spiffy flourishes. Mashed potatoes, beef stews, roast vegetables, and soups. Coffee, tea, and a light wine were also served.

She found herself one chair closer to Roaringman with each meal, whether by intention or providence she didn't know. He ate somewhat carelessly, often dabbing his chin to remove a bit of broth.

Though conversation at dinner was quiet, it was not subdued. The Sisters threw down their verbal gauntlets with ready ease, plowing a world of politics, food, culture, and sports. The Pittsburgh teams were loved in excess, thought Emma. Overpaid athletes from every geographical origin, drawing fame, fortune, and a lot of dollars to their concerns. It all entertained, and if Rome was not burning in so many other areas, it would seem germane. But she listened to the holy chatter largely with relief. These people were living as if their lives were authentic. She didn't Believe, but she believed in belief.

'What are you doing here?' were the first sonorous words from the Native American physicist she found herself sitting next to.

Emma turned slightly, and their eyes met.

'I'm eating. What are you doing here?'

Roaringman's shoulder dropped, his head tilted, betraying his amusement. 'I do apologize. Seeing we're the only two lay people amongst these religious, I should have offered greetings at some earlier moment.'

'No worries from my end,' said Emma. 'I'm Emma Green.' She held her hand out. He wiped his mouth, wiped his hand, and took hers in his burly palm.

'Grey Cloud Roaringman. I'm brother of Mother Jill.'

'Jill Happe. What tribe, if I may ask?'

'Blackfoot, out of Minnesota.'

'Never been. To Minnesota.'

'You know, I was trying to get Dylan to come for a fund-raiser, once. For the people. Bob, the rascal, Robert Zimmerman. Didn't show.'

'From Minnesota, yes?'

'That's right. Prince, F. Scott, Garrison Keillor, Charles Schulz, and my favorite, James Arness. *Gunsmoke* and *Thing from Another World*.'

'I've read some Fitzgerald. The big hits. Prince you can have. Dylan, when I can understand him, I love.'

Roaringman stabbed a forkful of cauliflower. 'Why are you here, Ms. Emma Green?'

'I'm, really, hiding, mostly,' said Emma. She reclined a bit, felt more exposed, and pulled her chair forward, sitting up 'properly', like all the nuns seemed to do.

'*You can run but you cannot hide,* James Taylor sang. *This is widely known.*' Roaringman muted a hiccup as best he could.

'Excuse me, ahh, Grey Cloud. I'm going to grab some tea.' Emma wasn't ready to bare her soul to this loquacious nepotized gadabout. She'd thought there'd by a possible parallel in their lay journeys. Something keyed into the search for faith. Her move to the convent was meant to be a balm for her disquieted, searching soul, a soul that had been violated with a strange force from outside, an *other* side, and had made her the agent of improbable, fast-growing, little deviant humans. That she loved, by the way. Roaringman's speech, his largess of presence, though not unkind, struck the wrong nerve. She walked past the tea trivet and headed for her room.

*　*　*

Riley Cardle pulled her Suzuki Sidekick in at the curb, across from the Regent Square Theater marquee. The marquee spelled out *The Ghost and Mr. Chicken*. 'It'll scare the laughs right out of you!' was rendered in smaller letters underneath. Cool theater, she thought. Foreign, classic, independent, and just weird stuff. Good mix.

Lars rushed to the car door, in a light tan jacket, shorts, and a cotton tossle cap. A few stray hairs waggled over his forehead, all of them green.

'Hello, Lars.'

'Hello Miss Cardle.'

'Call me Riley.' She pulled out and headed for the Parkway ramp. 'You dye your hair.'

Lars pushed the strays up under his hat. 'My sister. I'm gonna kill her. She painted my head while I was sleeping.'

'Sisters,' said Cardle. 'I have two and I hate 'em both.'

'You hate them. Actually?' Lars was staring at her.

'Both idiots. One thinks she's a princess and the other is a family despot.'

'Cripe. I'm gonna kill my sister but I don't hate her.'

'There you go,' said Cardle. 'Tell me some stuff, Lars. Remember, I'm trading my driving for your info.'

Lars fiddled with his seat belt and turned his face away from her. 'Ok, listen. I'm going to tell you the whole thing, the real thing. It will get me and other people in trouble. It's hard to do. My mom's gonna hate me and throw me out.'

'I'm listening. And I'm recording, just so you know.' Cardle opened a small pack on the seat that revealed her phone, the red record light flashing.

'I feel good because this story has to come out. So it's, like…' He blew out a breath that contained a sigh. Cardle looked across at him, this young kid with the weird hair, and took a breath of her own. She decided to change tack. So eager to get the story, she remembered how much better it was, how much more lucrative, to let the person release their tale in their own time and manner, to a welcoming ear. Her coercion would work against her aims. *Relax.*

'How about this. We have some hours. Let's drive to Greensburg, the Remediation Center. They'll have parking. We can sit and talk, after you see your friend.' She turned and smiled at him. Suddenly, the kid seemed like a young brother out on a limb. She clicked off the recorder.

'Should be some good places for eats out that way.'

*   *   *

Moss had mixed a variety of web-recommended fertilizers into the soil that held the Tree. The last few leaves had gone brown. He fought against calling in some tree experts. Everything would boil over and out, including his own culpability. Did anything matter at this point.

What was the purpose of burning down the Nature Center anyway? A feral impulse after he'd first bitten the apple. A royal plot that would propel him into some important stratosphere, he the bold implementer of some cosmic reckoning. Now, it made no sense, though it did add a nice felonious touch to his Catholic high school principal resume.

He stood up and gazed around Razor's room. Did he even know his son? Did he care about the things Razor had collected here? Movie posters, books, a basketball, a P-38 Lightning model airplane hanging from the ceiling. No; there was no connection, no family ties, no father-to-son or son-to-father conduit worthy of being defined as care, let alone love. Derealization had made him a living cripple, without so much as a limp to show for it. He felt like pounding his head against the wall, or taking an axe to the telephone poles outside, or wringing something's neck. This dark energy wanted out. He was losing the ability to check it. Well, he'd tried to find a way out of the trap via religion. Or at least theology. The apple tree and Eden he'd bitten into? Another dead-end farce that only honed his own stiletto-sharp confirmation that life was not about any Big Bang, or Big God. Big Deal. Big Joke. *God, don't help me here.* I'm on my own, like everybody else. Somebody's gonna get some of my free retribution.

*   *   *

Lars was puffing, in a hurry to get back to the car, where Cardle sat with her notebook and pen. 'They won't let me see him.' He opened the car door and got in.

'Did you give some advanced notice? Get family permission?'

'No. I'm just a friend who wanted to see a friend.'

'Lars. You can't operate like that in a place like this. The boy is in a coma.'

'No shit.'

'Lars.' She blew out a formal sigh of annoyance. 'You have to reach out to the Moss family – Ray Moss, right – you said. Then the family contacts the center. All sides agree a visit, despite the coma, is appropriate. You must have known this.'

'Maybe I did. It's a mess. Me too. And he might be dying. And his dad's a crazy ace.'

'What's his dad's name?'

'Gideon Moss. He's the Principal at St. Anselm.'

'St. Anselm. Swissvale. That's where that Green family is. The ones with the triplets, the three girls.'

'Yes. Three girls. Ms. Green is their mother. She was teaching there. Guess she's on leave.'

'I interviewed her, and Mr. Green.'

Lars fell back against his car seat. Cardle drove them out of the center's parking lot. They found a Panera's near the Westmoreland Mall and a table inside away from the front counter queue. Cardle got them both a hot chocolate and sat down across from the kid.

'So let's untangle this, Lars. You're friends with Ray. You know Gideon and the Greens. You know about the fire. Are there threads here, I can twine? If we bring these things into one, I might consider burying your identity. You'd have to somehow steer your mom from guessing, but at least there wouldn't be tacit verification that you were involved in a way you shouldn't have been. And, as I told you, I got a tip about arson already, anonymous, by someone who sounded young, like you. We could go with that hidden character as the main source. Our own little deep throat. You just corroborate, from a safe, legal distance.'

'I'm down with that.'

'Down?'

'I'm Ok with that. Start with this: it was probably Razor who called you with the arson thing.'

'Razor. That's Ray Moss.'

'Yes.'

*　　*　　*

The leopard pillbox slug had taken a random route through the edible fresh shoots in the gardens of Frick. After traversing various summer rain puddles, small episodes of water-melting had occurred. The puddle water, ingested, then merged with the slug's excreta, had disassembled each H_2O molecule, the hydrogen and oxygen heading their separate ways. The sum of the earth's water content had been thus minutely reduced.

Boneseed sixth was the fruit of life. A very difficult plant to germinate, once established it produced three to seven viable crops annually. Ingredients in its composition were likely to extend a typical human lifespan by several decades. It would be coveted, more than gold, more than power. Thus it would be an exemplary flash point the world did not need.

Boneseed seventh was the weaselmander. This creature was gentle like a lamb, cute like a kitten, friendly like a dog, easy to feed, healthy, playful, and had no natural predators. It was likely to be a popular pet. Kept well, in good environs, its lifespan exceeded 500 years. It was considered as fecund as rabbits, and this one, on this new earth, was already expecting.

*   *   *

It would have been nice to get a *fiat lux* before the *Fireworks* summit, thought Abel. Let me just check.

He tried sitting at his laptop, staring at the wall, and thinking about… sex. Sex with Emma. Lots of good stuff there. Nothing on the screen. He tried thinking about french fries. Eating french fries. Primanti's french fries. Slaw right on the bread. How about french fries after sex with Emma? Still no. He tried thinking about University of Pittsburgh's Womens' Volleyball team currently ranked number two in the nation. Nothing. He tried thinking about the times he and Emma had hiked parts of the Appalachian Trail.

He looked at his screen. Nothing.

He looked behind him. The three Green sisters were sitting cross-legged, there on the floor.

'Can we use the laptop?' It was Boyd. 'We want to check, Dad. Rumors about us being witches. Mini-Anti-Christs. Or aliens. It's all wrong. We're not troubled. Mostly curious. Plus we want to get some more material into the document. Will you let the Three Wise Guys read this?'

'You know what, gals? Don't sit behind me silently like that when I'm here trying to do my own thing.'

'We're sorry,' said Boyd. The others nodded, heads drooping.

'I need this thing, for a while. You guys. Maybe wash the dishes.'

Etta appeared in the kitchen doorway, waving a dish towel around like a military baton. 'Young Banshees! Get in here. Dragon, you wash. Miller, dry. Boyd, put away.'

The girls scampered into the kitchen. Abel watched them run, like six year olds. When they came out of the kitchen they'd probably be seven year olds. When were the black helicopters going to hummer in overhead and drop the SWAT team who will, in the name of the government, seize these 'assets' – his children – for research and security and to prevent nuclear war and alien invasion and armageddon…

And, of course, there it was.

fiat lux six

In the search for your true calling, you must forget fame, and adoration, and treasure, or it will be forever hidden from you. You must hide from the affirmation you covet. You must flee from the attention you crave. You must sit in the quiet corner, or under a growing tree, find your gifts and engage your talents. If no one ever says a word about them, or about you, and you finally lose interest in ever hearing about yourself, you have won. Then, you have climbed the greatest mountain of all. Then, your life will begin.

Well hallelujah and the Lord be praised. This does a lot of good.

*   *   *

'Ok. Recorder's on. Let's go, Lars. We have a half-hour, then need to get you home.'

'Gideon Moss wanted me to help tear a tree out of Frick Park. Wait. The *Black Squirrel*.'

'Can you get me a photo of Moss?'

'He's in the yearbook. I'll e-mail the photo to you. This weird Black Squirrel was down in Frick Park. This was last October. I think it has some cosmic connection to everything. Like, it was on the roof of the Nature Center, dead, the night we…the night we…the night we burned it down.'

'We?'

'Mr. Moss, Gideon, hired me. I know chemistry, combustibles. But, wait, first, let me finish. This Black Squirrel, if you know any stuff about sorcery and black magic, it's part of that scene. Never saw one in Frick Park then all of the sudden it's spooking me out. The woods were weird that day.'

'Ok, ok. I need, I want to get to the fire stuff. We don't have all day.'

Cardle stole a glance at her phone's clock.

'Ok. Razor asked me to help his dad go down to the park and dig up this tree, this apple tree. I thought the whole idea was nuts but Razor wanted me so I could let his dad know it was stupid. The damned squirrel bit me on the neck, and I went to the dark side in like, 30 seconds. Mr. Moss and I shoved Razor out of the way and dug up the tree and took it to his house. Next thing I know, he's calling me up to help him toast the Nature Center. Why not, huh? We went down there, it was snowing, and I climbed on the roof and basically torched the place.'

'So Gideon was the mastermind and you the flunkey.'

'I'm no flunkey, Ms. Cardle. You can check my report cards.'

'All preplanned, though. By you both. What for?'

'Great question. I still have no idea.'

'And a snowflake, the green hair?'

'Yeah. Something from the fire landed on me and my hair burned off and grew back in green.' He lifted his cap so she had a better look.

'And all this time you're just cruising with the plan. Never second-guessed what you were doing, who might be harmed, damage to the park.'

'Of course. I thought it was mad. That squirrel bite – it's still with me, inside me, in my blood. The green flake stuff, too. I'm been trying to figure out a way to locate where the green chemistry might be reacting down in the park. So you see my screwed up left and right brain consciences are hard at work, fighting each other while I try to live. And I'm here with you, confessing. So who's winning?'

'Lars. I admire your honesty. Don't know that anything here will stand up legally, in your favor. But I'll do my part to communicate everything as well as I'm able. And, again, won't use your name. But be ready.'

'Ready to be sent up the river.' Lars gulped down the last of his chocolate.

'Let's finish in the car,' said Cardle. 'We have to get driving in ten minutes.'

They moved to the lot. Lars got in and cranked his car window down. He leaned out and blew a breath. 'Too hot.'

'Keep this next stuff to yourself – defcon #5, so to speak,' said Cardle. 'So the Greens have these three girls, and they're very wary of saying much. The girls may be disabled, or otherwise suffering from growth issues. Tell me anything you can about that family.'

'Mrs. Green is a good teacher. She's away, after the babies were born. Not sure if she's coming back. Oh – and wait, yeah – there's the apple connection. So Mr. Moss ripped up the apple tree and dragged it to his backyard. Guess it's still there, though considering how whacked out Mr. Moss is, a good chance the tree is toast. So Mrs. Green came to me just before all this crap started and wanted me to help her dissect a half-chewed apple in the school labs. Insane. Never did figure out why those two got all hot and bothered about apples.'

'Ok, Lars.' Cardle started up her car, and pulled out onto Rt. 30 for the trip home. 'I'm going to write something up. Send me that photo of your principal. And listen, I'm not your guardian or anything. I recommend you see a doctor about your hair, and tell them about the bite. Dr. Haskley out of Shadyside is a good joe. I know his assistant, Carmen. You want me to set something up?'

'Don't bother.'

'I know a few lawyers. I'll get you some names.'

'That sounds like fun.'

'Maybe see if your mom will go with any of this.'

'Maybe.'

'Will you tell your mom you couldn't get in to see Ray?'

'I guess.'

'She'll wonder what we were doing all day.'

'Yup.'

'Got one more lie left in you?'

*   *   *

The Three Wise Guys were about to meet the Three Green Sisters. Abel began to feel like a sumo-wrestling event was commencing. Miller, Boyd and Dragon were on a developmental express that scared and tormented him. Any dream of a normal life was a distant memory, and the impossibilities were piling up at a breathless rate. Feeding the cats became a controlled ritual he savored. Seren and Dippity refused to get involved with the metaphysical. They might already be, maybe all cats might already be, halfway on the other side anyway.

The last *fiat lux,* the big deal about 'forgetting fame' and all that malarkey, made him angry. That emotion dissipated when he realized that his daughters' writings were appearing in the documents more and more steadily and in concert with the *fiats.* What should he do about that? What could he do? Let there be darkness, for a while, so he could get some peace. Not likely.

So the 'simple' plan, facilitated by Sr. Ignatius, is that Sister would arrive with the Charity convent van and pick up the girls and Abel early on July 4th, and drive them to Greensburg for the meeting. Pancratius had covered transportation and lodging for the Wise Guys, who would also arrive in the morning. They would all convene at the Motherhouse's St. Louise de Marillac Reflection Sanctuary, a place where they could gather in additional privacy, located away from the convent proper, set by a stream and shaded by weeping willow trees. A light buffet of food. coffee and tea would be on hand, along with bottled spring water.

Emma would be there, and, unusually, she'd asked for another participant, Grey Cloud Roaringman, a theoretical physicist. Mother Superior had advocated for Roaringman. Abel didn't appreciate that some stranger would be waltzing in, and that Ignatius and Sr. Jill had approved, and worst of all that Emma had started this chain. So there she was, sequestered away with all those women, trying to find a way to faith through the novitiate program, and she'd taken up with some guy, some fancy-schmancy science guru, the very kind who would refuel her technical-biological-physics logic, all sparked up with apple turbocharging. Yeah, she'd make a fine nun, that Emma. Sister Darwinessa.

Was there some silver lining he might comprehend here? He looked outside. The girls were sitting on the grass, gathered in a circle, discussing something. Etta was putzing around in the garden; red tomatoes and purple broccoli were coming up in fine bunches. More and more self-sufficient, the four-month old children required little from their grandmother. Or from their father, for that matter. No childhood to speak of, unless its compression had amped up its experience to some unfathomable, distilled place. 100% proof.

They looked happy, so that made him smile.

'Hey you guys. We have to get up really early tomorrow and drive up to Greensburg. We'll see Mom.'

All sorts of *yahhoooos* and jumps and somersaults ensued.

'Mommmm*!*'

Yup. Mom.

*   *   *

Gideon Moss planned to depart St. Anselm High School with some notable, ugly, flare. Leave a token of ruin that would serve as a fitting end to his career as impostor and interloper. He could dig around for some personal, incriminating dirt in the faculty offices. Drop caustic acid into the plumbing. Run a rare earth magnet over the school's servers. That last, even as a thought, kicked some adrenaline into his psyche.

A few workable scraps remained in his life. Maybe the tree's roots held some potency. Or its withered leaves. A little more investigation into that might serve. If there was some way still to cash in on this Eden miracle, it'd be worth delaying his volatile exodus from his office, and the community, and maybe even the world. But he wouldn't delay for long.

*   *   *

Cardle got another hot tip, by way of Carmen again, through Haskley, who'd been alerted to a convocation of religious higher-ups coming into Pittsburgh to look into the Greens' babies' situation. They wished to see him before departing the country, about the nature of the girls' accelerated gestations and development. Haskley surmised it was in search of the miraculous. Or, more often, in search of exaggeration that disproved the miraculous, was Haskley's take. No matter what he told them, they'd find a way to debunk it. Unless they were open to the admittedly strange facts. He'd need the best evidence, and he and Carmen were compiling it. She was lining up meeting options, also. The three prelates (he was told) would be in the area July 4-5.

She began to wonder if her story might reach a national audience. If she pitched it correctly, she might be able to sell it to a high bidder, to some news organization beyond Pittsburgh that would see its potential. Her *Post-Press* managing editor might think again about her worth. It was obvious these Green females were making some sort of biological history. One thing tripped her circuit-breakers, though: she didn't want to be the cause of the federal government marching into that family's life. Probably she'd watched too many movies where the men with grappling-hooks kidnap the savants to advance some pernicious deep-state agenda. Whether it could come true or not, Cardle got squeamish with that trajectory. She wrestled with a narrative approach that would expound on wonder, versus some deployable – *make that deplorable* – weaponizing.

*   *   *

Emma was not keen on Roaringman's physical appearance. He lacked facial hair, and had what looked like small scars under his chin. She squirmed watching him eat. His clothes were often wrinkled. He liked to wax about music and movies. Rarely talked about god, lower case or capital G. She did like his crow-black hair. So why was she asking he attend the *Fireworks*?

Because he could argue the science without the emotion she knew would crater her own voice. She'd asked Sr. Jill to see if he was interested.

The evening before the summit, he'd approached her at dinner. He'd cleaned up. His copper-brown complexion shone like polished leather. His dark eyes sparkled as he leaned down, gently placing his hand on the table to steady himself.

'Thank you,' he said. He moved to a far table and ate, the same sloppy way.

*   *   *

July 4th arrived. The evening's fireworks would ignite Allegheny County after dark. Explosive happenings: a scalding day, insects buzzing, hot dogs burning, lemonade spilled, babies crying, rain pelting, Russian invasion, fake *news, God save the Queen!*

Abel woke with a start. He could hear the girls downstairs, gabbing away with Grandma Etta, everyone laughing quietly.

It was, really, July 4th.

EIGHTEEN

THE DOORS WERE pulled back, wide open in welcome at the St. Louise de Marillac Reflection Sanctuary. The parties were ushered from the shaded parking area as they arrived. The three Wise Guys, Rabbi Winkel, Imam El-Muhammad, and Cardinal Mirangue, seemed to be getting along swimmingly, as one of them put it. 'We had a dip together at the Hampton Pool,' reported Winkel. 'Without our garb, just some vacationers from out east, was our cover.' They all grinned. Apparently, the language barrier was not problematic; all of them had dealt internationally with diverse missions and assignments. Today, they each wore their traditional vestments, the kind not meant for formal rituals, while still establishing their distinction from the adherents they served. Sr. Pancratius brandished a briefcase and looked like someone you didn't want to bother.

The Greens' van arrived last. Abel roused his brood out of the vehicle. The girls were all wearing country-summer light cotton dresses, longish ones that swirled about their knees, that, according to Etta, they'd all chosen themselves. They looked like elvish fairy children about to dance around the Maypole. Not necessarily a good omen, thought Abel. That considered, he could see the shine of their innocent and guileless naivete dancing right along with their uniqueness. Maybe via his *seedy*-vision, but clean and clear and, dare he say, sinless. Ignatius performed dutiful mop-up, maneuvering the kids as they converged, with big eyes, on the food table.

*

Emma was in a form of shock – actually befuddled, seeing how grown her daughters appeared to be. They were conversing. Moving about with young, intuitive reflexes. They were born at the end of February. They'd now spent around four months on the earth, after a short stint within her body. They were living miracles, but also sort of outrageous; her own flesh and blood, walking, talking girls, whose obvious and hidden wisdoms were both profound and appalling.

She didn't have many emotional options to deploy. She loved these daughters and would have stood in front of a locomotive to protect them. She suspected they'd have simply moved her out of the way and thanked her for the effort.

Today was like a coming out day for her metaphysical debutantes. Her heart beat with pride and some form of embarrassment, along with a renewed desire to hide away for a very long time. The apple tree in Frick Park... she wished she'd never followed that warm, ethereal glow up the hillside. For now, this present refused to become unstuck. Their reality would have to play itself out, while she and Abel and her girls played along. While the gods laughed or cried or stayed tuned to see how their precious humans would manage this thing. At least, meeting these deities after she died, if they existed, would allow her to give them a piece of her mind.

She took a deep breath and, as so often, found herself again realizing that a prayer would precisely fit the moment. A prayer. No. *Sorry, God.* She could recite the words, but they wouldn't come from her soul, or even her heart. Just from her mercenary mind, which was working overtime and powered by a super-fruit and pretty much so far down the rabbit hole it was surfacing, cart-wheeling, sling-shot out the other side.

Another deep breath. Her daughters were laughing, over by the food. Ok, Emma. Try to relax. Those kids are incredible, yes. But still kids. Sort of.

She found a chair in the corner, though the center table had name cards. She hoped they'd move to an open spot near the large windows, where you could better see the stream and trees and hear the robins whistling their song. Roaringman came in looking almost dapper. He wore a small Native American pendant around his neck, to go with a dark suit jacket.

Abel looked a little shell-shocked. Maybe a lot shell-shocked. He came over and kissed Emma on the top of her head. She held out her hand, which he took and squeezed.

'Hello darlin',' he whispered. The immediacy of their love spread up and across her face, a warm balm. If there was doubt, it crept away to rest awhile.

'I love you,' she whispered, noting the slight reluctance in her delivery. He loosed his hand and proceeded to the food table to point out their mother to the young women – their four month old daughters.

'We see her, Dad. We wanted to give you two a moment,' said Dragon. The girls then raced to swamp Emma with hugs, kisses, and more hugs. She embraced them all and her teeth gritted against her plain-faced joy. She shooed them off as the meeting looked to be starting.

Sister Jill directed everyone to sit. 'Good morning everyone. Welcome to the Reflection Sanctuary.' She took a moment to identify the participants, going around the table, where she stood at the head. The Greens were lined up on one side, the Wise Guys on the other. Roaringman sat at the long other end. Sisters Pancratius and Ignatius remained standing.

'We're honored to have you all as guests today. I won't be staying while you meet. Please let Sister Ignatius know if there's anything you want or need. There's food and drink, provided by our convent staff, as indicated by your dietary requirements.' She gestured at the refreshments. 'Sr. Pancratius, Deer Park Spring Water as you asked. Restrooms are just outside, in the entry area. There's no cell phone service here in the Sanctuary, so you won't need to turn off your phones. Please don't record the session.'

Sr. Jill continued. 'I hope you'll find the day fruitful. I will offer a short prayer. Imam El-Muhammad and Rabbi Winkel, I welcome you to add your own words if you'd like, after.' They both first nodded, then both shook their heads.

'God, watch over these children of yours. Let us find the light you provide every day. Most of all, let us find the ground we all walk in common, regardless of where our hopes take us. Amen.'

Sister blessed herself, bowed, walked past her brother Roaringman to whisper something, unlocked the stays and pulled the doors closed behind her.

'Listen,' suggested that sonorous Native American voice. 'Why don't we retire to the more comfortable seating by the window. There's three couches, easy chairs, a rocker. I like that rocker.'

Roaringman stood up and took to the rocking chair, a finely-wrought oak antique. After a few raised eyebrows, people stood, and soon the assembly was gathered nearer to the windows and appreciating the outside air that wafted in. The kids sat on the floor, below their mother and father, who settled together on a couch. Ignatius sat on a chair against the wall.

Pancratius. looking ever-so-slightly miffed at Roaringman's impudence, dragged a wooden stool to a strategic position, centered up behind them. She opened a thick notepad on her lap, pulled her round spectacles up tight, and set her pen to the page. Then she raised her head and snapped her flock to full attention.

'Listen up, please! I'm going to cover the methodology we'll use for this meeting. You've all had a chance to review it. Let's keep things tidy and keep things moving.'

She lifted the pad and read, gesturing towards the clerics.

'First, you three, Cardinal Ethan, Imam El-Muhammed, and Rabbi Ben, tell us what you're here to learn, and what you hope to take with you. Then Emma and Abel describe their experience. Then some questions. From all sides. Including Dragon, Boyd and Miller in these. Then, if all agree, as you have done but we can confirm here, now, our three guest religious will get an hour alone with the Green daughters.'

Everyone nodded.

'I wonder,' said Roaringman, 'Might someone join them, perhaps myself, least personally involved and I hope objectively-oriented, as a witness?'

'I don't mind,' said Imam El-Muhammad. He turned and presented a palm to Rabbi Ben and Cardinal Ethan.

'Sound idea,' said Ben.

Ethan leaned forward. 'I'd prefer not. I believe this opportunity requires the utmost respect and privacy.'

Roaringman acceded readily. Emma had been conflicted about that aspect of the *Fireworks*. Now playing out like a script she couldn't revise.

'Ok. Then. Let's get started,' said Pancratius.

The Wise Guys each had a turn. In sum, they expected nothing. They were here to hear. There was no plan or ambition to prove or disprove. It was obvious a very special event had occurred, an event that aligned very readily with one of religions' best-known canons. They only wished to apprehend what was recalled, ask questions, each from his own ecclesiastical station, and then return to their homes to discuss and discern what it all might mean. They would keep the proceedings confidential. This was not territory any of them were unfamiliar with, though, admittedly, this particular episode had jumped to the front of their duties. A phenomenon, they were willing to see it as, worthy of their attentions and possibly more.

They had titled the case *'The Square Miracles'*. Emma couldn't help but raise her eyebrows. She'd heard *Square Family Fun Day*, and *Regent Square Yard Sale* day, and the *Square Bake Off*. Never *miracles*. Yet. She was inside this miracle thing. Pushing for a deeper way in. Or out.

No questions, so far.

The Greens were next. Emma and Abel laid out the story as it happened to them, while everyone listened. One question, from Roaringman.

'What happened to the apple you saved?'

'It's in a fridge at St. Anselm. Or thrown out,' said Emma.

'Bad science,' said Roaringman.

'Tell me about it,' said Emma.

'And no doctors were able to indicate reasons for your altered physiologies, from the ingredients you ingested. From the apple?'

'No,' said Abel. 'To be honest, we've been racing to catch up since day one; October 1st of last year. You'll be meeting with Doctor Haskley, who can give you the medical data on Emma, and the kids.'

Emma looked down at the three full heads of hair, sitting at her feet. Where her psyche was treated to more 'fun' – Boyd was blond, Dragon had reddish hair, and Miller's was medium brown. She had a flash that she was Rosemary, she was Mia Farrow, the serpent mother, and these kids should be in a horror movie, *Rosemary's Babies*. They were begotten from her womb and now sprawled at her feet. Sitting in rapt attention. Maybe more like well-fed cheetahs, resting before the next hunt.

Ignatius raised her hand.

'I want to mention Gideon Moss. He's the Principal at St. Anselm High School where I teach. Most of you know he also, apparently, tasted the apple, an apple, from the same tree as Emma and Abel. He and I have had some general conversations, mostly about spirituality. He has talked around much of the Apple and Eden stuff. Because I want to respect his privacy, I won't say much here; not that I myself would have much to add. I'm happy to provide his contact details if you wish.'

'Thank you,' said Rabbi Ben. 'We're aware of his involvement to a point. We know he's dealing with a family crisis and don't intend to bother him for now.'

From across the room came a pronounced shuffling of papers.

'Any more questions?' asked Pancratius. 'No. Ok, let's take a 20 minute break. Have some refreshments. Then you kids – you and Ben and Ethan and El-Muhammed – will get an hour by yourselves.'

Boyd raised her hand and gestured at the Wise Guys. 'We want to know, respectfully, how to address each of you.'

The men looked at each other, sharing slight nods. 'Our first names are fine for today,' said Rabbi Ben Winkel. 'What shall we call you?'

'*Banshee Patrol!*' yelped Miller. The other girls laughed, with hands over their mouths. 'Call us anything you want: Caroline, Rebecca, Maggie. Dragon, Miller, Boyd. Three Green Sisters.'

The adults seemed stricken. Emma certainly was. Were these really their babies, born in late February? Had there been a switch in the nursery? She wished there was gin, or a more powerful drug, at the food table. She'd have gulped it down.

Everyone rose and stretched. Pancratius snapped her notepad closed, then picked up a bottle of spring water on her way out the door.

Emma walked over to her husband. 'Please. Tell me, Abel. What in the name of anything, anything at all, is happening?'

*   *   *

Lars Patton had forwarded the JPEG photo of St. Anselm High School Principal Gideon Moss. When Cardle had clicked on the image to enlarge it, she stared. This was the guy who'd kissed the Poor Clare, down in the privates of Frick Park.

*   *   *

The sisters were tucked in, sitting across one couch, and the Wise Guys were seated across from them on the other. Cardinal Ethan opened the dialog.

'So you girls were born end of February?'

'Yes.' 'Yup.' 'Uh huh.'

'How does it feel to grow so fast?'

'Good. Get through unable to hold your head up, past all that crying, and toilet-training, on to solid foods, talking and reading classic literature. Like *The Catcher in the Rye*.' said Miller.

The clerics took a moment, appeared to consider frowning. The Imam continued.

'You wouldn't mind slowing down?' asked El-Muhammed.

'It would be nice to live longer. Based on the speed of our growth, if we continue at this pace, we'll be past an approximated average life expectancy in about ten years. Kind of short.'

'Big word, *approximated,* sister,' snarked Boyd. Miller poked back at her sister.

'Pretty good for a four month old,' said Rabbi Ben. He paused. 'Do you all get along with each other?'

The sisters shot glances at each other, making a variety of serious faces.

'We're Ok. We fight, and say dumb things. Overall, pretty good…' Dragon continued, casting a teasing look at Miller and Boyd.

'Can one of you summarize what you believe you are?' asked Cardinal Ethan. 'I don't mean to sound rude, or as if you are from some other planet just landed. You're rather a living miracle to us.'

'What do you think we are?' asked Boyd.

The religious each tilted their heads slightly, furrowed their brows, and ran hands lightly across their lips. Rabbi Ben started to say something, as did Imam El-Muhammad. 'Go ahead, Ben,' said the Imam. The Rabbi proceeded.

'We have been given summaries from Sister Pancratius. And from your doctor, Dr. Haskley, and also some material from your parents – mostly your father – along with Sister Ignatius and Father Jack. We have conferred with our own, colleagues, if you will, individuals in the higher offices of all our religions. We have talked with each other on the way here.'

He paused to study their faces. The girls were listening attentively and politely.

'We can see you are unique, and that your biological development does not conform to anything seen prior. On this Earth, as far as records can supply that. We know of the apple, and how it was a catalyst for the events at hand. The best summary I can offer, that we might offer, would be to say that you are a Mystery before us, that has a certain goodness about it – your story and your lives so far, so to speak – that continues to suggest "open" vs. "closed" as we gently and cautiously and prayerfully and judiciously look to reach understanding.'

He leaned back, looking relieved, as though he had articulated some wellspring of pertinent truth. 'We don't intend to seek out the miraculous, nor to test you in any manner,' he said, then turned to his theological comrades. 'Imam, Cardinal, can you add to my thoughts, here?' El-Muhammad spoke next.

'I agree with Rabbi Ben. Islam does not reverence the same traditions as my two brothers here. Though this story is indeed included in the Holy Quran, the tree's lineage takes on a different significance,. We do, however, search for the holy where it is offered. In the case of you young children, or young women – I'm not sure which to name you – there is a Spirit at work. That is plain. I cannot begin to fathom its source or its future. But it is present, now.'

Cardinal Ethan followed. 'I feel grace, as seldom I have, in your presence. Too clearly for someone as acutely aware of my shortcomings as I am. This is not false modesty, Dragon, Miller and Boyd. I have a perception that false *anything* would not survive the three Green sisters' unique filters.' He paused and leaned towards them. 'I don't want to speak for the others. We must maintain our objectivity. You can see we are somewhat off our game. We want to believe, however – you and your gifts may be a deception.'

'What is it that you hope?' asked Dragon.

'We do not hope. Only pray we might perceive,' said Cardinal Ethan. 'But. I would like to ask you, again, what you three consider yourselves to be.'

'Shall I?' asked Dragon, casting a quick glance at her sisters. Miller and Boyd nodded. 'We're young, even though our growth rate is as maddening to us as to our family. But, my point is we have tons to learn. About this world, our lives, everything. It's coming onboard fast. We are able to take it in, and we seem able to…digest stuff.' She looked over to see Miller and Boyd exchanging wry smiles. 'Our best guess is this: we are *unfallen*. Since Mom and Dad bit the Eden Apple in innocence, without having a prior exhortation from God that they shouldn't, they received knowledge. Still working out whether it's just about good and evil, or general knowledge about everything. So, they kinda got a big dose of major stuff from the apple. So, we, born of their state – and take this with a grain of salt, please, reverends – and excuse me if that's the wrong usage, please, Imam El-Muhammad – are free of Original Sin, kind of like Adam and Eve would have been without biting the apple, but with the apple's gifts.'

Dragon paused, giving the Wise Guys space to respond. They remained silent, gaping with closed mouths.

'So,' said Miller, stepping in for her sister, 'we're just trying to let everything flow into and around us and not assume too much, but still be grateful and happy and also we don't want to lose out on what may be a speedier kind of life here. It's all so beautiful. Have you seen Regent Square? And Frick Park?'

The religious shook their heads to answer 'no', and, indeed, looked on from their stations with every kind of 'no' stirring in the logic of their minds. Faith would have to survive these Sisters. Faith would need some new structure. Faith would be tested, in a way none of them expected.

Behind them, Pancratius swung the doors open. 'Sorry to interrupt. Imam El-Muhammad, you had requested a short recess now.'

'Yes. Thank you. Zuhr, my afternoon prayer.' He proceeded out.

'You'll have another half-hour to talk with each other when he returns,' said Pancratius. 'Take ten minutes.'

The sisters raced out to their mother and father.

'What do you think, Ben?' asked Ethan. The Rabbi's face was unreadable.

'I don't know where to go with this. I guess I would say I don't want their story in my life, or in my people's life. Because it alienates centuries of a, maybe not fragile certitude, but the steadiness of a theology built from human to human through Yahweh's steering, merciful, just hand. Olam *Ha*-Ba is not reinvented because the Garden of Eden has been resurrected. If the sisters' story enters our Jewish narrative, and is embraced, even partially, the erosion might be incalculable. What are your thoughts?'

'Probably a more comfortable fit for Roman Catholicism and Christianity. Trepidation comes from the inability in this day and age to relate a story – and I understand the story's veracity is yet to be fixed, if it ever could be – to communicate something so significant and profound without it being twisted into endless forms. I mean, look at the Bible. How many interpretations are among us? How can we ever bring this, event, this happening, this reality resolving in front of our own eyes, into some construction that won't merely muddle into wild end-times ruminations, faith-rocking misfires, or stupefying incredulity?' Cardinal Ethan stood and flapped his crimson robe out to his sides. 'Do you see?'

'Spoken like a 21st century warrior,' said Rabbi Ben. 'So we're in a pickle. Let's see what El-Muhammad thinks, when we can talk afterwards.'

*   *   *

Cardle began to assemble her story. Fabrication will be required to draw a connecting line through the middle, to bring it all into one coherent narrative. With some fuzzy edges, sure, but Cardle believed she could make it happen. Tomorrow evening, she'd have a beer with Carmen, see what the religious contingents had wished to find out about the Green daughters' medical picture.

Ok, it's the 4th of July. I am going to sit out on the porch and watch the fireworks. Independence day – *Rah rah, yahoo, and all that other malarkey.*

*   *   *

Independence Day was a good day to get into the high school and plot the brutal finale Moss intended to wreak. Nobody'd be around. Moss threw some cardboard boxes in the car trunk, and headed over to McClure Avenue. He looked down at the keys to the school as he unlocked it, and wondered if he should torch the building. There was care, and investment here, he would admit. His *derealized* investment, but his. He got through the door, closed it, shut off the security alarms, sat down on the entry stairwell steps, and thought he felt a tear on his cheek.

*   *   *

Rika Newman was a painter. Frick Park was her muse. She loved nature, and studied it with care. At noon on the Fourth of July, she told her husband she was going into the park with her plein air acrylic paint materials to do some short studies. The Newmans lived in Squirrel Hill, and the park was at their back door, an urban forest full of birds, squirrels, chipmunks, snakes, turtles, frogs, owls, beavers, possum, deer, raccoons, salamanders, toads, bugs galore (a few of those she could do without), and a variety of lovely trees, flowers, and undergrowth. Areas of red clay added a background palette Rika especially liked. Rika's husband, Casey, also painted, but preferred house and cityscapes. He wished her well and sat down to read.

Rika had a small checklist in her bag, noting every species she'd seen in the park. She hadn't painted them all, of course; but knowing the breadth of the park's denizens was certainly another wonderful aspect of it. She knew all about the pollution and the human-tossed litter. Maybe her paintings could help those litterbugs reconsider. She set up near the Iron Gate trail, down some way from the playground above. It was nice to be able to hear the families cavorting not far away. Felt safer, though she really never felt unsafe in the park.

Just off the path, she put a rubber mat down to sit on, and pulled her knees up to set her blank canvas on her lap. A mountain biker raced past, with a quick wave and a shouted *'happy fooooouurrthh',* he and his greeting disappearing in a whoosh around the bend. She opened her bag. Two small jars of water, some rags, brushes, paints, a couple of canvases. She'd use cadmium green, as a base, for a quick start piece, warm up her hand, get the brush moving. The jars of water she set down on some flat rocks on the ledge behind her.

Ooops. Dropped the cap to the tube. Always happens, doesn't it, starting out. She set the canvas down and crouched down where the cap had fallen. *Hmm, humm...* Ah, there it is. Dirty. Best to dunk the thing, wipe off the specks. She looked. One jar of water was full. The other empty. At the bottom was a curious-looking snail, or slug. Really interesting, leopard spots. She'd add it to her species ledger. She tilted the jar so the creature could waggle its way out. What happened to the water?

*   *   *

Boneseed eighth was the snapper manta. The fresh-and-salt-water manta had been seeded in a pool under the Forbes Ave. bridge, a fenced-off area dammed with a row of rocks, where dogs could splash about in summer's highest heat. It was not ideal, with canine paws regularly agitating the water and often kicking close to the vulnerable young manta. This water flowed into Fern Hollow Creek, draining the valley, coursing out into the Monongahela and then Ohio Rivers, down to the Mississippi until it reached the ocean, the Gulf of Mexico. There it could reproduce away from these threats. The water's quality did it no favors. It studied a plastic shape that floated past and dropped over the rock dam.

The manta had a disturbing gift, a defense, that could come into use soon. It was able to emit an eardrum snapping shriek from its ventrals, via slits through which it forced bursts of compressed carbon dioxide. The gas-powered scream worked under water or above, when the manta raised itself up on its (eventual) adult musculature, via its wing-like cephalic fins, and engineered this startling geyser spectacle, a clamor of noise and pain.

Boneseed ninth was the upjaw-dropjaw. This creation seemed a cruel idea from a disturbed inventor. Elongated as an eel or fat snake, it had two jaws: one at the upper portion of its front end and one at the lower portion of its back end. To consume – to eat – it required the two jaws to meet, by curling back on itself, in order to grab, tear and macerate whatever sustenance it had managed to grasp. Its eyes were located inside large, ungainly ears, somewhere near the mid-section of its tubular shape. It was doomed to be a mean-spirited, pitiable beast.

Boneseed third, the batbird, had formed, gestated and hatched from its egg near the roots of the maple tree where it had been fertilized. Some green emanation of scent or spore had kept rodents from despoiling it as an egg. The grubs and other insects on the tree's bark provided early fodder. The young bird was strong, and smart, like a young raptor might be, as designed, since it would have to survive alone until its species could be established in this place, this new world, this Earth.

*   *   *

The Green sisters returned for the final part of the *Fireworks* summit. Ignatius closed the doors. The Wise Guys were curious about the *fiat lux* material, which Abel had been wary of releasing, eventually deciding he was unable to share it.

El-Muhammed opened the discussion. 'You've read the *fiat lux*, that your father has told us about?'

'We have. He didn't hide it from us. Probably didn't think we could read. Didn't say *don't read this*. So we all did,' said Boyd.

'What are your opinions?'

'It's a tricky thing. Dad typed it in a kind of trance, apparently. There hasn't been much new stuff in a while, by the way. Also, some of it came in non-complete. Fragments. The last one didn't seem to follow the others, as far as similar content,' said Boyd.

'Yeah,' said Miller. 'So we all thought, when we talked about it, that whoever was sending it – and *sending* should be in quotes here – wasn't playing with a full deck.' The sisters shared a small giggle at that one. 'No disrespect meant. We all think there's an extant cosmic sense-of-humor in the universe.'

'*Extant*,' said Dragon. 'Miller, you need to curb your enthusiasm for big, trying-to-be-impressive words.'

Miller gave her sister a slight, sharp glance.

'Anyway,' said Miller. 'Our thought, we sisters, is that the *fiat lux* material must be kept low-profile. We imagine what it would be like releasing fresh Christian-scriptural kind of writing, and it doesn't seem like a good step to take. Just as happened with the Dead Sea Scrolls, when newly-discovered spiritual sources appear, they shake up what is accepted and agreed upon. Even if somehow authenticated. And that authentication would come under whose auspices? Who would certify material that appeared on a computer screen, these days? We thought about the controversy and discord that would follow. Probably not a wise idea for the *fiat lux* to be released. Mom and Dad may think differently, so be sure to ask them.'

She looked at her sisters. 'All that said, we, my sisters and I, are going to review the *fiat lux* material carefully to see if it will help us figure out what we've agreed is our biggest problem.'

'Can't wait to hear what this problem is,' said Cardinal Ethan.

Outside came the faint sound of a siren.

'The problem,' said Miller, 'is that we don't know exactly what we're doing here. As in, *why* we're here, now.'

'God has a plan, right,' said Rabbi Ben, in the slightest of mocking tones.

'Yes, the old adage is like a catch-all for everything that works out, and disappears when you have to explain Hitler or tsunamis and that kind of thing,' said Dragon. '*Fiat lux* suggests an invasion of sorts, coming from creatures that the apple tree's appearance has initiated, things that weren't meant for the now, that heaven voted against including. So maybe us three, the *unfallen*, three Green sisters *Banshee Patrol*, have appeared on the scene, on the planet, to help mitigate these happenings.'

'That's our current best guess,' said Boyd. 'Even though *'mitigate'* is another pretty big word.'

'We are finding that, for the most part, our unfallen guesses get decently close to the mark,' said Miller.

'Which makes life both amazingly clean and clear and crispy,' said Dragon. 'But, and this is something we're also mulling, somewhat less positively to our thinking, is the idea that our acceleration and intellect are burning as high-octane, and how much fuel have we been allotted.'

'Better to burn out, than to fade away.'

The voice came from the doorway, which had been quietly opened from the foyer. Roaringman's head tilted in through the gap. 'So sorry to interrupt you. Sr. Pancratius has received word that a fireworks truck somewhere off Rt. 30 has derailed, spilling its combustible material across the highway, not far from the Motherhouse entrance. Nothing's on fire and nobody's hurt. So this is just a precaution. If there's some sort of risk, she'll let us know. She hopped down there to check it out.'

'Thank you, Roaringman,' said Cardinal Ethan. 'We'll duck our heads if any rockets come through the windows.'

'Neil Young,' said Roaringman, with a wink, closing the doors again.

'So it feels like this wonderful life may go by at light-speed,' said Boyd.

'Yeah. Way too fast,' said Miller.

They all took some breaths. The sisters seemed as perky as when they'd begun the session. The Wise Guys seemed to be flagging.

'I wanted to add something, dear Rabbi, and Imam, and Cardinal. Our thanks for meeting, of course…' said Miller, the sisters all nodding and smiling in a thankful fashion '…but also a note that our language today accelerated from this discussion. Like, the level of discourse with all of you has kept our own development progressing, and the big and small and other words and sentences we find ourselves using are a kind of surprise for us also. Do you agree, Dragon, Boyd?'

Dragon and Boyd nodded.

'We can't read any future with our unfalleness. We discern, we figure out, we guess and ask each other. But we're not some sort of angels or saints and we don't have access to the other side in any unprecedented manner. We're humans gifted with a special toolkit, still trying to open half the compartments and then trying to figure out what the heck the tools even are…!' All of them laughed.

'Let's conclude, then,' said Rabbi Ben. 'You are a gracious, curious, inexplicable bunch, that's for sure.'

The Cardinal and Imam bowed gently. The three clerics stood up from the couch. The girls sprung up and danced over to grab at the door handles and pull. The doors swung open.

*

Abel had brought the girl's musical instruments, as requested, and had just finished tuning them, by ear, as best he could manage (and hoping for some seedy assist), when the girls burst through the inner doors and raced to hug their mother and father. The food table was rolled out into this pleasant atrium area, and all took time for more drinks, and visits to the restrooms.

Sister Pancratius strode in with a report that the highway mess had been cleaned, but there would be no fireworks at the Greensburg Fairgrounds tonight. Then, to the delight of all, the Green sisters took up their instruments. Miller wielded the six-string banjo. Boyd wrestled the acoustic bass to stand-up. Dragon ran some notes off on the mouth harp. Abel spoke. 'The girls have written a song, I think kind of in your honor, gentlemen. And in honor of this gathering today. Did I get that right, ladies?'

'Yup!' They shouted.

Roaringman had mustered up a Native American flute. 'May I join you ladies, if I stay on the quiet side?'

'Sure!' they exclaimed. There was a final huddle to check their tuning. Then Miller turned to face the seated assembly.

'Ok. *Man, I'm nervous.* Ok. Today, we'd like to perform our very first original song.' Boyd poked her in the ribs. 'Oh – we're *The Banshee Patrol*, by the way – yes indeedy.'

She paused to see her compadres were ready. 'Hit it…..!'

Dragon started with a riff on the mouth organ, slow and peppy at the same time. Boyd checked in with a pumped, sly bass line. Miller came in third, a ringing banjo lilt that had people's toes tapping.

Then Miller sang, her sisters joining her to harmonize on the three-part chorus.

well the 4th of July
came a-rollin' right in
in a world full of grime
in a world full of sin
and a little bitty light
came from over on the hill
where Seton and her sisters
were fillin' in the bill

away with the merry
away with the glum
away with the chariots
we're stickin' to the sun
away in the cradle
the way we wanna fly
away to the places
the wind and rain and sky

the Wise Guys here now
wisdom in the room
words of their years here
a gentle kind of boom

a small kind of firework
we look to shine a light
we crawl from the ashes
and blow away the night

away with the merry
away with the glum
away with the chariots
we're stickin' to the sun
away in the cradle
the way we wanna fly
away to the places
the wind and rain and sky

we soar keen for answers
a glimpse will have to do
our rhyming gets shaky
our verses come unglued
we sing for the simple
the joy inside the notes
we sing as we simply can
we sing right from our throats!

away with the merry
away with the glum
away with the chariots
we're stickin' to the sun
away in the cradle
the way we wanna fly
away to the places
the wind and rain and sky

The girls finished, and blushed. Everyone clapped heartily. Sister Pancratius was glowing.

'That was so fast! Hope you liked it! We should book some gigs!' the sisters clamored in unison.

Roaringman had not lifted his flute, mesmerized by the Banshee Patrol's melody and craft. Abel thought, though, that song needed a bridge.

NINETEEN

Moss FILLED A cardboard box with his personal academic documents. Nothing too confidential here anyway, he thought. He took some time to rifle through the faculty and staff personnel files. No dirt he could use to shame or even embarrass his co-workers. The school janitor had been caught with some *Playboy* magazines once. Moss had given him a warning, then took the magazines home for his own personal review. It was the nuns, though, those walking embodiments of purity, sacrifice, and with those holier-that-thou habits draped over their bodies like shields, as if an archangel hovered above their haloed heads, that really fueled his desperation. He never trusted those nuns. Antioch especially. Or that secretary Schneikert. And of course, that damned alluring Ignatius. He knew they couldn't all be saints.

Sincerity no longer seemed a valid trait, in anyone, including – and especially – himself. Everyone was a walking fake, pre-loaded with ideas and hopes and assumptions and ridiculous road maps for how their lives were going to play out. That all amounted to zero. Razor'd have the right words here, from his Bard buddy – *'a tale told by an idiot, full of sound and fury, signifying nothing.'*

So there was nothing here to pin on the Sisters of Charity, or any other

St. Anselm personnel. He considered taking home anything he thought might indict himself, though there was probably nothing here that would have. In all the curious twists of this present catastrophe, he'd discharged professionally and adeptly his own duties as principal. He lifted his brass name plate – 'Gideon Moss ~ Principal' – and threw it in the waste basket.

Somewhere in his throbbing head, Moss remembered the refrigerator. Lars had told him. The apple he had bitten, what remained of it, that Emma Green had stolen and taken away, as if it were hers. That bastard. *No* – what's a female bastard. *Bitch.* It might still be here, in the school. He could take it, and if it had potency left, he could get another dose. His apple tree at home, Garden of Eden special variety, was about as alive as his son. This Emma apple, his apple, might have persevered.

Moss hurried to the faculty lounge and unlocked the door.

*   *   *

In today's climate, it's easy to identify and debunk narratives that take readers into spurious territory. Everyone is jaundiced from the overflow of attention-grabbing fictions and unverifiable exaggerations. The story I am about to relate may seem like such. I ask you, dear readers, to step away from your prejudices, your inclinations to doubt, and your mindful discrediting of tales that are written to waste your hours and bypass your brain cells. I will attest, here and now, to having experienced much of this story directly, in the first person, and to have gleaned recorded testimony from key individuals, who shared their involvement in what is perhaps the most disquieting chain of events to occur in our home neighborhoods, in our lifetimes. Know also that its climax, this story's denouement, will certainly be dark and possibly dangerous.

An unknowable menace, hinted at in the words that follow, hangs like a shadow in the center of this account.

Gads, that last sentence really takes the cake.

Riley Cardle had started her story, unsure where to lead it, but figuring she should go for broke, make it epic and ridiculous, and pull back after she'd considered what she'd composed. The opening paragraph set the stage for her calamitous tale. Sick, but delicious. She took off after it…

Frick Park's Nature Center fire, last November, is a still-unsolved mystery. Now, the events taking place before and after have transformed that occurrence into a minor feature, a dire set piece from a convoluted assembly of astonishing and fearful developments. How is this stage set, and what for? Three arrows point to a common middle. These arrows smite the Green family, of Regent Square; Gideon Moss, the Principal of St. Anselm High School; and an unnamed youth, who shall be called 'Tommy X' for the purposes of this story. Tommy X, an innocent recruited to not only assist in the Nature Center's inferno, but to steal a yearling apple tree from the park, for the most curious and, as we will see, calculating Mr. Moss.

In October of last year, a peculiar and previously unseen mammal appeared in the park. A black squirrel; this variety, this coloration, is steeped in dark mythology. Legend maintains a black squirrel might transit between the spirit world and our own. When it also bites a human, and this one did, it conveys whatever contamination it embodies, and so it also seems to have done. Our young Tommy X, bitten on the neck, seemingly received some other-worldly toxicant from this dark-hearted beast. His demeanor, his very conscience, collapsed like a broken shield wall, unmooring that inner voice we all hope to call upon, the one we might use against any wrong-footed influence that might be allayed. In this instance, Tommy X's resolve, his ability to choose what is right, was deflected. Put aside. Subdued and forgotten.

Moss 'hired' the young man as an accomplice. After the bite, once those animal teeth had sent its substances into his bloodstream, he bore no means of resisting. They clambered to the Nature Center on a cold snow-blasted November night, carrying their matches and wicks and plot most foul.

But Moss, himself a revered, respected community personality – what drove him to these actions? Moss had his soul turned inside out from something. A coveted apple? So it seems – though at this point our confirming sources have not come forward. Before the Nature Center episode, he'd corralled Tommy X and his own son, Raymond, to help him purloin a special apple tree from the park. Get this: an apple tree so young it barely reached their shoulders. An apple tree with only a couple of mature fruits hanging off its branches. An apple tree that no one else would take a second glance at.

Rereading this, Cardle halted.

Rats.

She wasn't facing down a necessary reporter instinct. Even with her new hat, with her taking major liberties with facts and assumptions, she had to do it: contact Gideon Moss. Lars Patton, she was sure, had told the truth, broken open by his youthful innocence and quick-fire intelligence, he'd made Moss out to be a character in turmoil, and not necessarily a villain. But Cardle couldn't go to print with such an exposé without giving Moss an opportunity to respond. There was the legal aspect, also.

Damn.

Why did these stupid formal details always have to show up and put the kibosh on a gripping story? Why did fairness and truth always have to meddle in the endorphin rush of some cleverly-wrought words set end to end that would make her some money and gain her some status and pump some thrill into the ongoing banality of existence?

Moss's high school e-mail was on the school website. It was July, school not in session. Hopefully he checked his work e-mails now and then.

*   *   *

Sister Ignatius was grateful the *Fireworks* summit had, as far as she could tell, achieved its goals. Pancratius had thanked her, Abel had given her a pack of Little Debbie peanut bars (she loved them), Emma had held her hand in silent appreciation, and the kids…well…the kids had revealed themselves, as far as they understood themselves, and suggested intimations of a way to proceed. To *love* it – life and people, is what they seemingly proselytized, as far as any epiphany Ignatius could glean. They did this not so much with words, but more with their manner and innate enthusiasm, which looked to almost spill out of them at points, an overflow of goodness and cheer. And the song, of course! All this said, she didn't know how the closed-door sessions had gone. The Wise Guys maintained their confidentiality; from her observations, and from the body language, facial expressions, the relaxed demeanor when the doors had swung open, there was nothing to suggest some unusual breech of decorum, theology, or respect had taken place.

Her problem, a nagging more than a crisis, was that apple in that fridge. She would go to the high school in the evening, when the community would be immersed in their Independence Day firework shows, and take a look. Just a look. This simple piece of fruit had transformed lives, in front of her eyes. She wasn't looking for faith-vitamins. She wanted to hold something that God had touched.

*   *   *

The Green sisters were tired after their long day. Abel fed the cats, and told the girls to watch a DVD, an idea they jumped at. Emma and he had a selection of classics and a few family movies. Abel heard the theme music from *Monty Python* starting up.

Wait a minute – a little brazen for girls four months old.

Then he smiled…there was no point hiding these three from so-called modern culture. The zeitgeist was seldom skewered with such love as it was by those British nutballs. He fetched a cola from the pantry, grabbed a bottle of Kraken Rum he kept (for special occasions) on a top shelf in the kitchen cupboard, and mixed a little spirit for himself.

Emma had looked so beautiful, sitting there quietly at the Sanctuary. Their words had been brief, but he thought he could feel the steadiness of their bond stay…steady. He took a sip of the rummed coke and melted into the couch.

*   *   *

Ignatius had returned to the convent. And decided not to wait for darkness. This was not a sin, where shadows were required to hide her actions. As far as her conscience troubled to consider the matter, there was no moral trespass at hand. She wasn't planning to take any nibbles. The thing should be inedible by now, even in the cold of refrigeration. So, just look, and hold, and appreciate.

She could see the high school from her window.

She knelt for a short prayer.

She walked down the stairwell, perhaps a bit unsteady. She'd be in its presence – seeing, perhaps holding, this possibly deific gift, this simple, wondrous, apple – in a few moments.

She decided to walk around to the front of the school: a verification she didn't need to sneak in the back way and use the more secluded door nearer to the convent, where no one could see her. The late afternoon sun warmed her shoulders. If there was a form of reverent giddiness, it was hers.

*   *   *

Moss opened the fridge. There it sat, staring at him, wrapped in foil, note intact. He lifted it out, gently opened the foil. The half-chewed red fruit looked strangely appealing. The red skin was broken open where he'd bitten it. The interior, the fleshy fruit, revealed no signs of rot or decay. It rested, calm, patient, as if it was waiting for his next move.

He pulled open a closet and found a Giant Eagle bag. He scrounged for a plastic trash bag, wrapped it around the foil-covered apple, and stuffed this into the Giant Eagle bag. That should protect it for the short ride home, against the fourth of July sunshine.

At the back door entry, he set the alarms, and disappeared.

*   *   *

Ignatius entered the high school and switched off the security alarms. The Faculty Lounge was unlocked. The refrigerator was empty. The apple was gone.

*   *   *

The din and boom of fireworks rolled in from several directions.

Moss unwrapped the foil, under the lights in his kitchen. The apple was desiccated, seen in this brighter illumination. He carved it gently into smaller pieces. He removed the seven seeds and put them in a small container, which he sealed and placed in the fridge. He lifted the largest section, and placed it on his tongue, not unlike a communion wafer.

He recalled what had happened in the park. He remembered that he'd fainted, and so lowered himself to the kitchen floor, where he fell, gently, into unconsciousness.

*   *   *

Boneseed tenth was the black rose. A plant that grew with sharp thorns, the black rose oxidized the soil around it, and, due to a unique chemical, molecular, and atomic reaction, fed radioactivity into its flower. The pollen of this rose would be carried by bees and their hives, where the radiation would violate the honey-making, causing mutation in the bees, and disseminating the radioactivity in whatever honey was produced.

Boneseed eleventh was the wheelbone. The wheelbone, so named due to its calcified exterior and circular physiology, was an anomaly among anomalies. The boneseed appeared human-made, a perfectly concentric circle. It grew to about the size of a small dinner plate, and was like a doughnut, a rounded tube with a hole in its middle. The wheelbone was an incubator. It gathered materials from surroundings, brought them into its exterior through micro-infusion, and served as an incubator for novel forms of life. The calculating *Selectors* who had stealthily managed the thirteen boneseeds into Time, unto the Earth, especially favored this nereBegat, as it would proceed with its own small-scale creation activities as it gathered streams of elemental resources from the soil, air and moisture in its vicinity. It was not mobile, but its offspring could be anything, from flying electric moths to x-shaped snakes. The single wheelbone spawned in Frick Park was exceptionally robust, durable, and fertile. It would begin producing new creations in a few weeks. Until it did, remaining hidden was its only need.

Boneseed twelfth was unusual even for its incorporeal origins, a late addition to the *master plan*, if the plan might be called such. The boneseed, long fertilized by the green snow of November, was growing into a kind of earthly horse. The creature was called a silvermare. The silvermare's inclusion was a more romantically-driven notion, if romance was a qualifier in the realms where the boneseeds were drawn up. This foal would grow to majestic proportions, and have strength and beauty like that of no other mare. The silvermare would be coveted as a unicorn might have been. The sheen of its skin could be mistaken for chrome, shining, like a polished metal in the glinting sun.

There were differing suppositions, from *Makors* and *Throwers,* as far as defining precisely what the silvermare's reason for existing would be, and what its survival might be predicated on. Some believed the silvermare could not survive on the Earth, that its inability to conceal its overt visibility would preemptively doom it. Others conjectured the silvermare had been engineered as a mount for boneseed thirteenth, and would ride down any challenges before it with a power that would not be stifled.

Boneseed thirteenth remains unnamed (and thus called nere-X); yet it bears ominous potential, considering its size and capability could include mastering and using, as a mount, a full-size earth-modeled stallion.

And with that, Dragon stopped her *Banshee* typing.

'We're *fiat lux*-ing, sisters,' she said. 'Should we let Dad read all this stuff?'

'I think we should,' said Miller. 'He took the burden before we could comprehend. We can explain things to him. And get his help. Geeze, we're, like, seven or eight years old.'

'I agree,' said Boyd. 'Let him read everything we've added to *Banshee Patrol*. Mom too. And if you guys think we should, Sr. Ignatius. I trust her.'

'Ok. I'll print it up for Dad. I wish I could take out all the goofy flowery prose that my fingers end up tapping into text. This *fiat* delivery protocol is exceptionally weird. Hey, but Dad managed it, without even trying.'

Miller was staring at the fresh *fiat*. 'Hey Dragon. A mare is not a stallion!'

Dragon peered at the last lines. 'Oh. Yeah. Whoa. Is that my error or the *fiat's* feed, as it were?'

'The silvermare would be female, a stallion a male,' said Boyd.

'Yes!' said Dragon. 'I got that. But what if I typed something that wasn't meant to be typed. Or the *fiat* sent something incorrect? Who's proofreading this stuff up there?' The sisters took a moment to look at each other, raise eyebrows, shove up their shoulders, and present flat palms to each other. Then they raced to tell their dad.

*   *   *

Moss's phone rang on the morning of July 5th.

He woke up, cold from sleeping on linoleum. *Must visit Ray*, was his first thought, his second a surge of optimism, hanging like a gossamer thread in his psyche. *I care.* He didn't want to track the explanation. He moved to a chair, and picked up the phone, rubbing his eyes with the back of his wrist. 'Hello?'

'Gideon Moss?'

'Yes'.

'My name is Riley Cardle. I'm a reporter for the *Post-Press*.'

'Hello, and good morning.'

'Yes. Good morning. Hope your holiday was good.'

'Not bad. How about you?'

'I'm not much for fireworks. But it was Ok.'

'Great,' said Moss.

'I'm writing a story on the Frick Park Nature Center fire, a follow-up.

Maybe you read the original article?'

'I did. What a shame, huh.'

'I'm calling to let you know that this follow-up feature is extensive, and includes material I have from meeting with Lars Patton.'

'Patton attends St. Anselm, where I'm Principal. Good kid, though he's been through the wringer recently.'

'Yes. He's confessed to the arson, you should know.'

'Ahh that's so good to hear, Ms. Cardle. He alluded to doing something, something not so good in his eyes.'

'He told you?' asked Cardle.

'No. But he and I went on a – well, a kind of sortie, is probably the word – earlier in the year. I was there when he was bitten on the neck by a squirrel. I suppose rabid, or at least unhealthy. I begged him to get medical care. As far as I know he did not.'

'So, Mr. Moss. My understanding from my recorded – deposition, if you will – from Lars Patton is that *you* were the instigator of the Nature Center fire.'

'Ahh. Poor Lars. I hope you were able to reach out to him about some intervention.'

'He was quite lucid. Well, let's say fairly, for a teen. Smart, precise memory. Did he and you talk about the fire?'

'No, we didn't. And I can tell you a bit for your report, that I'm needing to come clean about, though it's hardly worth a feature.'

'Go ahead,' said Cardle.

'I had asked Lars and my son – my son Ray who is currently hospitalized – to assist me in salvaging an apple tree from Frick Park. It was a kind of whim or lark for me, the idea of saving this thing from the public abuse it was sure to get in the park, which is busy with mountain bikers and picnickers and kids running through it, not to mention animals that could damage it and the hard-pressed environment, there, in Frick Park, as you're aware. Sewage overflow, and all. So, I cooked up a rather obtuse idea to dig up the tree and bring it to my yard, for care.'

'So you did that?'

'Yes. Dumb. Illegal? Maybe, probably. Not a felony but, for sure, basically a bad move. And I, a principal of a Catholic high school. You might mention my theoretically noble motives if this stuff goes to press.'

'Yes. Well. The problem, Mr. Moss, is that my story is built around your involvement in the fire. In fact, according to Lars Patton, your orchestrating of it, on a night last November. I was there.'

'You were?'

'Yes. And I have a photo of two sets of footprints in the snow. Freshly-made prints, from the look of them. The photo was taken almost immediately after the fire started.'

'A photo taken at night, with a blizzard and a fire raging. Ms. Cardle, I don't mean to doubt your evidence, or credibility, but might those tracks have been your own? Or mixed in with Lars?'

'Mr. Moss, are you denying you were involved with the fire?'

'I don't need to deny it. I simply suggest that poor Lars, with that bite, must have a confused memory. Still, I'm pleased he's confessed, and I'm available to speak up for him, to you and in court.'

'Mr. Moss. Were you down in the park a few weeks ago, with a nun, a Poor Clare sister?'

'I was.'

'Did you embrace and kiss her?'

'I did.'

'And,' said Cardle.

'And?'

'Is this something you care to expand upon?'

'Are you planning to write that incident into your story?'

'I'm not planning anything,' said Cardle. 'I just thought you should be able to respond.'

'Sister, that sister, is an associate at the school. I'm sure you'll dig up her name. She had expressed some interest in me and I have tried to counsel her out of the idea. We shared a regrettable show of chaste affection in a weak moment, for both of us. We understood it had nowhere to go and would be ended. Is this really something you want to put your byline under?'

'Mr. Moss. Serious allegations don't go away because one party muddles the truth. I'll finish my article and forward it to you for a review, and a chance to comment. Then we can determine what might come next, for you, and Lars.'

'Thank you, Ms...?'

'Cardle. Riley. Thank you, Mr. Moss.'

She hung up.

Moss stood up and stretched in the mid-morning sunshine. Having refreshed his apple dose, he was feeling a version of better. Better not to over think it, over qualify it, over analyze it.

He had some explaining he wanted to do, to many individuals. He'd start with his associates at the school. Throwing away his position there would have been a disastrous calculation. He'd regroup, take his files back, and regain his footing as Principal. He'd apologize to Ignatius, explain how the reporter was attempting to slander both of them. He'd mold the Lars duplicity around Lars' squirrel bite and snow flaking. The tree theft, he'd freely admit to. That wouldn't be a jail term. Maybe a fine – for trying to save a fragile fruit tree trapped in the shadows in Frick Park.

This new bite of the apple was startlingly invigorating. He was saved, for a duration. A specimen of the apple should go to a science facility. He'd get one of his academia-ensconced fraternity brothers onto that. The seeds he'd save like holy relics: an at-hand stockpile that promised an adrenaline shot of strength, wisdom, and self-assurance. There was a dark hope brewing once again in his head. For good or for ill, it was too early to know.

But...

He'd already forgotten: what was that first thought that came into his head, just as he woke?

What was it… *damn!*

*   *   *

Lars thought he should warn his mom about the confession, about the article, about his pending stint in some kind of juvenile detention facility – that was sure to be fun.

He couldn't do it. Couldn't tell his mom. Maybe he could hint something to Dixon, or Astrid. Not his mother. That was not fair. He regretted all of it – the expedition to Frick, the tree, the fire, the admission to Cardle. *Twisting in the cosmic wind, I am.*

There was a possible, partial redemption: even though the X-Tector build had failed, he still wanted to find the green flake exposures in the park. He resolved to head down there, regardless of the slim chances of stumbling on anything. The color green might have been a giveaway in the white snows of winter: now the park was greened-up, at summer's peak. Hopeless. But he could use his eyes, and search.

He lifted up the house landline. 'Is Dixon there, Mrs. Nickson?'

'I'll get him. How are you feeling? Dixon says you'll be back to school in September. So nice to hear.'

'If I'm not in jail.' He heard Mrs. Nickson laugh and knew the joke had landed. The *real* joke is that he might be.

'You stay away from that nook-u-lar weapon-making, Lars. I'll get Dixon.'

Lars was hoping to rope Dixon into helping. He'd be another pair of eyes to augment his own semi-desperate search. Plus the company would be good. Plus, he might also rope Astrid into coming along if she knew Dixon would be joining him. He cleared his throat, summoning his finest pleading tone.

'Dixon, my main man*!*'

'You want something. You fiend,' he replied, in classic Dix deadpan.

'I want to mount a soul-salvaging expedition to the dark underworld of Fern Hollow, and environs. I want you to come. I need to find some evidence that will throw off the authorities when they have me on the stand.'

'That bad, huh?'

'Aww, man. I spilled my guts to a reporter, dude. Not sure if she will use my name but I'm kinda recognizable, depending on what she publishes.'

'And what exactly is your criminal crime?'

'I don't want to tell you. Don't want you to carry it around,' said Lars.

'Should I be seen with you? I have chess club matches to get to, and a full life ahead.'

'Dude…'

'Of course I'll come, you dirigible. I'll even wear a green hat so nobody notices your hair.'

Lars grinned, big time. 'Ok, ok, ok. This is great. When can we go?'

'When do you wanna?'

'Tomorrow.'

Lars heard, through the phone, Dixon call out to his mom. 'Mom, we doin' anything tomorrow? I mowed the lawn!' His mother's voice was yelling back, unintelligible. 'Yeah, yeah, Ok, yeah.' shouted Dixon. 'Yup. Ok!' He returned to the phone call. 'She's cool. We were supposed to do some wacked-out museum crawl before summer ends. She and Dad are heck-bent on it, but it keeps being shunted back. So I'm good for tomorrow. You wanna meet at the corner of Hutchinson, at the entry sign?'

'Yeah. How's 9 a.m. for you?'

'Way too early. It's summer, wang-man. How about 9:13?'

'Make up your twisted mind,' said Lars.

'9:07, a compromise. Bring food and drink, I'm a special guest.'

'Better than that, I'll bring my sister.'

'What?'

'Remember Astrid.'

'Very funny. Bring her or don't bring her. We men will move at speed. If she can't keep up, she dies.'

They hung up. Lars felt a modicum of strange hope, to go with a compelling urge to go to the Greyhound Bus Station and get a ticket for somewhere far away, like Cleveland.

TWENTY

'DR. HASKLEY, IS there any similar case in all medical history that has relevance to what's occurring with the Greens?'

Imam El-Muhammad sat in the small office with his Wise Guy 'associates', along with Carmen Walker, and the doctor. His head had been awake with curious thoughts, many of them too somber for what he had witnessed.

The potential for a serious leak gnawed at him. He trusted the family, and the Sisters, and Roaringman. He trusted implicitly the Rabbi and Cardinal. He trusted himself. But the doctor's office, where a number of specialists had visited, and where the medical records were held, seemed a flawed, tenuous location for such a valuable, unique, and potentially charged inventory.

He had no idea how many individuals had learned about the Square's 'miracle children', but guessed more than a few would be keeping tabs, or at least circling at the perimeter, in the hope they might continue to study the girls' development. It was perfectly natural to do so; professional even. But the situation still required privacy, he felt. He wondered if the children should be moved to a more secluded location, where they could attain some sort of stabilized state, further from the public eye.

The Green daughters were a miracle, in every applicable sense. He couldn't guess why they were as they were. The apple story was all well and good and he did not remove that consideration from the make-up of the story. None of this was a threat to Islam. Gifted children in America would not send some theological shudder into the core of his faith. What he worried about was that the family might be put upon. The *tickle*, as he framed his concern, had two parts.

The first, he had probably over-considered due to the climate of today's superhuman ethos. Power-wielding personage taken in and taken over by governments with intent to forward the agendas of their given empire. If the Green daughters began to manifest something more than their awful intelligence and astonishing capabilities, if their instinct and insight continue to shatter convention and break the mold as impossibly young savants – they might be exploited, by intelligence operatives, armed forces professionals, and, worst of all, deep state agents. All seemed unlikely, after the light-filled and light-hearted interaction with these three, young, amazing humans. But the world was a curious place.

Second: he wished he didn't have to consider this element of the proceedings, and was as yet unwilling to share his concern, his *tickle*, with his Wise companions. He wanted to steer the conversation in such a way that some answers might resolve on their own.

'There's nothing at all, Imam,' said Dr. Haskley. 'Their gestation, their growth, their physical aptitudes. Off any chart I could present.'

'We have tried to consult specialists across many forums,' said Carmen. 'And all have been, well, just wide-eyed and kind of left with no, uhm, answers.'

'So if you were to sum up, for a medical journal such as *The Lancet*, how would you describe these three young females?'

'I wouldn't, and I haven't,' said Haskley. 'We have intentionally avoided public-forum follow-up. All the specialists signed and have honored non-disclosures. A local reporter hinted at some of the girl's uniqueness in the

Pittsburgh Post-Press article. Maybe you've read it: mostly accurate, the writer seemed to enjoy teasing the boundaries of truth in search of some kind of breaking news. Regardless, I am not in contact with Abel, Emma, or the family, unless they ask. The girls are healthy as buttons. Every test I did maxed the board. Their marks are – how do the British say it – spot on. The only thing these young ladies have that other humans do not have, is acceleration. They grow in normal ways, bones, muscle, mental aptitude, but they scream through time.'

'Scream through time. There's a notable quote,' said Cardinal Ethan.

'So,' said Imam El-Muhammad, 'you don't see them being able to fly, read minds, or leap over tall buildings in a single bound.'

Everyone looked at him, faces puzzled, then grinning.

'Who knows,' smiled Haskley.

'So the miraculous – the *truly* miraculous – is on hold for now,' said Rabbi Ben.

'Depends on your definition,' said Haskley.

'Well,' said the Imam. 'We appreciate your time today. We ask you not to share our presence, our mission, or our dialog with anyone.'

'We'll all be re-reading Genesis. That's a given,' said Rabbi Ben.

'Genesis?' asked Carmen.

'The apple. Frick Park as the Garden.'

'Say again?' said Haskley.

'I believe that was a bit of humor being passed around,' offered El Muhammad, casting a sidelong glance at the Rabbi. 'Again, we ask your discretion in all these matters.'

'We're happy to honor that,' said Haskley, standing. 'We're in the Greens' corner. As it appears you all are.'

'We are,' said Cardinal Ethan. With that, they shook hands and departed.

*

The Wise Guys would be going their separate ways at the airport, but agreed to continue discussion of the Square Miracles by correspondence, especially after they'd met with more individuals from their own assemblies, or in the Imam's case, Jammat, to confide, confer, and consider. Outside the doctor's offices, on the sidewalk, they waited for their transport, which Sister Pancratius had arranged before leaving them for her own flight home. While El Muhammed and Ben chatted, Cardinal Ethan took a moment to indulge in a small vice of his which seemed appropriate for this *Wise Guy* moment, and lit up a Camel.

He sent out a long, slow puff. The Cardinal had noted, as had the Imam, that the Rabbi had moved their conversation, by accident, from the miraculous to the Biblical, by mentioning Genesis. He hoped and guessed that Dr. Haskley and Ms. Walker would buy El Muhammad's suggestion that the Garden talk had been a passing joke.

*

Carmen and Haskley had bid the visiting religious farewell, then begun preparing for afternoon visitors.

'Carmen. I want to ask you something.'

'Yup.'

'That interview, by Riley Cardle, about the Greens. It seemed to have a slightly more informative inside track, about the kids. A few things in it Emma or Abel seemed to prefer not for public release. I'm wondering if you had any suspicions that one of our specialists might have leaked something.'

'Don't know how Cardle would even know who the medical people were, Doctor. Maybe the Greens said more than they intended. Maybe it just spilled out of them. Shall we look at the article? I saved it.'

'No. That's alright. I looked at it too.'

He pulled his glasses off to wipe the lenses, and looked at Carmen, with a half-grin.

'I thought the Imam, especially, was worried some federal knuckleheads would suddenly decide that Miller, Boyd and Dragon are not Barbies, but Barbarellas,' he said.

'Barbarellas?'

'Jane Fonda? Roger Vadim? Nah, you're too young. Forget it,' said Haskley. 'Get the file on Mrs. Porvaznick. She'll be here right after lunch.'

*   *   *

Emma and Roaringman strolled across the Motherhouse grounds, watching and listening as summer turned its fourth-of-July corner; the humid, long-drawn slog of August, with its stark another-year-is-coming-to-a-close realization and sense of loss already backfilling into the hours. Emma felt a camaraderie with Roaringman. She'd dared to address him as Grey Cloud, a few mornings after the *Fireworks*, and that had led them across some relational bridge. It felt right. Not the gateway to some romantic interlude. More a causeway to some of the philosophical intercourse they might ply.

'Do you think my daughters are... well, what *would* you say, Grey Cloud?'

'They are children, growing, melded to spirit, obviously. I have glimpses. I am reluctant to share what are meanderings and guesses. Especially with you, their mother.'

'Pretend I'm not their mother. Pretend I'm... Margaret Thatcher.' They both laughed. Emma figured neither knew a whit about Thatcher. Emma was evoking an over-bearing female notable on the fly, the first name to show up in her head. So much for seedy humor. It was stupid enough to shake Grey Cloud forward.

'Your daughters are touched with mystic powers. I felt like a child, in their presence. They advance before one's eyes. They came out of their closed-door session with more – something, what, maturity? – than when they went in. And, that song...'

'Yes. Their music, their joy, is contagious.' Emma led them down a stone path towards a bench under a willow, where they sat. A hidden brook murmured nearby. 'What is your opinion on Eden, and the apple tree, resurfacing in two thousand and seven? That's 2007 years since Christ was born, if you believe. Believe *that*.'

'You're a biologist. I'm a physicist. We're the guardians of science's gate; fending off the metaphysical nonsense where we find it, eh. *Diigis,* as the Navajo would say. Stupid! There is more and more crossover unearthed than one can even catalog.'

Roaringman reached down to pick up and play with a fallen twig.

'But I want to let you know. I am here at the Motherhouse because this very same threshold you are facing broke me. My theories began to erode my science. My theories moved me across inner and outer spaces. But. I was not well. Maybe am not well. I can't get these two pieces to play nice inside me, these two halves. My Native American heritage is content to leave much to Mystery. As are many of the great Christian mystics, and the eastern saints, Buddha, and Rumi, and so many.'

'I know the territory,' said Emma. 'Now, my own offspring are physical evidence that the Bible may be true. How do you like *them* apples?'

She looked at Roaringman to surmise if he'd heard the faint humor in that old-school American slang.

'You have to, maybe, shed your constraints. I found I was forcing two opposites to try to mesh. Like opposite poles on magnets. Here, at the Motherhouse, I am provoking a different approach. Let it all be true. Let the opposites exist in the face of each other. Our human logic is in no position to bridge this gap. Our human logic is far too authoritarian. You dig way down and realize your own subjective mind curates your reality. *Your* reality *only*. Only only only. Yes – the gift of sensing is our way from outside to inside. But science, science carefully explains how we are fed particles of light and waves of sound and ingredients of taste and degrees of touch, via consciousness, courtesy of electricity and molecular duties inside the blood and tissue of our brains…'

Roaringman stopped, a bit breathless. He snapped the twig in two.

'You Ok?' asked Emma.

'No. Let's get up and walk.'

They rose and proceeded under the treed canopy of green, beneath the skies of Greensburg, miles from where the three Green girls were mobilizing for their initial foray into Frick Park, where the young mortals would tread inside a newly resurrected Garden of Eden, the place that had beckoned to them from their windows not long after they moved to live beside it.

*   *   *

Gideon Moss sent a letter to Sister Ignatius. Hand-written, in pen, on actual paper, stamped, in an actual envelope. The non-digital undertaking was satisfying for that very reason. A hand-written letter surely had more presence and authenticity.

Dear Sister.

My behavior over the last several months, and more specifically, a few weeks ago in the park, was inexcusable. I've been upset by my son's condition, and other factors you know about, but I've seen how I have let down him, and you, and the school. Forgive me, Sr. Ignatius, for these transgressions. Let me know if I can make amends. I'm happy to sit down with any school associates and discuss what I've done and how I hope to do better.

Sincerely, Gideon Moss.

The second bite had refreshed something inside him. Still fractured, he wondered what it might be.

*   *   *

Lars and Dixon had a shiny August morning in front of them. Astrid had 'recused' herself. Lars didn't ask exactly what that was meant to mean. He wielded a backpack full of tech stuff, and Dixon carried food and water. They were heading into Fern Hollow, to hunt down monsters of any size or shape they encountered. Then they'd stop for lunch.

*   *   *

'You are hereby officially deemed *The Banshee Patrol*,' said Abel to his young charges. The girls, with his and Emma's blessing, were heading into Frick Park to explore the site where the Tree had grown, and to discover the overall Eden-ish-ness of the place.

Abel calculated they had reached a maturity level and physiological markers somewhere in the vicinity of eight or nine years old. Etta had rolled her eyes, but Abel understood the eye-rolls were a demonstration of grandmotherly care, not a prohibition. Etta knew her granddaughters could safely explore together in Frick, but 'in the daytime only for now, Abel'. Each girl had begun to demonstrate more specific proficiencies. Much of this he chronicled in the *Banshee Patrol* documents. There he also read what the girls had added, copious material, along the lines of the *fiat lux* deliveries, which seemed to have gone dry for him.

He'd typed out the following, the evening before the Frick Park expedition was to take place.

Dragon, Caroline, is the Tamer. She is the eldest, and probably most canny in her general insights. She plays the mouth harp and now carries it with her almost all the time. She has perfect pitch. Also plays the fiddle - one she found lying around in our attic. She's a kind of angelic Sherlock Holmes, perhaps. Without the pipe (so far!). Philosophical but grounded. She is able to mimic bird and animal calls; her deepening voice lends itself to this capability. She draws maps. Has a shockingly good sense of direction and formidable memory. She would scare me if she wasn't my kid.

Miller, Rebecca, is the Destroyer. She is whip-smart, inventive, with an engineering bent. Very athletic. She seems more calculating in her willingness to get directly to a point, no hedging, very matter-of-fact. She was able to use a neighbor's glass-blowing workshop to fabricate a glass-rod walking stick. She tells me it can catch and focus moonlight for various purposes. Do you believe these kids? She loves our cats, who still run away from her affections. She's akin to a modern day Dúnedain, one of Aragorn's ranger brothers.

Boyd, Margaret, is the Subduer. She is an astonishing math and science wizard; you'd call her a savant but all the Green girls are that. Let's say she's like a quantum computer in human form. She can perceive (and sketch out) perfect circles. She's kit-bashed a t-square and proportion wheel and abacus into what she has titled an 'aziwheel'. She spins it to do cross-discipline calculations when her own mind can't get there fast enough. This is rare. Can read barometric pressure, ID chemicals, and puzzle past biological screens. Drills into things. Hard. Loves candy. An Einsteinian Wonka, or Sabrina the Teenage Witch?

As far as I can understand from my own seedy-enhancement, from the fiat lux, and Banshee Patrol writings, and from the girls themselves, they are on this Earth to figure out the boneseed *problem. (This is a ton of exposition, reader, bear with me :). So, they need to start locating these illegal creations – termed nereBegats – and make choices about each creature's viability as a new companion to humankind's stint on Earth.*

So here I am, sitting with my two cats, pretty much void of energy, about to set them loose (the girls, not the cats) for the beginning of this too strange-for-words venture. I still would not be AT ALL surprised to wake up at Western Psychiatric, with Emma one strait-jacket over, and crumpled drawings of bitten apples scattered across our security-floor room.

More than anything, he needed a nap.

'Banshee Patrol. Line up for inspection!' he shouted. The girls, still in the last throes of childhood and able to be duly alarmed by a parent's raised voice, did so.

'Daaaad! Don't do that!'

'Just testing you,' he said in a firm-but-friendly tone. 'Now listen. You are not the Fantastic Three. You are not Wizards. You're not Archangels – and if you are, I don't want to know. You are three young girls with a lot of spunk and smarts and willingness. I'm not afraid for you. I only ask that you don't over-step your capacity on this first – what to call it – sortie.'

'Bad word, Dad,' said Boyd. Miller began goose-stepping in place, til

Dragon slapped her on the arm.

'Anyway, it's ten o'clock in the morning and I'm going to bed. Etta is here. Come back before three o'clock or you will all be grounded. *Please.* Understand that?'

'Yes Mon Capitan*!*' Dragon saluted. This time Miller slapped *her.*

'Ok, go,' said Abel.

The girls turned and yelped their way out the door.

*   *   *

'Let's hunt some orcs,' said Dixon.

'Wish there were orcs down here,' said Lars. 'We could bring one back and turn it from the dark side, and teach it to sing.'

'You're as warped and normal as you were before you got bit and got flaked.'

'I am. You sensing any weird green snowflake chemistry?' They were approaching the spot where the apple tree had been. Lars knew it had been carried off by Moss, of course. They scrambled up the rise, and heard voices. Young girls, maybe not quite teenaged.

*   *   *

At last, Gideon had a task that he was completely sure he should proceed with.

He removed the apple from the refrigerator and placed it on the kitchen table. In good daylight, he separated out a piece about the size of half a golf-ball. He still had the seeds and about a third remained of the full apple; these he returned to the fridge. He used the back of a wooden spoon to crush the section, not too much. He didn't want sauce. It was a crumpled apple mash. He dropped this section into a small plastic container and snapped on the lid.

He took it with him to the car, and drove to Greensburg, to the Remediation Center where Razor still lay in a coma. He was shown to

Razor's room. He asked for privacy. He moved a stool next to the bed, and bent over his son. He slid the stool closer to the head of the bed, in order to block the view of anyone in the hall outside Razor's room, who might see what he was doing.

He slid the container out of his shirt pocket and nudged the apple piece closer to the lid. He looked once over his shoulder, then leaned down as if to kiss his comatose son. There was no breathing tube. With one hand, he opened Razor's mouth. With the other, he held the apple piece, tapped the back of the container, and let it slip into his son's mouth.

Razor showed no signs of taking in the apple, nor of choking. Gideon sat back. Razor's mouth closed again.

Moss ran his hand though his son's black forelocks. 'Good looking kid.'

He stood, brushed down his shirt and pants, and left the room, and the building, and Greensburg.

*　　*　　*

Carmen Walker had contacted Riley Cardle and they met at a small pub on Penn Ave. They'd had a light meal and were enjoying drinks.

'So the religious people didn't deliver anything we don't know,' said Cardle, nursing her singapore sling. Carmen cradled a mug of dark beer.

'I've given you pretty much everything. Please be discreet – no hints that can lead back to me. I like the doctor and the family. The kids are a living miracle,' said Carmen.

'You said something early on about wanting to… what – make sure the wider medical profession had a way past the family firewall in case there might be something in my article that caught attention, or raised flags. My article ended up so tame I doubt it could have served in that way.' Cardle leaned back. 'I want to ask you a personal question.'

'Shoot.'

'Are you looking for ten or so minutes of significance? Warhol's dictum? That loon *was* a *dick*-tum by the way.'

'That's pretty stupid to ask, and suggest. Like, what are you writing this stuff for?' Carmen ran fingers over a napkin on the table. 'I was – I am – trying to make sure the Green kids are known, and unknown.' She paused and looked at Cardle. 'Stupid, also, maybe.'

'Yeah. I think so. Not much more coming from you, then, Carmen. We can wrap up our correspondence. I'll grab this check –'

'Wait,' said Carmen. 'Wait.' Carmen dipped a chip into their bowl of sour cream and held it near her mouth.

'Wondering if you'd be interested,' she said, without looking up.

Cardle's shoulder's slumped, her boundaries suddenly abrogated. It was a lovely arrow she'd just taken, somewhere near the heart: that admittance, that passage to a person's deeper, revealed self. It made rare appearances, and juddered one out of complacency.

Cardle nudged the chip bowl around the table, pondering a worthy reply. It was a moment. And she, the writer, at a loss for words.

'You're good-looking. Wanting to say that since I met you,' she said.

Carmen bit into the chip, smiling.

*   *   *

'Should we hide, or something?' said Dixon. 'Why am I spooked. Where's your nasty black squirrel?'

'Nah. Three girls. Pretty young.' They appeared, coming around a blind bend up the hill. One had a glass walking staff in her grip. All shouldered small backpacks.

'Hello!' said Dragon. 'You're Lars Patton, aren't you? You helped my mother in the school lab, with the apple segment. What did you think of its chemistry? I'd love to know. Boyd would love to know even more!'

Lars stood back, guessing correctly he was in the presence of the Green sisters. *Oh. My. God.*

'I'm Lars. This is Dixon. Dixon Nickson. Nice name, huh…'

Dixon shuffled back against the hillside. 'Hey, poison ivy. I'm outta here.' Dixon scrambled away, up towards the Firelane Extension trail.

'Don't go far, Dix! I'm coming!'

'I'm Dragon, my sisters are Boyd and Miller. Green. All Green.'

'Hi. Hey, welcome and everything. You're kind of semi-well-known.'

'World famous in Regent Square we understand.' The sisters laughed. 'You can call us the Banshee Patrol. We play traditional American tunes, along with some of our own stuff. Norman Blake, Doc Watson. Stuff from *Oh Brother Where Art Thou.*'

'Ummmm,' Lars managed.

'We're here on our first foray into what may well be the Garden of Eden,' said Miller. 'Right where we are – and do watch the poison ivy, everyone – was where the apple tree was, that my mom and dad bit into. Dad told us someone had nicked it.'

'Nicked it?' asked Lars.

'Southern hemisphere slang for robbed or burgled,' said Boyd. 'Hey, you got zinged, look at your hair. What happened?'

Lars felt unable to concoct an elaborate myth on the fly. But he certainly wasn't going to open his chamber of immediate semi-horrors, either, to what were as clearly savantian a set of personages as he'd even read about, much less met. They almost crackled.

'Ummmm', he mumbled again.

'Listen, Lars,' said Miller. 'We're on a sort of mission-oriented outing today, so won't stop long. But, considering our mother thought you were A-1 as far as science, maybe you'd like to participate.'

'What?'

'We need to locate thirteen weird chemical markers, either buried or recently stirred up, in what we're hoping will be confined to the park. Could be some scattered further, but our inclination…' here Miller looked at her sisters, '…is that the things we're looking for, boneseeds, or boneseed locations, were confined to the park's borders.'

'Ok. I get that. I mean the general idea, as far as it goes.'

'Boyd is our resident engineer, but having a fabricator who could tinker some of this stuff into hardware would be marvelous.'

'How old are you?'

'Born end of Feb. So around… ' Miller counted on her fingers, '… almost five months. We know we're not standard. That's a story for another day.'

'Well at least together you're over a year,' said Lars. The girls all laughed. 'Hey, I'll catch up with Dixon before he bolts out of sight. I have your mom's e-mail and she has mine. Let me know what I should do, or expect. I'm more or less game: just don't know what this is all about.'

'Can we give him the nereBegat list?' asked Boyd.

'Should be able to, Dad didn't say not to,' said Dragon. She extracted a piece of paper from her pocket and handed it to Lars. 'Keep this confidential, please. Thirteen nereBegats are arriving on Earth via the regeneration of Eden. We think the Nature Center fire might have disseminated the chemical-spawning ingredients. Anyway, all of these creations need to be tracked and evaluated. We're running out of time. You can see from the descriptions that there's some unknown consequences ahead, for the world, really, if they gestate, reproduce in numbers, and get out and start making the planet their home.'

Lars looked over the list. 'You sure I should have this?'

'You probably shouldn't,' said Dragon. 'The thing is, us three, we haven't learned mistrust at any major level yet. We're inclined to better scenarios and hold some instinct that trust begets trust, etc. etc., ad nauseam, ad infinitum, amen!' The sisters all laughed again. Lars remembered running that last line at Gideon back in the 'early days.'

'Keep that secret. Keep that safe!' said Boyd.

With that, the girls moved up the hill, in the direction of Dixon's barely visible forehead, which, upon the sight of them approaching, disappeared.

*　　*　　*

Riley Cardle and Carmen Walker spent an afternoon together, at the Carnegie Museum of Art.

Cardle had found herself a bit too eager to rock and roll with her new lady friend. She slowed herself down, recalling how easy it was to start organizing a relationship into best-case patterns, notably and especially as they served oneself. So she took a useful breath and promised to proceed with less anticipation. Let things brew in their own time. After all, concurrent with this romantic, lovely lead story, she still had to figure out how to cash in on the *other* hot story fermenting in her life: the *Greens*, the *Apples*, the *Fire*. She would enjoy the new friendship-that-might-become-more but would not shelve the writing. They grabbed a small lunch out on the Forbes Ave. patio.

'I have to tell you something. I've been holding back,' said Carmen.

'You don't have to. Just because, I mean, of this. This *us* thing.'

'It's the best reason,' said Carmen.

'Happy to listen.'

'The three religious who visited. They let slip something about the Greens. I mean, Haskley and I were already wondering why these guys were even visiting us. We knew the Catholic church would be interested if miracles were involved. And, sure, the Green girls are an anomaly. Their growth, motor skills, intellect. But that's just growth, right? Physical acceleration. Maybe a miracle. I'm not Catholic.'

'I'm with you. And I'm with you, which I like.' Cardle smiled. Carmen smiled.

'They implied something, crazy. That the fruit ingested by Emma, before all this started, was from Eden. You know, *the* Garden of Eden.'

*   *   *

Tuck Gonferally was a televangelist who preached that the words of the Bible were the literal truth. He preached it on weekdays at 3:30 in the afternoon, on cable channel 73, the channel called *The Love and The Hope*.

His show he'd titled *Fiat Lux,* after the Latin for *'let there be light'*, which he thought modestly clever and was fond of saying out loud.

Fiat Lux was staged at a Rt. 22 studio that broadcast Tuck's show and a number of other religious programs. On camera, he wore a white suit with a dark blue tie. Tuck never watched replays of his sermons, and never watched other televangelists, because so many of them were, quite plainly, fake. First of all, they seemed to love money. Give us money, send us money, the Lord blesses you when you keep our mission bankable and solvent. Secondly, some of their bible-based logic came from the Moon. They warped the scriptures to fit the most outlandish of claims, and often had PowerPoint slides to drive home a ridiculous point. Thirdly, he judged them, yes he did, in spite of the Bible's own edict, *Judge not let ye be judged.* He felt he had to deflect the flock(s) from this type of off-kilter pontificating.

Now someone had given him a story. It was an intriguing tale about a happening, a local happening, that could mean big things for his congregation, and really all Christian believers who looked to the Bible for their spiritual nourishment, and, through Tuck, teachings that could lead to more. It had something to do, apparently, with the End Times. It hinted at some kind of verifiable evidence that Revelations and Genesis were not fictional ramblings of grand imagination, but God's front-facing testaments with 'practical value', as Tuck liked to put it.

He was wary, because his standing outside his broadcast medium had been so abused by association with stereotypical televised orators. He had to be sure the story had legitimacy, and he expected to be shown proof. But his own faith was secure. God prevailed.

Regardless of how it worked out, he'd thank Father Jack, for the tip, and for being a friend across the quiet middle ranks of clergy who shepherd their small flocks with care and zeal.

*   *   *

Gideon's phone rang.

'Hello'.

'Hello, this is the Remediation Center. Mr. Moss?'

'Yes.'

'We have good news.'

'Yes.'

'Your son Raymond woke from his coma, this morning.'

'Goodness! How is he?'

'He's groggy. Or was. Now, he's been asking to be taken home.'

'Oh. My. Wonderful news. Is he able, do you think, to be released?'

'We would keep him for observation. For a few days.'

'Oh. Such great news.'

'We think you should come out soon and see him.'

'Well I will, of course. So grateful, what you've done there.'

'He's become a bit…demanding. About getting home.'

'What. You mean he's…not himself?'

'We didn't know him, Mr. Moss, so can't say. You'd be able to.'

'Of course. I'll come out today. I should be able to be there in two hours, maybe.'

'Good. We appreciate it.'

'Yes, of course. Tell Ray his father will be there soon. Thank you again. Wonderful news.'

'Ask for Ms. Smith-Jones when you arrive. She's been attending to Ray throughout this and you and she will be able to discuss the best options for him.'

'I will. Thanks. Goodbye.'

TWENTY ONE

RAZOR MOSS WAS pacing on the wide porch of the Center, accompanied by two burly guard-attendants. A nurse stood behind in the shadow of the building's entrance. Razor's hair was down over his eyebrows, shiny black. His teeth hid behind a tight-lipped grimace. He gripped a plastic bag, over-stuffed with clothes. Gideon walked to the portico.

Razor saw him.

'Exit, stage left, this asylum. *Now, Dad!*'

Razor launched himself down the steps, past Gideon, and got in the passenger seat of the car. Gideon walked around and motioned for him to roll down the window.

'Just wait a few minutes while I talk with the nurse.' Razor squeezed his eyes shut. Gideon walked up the steps to see the nurse.

'Mr. Moss. I'm Ann Smith-Jones.'

'Hello.'

'You can see your son is agitated. We wanted to keep him, at least for a day or two. Go through some therapy suggestions. Check his vitals. He was having none of it.'

'I'll bring him home. He's probably in a messed-up head space.'

'Do you have someone there, if you're out, for work or whatever?'

'I'm Principal at a high school, St. Anselm's in Swissvale. I can take care of this.'

She handed him a card. 'Here's some contact info, including an emergency number. We see this reaction occasionally from brain trauma. Cognitively he seems "with it", so to speak. Which is healthy. His mood is the issue.'

A shout. 'Dad! *Let's go!*'

Razor yanked his head back through the window. Moss saw his lips moving – ranting to himself.

'He looks anxious,' said Gideon. 'We'll get him home. Thanks for all you've done. All invoices to the insurance company.' Gideon walked down the steps and got in the car.

'You might show some appreciation for those people, and to me for paying your tab and picking you up.'

'Shut the fuck up.'

*   *   *

'So in your lingua franca, the devil, or satan, is a prime mover in stakes such as those we're discussing,' said Grey Cloud Roaringman.

Emma and Roaringman sat in a quiet hallway alcove, some distance from the chapel and the to-and-fro of nuns. Both had cups of tea. They'd often talked daily since the *Fireworks*. Emma appreciated Roaringman's wide-ranging take on the current proceedings. His science acumen was especially delightful, since Emma's seedy-brain could go round for round with him on theoretical physics. They circled back constantly, though, like water to a drain: was a miracle at hand? A spiritual event? Or maybe everyone had popped their corks.

'I don't have to tell you perception is everything,' he reminded her.

'That's one rabbit-hole I refuse to head down, Grey Cloud. Every one of us, every human, is padlocked into a solitary experience. Alone, essentially. A mental construct, living on the scraps our senses provide. But that's Alice, that's Wonderland, and that's useless.' She took a sip from her cup. 'Anyway, the bad guy with horns is as fictional to me as the good guys with wings. Even though I'm playing a damned big role in this fresh new-age Gospel.'

'Ok, getting back to the bad guy element. In the Blackfoot tradition, and those of many of my Native American brothers and sisters, it is a *trickster* that brings about these machinations. Not so much someone trying to put his foot on your neck. I mean, what did the serpent have to gain when your cousin Eve chewed up that apple? It didn't get any fresh standing with the Creator. If anything, it would have had worse standing. God could have pinned *its* neck and said, *you* are banished, for tempting them. And brought his humans back.' He took a sip.

'Why would the Creator set up this untoward scenario of temptation, knowing the outcome, unless it had a point?'

Emma looked at him. 'I don't get the point of visualizing all these god stories, over and again. Honestly, I'd be glad to know heaven exists. My girls, this Frick Park apple; what does it prove? That there's a loving god? That the Bible is true? I don't see how. I just don't.' Emma set her tea down and put her head in her hands. 'Becoming a nun isn't a way for me. Is it?'

'No more than me,' said Roaringman with a quiet smile. 'Let me get back to this point, about the trickster. Let's suppose there is a god, a G-O-D type god. Really powerful, created the Universe, and other universes, has always existed, always will, created, controls, and knows everything. The key, I believe, to this Creator's elegance, would be its awareness that it could mosey along in eternity and watch the endless course of time flow forwards, backwards, down and up. What would it miss most? Free Will. Free beings who are independent and don't kneel at its altar just to worship and sing praises and not have an opportunity to engage in the very things this Creator finds most enduring and, even, let's say to make a point – for the Creator – transcendent.'

Emma lifted her head. 'I'm hanging on. Take me somewhere.'

'So don't create evil. Don't drum up some pointy-ear mastermind who invades and erodes in order to have some of his new beings end up burning forever in hellfire. But introduce rogue factors, unknowables, mysteries, chaos theory, and tricksters to ensure the *free wills* it has engineered into being won't be wandering methodically into each new day with nothing more on their plates than some rote repeating of the day before. Life must be unbounded to be glorious. I think the Creator saw that requirement. The need for eventualities that undo the complacency of normalcy. That's what brings succor to our human days. Not working out the minutiae of scripture or sanctifying an object in some special rite when all things are sanctified from their inception. Free will to option one's way through with eyes and heart open. God? Yes! God! No! God? Maybe? Free Will? Yes. That's my agnostic theorem. For the moment.'

'Some of that rings Ok,' said Emma. 'But free will itself isn't a tenet of science. And there's chaos. Chaos has some traction. And real evil. How is the holocaust or AIDS or crippled children a sign of a trickster? How is it evidence of free will? And are we unable to get anywhere near some logic that will make this palatable?'

'You can't expect too much from Mystery, Emma. It's all we have, in the longest run, til we come up against our own mortality, and get to see what's behind the curtain. Why I'm a theoretical physicist currently residing in a convent.' With that, Roaringman exhaled a portentous laughing wail. Then gulped the last of his tea.

'I see where you got your name,' said Emma. 'Think I'll use my free will to grab some lunch.'

'And I a nap,' said Roaringman.

*　　*　　*

'Decomposing. My story is now decomposing. Once God sneaks in, everyone goes bonkers. The Christian right will cry blasphemy or get me on a stage for the washing of my holy keyboard. The non-religious will go for my legitimacy as a reporter, whatever's left of that,' said Cardle.

She paused. 'Or else I'm just making excuses. I've literally lost the plot. Or I'm simply chickening out.'

She and Carmen were not as amenable as Cardle had imagined, at first blush. They had political differences, and other inclinations maybe not so compatible. Cardle was grateful they seemed mature enough to step back, go slower, and maintain something that could be very agreeable, if they didn't rush things.

'You're over-reacting, Cardle,' Carmen said. 'Couch the story in your own cynicism, and include an escape hatch of wonderment at how it could all be happening. A lot of it is really, truly, a miracle. Those kids are exceptional beyond anything I've ever known, as far as speed of aging. It's frightening. I feel for them, and the family. They won't live long lives.'

'So what do you suggest?'

'Write it all out, as true as you know it to be, and let the world decide.'

'I feel like a Christian Rushdie.'

'Hey, if you get that kind of attention, being killed off will be the least of your worries,' said Carmen. She followed up with a small grin. Perhaps they did have a thing. Cardle leaned in to kiss her new friend.

*　　*　　*

Abel Green was watching the clock, with his mother-in-law Etta. The girls had been gone for an hour. He wanted them home, and felt like a fool for letting them go into the park by themselves.

'Abel, relax. At first I thought you should be arrested,' she said. 'They are Ok, down there. Daytime, all three. The park is not the Amazon jungle. You will need to set them free early. That's obvious. Get used to it.' She sat down. 'I think I already am.'

He walked over to the window. The sycamore trees threw down soft sidewalk shadows in the late summer's morning light.

*　　*　　*

Father Jack knew sin. Just about everybody in the parish made contributions. He'd heard them all at confession, though the Sacrament was dwindling, mostly kept by the more traditional segment of his parishioners.

There was something so beautiful and important about the Greens' miracle. He had made a curiously calm decision to trade one sin against his ledger of being a clergyman and sacrificing his life in God's service. He prayed for a good way to make the sin useful, which was the only reason he had considered it anyway. The answer had come when he'd seen his buddy Tuck Gonferally doing his thing on TV. Tuck was the only Protestant televangelist he knew who didn't spew wild Biblically-imagined wrath and prosperity screeds all over the airwaves. He and Tuck had played golf together a few times, at a local course, on Sunday afternoons when the weather cooperated.

So after a game, they'd talked in the course parking lot, leaning against their cars. In the end, Fr. Jack decided he'd tell the Eden tale through Tuck.

Introduced on Tuck's show (Tuck called the show *Fiat Lux,* which was a lovely coincidence) it would be another pitch of the Christian message. But it was happening in the now. And it was real. And whether Frick Park was the resurrected Eden or not, there was nothing it the narrative that contradicted the Bible or the Faith. To Jack, it was like a tremendous booster shot or mega-vitamin that only a few knew about. It simply didn't seem fair that this gift, this grace, should be unshared.

He didn't want to bring calamity to the Greens. So he'd never reveal their identities. But he would assure Tuck, bound by his own vow to the priesthood, that he was witness. A convenient blind for him, the Greens, and the Catholic Church, is that this story would appear on a 'non-Roman' religious TV show: not considered the cornerstone of theological veracity by many. *Well, Catholics, anyway.* But, thought Jack, Tuck was different. An honest man in a non-honest landscape. The story might not have legs. God could decide, then, how far the message might reach. Jack's small sin could lead to big restitution, in a world starving for the Good News.

*　　*　　*

The Green sisters, the self-titled *Banshee Patrol*, were on the move. Their keen, unfallen capacities gave them considerable advantage over normal human comprehension, and teased them with a bit of foresight. Not an actual ability to know any future, but to analyze and predict with, ironically enough, scientific accuracy.

'We're not superheroes, sisters,' Dragon said. They were walking on the Tranquil trail towards the eastern section of the park, where the lower Nine Mile Run trail dovetailed with the Braddock trail, in a pinched dogleg that ended near the busy Parkway East, and exited out onto Braddock Avenue.

They had an idea of what identifying nereBegats might entail; they needed this walk to take first steps in this new Eden and see what transpired. The summer woods leaned over them, as glad to be above them as they below. Some of their parents' affection for these paths must have DNA'ed its way into their own hearts.

Buggy bogs on the right, a steepening hillside on the left, led them to a culverted stretch of the Nine Mile Run stream. Though the pollution had been reduced by diligent and caring park lovers, along with municipal resolutions that were slowing coming to bear, there was still junk visible in the rocks and flow.

Boyd crouched down next to the stream. She dipped her finger in the water and took a quick lick. 'Sodium, potassium, magnesium. Traces of nickel, chromium, manganese, maybe cobalt. Oxygen and nitrogen isotopes in nitrate, as nutrients, maybe.'

She brought out her aziwheel.

'Nitrate concentrations about, ahh…2.39 milligrams per liter,' she said, spinning the wheel with diligent indulgence.

'Any phosphates?' asked Miller. 'Phosphates would be a plus, right?'

Boyd finished some calculations, made a few scribbles in a small notebook, and stood. 'High levels for this water. Not looking great.'

'Hmm. Well. Environmental protection isn't our task. For the short time we're here,' said Dragon. 'Any non-standard chemistry that might speak to nereBegats?'

'No... *oh, look... look out...!*'

The girls ran, as fast as their feet would carry them.

The brackish creature moved wickedly, agile, blistering through the undergrowth, its stingers out to each side, venomous spikes rippling in a deadly array. A dark slithering shine, blood red, flashed off its strange hide. Not an insect, this thing: more like a small fierce python, unleashed, eager for victims.

'Looked like a *banedagger* – stung means dead,' gasped Miller.

'Unless you get re-stung,' yelled Boyd.

'*Insane...*' roared Dragon. 'Run, run, run – ruuuuu*UUUNNnnn...!*'

Stream on the left, hillside on the right.

Open territory ahead.

Safety.

The banedagger did not make it there: Miller Green thrust a glass rod through its middle.

*

'We need to put in some exercise time, sisters,' panted Boyd, pulling in deep breaths as she bent over. 'Almost didn't catch this thing.'

'Banedagger,' said Miller.

'Are we sure?' asked Dragon, stooping to study the hideous remains, which twitched slightly when Miller pulled the rod from its mid-section.

Boyd ran a finger across the end of the glass and sniffed. 'Not a chemistry I recognize,' she said. 'Banedagger, I agree. Based on the *fiat* description, and its behavior, and its presence out of the blue. Was it aiming to attack us, before it turned tail?'

'Hard to tell,' said Miller. 'This place is new to us, new to the nereBegats. We're all fresh arrivals to an unknown place.'

Boyd began, suddenly, to sob. She sat down on the grass next to the path. Miller leaned over.

'What's wrong?'

'Only one of its kind. Ever. Extinct. At our hand.' Miller rested a palm on Boyd's shoulder.

There were voices; a family of day walkers was moving down the trail towards them with a young boy on a bike in front. Dragon grasped the banedagger by its hindquarters and dragged it off the trail into some shrubs. She stood over it, hoping to hide it. The biking kid pedaled past, followed by the father and two other kids. The young mother stopped.

'Is she Ok? You all alright?' she asked, looking at Boyd.

'We are. Thanks. She's sad about the banedagger,' said Dragon.

'Ahh. Ok. Hope she feels better.' The mother moved along after her family, with a single glance back.

'Dragon, we need to get this thing out of the park, and up to the house, and I have no idea how, without anyone seeing it.'

'Let's hide it til night, somewhere across the stream, over by the Parkway, past the bog where nobody hikes. Then Dad can come down and get it. I guess.'

'*Ick.* He won't be happy.'

*   *   *

Their car was hurtling down the Parkway East off-ramp onto Braddock Avenue, Razor battering Gideon with insults, suspicions, and threats. Razor threw in numerous quotes from Shakespeare, twisting the blade with surgical precision.

'*Hang there like fruit, my soul, till the tree die.*'

'The tree isn't dead. It's sick,' said Gideon. '*You're* sick.'

'You are correct. Sick of you and control and stupidity and your petty world. For your refuse, your indolence, your keeping me from the theater, for all the eggshells I've had to walk on to keep you from wailing at the world every day and night. Sick, indeed, that is me. Now shall I sic my bad self on you, father-man.'

Gideon parked outside their Whipple Street home, and tried to hustle Razor inside.

His son raised his arms high as he waltzed towards the front porch. '*The milk of human kindness.* Face it, *Papa,* you're singed on both sides. Burnt, crisped, minus the leavening butter.'

Gideon swung the door shut behind them, as Razor wailed his way inside. He flung his bag of clothes onto the couch, where half of them spilled out onto the floor.

'Ok, listen, son. You've been in a coma, you just woke up, you –'

'Get out your rye, *Paternum,* let us throw down some dram…'

Razor stumbled and fell across an end table, knocking a lamp to the floor. Its bulb popped with a crunch. 'Hey, sorry, Poppsy.'

'Listen. Sit there.' Gideon raised the table and lifted the lamp. 'Just sit. Please.'

'*Huuu uhuu…so pleased to sit for you…*' mumbled Razor. He slumped onto the couch, brushing the hair out of his eyes.

Gideon pulled a chair up to sit across from his son. 'Do you want to talk to your mother?'

'No, no.' Razor grabbed the half-empty clothes bag and kneaded it, staring at the floor. 'You're reading this all wrong, oh Father.'

'I am? You're Ok?'

'Oh yes.' He looked up.

'That apple – that's what you fed me, right? – that apple has recuperative powers, for children whose fathers have assailed them with a brick in the back of their skulls. It's a remarkable elixir for one's cerebrum. You recall everything you learned. All the knowledge you may have forgot. A jolt of some hyper propellant for your personal passions. Or addictions, is that not true, Father? Did it sting you thus? Blessed with insights and out sights and front sights and back sights. All this play you've been craving to accomplish, is neatly seeded onto me. With Razor-edged takes. How's that make you feel?'

'You're my son, you're underage, and I'll put you in a home if you don't start to –'

'Don't *what?*'

Razor hurled the half-full bag of clothing at his father, hitting him in the face.

'Cheer up, Dad. It's not all so fraught. I'm on with the mission. I don't believe you ever even figured it out, despite all the advantages channeled so vigorously into your slow-witted head.'

Gideon stood up, stood over his son, and struck his son's face. Razor lurched back. Then, slowly, brought a hand up to his reddened cheek.

'You're decrepit,' said Razor.

Gideon stumbled back and sat. Ashamed he'd just slapped this boy, this man, this son, just home from weeks, or was it months, in a coma.

Razor leaned towards his father, and rapped at his own chest. 'Get used to this *me*. Your very own Mossenstein. You raised me, loved me, then coma-ed me, and then you *appled* me. I'm a rare breed of Moss. Younger and smarter and stronger than you shall ever be.' He felt at his cheek again. 'You'll play a key role here, Father, as we move to assure all the revelations brought forth by your Nature Fire are revealed. This appears to be the task laid before us, Mr. Gideon Moss.'

Razor rose and stood over Gideon.

'Strike me when you will, Father. Be aware of the suffering we'll know when I strike in return.'

He walked towards the kitchen, turning to say something over his shoulder. 'I love you. Crazy, huh.'

Gideon heard one last verse, as his barely recognizable son made his way to the refrigerator…

'*…hell itself breathes out contagion to this world…*'

*　　*　　*

Abel didn't like hiking into the park, after dark, to find some bizarre cadaver hidden by his gifted, lethal daughters, with the directive to drag it back up to their house, refrigerate it, and get it shipped off to a bio lab as soon as possible for an autopsy.

'Get to bed, girls. It's after 8:00.' He heard various feet pattering across upstairs hallways, along with some snickering.

'Thanks for going down, Dad!' one of girls yelled to him.

Fortunately, his older neighbor Dan, who'd been such a help when the girls had been brought from the convent, had agreed to join him, at least to hold the flashlight. Miller had provided a detailed map. They brought a sturdy plastic garbage bag for haulage. It was a scene out of some cheap horror movie. Dan and Abel headed out the door, shaking their bemused heads. Etta didn't ask what was going on, but wished them well.

It took twenty minutes to get down into the hollow and another ten to reach the rising slope across the stream. The girls had hidden the strange creature behind some downed tree trunks. They found it and avoided looking too long. Not a pretty sight when alive, Abel supposed, its appearance in death was nothing if not creepy. Dan thought it was some sort of escaped eel, which Abel didn't argue with. Fortunately, it had not been disturbed, nor did it reek. In the end, the banedagger was not a huge burden to bring back. Abel used gloves to lift it into the bag. He carried it, while Dan led the way back with the light.

*　　*　　*

'Good morning, Mrs. Green.'

Abel phoned her after morning Mass; Emma was asked to attend these to stay in configuration with the novitiate program. She'd been to enough Masses with Abel to get the holy gist. They were an occasion to meditate. Seek out the tiny cracks of light Leonard Cohen had evoked in his much-quoted line ~ *'There is crack in everything. That's how the light gets in.'*

'Good morning. How are the girls?'

'Well, the Frick Park expedition ended up a near-disaster. They dealt with a venomous nereBegat.'

'*nereBegat?*'

'Remember them, named in the *fiats?* Let's just say this one was ugly, lethal, and is now dead and stored in our basement fridge.'

Emma considered fainting. She drew breath. 'Ok. So…?'

'Well, the girls were exuberant but chastened. Boyd, especially, was sad, said this thing never had a shot.'

'Whew.'

'Anyway. Here's my even weirder thing: can you accommodate this creature? Up there somewhere on campus there must be a biolab. And medical facilities for the Sisters. We need a semi-private autopsy.'

'God,' she said. 'How many times have I said *"god"* since this started. He started it. His fault.'

'*She*, remember?'

'*Ha ha,* she replied.'

Emma leaned against her hard-backed chair. She reflexively turned to make sure a cat wasn't behind her. She missed Seren and Dippity.

'It's called a banedagger, according to our *Banshee* files. But here's a seedy idea that might make this escapade more palatable for you,' said Abel.

'Ok.'

'The thing has sets of double stingers. According to *Banshee* via *fiat,* there's an antidote delivered in the second sting, after the initial one – *if* you can corral the thing to get the life-saving sting number two. See why it wasn't a great fit for worldwide inclusion. But, maybe, and this might be why it *should* have been allowed in, the antidote could be a potent antitoxin for a variety of poisons. That's what the girls, think, anyway.'

'Ok,' said Emma.

'So if the antitoxin is still viable, or identifiable chemically, we might have a new vaccine or some such.'

'Sounds like a dreadful long-shot. What am I supposed to tell the admin here? We have an alien to dissect, excuse us, please.'

'That won't go over well. Here's another long-shot, from the girls again. See if your pal Roaringman can cajole his Mother Superior sister into requesting some lab time. He's a pretty esteemed scientist. Not too out of place for him to get some university resources. Is it?'

'He's a theoretical physicist. That barely flies.'

'Hmm. Well I can't leave this thing in the fridge.'

'I'll ask. All I can do,' said Emma.

'Hey, I hope you're Ok. You can move back here any time. You think there were fireworks last month, out there? Here it's heating up for who knows what.' He paused. 'More than all that, I just want to hold you.'

She held the silence a moment too long. 'I miss all of you and love all of you.'

'Ok,' he said. 'I gotta do some CMU work, believe it or not. Signing off.'

'See you. I'll call if I get permission on that thing.'

'Please do. Bye.' He hung up.

She looked out the window, a lovely end-of-summer gold lit the Motherhouse grounds. Roaringman sat on a bench, smoking a pipe, talking with his sister the Sister, Jill.

*　　*　　*

Cardle finished her article. She printed it out, rather than sending it electronically to her editor, and took it downtown to the *Post-Press* offices. She left it in his Inbox with a note inside.

'Karl. Take a very close look and get back to me. Thanks, Cardle.'

*　　*　　*

Tuck wrote up the script for his next show, which included a small preview of Father Jack's story. He hoped to find a middle ground, delivering the content with some sort of respectful calm that would help reduce the sensationalism inherent in the message. God was messing around with physical incursions, in our time, in our place. Beautiful, astonishing, nerve-wracking, and completely wonderful.

*　　*　　*

'Here you are, my very own Lear,' said Razor. He and his father sat in his bedroom staring down the tree. 'First, we might try to resurrect this bonsai you have practically killed, here. Though I do harbor some blame, having ripped it out of our yard. We would need a private greenhouse – a safe house – and an expert to make sure we salvage this tree. The monetary potential is quite favorable.'

'There's no way to get a greenhouse nor hire a botanist without the whole thing exploding, Ray.'

'Am I *Ray*, now?'

'Yes. Until you get back whatever part of your cranium you left somewhere else.'

'That would be humorous, Father, if only it was. How much money can we access?'

'Listen. Just for a minute, stop that runaway train in your head and let me explain what's going on. You've been in a coma for several months. Can I just talk?'

Razor leaned back. '*I scorn to change my state with kings.*'

'First of all, please don't ask me about money. We have enough to get by. The diocese of Pittsburgh is not rife with cash. We can't use savings to buy space in a greenhouse or hire a botanist. Both for privacy and because we'd be broke. My job is hanging by various threads already.'

'*Done to death by slanderous tongues…*'

Gideon bit at the end of his thumb. Was his son completely gone? '*Tempest.* That one I know.'

'*How sharper than a serpent's tooth it is to have a thankless child.*'

'You want to take up theater. I'll help you. After all this settles,'

'When all this settles, the world may not be what you expect.'

'You know what, Razor. I really don't give a damn. Do whatever you want. You're not getting my money. What the hell *do* you want?'

'I've been running you down, Gideon. I needed to vent, set some of my pain free. You know you've been an undependable factor in my life since the day I was born. You love me, though. I know that. We're *appled* now. *Blood-appled,* a family tie like no other.' Razor took a moment to snicker to himself, then continued, his voice darker.

'You must do me this favor, Father: don't harp about your derealization. Whatever happened, *happened.* Other people go blind, have limbs removed, see their children die of cancer. You have a mental shade, probably permanent, over everything in your life since whenever that lady proffered you that joint. So put that away, permanently, and we'll get on with this task, this thing from the other side.'

Gideon went blank.

He stood, and stepped over to his son, and lifted his hand to slap, again, harder, or get a brick and strike this child.

'Come not between the dragon and his wrath!'

With a snort, Razor stood and shoved his father, who stumbled against the bed, and fell.

'The fire you set at the Center. Explain your motive!'

Gideon ran a hand across his mouth.

'I don't know. It came from the apple. A decree. A commandment. An edict. I knew it had to happen. So beware, son. If we are following decrees from off world… well, you see how it shakes out. I'm hanging by a thread and you're not helping.'

'Hanging by a thread. Hanging by a thread. Everything's hanging by a thread. You're going to have to man up, then. I'm not sure, about the next step, considering we don't actually know what's been happening around here. Here's what I think: your big fire set up some awakening in the woods. Some unearthed potentialities. Either environmental crashes. Or growth bombs. Or mutations. Wherever the apple tree came from, resurrected if you will, this stuff will come from. In my current comprehension, what I'm getting, what I'm feeling, is that these things could be good or bad. So perhaps *our* task is to see this new equation gets a chance.'

'A chance?'

'You know, to survive long enough to establish themselves, or to register long enough to be incorporated into the ecosystem.'

'To make an impression,' said Gideon.

'To stake a claim,' said Razor.

'Why should we bother? The tree in this room could set us up for life.'

'If it fruits.'

'You almost killed it, ripping it out of the dirt.'

'You almost killed me, knocking me into that brick.'

'What are you suggesting we do, Ray?'

'You have the seeds. To the tree.'

'Yes.'

'Good. Let's establish if this thing will survive, with water and sunshine, right here. Or die. We'll replant some of the seeds somewhere after we handle this mission from God.'

'Mission from God?'

'We're on a mission from God, Gideon. Who else could've approved a reawakening of the Garden of Eden?' Razor grabbed a jacket out of his closet. 'Let's go to Giant Eagle and get some food. I'm starved. Drip-fed, in case you forgot, at the Remediation Center. Liquefied nutrition. I should put you on that diet. The "try to kill your offspring" diet.'

'I didn't know you'd hit your head, son. When I shoved you. I'm sorry.' Gideon stood.

'Can't linger at Giant Eagle. I need to get back here. I have to start prepping to open the high school. September. Keep my employment. Unless you want to chuck everything.'

'No, no. We'll maintain a semblance of propriety until we figure out what to do next. Mission from God. *Blues Brothers*. Dig it.'

Gideon got up, weary resignation in his voice. 'It's all ridiculous.'

'Misery acquaints a man with strange bedfellows,' said Razor, stalking out the front door.

*   *   *

While Abel drove the banedagger corpse to the Seton Hill University campus, the three Green Sisters met with Lars Patton, on their Gamma Way front porch.

'You three should enter the Millennium Prize Problems competition,' said Lars. 'Six math problems no one has been able to solve. It's ongoing and open-ended,' said Lars. 'Clay Mathematics Institute runs it.'

'You're right. There's six.' said Boyd. 'Birch and Swinnerton-Dyer conjecture, Hodge conjecture, Navier-Stokes existence and smoothness, P versus NP, Riemann hypothesis, Yang-Mills existence and mass gap. We dabbled in some of them. Above our pay grade. For now.' She smiled.

'A cool million for each one you solve. Think how happy you'd make your dad.'

'He'd freak out. Already pretty freaked out. Think we'll stick with searching out thirteen strange metaphysically introduced mutant creations before we start doing *really* weird stuff,' said Miller. Dragon covered her mouth, laughing.

'Ok, ok,' said Lars. 'Hey thanks again for inviting me into this circle. You got to know I am operating in some moral middle. The squirrel bite and the green snow flakes, have – speaking of mutation – mutated my ability to tell right from not right.'

'That's Ok with us,' said Dragon. 'We're unfallen, and so maybe naive mostly, as to who is doing what for whatever reason. You don't have to be secretive about this. Just don't go blabbering to some reporter. Mostly because our dad and mom are worried about publicity, and people thinking we should be put away, and also we think some of the Wise Guys we talked to are worried we might be drafted for Army service.'

'Really?' said Lars. 'Man. I need better invectives around you three.'

'Invectives is the wrong word, Lars,' said Boyd.

'Ok. Down to business,' said Dragon. 'We need a kind of divining tool. To locate the boneseeds. Did you read our list?'

'What is that? What's a diving tool?'

'Not diving. *Divining.* They were used to find water. Two sticks, in the beginning, historically. Also called dowsing sticks. Of course, the science is suspect. However, there have been instances where they've proven accurate,' said Dragon.

'Hold the sticks over the ground, walk around holding them out horizontally. When there's water below, the sticks drop, or bend, downward,' said Miller. 'That's what *wiki* says, anyway.'

'The general idea should work for our boneseed detector. I was able to identify a few unique markers in the banedagger's constitution. Three. Let's call them X, Y and Z,' said Boyd. 'We'll incorporate sensors to flash when the X, Y, or Z chemistry shows up. Now, here's a schematic for the build.'

On the porch floor, Boyd unrolled a large drawing. Lars leaned in to study it, eyes wide.

'Wow.'

'So do you think you can get this built by, say, next Monday?' asked Dragon.

'I think, maybe. Wild. Wow. Dependent on squirrel and flake boosters staying steady, and back and forth conscience staying true.'

'You worried you might – *what* – give us up to the authorities?'

'No. Might rush over to Gideon Moss and tell him everything.'

'Gideon Moss. Really?' said Dragon. 'Go ahead.'

'You're kidding.'

'Not really. We haven't met him. Is he that bad? What do you think he'd do?'

'I have no idea, but he's currently minus a full deck – if you know what I mean. At least ethically speaking. So to speak.'

'Well we heard he bit the apple; maybe it knocked his scruples into some weird orbit. You have to give people some leeway.'

Lars shook his head. Gideon Moss may have bricked his own son into unconsciousness. Generally speaking, he didn't ooze good character.

'Ok. Well. If you guys don't mind. I'm still influenced. I mean, look at my hair.'

The three Green sisters took a cursory glance at his head and got back to business.

'We're not saying rush over deliberately and tell him what we're planning. Just don't worry about it. Get this hardware done, then we think we can trace the boneseeds to their origin points, and, if we're lucky, trace their migrations throughout the park.'

'What if they've moved out of the park?'

'We'll take it as it comes,' said Miller. 'One thing we might relate about this whole saga, is that the boneseed nereBegats – that's what they're called by the way – the nereBegats are not intrinsically bad. Some designers on *the other side*, if you will, thought their crafting was being ignored, or not fairly considered, for inclusion in the general evolution-to-come. We're guessing even the dinosaurs just snuck in, with the caveat they'd be extinct long before humans could be around as prey.'

'Hmmm. Lot's of history and science teaching is going to go down the drain, I guess,' said Lars.

'Anyway,' continued Miller, 'the Throwers and Makors and Selectors from up there – and by the way, can we use *upstairs,* sisters, as a working term, instead of *other side,* which sounds spooky? Reminds me of *The Outer Limits*, that weird TV show.'

Dragon and Boyd both nodded, 'Sure.'

'The *upstairs* inventors and engineers were artists, editors, producers: the original content developers. The Universe had a fair amount of tweaking needed to achieve balance. You can't blame these individuals for wanting to see their work included.'

'Or at least short-listed,' said Lars.

'So we don't know all of this, exactly. Some we intuit, some we get from the *fiats,* some from talking to each other. Main point is to be able to evaluate the nereBegats in the here and now. Maybe some deserve a second chance. Free will, evolution, chaos, etcetera: though the draft version of the Universe has played out decently, we don't think God and his team expected a granular level of control and development that would exactly follow some micro-managed path. They wished for humankind to be on a journey that would be expansive, intriguing, mysterious in all the best ways.'

'Yeah,' said Boyd. 'We think the thing that has really gone bonkers is the balance of selfish versus selfless, really, more than any biological or scientific or environmental crisis. Like, climate change. Really brought on by selfishness.'

'But, but, but,' reminded Dragon. 'We prefer not to judge. Unfallen is an incredible gift, that we have, for however long. So breathing the sweet air, laughing at the mad humor, eating the great snacks, playing our music; we made a pact to try not to judge. We don't really know what it's like to be born with Original Sin. We've been dangerously close to suggesting that this particular theology should be reconsidered. Original Sin. Unorthodox considerations come sneaking in from every side. Hey, but we're five months old.'

'Five months going on eleven years, though,' said Boyd.

'Staying on our mission keeps us focused,' said Miller. 'As far as we know it to be our mission.'

'We need a mission statement,' said Dragon.

'Do you guys have cherry coke in your fridge?' asked Lars.

*　　*　　*

Sister Jill had gotten permission from the Seton Hill University Provost to access the science labs. Emma and Roaringman had escorted their strange bundle, chilled, in a styrofoam cooler. Abel had not stayed to chat, preferring to leave the gruesome banedagger innards investigation to his crack(ed) away team.

'We need some kind of forensics personnel, Emma,' said Roaringman. 'I'm way out of my station. You teach high school biology. Your husband seemed to believe this animal is actually an unknown species, magically manifested in your local park. Talk about theory.'

'That's right. You never heard about the *fiat lux* material. That was closed-door at the summit. Not to get too deep, but my girls and my husband have all been recipients of – how to put this gently – data. Heaven sent bytes of information. Do you believe it?'

'Data. Hmmm. Maybe stop there, so I don't get indigestion, and let's just see if we can dig up a forensics person. How shall we label this?' asked Roaringman, as they wiggled the cooler to fit in an oversized upright refrigerator that, along with specimens, held a half-full bottle of Sprite soda and some crumpled brown lunch bags.

'Do not touch under penalty of eternal damnation?' suggested Emma.

'Something harsher.'

Emma grabbed a marker and wrote on a piece of scrap cardboard. 'NOT to be opened. Contact Biology Department for more information. Thank you.'

'That's pretty tame.'

'Make it mysterious and the students will be all over it. Happens in every sci-fi movie. Some poor soul opens something they weren't supposed to. Then people die.'

Roaringman laughed. They wrapped the cooler with an additional layer of plastic, duct taped it all around, and taped the note to the top.

'Let's get outta here,' murmured Emma, in her best thriller movie voice.

TWENTY TWO

Friday. Tuck's show was about to start. Jack set his double-shot-of-gin next to him, and leaned back in the Rectory's television-equipped lounge. *Buckle up,* he thought.

Tuck began…

'People of God, I'm so grateful that you've tuned in today. We are blessed to stand before you. God, Jesus, I ask you for the grace to speak only truth. Reach our souls with your message of love. Teach us how to care within our means, and how to care beyond them also.

He paused for a beat.

'Send no money to me, or this show. Send it to a charity that feeds the poor, visits those in prison, cares for the sick.'

'Some of you know that I have associates who worship from across the aisle. As in our prayers for a society that works in bipartisan fashion to govern in service to the people, we, in our own denominations, all of us Christian, reach across from our own pews to uncover the spiritual commonalities that embolden our faith journeys. We truly gain from these associations and we can be assured the Lord blesses them. We "farm our faith and knead our doubt", as I have often said. We spell that word k-n-e-a-d.'

'I am going to share a very special testimony today. I don't ask you to embrace the words I will deliver. I only ask you to know the testimony was given to me with the utmost humility, and with the respect and devotion to scripture we all hold as sacred, and to listen with an open heart.'

'I'm going out on a spiritual limb here, since it will bring controversy, and perhaps trouble some of you. Know that I firmly believe this testimony to be nothing more and nothing less than a grace for our times, from our Lord and Savior.'

He paced across his televised stage.

'A few months ago, in this part of our beautiful state, not so very far from our own city, two people, a man and a woman, stumbled on a small tree, hidden, out of the way, in the woods, in a park. The tree held three apples. The man and woman partook of the fruit.'

'Yes. You know the story.'

'This tale could end here, and already contains some heart-warming, soul-warming simplicity in its mise en scene - that is, how it allows us to imagine, before the serpent shows up, the sylvan pastoral peace that went before the fall.'

'In this case, there is no serpent, and no fall. There is the knowledge of good and evil, gifted as in Eden perhaps, and the bounty of a miracle dropped in our communal laps –'

Suddenly, the TV feed went to a blank. A static message appeared: 'The Love and the Hope will be right back. Please stay tuned. Praise the Lord.'

*　　*　　*

Razor listened to Gideon's entire account, since his fateful day slipping in the mud in Frick. He was questioned at every turn by his son, who had become a twisted mirror of his own twisted persona.

'Please text Lars and tell him I'm out of my coma. We'll want to talk to him. Maybe recruit him again. I'm thinking we can recalibrate that squirrel bite. What about we give him a lick of apple?'

'God, Ray. He's been bitten by a squirrel and then had his head cooked by a weird chemical. Do we really want to mix the apple in here? We have no idea how his body would take that. Could kill him, for God's sake.'

'Notice how you keep saying *God*, for god's sake,' said Razor. 'No, we don't want to kill Lars. Maybe just a sip of some of its juice. He might be the science that leads us to the creations. Something's happening down in the Frick Park, right?'

'I never really got that. I didn't know what the fire was supposed to do. Or why I did it. Only knew the tree was precious. And might cure me. Since God doesn't seem to want to.'

'You're not authorized to speak about derealization, even as an insinuation. Text Lars. I'm going to call the reporter you spoke with and blackmail her. Then I'll make us some lunch.'

* * *

'Hello?' answered Cardle, when her phone buzzed.

'Riley Cardle. The reporter?'

The voice sounded strangely familiar. 'Yes. Who's calling?'

'My name is Razor, Razor Moss. Son of Gideon.'

'Whew. Wow, Ok. What can I help you with?'

'A warning. If you print the libelous article accusing my father of arson.'

'You're threatening me.'

'If you print it, your Point Breeze apartment will burn.'

'You're threatening me. I'll call the police.'

'Call them. I'll deny I ever called you.'

'You'll hear from the police.'

'Listen for matches being struck.'

He hung up.

* * *

Wow and *whew*... Lars had gotten great news – Gideon Moss had texted: Razor had woken and was home! Lars' fingers shook as he keyed in his reply. 'Can I see him?'

'Yes. He'd like to see you. Can you come over now?'

Lars covered the schematic on his workbench and raced up the steps.

'Mom – Razor woke up!'

'Awww, that's good news. You going to see him?'

'I am outta here…!'

*   *   *

'Reverend Gonferally,' said the Station Manager Humphrey Moore, 'we've given you plenty of leeway. Especially in this low-rated time slot. You have never strayed from the Gospel message. We don't pre-check your shows for content. I have to tell you that we were surprised to get phone calls to the station, almost immediately. Can I see the script?'

Tuck moved to the podium and handed it to Moore. 'I know. It's a risk, perhaps.'

Moore studied the sheet. 'You really want to offer this?'

'I wouldn't be presenting something that wasn't true.'

'Hmm. You've been good. But your source is unnamed. Can you identify them?'

'I can't divulge.'

'Hmm. Hmmmm.'

They had been on the static card for five minutes.

'Ok,' said Moore. 'Go back live, and wrap it up as you want. Don't deliver the last part here, til I get a chance to share it with the board. Do you have something for twenty minutes, to fill?'

'Actually, I'd rather you stuck with the card and just hold til the next show. I don't think I can come in, and just pretend I'm teasing the front of something profound, and then not saying it.'

'Ok. Listen, this is compelling material. I'm interested in knowing more. Maybe some idea of your source.'

'Thank you, Humphrey. Praise the Lord.'

*　　*　　*

'Who's the bastard?'

Carmen was up in arms. Cardle had gotten the story back from her editor, and he'd approved it, with the caveat that she definitely get a statement, or at least rebuttal, from Gideon Moss. 'Make sure you state that you gave him an opportunity to respond. Remember Watergate. Or at least, the movie.' Her editor was in love with Woodward and Bernstein's epic bring-down of Nixon's corrupt administration and seemed to think even the rangiest story might break open into that kind of 'big thing.'

Now, this Moss character's son, fresh off a coma, was threatening to burn down her house.

'Who is the bastard? Give me his phone number.'

'This is getting sticky deep,' said Cardle. She handed across her phone. Carmen dialed Razor's number.

'Hello, Moss? Ray Moss?'

'Cardle. You sound annoyed,' said Razor.

'Is this Ray Moss?' asked Carmen, her voice hot.

She punched the button for speaker phone, so Cardle could hear.

'Who is this?' said Razor.

'Carmen Walker. You called and threatened Riley Cardle, about the newspaper article.'

'She chicken to talk? She hiding?'

'We're lining up lawyers and the police. Get ready to be busted.'

'Your buddy Cardle spent a long afternoon recently with an underage teen. Lars Patton. He's what – maybe 16 or 17.'

'Didn't your mother teach you ethics?'

'Let's all go lawyering, if you wish. Some nice touches by your friend Cardle – molesting minors, spying on nuns, writing unsubstantiated claptrap so she can make some cheap cash, make some cheap noise.'

'You don't have any idea what's coming down, Moss. Your family is already known for its arson habits. You're toast.'

'Listen for matches being struck.'

The phone went dead.

Carmen stared at Cardle, steaming. 'He's an A-grade asshole. Must still be concussed. You should call the police *now*.'

'I will, but let's go a little slower. I got to make sure I have answers to the accusations,' said Cardle.

*   *   *

Boneseed twelfth, the silvermare, had surfaced in the furthest, most isolated section of Frick Park, below the slag dumps and rocky hillsides above Nine Mile Run, where debris from decades of industrial waste mixed with just-hanging-in-there weeds and shrubs. The young creature was frail, the water in the trenches less than pure. It wobbled forth, weak and unprepared, though its chrome hide already shone like a skin of light armor. Several rodents approached it as a possible meal. Fortunately for the silvermare, its hind legs already packed a strapping kick. One or two rats were dispatched, and a possum steered clear.

But the beautiful beast was lost. No mother, father, or kin to protect or teach it. It had, perhaps, spawned too soon. *Boneseed Thirteenth* might have orchestrated some sort of defense, for this nereBegat and indeed all of them, in these earliest and riskiest days. The silvermare was also highly visible, even as it tried to move into thicker woods and a modicum of safety. Soon enough, some human would spot it and either capture it or worse.

With a measured gait, it paced slowly along the stream, back towards a more dense part of the forest, where it might hide and gain strength. A leaf here, a sip of water upstream, a delicate and cautious ingestion. It raised its chrome head in the gloaming of the evening, and sounded out a melodious, singular *neeeeighhh*. The owl turned its head. The fox listened. The silvermare stooped again, appreciating the song in its own voice, and licked a small slug into its mouth. The slug was the leopard pillbox slug. Once ingested, it separated the water molecules inside the silvermare into hydrogen and oxygen. Both the silvermare and slug perished.

The creature's carcass was mistaken by walkers for discarded foil, or the reflection from some partially-submerged metal. It slowly decayed, reduced to a green-silver dust which dispersed in the wind and the rain, a melancholy swansong to its short life.

*   *   *

It was time. Emma knew it.

Despite her hopes, there was nothing here at the Seton Hill Motherhouse that had provided her some novel horizon of headway. She could *dick around* forever, streaming ruminations within philosophy, science, theology, psychology, and the remainder of an endless list of what ultimately were distractions, not solutions.

It was time to get back to Gamma and face the celestial music. Her husband was in deep, and needed her. She needed him, in whatever form their marriage and love would now take. And her girls, her flesh and blood offspring, those three miracles-within-a-miracle: she could see them and hold them and laugh with them and cry with them, and if it came to it, considering the forces in play, die with them.

She let Roaringman know she'd be leaving the Charity Motherhouse, and asked him to take over the autopsy on the banedagger. He refused, and let her know her assumption that he might was an encroachment on whatever bond they had generated. She was mildly surprised, only mildly, as she felt an increasing detachment from people in general. She and Grey Cloud had shared significant interchanges. Both would move on. Emma had no idea how her own family would register, how they'd see her and she'd see them, now, in her malleable, un-wrought, over-fated condition.

The head of Biology at Seton Hill, Daniel Greystone, told Emma the cooler-with-X could remain til the end of September when the University's fall classes would be in session. Student research would grow as the semester went forward, and lab spaces and equipment would be reserved for their use.

She thought of bringing it back to Saint Anselm, and just as quickly dropped the idea. She remembered that she needed to contact Gideon Moss and let him know she'd like to return to work. She hoped Sister Antioch might be an intermediary. She still wanted to avoid Moss. It wasn't Moss in himself: it was his connection to all things Eden she didn't want. She'd have enough of that at home.

Sr. Jill arranged to have her taxied to Regent Square. She only had to call Abel.

'Helloooo.'

'Honey! Hello. I love you.' Abel's voice broke happy.

'You have room there? I hear the house has some resident lodgers who refuse to stay young and are crowding up the works.'

'Oh, Emma. You jest not?'

'I jest not. I jest want to join the – what is everyone calling everyone – the *Banshee Patrol.* I can be, like, a den mother.'

'*Ahhh,* Emma....'

'Hey, listen. You have been so kind and understanding. Not expecting a red carpet. Haven't figured out anything.'

'Not becoming a nun, then.'

'So many good souls up here one begins to do penance by comparison alone.'

'How about your theoretical gentleman acquaintance guy?'

'Roaringman is quite a fellow. We can invite him over some night. Wine and cheese and quantum mechanics. Seedy heads can actually work out some of this. Mine did, so yours should.'

'Listening to him and the girls talk relativity would be a riot.'

'Oh God,' said Emma.

'We try not to overuse that around here.'

'Ok, Mr. Green. On that metaphysical delectation, I'll say goodbye. Sr.

Jill has arranged to get me back to Gamma. Probably this weekend. Friday if that works for you,' said Emma.

'I'll have to check my bowling schedule…' Emma could hear her husband succumbing to the idea their full-on contentment might return, over the phone line, though it was silent. She wouldn't try to guess. It was Ok to be so loved, that she never doubted. The rest, well, it was the rest.

'See you then wife. In the flesh,' said Abel.

'In the flesh,' said Emma.

*   *   *

Lars knocked on the door of the Moss Whipple Street home. Razor answered it.

'Lars, come on in, my friend.'

'My friend?'

'*Yes, yes, yes,* don't dally out there in the heat. Come in and let's make the future.' Razor waved Lars into the living room. Gideon stood by the bookcase, his hands in his pockets.

'Mr. Moss, hello,' said Lars. 'Thanks for the money. Really helped.' Gideon nodded, slightly. 'And Razor, you nutball. You actually woke up. Everybody thought your brain was fried,' said Lars, taking a seat on the couch.

'I'm renewed, and we three are all apple blood relatives, if we consider your squirrel bite and your green head to be affliction by association.' He grinned.

'Lost here, fellows.'

'Lars Patton, did my dad never even explain why he wanted the tree dug up? Father, will you elucidate for Lars?'

Gideon rubbed at the back of his head, and crossed to the window.

'We can't keep Lars in the dark,' said Razor. 'He was your right hand collaborator. He's like your adopted son, is he not? *One touch of nature makes the whole world kin.*'

'You know, Ray, Lars doesn't want to listen to your Bard-speak,' said

Gideon. 'Why don't you can the drivel?'

Razor leaned towards Lars. 'My father, I love him dearly. But we're at a crossroads. Since he won't tell the tale I'll give you the full staging, as far as I am able, as far as the apple and the tree and the fire and your rather gormless green hair.'

'Don't look so bad,' said Lars, running his hand through his scalp. 'Getting kinda used to it.'

'Father hired you to purloin that tree because it's straight out of the original Garden, as in *Eden*. He had a bite of that tree's apple, and was krelled in the cranium.'

'Krelled?'

'Obscure reference to *Forbidden Planet* movie, where advanced Krell civilization rocked-on with brain-boosting apparatus. We could watch it tonight, if you want. Based on *The Tempest*, by William Shakespeare. Did I tell you how father never let me do theater, because he's *derealized?*'

Gideon left the room.

'Dad's touchy. Listen, Lars. This whole thing has gone rather mad. I'm not back to where I was. I won't tell you how I hit my head. What I want is your assistance figuring out what the green chemistry in your Nature Center fire affected in the park.'

'Hey, we *both* want to know that.' Lars interlaced his fingers. 'Feel bad for your dad, dude. And you. I'm so glad you're up and around, anyway. I should leave soon. You both need to recover. Rest. Something.'

'Unfortunately you informed to that reporter. In her story, she's planning to implicate my father in the crime.'

Lars made the kind of face that combines innocence and guilt in equal measure.

'I've threatened her,' said Razor. 'If she publishes – we'll burn down her house.'

Lars stared, then swallowed. 'Well, it all happened. Facts are facts. In case you didn't figure that out by now.'

'What would be fortuitous is if you deny everything she prints and testify that she tried to come on to you, sexually, when she took you to Greensburg. Your word against hers.'

'Man. What are you talkin' about? I'm not even *in* her story. She promised to hide my identity.'

'My father thus takes the rap. You remain innocent, uncompromised.' Razor paced, hand to chin. 'Lars, you have to realize you *will* be found out, and implicated. That reporter can't accuse Gideon Moss of arson without a source, in a public forum. I'm surprised she's even thinking of publishing.'

'I'm already doomed, Razor,' said Lars. 'My Mom's gonna bust a gut from all this. I'll be expelled and probably end up in a circus freak show or something. Can't we derail this whole mess and return to civility and whatever they used to consider normal?'

'There is nothing either good or bad, that thinking makes it so.'

'Yeah. Why don't *you* run off and join the circus. I gotta get home.' He stood up. Razor followed him to the door.

'Lars. Here's my proposal. You call the reporter, you deny the Cardle story, which clears my father, for now. Tell her she should never had tried to seduce you. You let me know if you get any ideas about what the green snowflakes caused in the park. If you come through, we won't have to burn your house down.'

'You're on a real kick. What happened to your head, man? I'm the one who's supposed to be wrestling with my conscience.'

Lars stepped out onto the porch.

'Do you know the Green sisters? The three girls born in February and now, like, ten years old. They're on to all this stuff. You should talk to them and leave me alone. Because, Razor, you are definitely crazy.'

He started down the front walk and turned.

'Don't burn my house down, man. Get some help.'

'I don't want to cause you pain,' said Razor. 'This is something for my father. And me. We seldom got to play catch while I was growing up.'

He called out as Lars walked away. 'It's also for the Universe. Will be cool, once we figure out what the fuck it is.'

*   *   *

Tuck Gonferally called his clergy friend Father Jack Murray and arranged a meeting. They met at the Schenley Park Golf Course Clubhouse and sat near the big windows, where you could see downtown Pittsburgh and watch golfers miss practice putts.

'I have to bring you on the show, Jack. Our Board will not allow this to go forward unless you agree. They're not asking for identities or locations of the so-called Eden story. But they feel, understandably, this is a serious proclamation to set forth without attestation.'

'Oh Tuck. I'm not sure I can deliver.'

'Well now, we're stuck. I mean I'm stuck, in this middle. How can I go on again and tell my audience last week was a ruse?'

'You can't. But we did agree, that I'd be left out. You made the choice to go forward knowing that.'

'All I'm asking is you talk to your Bishop. He's in on some of this, right?'

'Yes and no.'

'Well, call the Pope, then. Or me and my show are a goner.'

*   *   *

The batbird took to the air, its four wings providing ample loft and enabling precise navigation. Its internal 'radar' imbued it with directional virtuosity. It could rise, flip, drop, and twist in tight spaces without impacting solids. But it was still young, and didn't fly far before tiring. Other birds, some small mammals, and one bull mastiff terrier on a leashed walk in the park near the area being cleared for the new Nature Center, wondered at the disorienting pitch of audio they felt in both their ears and their muscles.

*　　*　　*

The Green sisters got permission to visit Lars at 444 Hutchinson. Dan Vaz would drop them off after their band practice. The girls had come up with several new songs, along with covers of the Kruger Brothers, Doc Watson, and more Gordon Lightfoot.

August was winding down, with September, and the start of school, around the corner. Lars had recused himself from everything but his HUX lab and food his sister tossed down to him. Going back to school seemed almost ludicrous. But, technically speaking, he had no excuse. The green hair hall pass would no longer cut it. And what was he supposed to do about Razor Moss? Lars wasn't going to retract his confession. If the Cardle article was printed, Razor might torch his house. That premise was easy to visualize, considering he himself had been party to the Nature Center fire. More than party ~ *he'd lit the bloody match!*

His narrow way out was to get some trade-able assets from the Green sisters. What did they know about the new Eden? Would they tell him? If he could finish the X-Tector, using their schematics, he'd have a way to placate Razor. He'd get the Green sisters to let him borrow the thing, and he and crazy Razor could do an expedition in the park, of their own.

The X-Tector build was going halfway well, with his magnified mental capacities. These Moss threats were screwing with his focus, though, and with schoolwork joining in it was going to be a hellish compendium of manic bedlam. With Lars positioned at bedlam central.

He couldn't tell his mom about any of this. Astrid, of course, with her sixth sense and unfair sibling-based intuition, probably knew everything. *Compos mentis.* He needed full control of his mind. And he had green hair.

'Lars, your posse is here!' shouted Astrid from the stairwell.

He stood at the bottom and called out his welcome. 'Hullo, Miller, Boyd and Dragon!'

The girls, now looking like eleven or twelve year olds, dashed down the steps. 'Your mom is really cool,' said Boyd. 'She warned us about your explosive proclivities.'

'I'm harmless. In the deadliest of ways.' He grimaced at how stupid he sounded and flushed red.

'How's it going?' asked Dragon.

'Not great, but not terrible. The inceptor-unit needs a triple relay, which I ordered from Amazon yesterday, rush. I'm housing it inside two old walking staffs of my dad's. Bit of a steampunk look.'

'Nice,' said Miller.

'So, sensing calibrators at the ends of the two sticks. Reader-meter up here, you can attach to your belt or backpack with this cable.' Lars demo-ed what by all appearances was a simple-looking apparatus. It made short beeps and vibrated to test pulses, as Lars manipulated various controls. He showed them the small, rechargeable lithium battery housed in the meter.

'Divine divining rod, sisters.' Dragon shared a pleased look with her siblings. Lars wasn't sure exactly what he had been fabricating, to be honest. He thought it best to follow the sketched plans and hoped it would function. His understanding of the science involved was adequate; it was the metaphysical, Black Squirrel aspects that left him in the dark. There was crossover here, two worlds colliding, combusting in awkward and unpredictable ways.

'I want to ask you. You're the Green sisters, and you're in the center of all that's going on, in the park. Not sure you know what happened to me down there.'

'We know you helped our mother with the apple investigation. Think that apple's still up in the school fridge?' asked Dragon.

'Could be,' said Lars. 'But, listen. I'm caught in some stuff. Sketchy stuff.'

'Can we help?' asked Boyd.

'Maybe. How much do you know about the Mosses, Ray and his dad?'

'Gideon Moss had a bite of the apple too,' said Dragon.

'What does that mean?' asked Lars.

'Hmm. I'm thinking we need to clarify some things. You and us,' said

Dragon, glancing at her sisters.

'It would help me, a lot, right now, to hear what you know, and I can clear up my end. I'm involved with the tree. The apples.' He paused. 'And the fire.'

'What fire?' said Miller.

'Cripe, I forgot you guys weren't even born yet.' Lars sat down at his work bench and ran a soldering iron against the end of a brass wire. He watched it melt and smoke.

'Ok, ok.' He took a moment to glance up the stairwell. 'Sorry there's no chairs.' The girls dragged a low bench over nearer to Lars. Miller sat on a wooden crate. 'First of all,' said Lars, 'I know the apples are, like, important. I helped Gideon Moss rip the apple tree up from Frick Park and take it up to his house. It's probably still there.'

The sisters listened attentively.

'But, and God this is the crazy part, I was bit by a black squirrel that night. It messed with my head. And pretty much voided my conscience. I think that rodent came directly from Hell.'

The sisters nodded.

'So after that bite, I agreed…' He paused again to check the stairwell and listen for noise. 'After, I agreed to help Mr. Moss burn down the Nature Center. It was old and practically falling down, and there was no danger of anyone getting hurt. But still, this was *me*, doing this. Kind of stuff idiot bad guys do in movies.'

The sisters listened in silence.

'And that night, some weird green snowflake landed on my head, and now my hair is green and I'm about to go to jail and have my house burned down…' Lars attempted to look both guilty and redeemable.

'You're between a rock and a hard place,' said Boyd. 'I can't speak for my sisters. We don't put a lot of energy into judging. We're very young. Very impressionable. Apparently we know things that people don't get to understand except rarely, some spiritual notions and some additional human-oriented exposition. Am I getting this more or less accurately, Miller and Dragon?' They nodded. 'So to summarize, we wouldn't know what to do with your implied guilt, nor recommend any plan to rescue you. Our ideas are amalgamations across unusual platforms, and we're taking one thing at a time, more or less, though at an experienced speed that also probably differs from a standard human's experience. Not to position us above anyone!'

Lars wanted to smile. The sisters were like a comfortable blanket, surrounding his confusion with detached warmth.

'I'm really out of things to say. Without sounding even stupider,' he said.

'I would propose this,' said Dragon. 'Let's set a date to field test your X-Tector – cool name, by the way – down in the park. Maybe we can use some of that time to explicate our story and hear more of yours. In the end, the task of locating the nereBegat markers, via your neat invention, is our priority.'

'*Explicate?*' said Miller, laughing.

'Yes,' said Dragon. 'We think the boneseeds are releasing now and if we miss a given intervention, these things could travel beyond the park boundaries and get out in the world, and that'd be that.'

'We'd never catch them,' Boyd said, 'or identify if they were appropriate for joining the Earth's species.'

'So you think the green snowflakes set all this in motion?' said Lars.

'Seems so,' said Miller.

'So I pretty much shouldn't go to jail – I should be drawn and quartered by a couple of celestial chariots. Holy double-frickin' mother of feldspar…' Lars tapped two fingers against his forehead. 'And now I sound like Dixon.'

'You will let us know about, maybe, next Saturday for field tests?' asked Dragon.

'Anybody down there want a baloney sandwich?' Lars mother yelled down the stairwell. 'Lars, show those ladies some hospitality. Send them up here. I have some sassafras root beer and potato chips.'

The Green sisters' eyes lit up. They stood and followed Lars up the steps into the kitchen.

*   *   *

The Bishop greeted Father Jack with a cursory hello and led him into the room where they'd met Pancratius some months ago.

'What's on your mind, Jack? I have quite a bit to get done this morning.'

'Well, it concerns the Green sisters. The situation that brought Sister Pancratius to Pittsburgh.'

'I'm not really in the know. You need some ecclesiastical green light, here? Would it not be wiser to consult the group you were part of? It's been largely kept – the incidentals of their story – from the rest of us.'

'Yes. Well.' Father Jack found a kneeler below the stained glass window. He knelt and bowed his head. "Bless me Father for I have sinned.'

*   *   *

By the pricking of my thumbs… something wicked this way comes…'
Gideon stared at his young, wounded, recognizably unmoored only child, who was again tossing out theatrical quotes the way some people seeded their lawns. How does one get to these stations in life, he wondered. For himself, not his child. Somewhere in the middle of this mess, he had to reestablish his ability to serve as Principal of St. Anselm High School. The apple-boost he'd had was helping him, just barely, survive this new edition of his son. And indeed, he was culpable in raising Ray from the *(practically)* dead. Which in retrospect, though done out of familial love, had turned into its own fiasco-cum-disaster.

'Do you want some soup?' Gideon asked. 'I can heat up some chicken noodle.'

'I'm too pent up to eat.'

'Why are you pent up?'

'Because we're awash in mystery, and awash in new energies, and are these energies darkness or light, and are we able to do some bad damage for the winning side. Or good damage for the losing side.'

'That's a mouthful.' Gideon reached for a box of instant soup and tore open the package. 'Well, I'm going to eat.' He microwaved the food, and sat at the kitchen table. He stared at his 'nuked' soup as it cooled, vaguely recalling something of what had once been their life.

Razor wandered around the kitchen, tapping his hands on the cupboards. 'I'm going to lose this advantage you've conferred unto me, Father, from the very special apple. And maybe I'll die. Or slip back into a coma. Thus the reason for my urgency.'

'What's coming that's wicked?' asked Gideon, slurping his hot soup straight from the cup.

'I like the verse. Nothing wicked this way comes. Though maybe a jail term. Maybe some metaphysical false-starts from your fire. I can't delineate the near future.' He sat down across from his father. 'When I woke up, from the coma, I felt the world had restarted. Felt pushed, by some inner voice, to join and accelerate your campaign. But you don't know what this task is. And your attention to your own fate muddles it further. Perhaps we're both in a trap.'

'We may be. I don't want you in here with me, Ray. Razor. My son. We have a dying tree and we might have some role in establishing whatever Eden is attempting to make happen. More and more, I think the Green girls are the key. We need to hear from them what's taking place, and get an idea of the stakes.'

'Lars is our conduit. I prefer not to threaten him. But time is of the essence.'

'It may be. What about the article, the fire piece that will nail me?' said Gideon.

'Yes. That's a problem. Perhaps we should both visit Cardle in person and lay out our terms.'

Gideon heard a knock on the door, and opened it to see two uniformed

Pittsburgh Police officers, and a plain-clothes detective.

'Gentlemen, ma'am. Come in,' said Gideon Moss.

*　　*　　*

Emma came home. Abel opened the front door. The house was a mess; furniture moved, books everywhere, various clothing items strewn around. She dropped her suitcase on the couch and dropped her body into the cushions. Both cats stared at her. *'Kitty kitty kitty…'* They were unamused and wandered away to consider what they thought of her.

'The cats hate me.'

'*I* love you.'

'Where's my mother?'

'She headed out for a walk. Wanted to give us some space.'

'Where's our daughters?'

'In their rooms. *They* wanted to give us some space.' Able sat down next to his wife. She smiled at him, tears welling. 'You're too good to me.'

'I am.'

She pulled back to check his insinuation. He meant this.

'A thousand things you have missed here. Our girls roared through their young youth and are cartwheeling into their teens. You will need to address female biology.'

Emma smiled back greater tears. 'I can imagine my mother would have given it the old college try.'

'Yes. So you see why I'm glad you're onsite, with 24-7 mom availability.'

He pulled her close and kissed the top of her red amber hair. 'And I am in arrears – if you'll excuse the term – of showering kisses across the lovely terrain of your body.'

They fell together and, once again, appreciated each other's mouths, and arms, and hands, and lips. The cats, observing from a perch in the next room, were silent.

*   *   *

Father Jack had been informed he would not be on Tuck's show, nor be able to say Mass for two months, as discipline for breaking the confidentiality of the 'Square Miracles' events. Bishop Garner had contacted both Sr. Ignatius and Sr. Pancratius about Fr. Jack's lapse. They were merciful, but Pancratius was strident in her argument that the situation could become unwieldy, and rapidly, if connections were made to the Green family, or any of the associated individuals, occurrences or pertinent locations. Fr. Jack seemed reluctant to admit how much he'd revealed to the televangelist (a qualification that had raised a bright red flag), and in fact, he hadn't been part of the *Fireworks* summit, nor had any ongoing doings with the Greens. Nevertheless, it had been an unusual trespassing of good sense and would rock parishioner trust if it all came to light. Tuck Gonferally, in a letter from the Diocese of Pittsburgh, was asked, cordially, to say nothing more about the Square story. He was also informed that Fr. Jack would be unable to see him, including for golf, until the following spring.

*   *   *

It was the Labor Day holiday, a three-day weekend. Lars finished the X-Tector. School started on Tuesday. Lars had had no additional contact with the Moss 'boys'. He texted Dragon and asked when she wanted to get into the park for some trials. Fall weather was freshening the air.

*   *   *

Emma and her daughters had no barriers between them; Miller, Boyd and Dragon were in awe of their mother, in all the ways a child can be, but in this case compressed and contained then released and bestowed with heaps of pent-up affection. Abel observed it all with the widest of grins.

They decided to mount a family picnic in the park, before Emma had to go back to teaching after the weekend (for which she was ill-prepared but determined to do). No miracle-working, no visits to the Garden.

Miller had to leave her glass walking staff at home, and Boyd her aziwheel, though Dragon could bring her mouth harp to provide a bit of musical cheer. Etta and the Vazyovichs would join them, a last hurrah, as the girls no longer needed – if ever they had – chaperoning. They would march into Frick Park and reclaim it: a longish hike down along the Tranquil trail, towards Commercial Street, pick up the Nine Mile Run trail, right turn onto the Deer Run trail, then finishing on the Iron Gate trail, where they could top out at the Squirrel Hill 'Blue Slide – Crazy Park' playground. Water fountains, restrooms, monkey bars, see-saws, ladders, and a famous cement slide that wasn't so much enjoyable as a necessary rite-of-passage for Pittsburgh kids. The ride was cement-bumpy, was not slippery, and fairly short. But it was still cool.

Abel was steeped in a rare contentment. This stolen bit of normalcy could be meted out in the days and weeks to come, as the Greens' headed into their unknowable future. A small caveat appeared when Emma and Able were informed that Lars Patton wanted to show them the X-Tector invention he'd prototyped.

'*Nope!* No hocus-pocus, all non-earth predicated activities are prohibited. Text Lars to test it himself and get back to you,'

'Ok, Dad,' they all nodded.

*　　*　　*

Standing at the front steps to the Moss home, the two police officers and a woman dressed in plain-clothes flashed their credentials.

'I'm Officer Johnson. This is Officer Marshall. Detective Baker.' They nodded their 'hellos'. 'We've received a complaint from Ms. Riley Cardle. Your son Raymond allegedly told Ms. Cardle he would burn down her house if she printed an article, in which you, Gideon Moss, are accused of starting the Frick Park Nature Center fire.'

'Come in,' said Gideon Moss. The three officials moved to the front hallway. Razor watched from behind his father.

'Hell is empty and all the devils are here,' Razor said softly.

'What was that, son?' said Officer Johnson.

'My son is just out of a coma, three days ago, recovering from a traumatic brain injury,' said Moss. 'Ray, can you leave us for a moment?'

'I would never leave you thus.'

Gideon opened his hands to the officers. 'You see.'

The detective moved forward slightly, around Moss, to address Razor.

'Raymond Moss. Did you call Ms. Cardle on Thursday of last week?'

'I'm just out of the Remediation Center. I have loose screws.'

'You identified yourself to her and made this threat, according to Ms. Cardle.'

'Loose.'

'We'll need you both to come down to the station and make a full statement. Mr. Moss, you can supply medical documentation, for your son's condition,' said Officer Johnson. 'We'd also like to get a statement from you, Gideon Moss, concerning the Nature Center fire. According to Ms. Cardle, you are implicated in this event, which occurred last November. You should know that the investigation into the fire has never been backgrounded. Significant traces of explosive materials and combustibles were found at the site. We've known it was arson.'

'Cardle called me and accused me. I explained about the teen who lit the fire. She was having none of that.'

'We'd like to see both of you at the Squirrel Hill Zone 4 Police Station, on Northumberland St., on Tuesday at 9:00 a.m. Please be there promptly and bring any pertinent information concerning these accusations. Also be aware Ms. Cardle's telephone number will be on a trace alert, so that any calls or texts you might make to her between now and Tuesday will be intercepted by us, and may be used in a court of law.'

'Tuesday is the return of students for the new academic year, at St. Anselm High School, where I'm Principal. Can we move the meeting date, or time?' said Moss.

'No,' said Office Marshall. 'Good day to both of you.'

With that, the three turned and departed.

'Where is God in all this, I wonder?' asked Razor, staring after the officials with a face Moss had not seen before. 'We could use a little help from the big deities, yes, Father?'

*   *   *

Ok, the police are on this. I feel better.

Riley Cardle was still not sure what the knock-on effects would be from her article. It was a combo smear-and-release, so to speak. It would certainly garner attention, and readers, and maybe some notable buzz for her reporting work. Or it could combust into a big legal and personal mess. She decided she'd go for it. No charges had been filed against either Moss. But she knew charges *would* be filed. So it should be safe to publish. Bernstein and Woodward didn't have criminal indictments in the bag as they began to name names. Watergate would never have broken open if they hadn't taken those risks.

She laughed at how, in the current political and news environment, the Watergate crimes seemed so petty and JV squad-ish. She hoped the country and its politics would stay on the decent side, even if she couldn't manage it in her own profession.

Buy tickets for her and Carmen to fly to Utah. Cardle made a note to do that. Carmen loved the National Parks. They could get away for a couple weeks after the story was published, get outta the hot kitchen, as it were. Bryce National Park had amazing hoodoos, peculiar rock features eroded over eons, surrounded by a maze of trails inside red canyons, under overhangs, and past gnarled bristlecone pine trees. They could get to know each other away from all the madness. For a while, anyway. Even though it would pretty much empty her bank account, it would be worth it. Not even to mention avoiding a Moss-instigated inferno.

Ok, call my editor. Do a rewrite that specifically nails Gideon Moss with the crime, and confirms him as mastermind. I'll need to identify Lars Patton in this. Poor kid. Dumb kid. I should warn him. I can't. Time to jump into my own little fire. Finish off this fiasco, for all parties.

*　　*　　*

Tuck prayed, asked for anything he could get. Seemed that God didn't mind the story coming to light. Tuck should go ahead, and even use the censorship at his own station as a calling card to be invited as a guest speaker elsewhere. His revelatory dispatch would trend well on a more *'End times ~ Revelations'* type broadcast, where this spiritual epiphany would really land. He wouldn't do it for publicity, or fame, or ratings. And he wished he wasn't endangering the vocation of his good friend Father Jack. But why should God want to sneak this miracle in, for only a few to gain from? Right in our neighborhoods, right in our laps. We've gone two thousand plus years without this kind of visit. We need it, oh Jesus, oh yes, we need it and thank You.

*　　*　　*

Sister Loyola Ignatius was prepping for the high school semester, as were other faculty and staff. Gideon Moss was returning as Principal, and she wasn't sure how she might personally and professionally navigate their necessary academic association. She wouldn't quit. She thought of reading him a version of the riot act, as a kind of first-strike warning should he step out of line in the slightest fashion. All roads led to problems. He might accuse her of some sort of seduction episode. He might bring the school to some new nadir, with his faith and constitution so riddled. Or he might just be a human she wanted no part of seeing or working with. And that last was the *rub,* as the English put it. Charity and forgiveness required she find a way to his good heart. Bypass his human frailties and stir the grace buried in him, as in everyone.

Father Jack might have some guidance. She set up a meeting. She surmised that Jack himself could use a talk, after partially disclosing the Greens' adventures to a *televangelist,* of all people.

*   *   *

The batbird nereBegat flew away, north, towards Lake Erie, and past there, into Canada, then east towards Greenland. It reached colder air, and, using its unique radar, hunted a pocket of warmth. It was September. The wind picked up. Ice came down, suddenly, on its leathery, feathery wings, all four. It fell from the sky and froze to death.

Boneseed tenth, the black rose, was growing through the soil, in a small alcove below the Rollercoaster trail. Poison ivy and a circlet of small white flowers grew near it.

Boneseed sixth, the fruit of life, sprouted not far below Gamma Way, under the great sycamores near the Green residence.

*   *   *

Lars roped Dixon into his X-Tector prototyping excursion. 'Necessary for your continued membership in the HUX Exploratory Space-Vacuum Zounds Fraternity,' stated Lars solemnly, when Dixon once again threw up the weak excuse of a chess club gathering.

They headed down into the park. To avoid the crowds, they'd selected the area under the Parkway East bridge as a good place to do their first 'divine divining'. It was technically still Frick Park, though less frequented due to the slag and trash and less sylvan feel of the area, compared to the beauty centered all around Fern Hollow.

*   *   *

The Green entourage left for their hike. Etta and the Vazyovichs would drive to meet them at the playground, so their less-young legs wouldn't tire from a too-lengthy stroll.

Boyd led the way, with Emma and Dragon behind, and Miller and

Abel in the rear. All carried backpacks. Abel started whistling the *Colonel Bogey March* and soon they were all humming, harmonizing, and adding a sturdy drum beat. Dragon pulled out her mouth harp, taking the whole thing to epic proportions, until Emma suggested they chill it back for other people trying to enjoy this last bit of summer.

*   *   *

'Dix! The sticks!'

Lars yelped. The X-Tector, divine model-A.1 prototype, was zinging. The register unit at his belt was sending a strong wave of pulses. As Lars moved the sticks he held out in front of him, the pulses weakened or strengthened.

'Can I try?" asked Dixon.

'No! This actually works!'

'Did you think it wouldn't?'

'*How the fu…* how in hades was I supposed to know!'

They were walking on the last bit of the Nine Mail Run trail; it would soon meet Commercial Street, and led them downstream to the area they thought to use for testing.

'God *damn!*' said Lars.

'Can you for once stop swearing.'

'Dix*!*'

'I get it. It's exciting. What the fig are we supposed to see?'

'I think it might be in the water.' said Lars.

'Pity the critters that have to drink that stuff,' said Dixon. They moved to the water's edge. The pulses grew louder.

On the trail behind them they heard a group, whistling, coming in their direction. From the water, a large grey-blue manta leapt into the air, raising volumes of liquid, and draped with a plastic grocery bag. At the apex of its arch, it emanated an ear-splitting screech. Lars and Dixon crumpled, grabbing their heads and pitching into the mud beside the water. Dixon was bleeding from his ears. The family behind were suddenly in a circle around them.

'Lars, it's Emma.' Mrs. Green was leaning over him. All had flat palms over their ears, feeling the same exquisite spike of pain. Emma reached for Dixon. 'Dixon. It's me, Mrs. Green, from the school.' She cradled his bleeding head. All could hear the pulses of the X-Tector.

'Abel, we have to get him to help,' she said.

Dixon stirred awake, folded into a fetal curl. 'Oh God, *oh fuck…*'

'He never swears,' said Lars

Abel lifted Dixon up to sit. The boy started crying. Abel spoke to Emma. 'Get him out onto Commercial. Flag down a car.'

'Lars - what about you?' asked Emma.

'Ahh.. it's hurting less.' Lars tilted his head to the side, tapping at his ear, as if to drain the pain out of his head. 'Starting to be able to hear you.'

'Dragon, Miller, Boyd, you all Ok?' Boyd had taken over use of the X-Tector. Her sisters were at the water's edge, studying the swirl of eddies that didn't seem to coincide with the current. The water flowed strongly, moving into three large concrete pipes that ran under Commercial Street. Metal grates captured the solids, both human and natural made dross, creating a kind of ugly dam, which the water struggled to flow beyond.

'We're Ok, yes. Something's in the water.'

'We have to get Dixon to a hospital. Can you take care of each other?' asked Abel.

'Yes. We think it's the snapper manta. Another shriek could bust everyone's eardrums.' said Boyd.

Dixon moaned. Abel lifted him to his feet, as Emma steadied them.

'Ok, be careful, you three. Lars?'

'I'm coming,' he answered.

Abel, Emma, Lars, and Dixon hurried off towards the road.

*

A grey-blue fin, a leathery wing, splashed briefly above the water's surface; the thing was swimming close to the metal grates that blocked it from advancing downstream, to the river, to the ocean. If it got past, based on its speed, it would outrace the sisters and reach the Monongahela, where their ability to catch it, and pass judgment on its continuing existence, would vaporize.

Boyd parked the X-tector in her backpack.

'Wish I had my glass,' said Miller. 'I don't want to spear it, but that sound.'

'Yes. Be ready to hold your ears and exhale,' said Dragon.

'I'm going to head downstream, to Hidden City, in case it gets through,' said Miller. 'Not sure how I can corral it. So follow if it gets past here.' She raced off, on unfallen legs at unfallen speed.

'Look. It's starting a whirlpool, like it might jump again,' shouted Boyd. 'We better follow Miller. No way we're going to trap it here.'

The snapper manta sprung in a mighty leap from the stream, accompanied by a skull-splitting, brain-piercing sound, thrusting with all its unholy strength to surmount the barrier that kept it from its future.

Out on Commercial Street, Emma waved her hand, trying to flag down a car. Everyone bent, suddenly, and covered their ears. Above their heads, they watched as the shrieking manta propelled itself in an unwieldy flight over the road, then plunged back down into Nine Mile Run. A tremendous splash followed.

A car, its driver distracted by the clamor and implausible sight, veered suddenly, braking and skidding. The vehicle hit the wooden parking fence near the Frick Park entrance sign, snapping it. The engine sputtered, then kicked back on. The driver, an elderly man, appeared to be knocked out. Abel and Emma attended to him as best they could, then helped Dixon get in. Lars followed, and they all careered up the hill towards Shadyside Hospital.

*

Miller had almost reached Hidden City when she stopped to catch her breath. She hurried under the rusting iron railroad trestle, and jumped down into the water of the outflow, where Nine Mile Run met the Monongahela River. A few fishermen and women had lines cast nearby from the Duck Hollow landing, some looking uneasy at the noise they'd heard coming from upstream.

The manta was swimming with its growing might, tensing its lungs for a penultimate release of sound, one that might break any further obstacles choking its journey to freedom.

Dragon and Boyd were not far behind, but unable to match its frenzied speed. They glimpsed splashes and eddies, and swirls of churned water convulsing in the thing's wake.

'Must be pretty amazing biology,' panted Boyd.

'Killer, possibly, if you are close enough when it screams,' yelled Dragon over her shoulder.

The manta plunged forward, under the railroad bridge, bracing its newborne musculature for a powerful hurdle beyond this gateway and into the river.

Miller had waded into the center of the outflow, hardly to the level of her knees here, spread by the submerged flats before deepening again towards the river's middle. She stood poised against a thing created outside of time, released into an unforgiving present.

The manta rose, then pumped its fins against the water with otherworldly brawn. It rose directly over Miller, who knew only to drop and hold her ears. The sound shattered stones, cracked an iron abutment of the bridge, and threw a dozen fisher-people down into the shallows. The echo resonated up and down the Mon valley, juddering the Homestead High Level Bridge, terrifying the occupants on it, and sluicing water upon the near shores.

The manta fell, driven by its inertia, smashing into the water, water shallower that it could have known. It skidded under, bayoneted by razor-sharp fish hooks, which broke from their lines and rods, as it furrowed into the sludge. Open-mouthed, the creature swallowed volumes of the river's bottom-dwelling detritus: bits of discarded tires, rusting cans, rotting bones. It turned upside down, thrashed in pain, and choked, its short life disappearing into the murk, to be carried down and beyond the dams, to the Ohio and Mississippi, where it could at last join the salt water of its hoped for destination. It would not survive its wounding.

Miller raised herself from the muck. On the shoreline, people were helping one another, their ears bloodied. Miller felt a small trickle from her own ear.

'Miller!' It was Dragon, soon followed by Boyd, both reaching for their sister.

'I'm Ok. That poor thing, though. It was floating downstream on its back.'

'Oh, geeze,' said Dragon.

'It caught fishing lines when it went in, would be bleeding all over. The water was too shallow. Where it hit.'

'It's awful…so sad,' said Boyd. She turned away from the river.

'I don't know what we could have done for it, anyway,' said Miller. 'Man, that thing packed a punch.'

They stared at the scene, watching cars slowly continue their journeys on the overhead bridge, and nearby, people leaving the fishing dock by foot or vehicle. Red and blue police lights flashed from across the river at the Waterfront shopping center.

'This is gonna make the evening news,' said Dragon.

'We better get back. Hope Dixon is Ok. Wonder if Etta and the Vazyovichs heard that shriek up in Crazy Park?' said Miller.

'They had to,' said Boyd. 'Hey, look.' She pointed to the middle of the river. The Green sisters had exemplary vision, well beyond 20-20, and thus were all able to read the small text that appeared, worn and faded, on a piece of what appeared to be perspex, a transparent material used in WWII aircraft cockpits. It had snagged on one of the broken fishing lines and the fast current had pulled it up from some place under the river's base.

'Northrup B-25 Mitchell,' said Miller, her face as blank as her tone.

'Are you kidding me? You know that stuff?' said Dragon.

'Dad's DNA, must be,' she said.

'How'd it get in the river? Ask Dad's DNA about that!' said Boyd.

'No idea.' They turned to retrace their steps, passing a throng from Hidden City who wandered cautiously toward the dock where something big had obviously happened.

*   *   *

'Father. The Green sisters. Lars said they would know. They're on the *inside*, you see, while you're on the *outside*, of the same grand theater playing out here. You are a pawn, they are queens. Until you get what they have, you won't be able to win this game.'

Razor paced in the bedroom where the tree stood in its bucket, its brown leaves hanging in the stale air.

'We'll take this tree back to where you pulled it out. There's a chance the soil there is the magic. If it regains its health, we get more fruit. You have the seeds?'

'Yes. I carry them. Right here,' said Gideon. He patted his shirt pocket, from which he then took out a small vial. Inside were a few seeds, maybe five. He shook it gently. 'I don't think we can go to the police appointment, Razor. They have Lars' testimony. I'll lose my job, regardless.' He shook the vial again 'These are precious, and I'm keeping them with me.'

Razor looked out the window, his eyes glazed. 'The article will paint you as a criminal. We should consider action against the reporter.'

'We're not about to murder someone, Razor.'

'This story has not enough tension, my Father. It's leading nowhere. It needs a *villain*.'

He turned and faced Gideon, running a palm across his drawn face. 'We will eat the last of the saved apple pieces. We will take the tree and replant it near where it grew from. Where the poison ivy is most rampant. A place where no one will find it, and if they do, will take no notice. Autumn comes and then winter will follow. We can watch over it. When it fruits in the spring, we will harvest the fruit.'

Razor stretched his arms over his head. 'Tomorrow, apple-enhanced, we will visit the Greens.'

'I'll get a bucket,' said Gideon. 'You understand that if we don't go see the police on Tuesday, I may be arrested.'

'A second helping of Eden apple will help us know how best to proceed,' said Razor.

'It might. It threw my mind into places it had never touched. But look where I am now – about to lose my job and be thrown in a cell.'

'We have to believe in the apple's power, my dear Father. We'll know what to do. Now go get the bucket.'

Gideon looked at his strange son, now a dark reflection of the boy he had once been, and walked down the stairs.

TWENTY THREE

RILEY CARDLE'S STORY went to press.

Her feature-length story was titled *The Frick Park Nature Center - the buried secrets haunting an icon's Death.*

The subheader read: *Strange mysteries, still in play, are coalescing around a group of individuals, all from the Park's neighborhoods, who may be the movers and shakers in this still-unsolved drama. Riley Cardle digs into the disturbed heart of the proceedings, unveiling clues, identifying characters, and predicating where it all might lead.'*

It appeared in the morning edition of the *Pittsburgh Post-Press*, beneath headlines about a train derailment near McKees Rocks, and the unusual disruption that had lit up Duck Hollow yesterday.

*   *   *

On the same day, Tuck Gonferally delivered his Eden sermon on the *Creation Calling* show, on Channel 55. The show's producers were keen to shore up their failing ratings, and Tuck's presentation, they were hoping, would light up the phones with both positive comments and pledges of money.

Tuck's sermon related how a 'Pittsburgh couple, husband and wife, had come upon an apple tree, eaten the apples, and been boosted into an almost angelic orbit'. As he paced the stage, he talked about a *'Regent Square'* miracle (apparently Fr. Jack had accidentally leaked that single identifying location.). He spoke of a new time on Earth, soon to be visited by the cherubic-seraphic offspring that would come from the couple's 'unification' (the best term he could manage on the G-rated broadcast). God had dropped a special grace into their worlds.

As he told his audience…

'We don't have to kneel before this wonder. We don't have to suddenly repent because the end is nigh. We don't have to rush to Regent Square in search of holy relics and physical healing. What I hope we can do, is say a simple prayer of thanks, that we've been given this great blessing, and that we can ask God to watch over all the individuals He has selected for these events, and that God will nurture whatever mission they are reckoned to achieve, and whatever meaning they are able to supply, and whatever faith they are able to boost. We live in an age where science beats down the doors of belief with an onslaught of logic. We live in an age where the scriptures are placed on a quiet shelf, for a quaint reconsideration in challenging times. We live in an age where the very idea of a miracle, a real miracle, taking place in our midst, simply cannot be true. I tell you, from my heart, with all that I cherish as trust between God and myself and all of you, that it is true.'

* * *

Carmen Walker had gotten permission from Dr. Haskley to travel to Utah for a three-week getaway.

'Just don't get a new job out there, Carmen,' he pleaded with a smile.

Cardle's article suggested, based on the deposition of an unnamed under aged accessory-to-the-crime (Cardle had been unwilling to identify Lars after being informed she might be threatened with litigation since he was a minor) that Gideon Moss was the fire's perpetrator. A lawyer allegedly representing the Moss family, Sean Rosmarin, contacted the *Post-Press* offices the afternoon the paper went out.

The administration, faculty and staff of St. Anselm High School soon got the word, via texts and phone, that their Principal was under suspicion for the crime. Sr. Ignatius offered a prayer for Gideon, then began an immediate search for a temporary replacement. She understood it could, in fact, be Gideon who had committed the deed. She understood, to a point, the mitigating circumstances that could have led him to do it, including coercions that no earth-bound police investigation would be able to comprehend. Perhaps she could serve as a trial witness.

* * *

Dixon Nickson was released from the Emergency Department at the hospital after treatment for an 'almost busted' ear drum. Etta and the Vazyovichs had returned to Gamma Way (after Dan had taken one ride down the cement slide). The Greens hoped to use the remainder of the Labor Day weekend for what they trusted would be some rest. Lars left the X-Tector with Boyd, suggesting the girls would be better equipped to handle the next 'beastie' the contraption found.

* * *

Gideon and Razor Moss sat on the floor, opposite one another, surrounded by cushions, leaning against the couch and an easy chair. Razor had queued up music from Wagner. Each had a half of the remaining portion of the Frick apple.

'Ready, Father?' said Razor. Moss nodded.

'See you on the other side, then.'

Razor slid the apple piece into his mouth. Gideon did the same. Slowly, they slumped to the floor.

* * *

Tuck's show drew solid ratings and the show was rebroadcast the next day to a bigger audience. A number of viewers contacted the station, either by e-mail, text, or phone.

Some of the comments were as follows:

'The Bible does not mention any repeat performance.'
'You are a bad person. Bad, bad, bad.'
'These children you allude to, where do they live? We wish to visit them.'
'See your minister, Tuck. Then a psychiatrist.'
'Resign from your job at the station. Sooner is better.'
'Please sell this show as a DVD. We'd like 50 copies.'
'Can you name any real person who can corroborate this story?'
'Science fiction.'
'We are seeing His love, here and now. It's wonderful.'

Tuck felt good about the results. He was not expecting a glorious round of tribute. He didn't expect God to grant him a vision, but knew in his heart the telling was worthy. A jolt of juice for the faithful, that was all it was supposed to be.

* * *

Word got to Bishop Garner that part of the Greens' story had been televangelized. *Tele-vandalized* he murmured to himself. The best course seemed to be to do nothing. There had been no direct connection between the Catholic Church and this episode. Of course, the identification of Regent Square might lead to some sleuth figuring out more specifics, including identities, that were part of the tale. But for now, from his offices, it was officially *no comment,* although no one had yet asked for any.

Father Jack was privately pleased. He wondered how long he could maintain his ministry if he fed more of the story to Tuck, bit by holy writ. A kind of wind was picking up in the sails of its spiritual potentialities. It could unfold as a modern-age tool for reviving faith, a battery-jump for the latent electricity in the most withdrawn of souls, a shot of 100% proof saintly bourbon in the tepid mixes the flock is too often asked to swallow…

He must find a discreet way to again meet with Tuck. A slow feed of more details could grow this testament, helping to expand its reach and verify its tenets. Oh, and he would pray about it first.

*   *   *

'So Ok, young ladies,' said Abel, as they sat on the porch, Emma, Etta, and the three sisters, enjoying the last vestiges of summer, and possibly the last vestiges of the girls' childhoods, 'tell Mom and Grandma and me what you think is occurring, and what we should expect, and what we can do to help.'

'It's not complicated,' said Boyd.

'It's fairly straightforward,' said Dragon. 'We seem tasked to locate the nereBegats, and then cast a verdict as to whether they should continue down here or be dispatched. *Down here* means on the Earth, and in our physical universe. According to the *fiat* list, we've only accounted for the banedagger and the snapper manta. With the X-Tector Lars built, we're planning to get into the park every day –'

'– and for as long as you'll let us stay down there at night,' interrupted Miller.

Dragon nodded, and continued. 'Yes, night, too, and get after the remainder of these things. We think some may already be outside the park. Nothing to be done there, other than keep an eye out in the news. Unless contacting some federal authorities to join the search would help.'

'I doubt it,' said Emma. 'The amount of explaining involved is not going to lead anywhere useful in that regard.'

'I think I'll go make supper,' said Etta, hands on her knees. She rose and went inside.

'Mom is right,' said Abel. 'New species are one thing, naturalists will jump on anything unusual in their vicinities. But we have relatively small, solitary spawnings, creatures maybe struggling to figure out how to even eat and breath. We have those two plants, the *black rose* and the *fruit of life*. We have the *wheelbone*, which may be stationary. A small shiny horse, the *silvermare;* I still can't believe that one made the cut. Point being, these things, though theoretically designed to flourish without begetters or special food or protection, are going to be very, very difficult to find. With or without your X-Tector.'

'So, our daughters in Frick Park at night, Abel. What do you think?' asked Emma.

'I think yes,' said Abel, looking over his young teenaged-in-appearance daughters. 'I can go down with you, but with your abilities, I'd probably be a burden. I can't run – or think – as fast as you can. So yes, tonight would be a good beginning. All of you should take the phone we bought you. Mom and I will keep ours at hand.'

'Ok,' said Dragon. 'This is great, dear Mother and Father. We're aware it's hard for you. But you have some idea now we're not frightened by the creations nor the task.'

'No, you're not,' said Emma.

'Let's grab our kits,' said Miller. The sisters hurried back into the house.

'Those are our daughters,' said Abel, stretching his arm to touch Emma's shoulder.

'I know. Words are useless,' she said, pulling her hair back into a knot. 'I want to know where God was hiding when somebody upstairs engineered this coup.'

*　　*　　*

Gideon Moss woke. The scene was a blur. Above him, a ceiling, a disorienting wash of empty. He struggled to wake, to be sure he had not died, and inhaled a full breath of air. Rubbed at his eyes. Blinked. Looked again. Beheld his son, slumped on the floor across from him, in a ring of green fire. 'I will find the nereBegats and forge their destiny,' said Gideon, forcefully, in the quiet of the room. He lifted a weak hand to his forehead. 'Talking out loud. To myself. Again.'

Razor opened one eye, slowly, stared at his father, spoke. '*A sharpness fiddles with the mind that beckons.*'

Gideon sat up. 'Your mind, wounded when you struck the bricks, I pushed you,' he said. Something of a confession. Something of an apology.

Razor felt around the top of his head. 'I'm damaged. In a waking coma. It's good, Father. It's good.'

'Which Shakespeare are you quoting?' asked Gideon. He nodded his head, wiggled his shoulders against the trance.

'Not awake. Ask me later. I'm thirsty.'

'We should not leave the house.'

'Two apples bites too many. Would we kill, with this?' asked Razor.

'We need time, let our blood cool. This is Eden chemistry – and *nereBegats* – I hear that word, in my head.'

Razor lifted himself up on his elbows. 'The tree, needs to go back to the park. It can grow there.' He glanced at the tree. 'It'll die here.' He began doing slow sit-ups.

'We'll visit the Greens,' said Gideon. 'The three sisters. Find out what nereBegats are. They'll tell us. They'll know.'

He took a deep breath, then stood.

'Raymond. I will love you. If this kills us.'

*　　*　　*

The three Green sisters, the Gamma Way renowned *Banshee Patrol,* the unfallen trio of fast-growing, un-fearing, faith-fired females, were kitted out for their fateful mission.

All had head-mounted flashlights. Each wore gloves and jackets; the September night had turned chilly. Boyd wielded the X-Tector. Miller carried her glass walking staff. The full moon's shine, caught at the right angle in its crystals, could be narrowed into a blue-brown beam of moonlight. Dragon kept her mouth harp in her breast pocket. She thought that, in certain circumstances, the notes from it, played in the right way, might tranquilize some of the nereBegats. This Boyd doubted, her science acumen more and more surgical, spearing false futures as if they were party balloons to pop. A first small crack in the girls' homology, her sister's doubt intrigued Dragon more than bothered her. They needed to get some distance from each other, she felt, and not move through their potentially short lives as a single animate mass of wholeness, thinking the same kind of thoughts and pursuing the same kind of deeds. She explained this concept to Boyd and Miller, who nodded, eyes soft in agreement.

Emma and Abel let Etta know the Banshee Patrol was mobilizing for what could be an overnighter. Etta ran her tongue ruefully against the inside of her cheeks, sighed mightily, and said, 'Wake me when it's over.'

The girls waved at their parents, headed out the door, and turned towards the sycamores, the white trunks like pillars of some great shadowed hall. The moonlight danced briefly on the girls' shoulders, winking out as they disappeared over the slope.

*　　*　　*

Gideon and Razor had both dressed in black. They wanted to be invisible, both thinking their spiked apple supplement might possibly bestow that sort of power. If it did, they couldn't determine a way to bring it about: thinking with effort seemed to brutalize their over-cooked brains, as if the capacity for incredulous fruit-induced brilliance was being undermined by the extreme dosage they'd ingested. It made them breathe faster, and sweat more, and their vision had quickened, feeding photons through their synapses as small darts of sharp light. The power at hand was overloading the circuitry it must run on.

They drove down Commercial Street and parked under the great concrete bridge, its broad pale columns reaching upwards into darkness.

Above, on the roadway, the ceaseless traffic pelted them with its dissonant, mechanized din. Shadows were splotched across the lightless way forward into the park, the Nine Mile Run trail. From the car they brought the tree, flashlights, a small shovel, and a canteen of water. They'd proceed up Firelane Extension, then find some alcove not far from the heart of this preternatural new-age *Eden*, the *ground zero* where this had all begun, where Gideon had fallen, and bitten into his own abbreviated eternity.

As strange as their visual acuity had already become, a startling form of night vision now kicked in. Things took on an infrared-like boost. Colors jumped around, and helped them discern distance and material. Their hearing, also, began to refine. Their earthly bodies were acclimatizing to unearthly chemistries. They put their flashlights away. Off the trail, behind a clutch of thorned shrubs, they identified the spot to plant their tree, a stone's throw from where it had first appeared. They dug a hole, planted the tree, and watered it with the canteen. Razor, gloved, transplanted several plugs of nearby poison ivy around the small trunk. Satisfied, they circled down to Falls Ravine trail, intending to scale the far side steps up into Regent Square, and Gamma Way, where the Greens would be settling down for the night.

*   *   *

Miller, Boyd and Dragon were soon in Fern Hollow. The evening's forest sounds played at the edges of their hearing.

'Up to the Eden tree site first, sisters?' asked Miller, who led.

'Sounds good,' said Dragon, quietly. 'Let's be careful not to make too much noise.'

'We're pretty quiet,' said Boyd.

'Just don't want to disturb the peace,' said Dragon.

'I think we're about to do just the opposite,' said Miller. Dragon touched her on the shoulder, and they kept walking.

As they climbed the gentle slope, they began to notice a soft, barely discernible green glow, off and above the trail. The X-Tector began a steady, faint pulse.

'Up there,' gestured Boyd, pointing with the X-Tector rods she held out in front of her. They all switched off their headlamps.

As the sisters moved towards the glow, the pulse grew in frequency and volume. 'The X-T was not engineered to generate a visual response to its own tracking emanations. Which means it may be *us*, related as we are to all the park's miracle components, who are causing this nereBegat to light up. To identify its own location. To glow.'

'Wow. This makes thing a bit easier. Maybe we didn't even need Lars' handiwork,' whispered Miller. 'Still glad we have it, though. We don't know yet if our presence is causing the glow. Not even sure that's a nereBegat up there, yet*!*'

*　　*　　*

Beneath the moonlight-illumined tangle of branches, Razor and Moss blinked hesitantly at the unusual thing seen with their unusual eyes. Three barely visible halos, green hued, floating gently in lockstep, moving in single file up from the trail, towards the zero ground.

*　　*　　*

The sisters heard footsteps, then felt a muted gloom descend over them, like a great woolen shroud.

'Something's nearby, coming towards us,' Boyd murmured.

'People,' said Miller. 'Most likely. I'm getting a sense that nereBegats may be *drawn* to us, somehow, also.' She glanced at the X-Tector. Its pulses were steady and getting stronger. 'Should we hide?'

'We haven't so far,' said Dragon. 'Squirrel Hillians out for a late walk. No flashlights, though. Slightly weird. Stay frosty.'

'Let's go,' said Miller, pointing.

*   *   *

The upjaw-dropjaw had begun its slime-facilitated crawl down from the South Clayton trail some days ago. It had managed to corral, choke, and eat a few victims, though the torment of distorting its malformed body to manage a teeth-sinking bite from two separated mandibles, and the effort required to finish off its meal – harnessing a grueling mastication to enable digestion – caused it to wonder why it had been born. It was a restless beast, writhing downhill towards another night of physical and existential discontent. There was something drawing it, inexorably, to a small alcove about Falls Ravine trail, where some residue, some hint, of its origins, must have persisted. Maybe it could find the instigator of its sorry plight and repay it. The delicious cracking of soft bones and tearing of moist tissue would make up for a portion of this cruel inheritance.

*   *   *

Razor and Gideon Moss, senses sharpened through metaphysical substances, perceived they'd stumbled, as if fate had arranged it, on the three Green sisters. The halos were mesmerizing: it was apparent each girl possessed her own. Gideon and Razor could track their smallest movements. Conveniently, they'd no longer need to visit Gamma Way, and confront the parents. Their night would play out in a pageant of dark beauty, where chance and providence melded into a single pleasing aggregate. *'Fate, show thy force.'* swore Razor, his brow on fire.

*   *   *

The green glow seen by the sisters emanated from the black rose. Boyd knelt before it. Miller pooled some of the filtered moonlight through the glass rod, illuminating its flowers, its thorns, and its red green stems.

'It emits a small bit of radioactivity. Only the flowers. The danger is the bees harvesting this pollen and producing radioactive honey, and the uncontained spread, and harm to bees and humans,' said Boyd.

'You do know your science, Boyd,' said Miller. 'Should we dig it up? Do we need hazmat suits?'

'Don't touch the petals. It's oxidizing soil and transmuting the photosynthesis with radioactive carbon dioxide. Not really dangerous, yet, because it's young. Output is modest.'

'We should dig it up, sisters,' said Dragon. 'At the very least, it needs to be quarantined.'

Through the green-shaded darkness human footfalls came near. They all turned, hailed by two figures: a tall, stocky man, and another, younger, fidgety and potent.

'Greens,' said a voice.

Miller turned the glass rod to shine on their faces. 'Who are you?'

'Gideon Moss.'

'Razor Moss.'

'Hello,' said Boyd. 'You want to keep back from these roses. Radioactive.'

'We have questions,' said Razor.

'We want to know what's happening in these woods. Since *Eden* has surfaced,' said Gideon.

'And since the fire,' said Razor. 'What did the fire bring about?'

'You know quite a bit already,' said Boyd. She switched on her headlamp, unbuckled the X-Tector from its belt harness, and handed it to Razor. 'We use this to find the nereBegats.'

'What do you want to know?' asked Miller.

'What are *nereBegats?*' asked Gideon.

'Thirteen boneseeds were woken when the Nature Center fire's components reached them. The nereBegats are, let's say, *unapproved* creations from the other side. Beings designed them, beings from the *other side* – if you take my meaning – beings determined that the nereBegats be included in the make-up of Earth's original compact,' said Dragon.

'*Other side.* Other side. Stop hedging. Be specific,' said Razor.

'Whatever you want to call it. Whatever is not here, on Earth. Whatever is way up there, way out there, as in not from our physical universe,' said Dragon, waving her arm towards the treetops. 'It's not easy to explain.'

'You're getting wordy again, Dragon,' said Boyd. 'Let me try. Inside Frick Park are thirteen illegal aliens that may be a mortal risk to the Earth – to humankind – if they are not reviewed.'

'You three, you children, are in charge of this – *this judgment?* This *assessing* of their viability?' asked Gideon.

'It's a bit tricky, as you can imagine,' said Miller. 'Why do you want to know?'

'It may be *our* task,' said Razor, 'my father's and mine, to prevent your interference in this single chance these creations have. Who are you three to cast such a momentous verdict?'

'With due respect, who are you to suggest otherwise?' asked Boyd.

'We want a list, the names and form of all the nereBegats,' said Gideon.

'We'll take this shrub, this glowing rose. We'll take this machine, also,' said Razor, swinging the sensor rods in a broad circle. The pulses responded to the black rose, then thrummed loud, as Razor jerked it towards the back of the alcove.

'It's called the *X-Tector*,' said Boyd. 'Lars Patton built it. Sorry, we can't lend it out right now.' She squinted at the darkness where Razor had directed the rods. 'Something out there. Near.'

*

The upjaw-dropjaw drew close, its approach masked by the human voices. It flexed its lithe, strange body, and sprung, wrapping its length around the neck of Gideon Moss. Moss thrashed, as the beast's upper and lower jaws met, clenched, clamped, squeezed – their double row of serrated fangs sinking deep into his fleshy back. Gideon's mouth opened, but he had no airway to scream.

Miller wielded the glass shaft, wedging it beneath the rippling, slimed coil of the creature, and tried to prise it from Moss. It clung tight, snapping with cruel bites as it fought Moss's wild flailing. Dragon and

Boyd pummeled and pulled at the tendril-like body, until Miller's glass rod finally wrestled it free. Gideon fell, his upper body bleeding profusely. Razor staggered back, stunned.

The upjaw-dropjaw writhed like a corkscrew, maneuvering to pounce again. Dragon and Boyd slammed a heel over each of its necks, as Miller plunged the glass through its middle. It shrieked, twisted in a vain attempt to find flesh, shivered in a last wave of pain, and was still. The bitter green pallor dimmed and passed with its last breath.

Razor's eyes fluoresced in awakened terror. He swung wildly at the sisters. The X-Tector flew out of his grip, landing in the shadows. He shuddered, then flung himself upon his father.

'Dad…*oh please, Father…*'

Eyes welling wet, he rifled through his father's pocket, found the vial with the seeds, opened it, and poured the contents into Gideon's mouth. There was no reaction, no movement, No breath. *'Dad…………………'*

He lifted his father, cradled him, kissed him lightly on his forehead, whispered softly in his ear…

'*…look to the angels…they're near, my Father…they're here…*'

He stood, unsteadily, setting his hand against the slope.

His voice trembled, and then burst –

'You will see me..!'

The shout echoed up the slopes, as he bolted away into the night.

*   *   *

'You think the gals are Ok?' asked Emma. They were lying in their bed, fully clothed, the overhead light bright above them.

'I won't get any sleep, that's for sure,' said Abel. 'What time is it?'

'9:30,' said Emma. 'Should we phone?'

'Not yet.' He stood up. 'I'm going downstairs for a shot of something. Want anything?' They heard the back door open.

'*Early!*'

Abel and Emma hurried down to meet the Banshee Patrol. The girls came in, looking strained, calm, and spent.

'You guys Ok? You don't look it,' said Abel.

Silence and grim smiles.

'Mr. Moss is dead,' said Dragon.

'What??' Emma and Abel turned to gape at each other.

'There are bound to be things, hard things, as this plays out, Mom, Dad,' said Miller. 'Sorry you have to be… privy.'

'Gideon Moss dead. Is he down there? What happened? Did you call the police?' asked Abel.

'We thought about it and decided against it,' said Boyd. 'We left a note, an untraceable note, on his body. The creature that killed him is there, dead. It'll be obvious that its bites killed Mr. Moss. His son, Razor, was there too.'

'Was the only way we could think to avoid postponing what we need to be doing,' said Dragon. 'We're running against time. Can either of you suggest how to get the police down into the park, so they deal with the body before someone finds it in the morning?'

'Or a creature desecrates it,' said Boyd.

Emma wanted to comfort the sisters, at least say something, but could only manage silence. Abel logged into his CMU VPN messenger app. He encrypted a short description of what the girls described, and sent the communication out through various nodes and back around to the Squirrel Hill police.

'It should get to them anonymously,' he said. 'What's to stop Razor Moss from providing your names?' asked Abel.

'Nothing,' said Miller.

'What happened? Can you tell us?' said Emma. She put a finger over her lips. 'And keep it down so we don't wake Etta. She'll have a heart attack. I might have one anyway.'

The sisters told the night's story. Their account of the upjaw-dropjaw, though it had been described in the *fiats*, was bewildering; both its behavior and in its unfortunate physiology.

'Makes you understand why some of the nereBegats were forbidden, placed on the 'no-fly' list, to be locked out,' said Emma. 'Eyes inside ears. Separate jaws at either end of its pathetic body. Terrible way to have to exist.'

'We felt sorry for it,' said Boyd.

'Maybe it was happy – or could have been,' said Abel. 'We can't know.'

'I doubt that, Abel,' said Emma. She turned away.

'One last thing,' said Abel. 'That nereBegat is lying there, the upjaw-dropjaw. And the radioactive flower, too, the black rose. The police might be exposed to radiation. Somebody's going to ask hard questions, if this unravels. Not sure what we'll do if the trail leads back to us, back to you girls.'

He paused, continuing with a softer tone. 'Will you be able to get done what needs done?'

'We brought the rose back. It's over the hillside, behind the house, replanted,' said Boyd. 'Radiation is very low at this point. Tomorrow we can bring it into the basement. Make a small containment for it.'

'Madness. *Madness.* We have to send Etta back to Lancaster,' said Abel, looking for Emma.

She sat near the window, a blanket over her shoulders.

'I can't believe. Gideon Moss,' said Emma. She bowed her head.

*   *   *

The police found the body, the creature, and the note. The strange species found next to Moss's body had mushed into a soupyness that made it less distinguishable from the something it must have been. That it appeared to resemble a snake that had suffered significant birth defects was all the forensics people could deduce.

*　　*　　*

Razor Moss agonized in the abrupt silence. His father, his derealized, long-suffering, imperfect-parenting Dad was no longer part of the Earth's being.

Was there any way to take meaning from the last few hours, weeks, months? The slow draining of whatever merit their relationship held; then the insidious introduction of the Eden elements, ending in his own coma, and forced awakening, and deluded commonality with his father's ineluctable quest.

These things came – oddly – very clearly; unmarred by his recently-acquired less-sound, hardly-hinged, skull-cracked, apple-disrupted brain. *Where did the blame lie?* The Green sisters had tried to save his Dad.

Lurking in the center of his confused chest, was the dark erosion of faith in the things he'd trusted before the curses rained down. His untethered state easily transported his thoughts to nefarious conclusions. His father had deemed the nereBegats worth a judgment, as did the Greens. Whose perspective would champion their cause? Did any of it make any difference? A shocking, additional layer of thought hove into his mind: was this derealization? *Was he now afflicted?* Or was everything a distortion and magnification of the apple-threaded madness that had befallen the Moss brood, the once and future Moss family malediction?

He felt an unholy urge to kill, something he'd never known before. A lust for revenge, not against the Greens, so much, as against existence. But the Greens were handy, as a higher mark for a higher pain.

He shook the vial in his hand. A single seed had not dropped into his father's un-breathing mouth. This might come in handy.

'*If you have tears, prepare to shed them now.*'

*　　*　　*

Riley Cardle, sharing a room with Carmen Walker at the Bryce Canyon Motel in Utah, was contacted by *Good Morning America*. The broadcast hoped to record a small 'Americana' type piece for their program. Cardle agreed, and a time was scheduled when she could get to a dependable internet connection to do the show.

*   *   *

Abel woke early. Yesterday had been hard and the night unrestful. The girls must have still been sleeping, and for that he was grateful. Emma was not in the bed; he heard her, downstairs, brewing her morning coffee, chatting quietly with her mother.

He was too tired to open his laptop, opting to instead exercise his seedy-charged mind for answers, though even it seemed to be overwhelmed with the stark realities unfolding. He wanted a nereBegat status report.

Three creatures, they knew, were dead: the banedagger, snapper manta and upjaw-dropjaw. He pitied that last thing, also, just from the description. Better off dead, though, than running around these parts. The black rose was accounted for and soon to be radiating in their Gamma Way basement. How serendipitous. Good reminder – will have to keep the cats from thinking it's their new litter box. We'll be brewing our own little feline nereBegats if that happens: a set of their very own *nereBcats*.

That still left nine, loose in the world. Maybe long gone from Frick Park already. He rolled over and looked for a bit more sleep.

*   *   *

Miller, half-awake, had risen before her sisters. A dream faded, of her Dad asking for a something. Asking, and fading.

She found herself in front of the used laptop their father had procured for them to *'banshee their thoughts into fiat being.'* Her hands clicked over the keypad, her eyes she could hardly keep open.

Last night was an ugly, heart-rending blur, and sleep had been a balm. She'd get this done, only partially conscious, then go back to full unconsciousness.

311

fiat lux six point five –
Banshee Patrol – nereBegat status update

LEOPARD PILLBOX SLUG
deceased
KLATCH
deceased
BATBIRD
deceased
GIANT CLOUD TARDIGRADE
at large
BANEDAGGER
deceased
FRUIT OF LIFE
location unknown
WEASELMANDER
at large
SNAPPER MANTA
deceased
UPJAW-DROPJAW
deceased
BLACK ROSE
contained
WHEELBONE
location unknown
SILVERMARE
deceased
NERE-X
at large or unspawned

Yawn.

She looked at the screen.

Seems Ok. *Thank you, mister Lux, upstairs, or wherever you are stationed.*

She underlined the five unaccounted-for nereBegats. One was a 'harmless' plant (the fruit of life); one stationary – though exceptionally perilous, should it set its biology to work (the wheelbone); another seemed harmless, though needed to be contained before its rabbit-like fertility was set loose (the weaselmander). That left two that seemed most urgent to find and conclude: the giant cloud tardigrade and the nere-X. The nere-X haunted her: it was *boneseed thirteenth* and in the *fiats* hinted to be some sort of powerful guardian, even if late to the proceedings. Perhaps it had been gifted with a human-like mind, that could plot and weave its way out of the new Eden and settle the nereBegats permanently in the present.

Miller yawned again and went back to her bed. It was just after dawn, the air still, and autumn's leaves ceding into their browns, oranges, and reds. As if the brief *fiat* session had all arrived inside a dream, she was soon asleep.

*   *   *

His father had perished before his eyes. But Razor had not contacted the police. His energies would be spent on a singular quest. He pondered ways to strike. The police, the same officers, Johnson and Marshall, had come to his door that morning with the news. Each carried his cap in his hand, and each expressed sympathy. Razor feigned proper shock. Then the questions: *What were his father's movements of the prior day? Why had he gone to the park? Was he with anyone? Did you go?* Their presence agitated Razor; he told them his dad had gone out for a night time stroll, alone, as he often did. Razor referred their queries to his mother. They apologized again, said they understood, and would come back another time. They supplied Razor with support phone numbers and let him know a case worker would be in touch soon. They raised their caps to their chests, in a token of respect, and left.

Razor closed the door and lay down on the floor in the middle of the living room rug. He stared at the light fixture above, commanding it to shatter, in homage to his father's utterly realized soul.

*   *   *

News of the death of Gideon Moss spread through the community. He had apparently been bitten by a snake in Frick Park, and perished from loss of blood. No one could think what species of dangerous snake it might have been. The park had none that were venomous and none that were more than medium-sized. The high school delayed the return of all students for a week. A Mass was said in Gideon's memory. Another would be said when the students returned. There was no mention of the odd late night excursion that set the tragedy in motion.

Sr. Ignatius prayed the rosary for this curious man. She grasped that his story had corridors few had reached. She had made an effort. What part he had played in the Square Miracles, she chose not to pursue. *Amen,* dear Gideon Moss.

*   *   *

Cardle's taped television appearance catapulted the Green-Moss-Nature Center story to a national audience. But it came off as mostly quaint. With a regular diet of international conflicts, celebrity break-ups, political messes and sports incidentals to choose from, the public had twenty-four hour access to a buffet they consumed as their ever shortened attention spans dictated. The far-fetched story of a Pittsburgh Nature Center being metaphysically combusted, with a dollop of fanciful child-prodigy mania as a chaser, simply didn't catch the wave of buzz it needed to go anywhere but away. An appearance on *Oprah* was floated, then cancelled.

*   *   *

But Tuck's star was shining. On selected evenings, he and Father Jack met outside the golf clubhouse, and discussed more of the Eden story. Jack had hurdled some levee and was not going back. Tuck rode a standing wave and was not jumping off.

*   *   *

Gideon Moss's Funeral Mass was to be held at St. Anselm Church the following week. Lars planned to attend. Father Jack was giving the sermon, and his were pretty good, for a priest. (Though, Lar's mom informed him, for some reason Father Jack was not permitted to officiate the Mass. Weird, as with everything else these strange days.)

*   *   *

It was a quiet afternoon. Abel and Emma sat together, rocking gently on the porch swing, her head on his shoulder, both drifting in and out of soft dreams. Through the screened window, coming from somewhere in the house, Abel heard the tune, recognized it and the words.

'*The legend lives on from the Chippewa on down…*'

It was the girls. Dragon singing. He realized her voice had moved down a register.

'*Does anyone know where the love of God goes, when the days turns to minutes, to hours…*'

Emma stirred, and pulled Abel closer. 'Maybe that's how they grieve,' she said.

*   *   *

Away from the thickets and woods, the giant cloud tardigrade found itself up near a wide field. It was morning, indeed, the first mornings ever for the creature, still feeling its way around this new universe. Its toxic excretion cloud had eliminated some irritating wasps that must have found it interesting as a potential food source. Or perhaps they were drawn to the slightly sweet odor of its poison gas. A few mammals had also collapsed in its gaseous wake, though the tardigrade itself only wished for greens to eat, and a modicum of peace.

It waddled through a gap into a fenced area where grass grew in abundance, though it was pockmarked by mud divots. Almost like a cow, it chose a spot to graze, then settled itself in a corner.

It was suddenly awake, a new sound filling many of its audio receptors. And just as suddenly, a flotilla of beasts, nosing at it, pawing at it, threatening it. It released an excretion, and the dogs fell away, gasping, panting, dying.

315

Worried owners raced to see what was causing the commotion. Most had to turn away, the acrid sting of gas reaching their lungs. There was much yelling, some screaming, and loud barking. The tardigrade tried to move away, its reservoir of defense used up. It felt the bite of jaws, and another bite, and then nothing.

The dog, Jasper, a bull terrier, knew the strange creature was dead, and hurried away, back to its owner, and safety. A few of the other dogs, small and large, raced in to finish the kill. The last of the toxic cloud rose up into the winds and drifted into nothingness.

*　　*　　*

Etta Zenovick, Emma's mother, left Gamma Way and returned to Lancaster. She'd been a tremendous help and made certain her daughter knew she was on call if they wanted her back. The house seemed emptier in her absence, but both Emma and Abel were grateful they'd once again have their home to themselves, along with three girls who just so happened to be born in February and were teenagers on the brink of womanhood. Just your plain old All-American white-picket-fence situation, thought Emma. Yeah, *right.*

*

The Green sisters spent Monday morning in the basement, constructing radioactive containment and a soil carrier for the black rose. Emma spent some time trying to find a science facility that could take advantage of its possible energy benefits. There was also the vaccine in the banedagger. She called the Charity Motherhouse and asked for Roaringman. He had departed.

'May I speak with Sister Jill, then?'

'Yes. Hold please.'

Someone somewhere would be interested in this miraculous menagerie of unrecognizable biology. She was past worrying whether the world would care, even. As long as the thread didn't connect these beings to her daughters, her family.

'Hello. This is Sister Jill.'

'Sister, hello. It's Emma. How are you?'

'I'm fine, thank you. And you?'

'We're Ok. It's been slightly wild. No – completely wild.'

'Hmmm,' said Sister.

'Well, you know more than most so I'll leave it at that.'

'I don't know as much as you might think. How can I help?'

'I'm hoping to locate your brother. We have some science opportunities. I know biology is not his field but I thought he might be a good person to introduce the, ahh, the research opportunities, without the whole back story having to be told.'

'He may. Can I have him call you?'

'Yes. Please. Let him know this won't be a pitch, please, to pull him back into the Square orbit. I'm hoping he'll know some academics who might fit a certain – personality type – for the job.'

'Personality type?' asked Sr. Jill.

'Well. I'm not going to kid you, Sister. I'm hoping this can happen without the *Eden* angle writ too large,' said Emma.

'Probably wise. I suppose some good might come of this research?'

'Much good. And down the Emmaus Road, there may be some angel dust for your efforts and the wonderful help you've all provided.'

'Angel dust. I'll see what Grey Cloud thinks.'

'Thank you.'

'Goodbye.'

The Emmaus Road… Emma recalled a talk about it at the Motherhouse. She now walked this road, and as yet had not had the company there she sought. Her blindfold remained, even as her gifted children, her very own flesh and blood, danced in the light.

*　　*　　*

Razor Moss had no plan. No ideas. No future. No connection to his past. He felt like a wild card in a deck of all black. No hearts here. In a place of normalcy, in that foggy past where he was Ray, he would have had himself admitted and sedated, at least for a while. But his father's death required some sort of karmatic reckoning.

For all his father's long, trenched, narrow, existence – at least the part Razor had shared – Gideon had never flagged in trying to come up for air. Razor could see that more distinctly now. A lot of his father's failings now seemed so petty. Things even God wouldn't bother to bother about. Gideon had wanted nothing but a chance, and the derealization, wrapped so early around his youthful soul, had forfeited that baseline. A baseline already hard enough to survive if you were a so-called *normal* human.

But what to do. What to do. He stared at the last seed in the vial. What to do.

*   *   *

'We should get back into the park. Soon,' said Boyd.

Emma and Abel were sharing dinner with their kids. Her stomach feeling less than hardy, Emma opted for a warm bowl of cooked oats. The others had a corn and rice soup. The table was subdued.

It was the end of the holiday weekend, a Monday. Emma should go back to work tomorrow. Because the students' return to the high school was delayed a week by the death of Gideon Moss, she'd have some extra time to prep. She needed to reconfigure her head, to once again teach teenagers who were there to learn the hard science of biology. St. Anselm's faculty were asked to seed their instruction with Catholic theology. She wasn't sure she could manage it.

Seeded, by the *seedy*. So that's where she was, even more unsettled now than prior to last October 1st, when she and Abel had taken a small bite out of eternity. Was anything proven as far as God's existence? Was there a bearded old man, or beautiful young goddess, sitting enthroned above watching over the minutiae of every quantum occurrence? Why was it such a hard sell for Emma, having been graced with a direct feed from the other side, from *upstairs* – as the girls had begun to label it – from the *official* Heaven of heavens. The real one, where you ended up as long as mortal sin didn't stain your innards.

She rested her head on her hand, and looked at her daughters, and at her husband. It was all miraculous. Before this all started, it was all already miraculous. Maybe that was why she couldn't reach some higher ledge. Perhaps she was already there. Had *always* been already there.

'Yes, you should go down tomorrow,' said Abel. 'Early. Come home for dinner than head back out, if you have the energy. Night should allow that green glow to work in your favor. What's the ledger, now, on the nereBegats?'

Emma took a spoonful of oats and tried to concentrate on what she might do for a syllabus, for her classes, next week.

'The cloud tardigrade is gone, sadly,' said Boyd. 'We lost so many before they had any chance.'

'It is sad,' said Miller. 'None of these things asked for this. Someone has some explaining to do.' She pointed at the ceiling. 'Up there.'

'Boneseed sixth is the fruit of life plant,' said Dragon. 'It's not a risk, but would be a wonderful thing to bring under our care. Seventh is the weaselmander, also fairly docile and harmless til it starts reproducing. Would be good to contain that. The black rose is in our box downstairs. We think it'll survive. Mom's looking into people that can see if it might be a source for low-risk nuclear power. Right, Ma?'

Emma looked up from her bowl and nodded, her mouth full.

'The wheelbone is a bit of a worry,' said Boyd. 'Theoretically, it's an engine of creation in itself. Wacked things could be generated and scurry off. Potentially disastrous. We have to find it soon.'

'You sure we shouldn't head out today, Dad?' said Miller.

'I'm just worried you are too beat from the Moss episode,' he said. He paused for a moment.

'You guys did a great *Edmund Fitzgerald* this afternoon.'

Miller, Boyd and Dragon all presented faces on the verge of something. Emma at first thought sorrow; but it was not quite that. It was more of an assured expression that understanding would come. It almost felt directed at her, though their eyes did not stray to her.

'Thanks, Dad,' said Boyd. 'Dragon could make a living imitating animals, birds, and rock stars. You should hear her Dylan.'

Abel broke into a quiet grin. Emma poured more milk on her oats. Her mouth felt dry.

'There's still *boneseed thirteenth*,' said Miller. 'That spooky number. I'm wondering if it's a feint. We know the *fiat* material didn't always arrive in logical fashion. Maybe Thirteenth is not happening, or never made the final cut. We'll look, but I don't have a sense of finding, for what it's worth.'

'Well, take today to regroup, rest, and consider,' said Abel. 'Believe it or not, I have to go into work tomorrow. My bosses have been exceptionally generous, Roman especially. But I do have a job and the grace period the university gave me is getting *extremely* frayed. Regardless of the three little angels floating around in my kitchen.'

He winked at them. 'You guys are still into eating and all that, right?'

They all laughed, quietly, except Emma, who smiled politely.

*   *   *

'Tis one thing to be tempted, another thing to fall.'

Despite his uncanny, wavering, apple-boosted senses, Razor had no way to locate any of the nereBegat creations. If he were to make any difference in this theater, he needed to find and follow the Green sisters, when they once again entered Frick Park. Camping out below their house, hiding down the slope, seemed the only solution. Unless. Unless. Unless he boldly offered to join their mission, praying they'd believe his intentions.

They might; except *he* didn't know his intentions.

He decided to pursue that course. A small olive branch would be identifying where the original Eden tree had been replanted by him and his father. He'd suggest the sisters come and see if its location, where it resided, this dormant, unearthly power, was within their unfallen natures to bless. He would go to their house this evening.

*   *   *

The weaselmander seemed to emanate joy. Like an otter it was, sliding down the rocks and scurrying back up for another ride, wholly satisfied by this experience of existence. It would not be long before it could self-perpetuate, and share the pleasure of being alive with offspring. It rolled onto its back and kicked its paws in the air.

Twenty Four

Monday evening felt portentous, the air disturbed. The Green sisters were agitated, Abel could tell. They usually emanated a form of calm that reached others in their proximity. Now, they sat quietly on the floor, each with a book, but not appearing to read. He'd just finished a look at the *Banshee Patrol* document; it had entries from each family member except for Emma. Or, to put it correctly, entries were 'attributable' to members. He shook his head, remembering the first, from many months ago, and shook his head again recalling the last, which he'd just seen.

fiat lux seven

Boneseed thirteenth will be the first. The last, first. Boneseed thirteenth will watch over its charges, and bring them to fullness. Boeseed Thirteeh is made in the image nd likeness. Boneseed thirteenth must not bbe hinegegzed onese ad thrihth een ehfoy sjoue rksdjkjk

Like some of the earlier *fiats,* it was broken. But this was the worst he'd ever seen. When this 'feed' from the other side was defective, a house of cards analogy triggered in his mind. For all they'd experienced, no saint had come marching in; no beam of angelic light had burned certainty into his soul; no one had turned water in wine. His Belief was secure. When the *fiat* stumbled, it was the great *Eden-Apple-Seedy* story that seeped instability, even with his miracle daughters sitting before him in the same room.

There was a knock on the front door. Kind of late for visitors; a work day and school day pending for many in the morning. Who could it be? Emma opened it. On the porch stood a brooding boy-becoming-man, a strange, awkward smile on his drawn face.

'Ray Moss,' said Emma. 'Razor.'

'Emma,' he said. 'Ms. Green.'

Emma looked over her shoulder at Abel, then motioned Razor inside.

'It's late. Come in, sit down,' said Abel.

Razor removed his long trench coat, slung it over the back of the couch, and sat. The two cats wandered over to rub their heads against his ankles. Razor leaned down to pet them.

'Would you like something hot?' asked Abel. Razor shook his head.

'Sorry about the late hour,' he said, without looking up. He lifted one of the cats to his lap. The other cat jumped up behind him. 'I just wanted some company. You knew my father.' He looked at Emma, then the girls.

'We're so sorry,' said Miller, Boyd and Dragon simultaneously.

'Yes, Ray,' said Emma. 'Razor – we're so sorry and the way he died is tragic. You have company, at your house? Relatives?'

'The police have been over,' he said. 'My mother was not close to my father, for many years. I'm pretty much by myself.'

'*Ohh,* Razor. Were you thinking of coming back to school, after this extra week off? Maybe it would be a way to take your mind off things,' said Emma.

'Considering it,' he said.

'Why don't you come with us tomorrow, Razor?' said Dragon. 'We're going back to Frick to try to find the last of the nereBegats.'

Abel sat down on the floor beside Emma, listening. It felt as if he and his wife were receding from any part of the last act, and could only witness it.

'Yes. You have had some apple, right?' asked Boyd.

'I've had two doses. It's electric.'

'We don't know,' said Miller.

'But you're unfallen,' said Razor.

'Yes. Unfallen. No Original Sin. Extra stuff, fairly comprehensive, from the apple, through our parents. Yours would be direct.'

'It did something to my father. And me,' said Razor. 'Guess you knew that.' He paused for a moment to place the cat on the floor. 'Dad was diagnosed as having derealization. Have you heard of it?'

'Yes. A terrible affliction, from what we've read,' said Boyd.

'Yes,' said Miller. 'Mix that with a bite of apple and it's understandable your dad would have suffered hard places.'

'He did,' said Razor. 'I will come with you. What time tomorrow?'

'Meet us at Falls Ravine, at the trail head at 9:00.' said Dragon.

'I can show you where my Dad and I replanted the tree.'

'That'd be great. Thanks, Razor,' said Boyd.

Everyone stood to see him out the door. He left, a silent figure, the night closing around him. Abel closed the door.

'Poor kid,' whispered Emma.

They stood as a family, together in the living room, Abel's arm around Emma's shoulder. 'Good luck, ladies,' said Abel. 'May the Lord be with you. Tomorrow, especially.'

*　　*　　*

Boneseed thirteenth had received, like all the others, the chemical prompt from the Nature Center's green fire. Its composition and cerebral capacities were the most complex of the long-buried nereBegats. Its instincts and bearing would have enabled it to rise up, nurture, protect, and usher the remaining Twelve forward into uninterrupted existence; positioning these creations to thrive and take their places in the pantheon of time and space. But something had failed it, something had weakened it, and something ultimately prevented its gestation and birth.

Beneath the soil of Frick Park it would now forever lie, a black husk of decay, a withered compound of unknown chemistry and biology. The foundational key to bolstering the nereBegats that had been raised, *Thirteenth* had fallen.

*   *   *

Tuesday morning arrived. Miller, Boyd, and Dragon, refreshed and enlivened by their long sleeps, were mobilizing on the back porch. Boyd again carried the X-Tector, and Miller her glass rod. They all shouldered small packs. Emma and Abel watched them over hot cups of coffee. Emma ran her hand through the wisps of steams rising from the cups.

'It's almost a year since this all started,' she said.

'Yes. Your birthday. And *thirty*, it appears, is waiting only three weeks away.'

'At least you remembered,' said Emma.

'October 1st. Not likely to ever forget your birthday, dear.' He smiled and pulled the hair back from her face. 'We should do something special.'

Emma looked across at him. She knew there was a certain emptiness in her glance. She wrinkled her lips and smiled back. 'Thirty years old. Absurd.'

Abel took a sip of his coffee. 'Should we do anything about the Tree, do you think? Now that we know it's been replanted?'

'No,' said Emma. 'Let someone else take the next bite.'

The girls walked to the porch for inspection.

'Ok, Dad, Mom. We're going to try to wrap this up this trip.'

'Good, because I'm going to work. The world doesn't stop just because you three are saving us from some unprecedented, infinitely-important mission to save the Universe.'

'Ha hah, Dad,' said Miller. 'We'll check in by phone if there's a major incident. Not stopping back for dinner, though.'

'Yeah, we packed plenty of food,' said Boyd, whacking at her pack.

'Keep half an eye on Razor, please,' said Emma. 'I can't really read him.'

'He'll be Ok,' said Dragon. 'There's three of us and one of him. And the poor kid's been through the wringer. It'll be good for him to amble around with us. We're sympathetic ears, if ever there were any.'

'Six ears, in total,' said Boyd. 'Six times the usual empathy.'

'Get out of here, you delinquents,' harped Abel. 'And don't come in all muddy when you get back. Take your boots off.'

'Yes,' said Emma. 'Please be careful.'

The three Green sisters headed out, over the hill and down into the park.

*   *   *

Razor paced in the soft grass, still wet with morning dew. He saw the sisters approaching. He slid his hand inside his jacket pocket, running fingers over the pair of garden shears he'd brought along. *We are such stuff as dreams are made of…* In all his remembrances of Shakespeare, this line had boiled to the top. He hated it. As if nothing had any concrete reality. As if nothing had substance. As if his actions held no resonance, no meaning.

There were the sisters, looking more and more like young teens, fourteen or fifteen, and not overgrown, impossible children. Dragon, especially, moved with a more feminine carriage. *There is no darkness but ignorance. Sweet mercy is nobility's true badge. So foul and fair a day I have not seen.* The lines were running together. He'd just have to wait and see. If nothing else was left, it was good theater, and the stage set.

*

'Razor, good morning,' said Dragon.

'Hello. Grass is wet,' said Razor.

'We have good boots. Mom bought them,' said Miller. 'How are you?'

'I'm Ok. I appreciate your trust. I'm not unwell. I'm not *well,* either.'

'We're heading up past the Nature Center area first,' said Boyd. 'Kind of been neglected in our park roaming.'

'The new center is looking spiffy,' said Miller.

'You're expecting we'll find nereBegats up that way,' said Razor.

Boyd lifted the X-Tector and switched it on. It pulsed quietly. 'Not sure, but if we start up there, we can do a wide circle over toward Clayton, then under the Forbes Bridge, and go up towards Reynolds St. and Point Breeze. We could shoot over to the East End Food Co-op for lunch, if you're cool with that. Our dad's friend, Big Fuzz, works there.'

'Unless we're lugging around some metaphysical beastie,' said Dragon, smiling.

They trekked up Falls Ravine, and, as they approached the Nature Center construction site, the X-Tector's pulses grew louder and more urgent. There were machines, orange tape, and plenty of noise.

'Easier after dark, when we get the green glow,' said Miller. 'I wonder if the construction work has moved or damaged a nereBegat. It's got to be in this vicinity.' She tapped the glass rod at the edges of the scattered dirt.

They searched to no avail. It seemed best to return after the workers had left for the evening, when they might sift through the muddied clearing and piles of wood, piping and stone.

'Let's get back here after dark,' said Boyd. They continued on towards North Clayton trail, which overlooked Forbes Avenue, a busy 4-lane commuter route into Squirrel Hill. They reached trail's end and took a short cut underneath the bridge. Working their way down the slope, they reached the Tranquil trail. On a school and workday Tuesday the trail was largely empty. The valley narrowed. The X-Tector showed signs of a signal, up the slope towards their right. Via the Kensington and Solstice Trails, they clambered up onto Cowboy Hill. The houses of Point Breeze began to show behind the trees.

'Pretty good signal here,' said Boyd.

Razor had stayed behind the sisters, but came forward, gesturing. 'I see it.' He pointed up into a tree. A chestnut-brown animal peered at them, a mischievous smile poking through behind its whiskers. It raced to another branch.

'Good eyes, Razor,' said Boyd. 'It's our weaselmander.'

'Appled. That's the thing,' he answered. They moved to the tree's trunk. Boyd began to whistle, til Dragon stayed her with a gesture.

'Let me,' she said. She trilled a call; the weaselmander's soft ears perked. It tilted its head on its neck, and scurried down the trunk. Razor reached down to pet it, to the accompaniment of a loud purr. The nereBegat rolled on its back, and batted at Razor's hand.

'It's beautiful,' said Boyd. 'We'll need to bag it.'

Razor turned with a grimace. 'Why?' The weaselmander jumped away, then nestled itself against Boyd's ankle. She shut off the pulsing X-Tector.

'It's very fecund,' said Dragon. 'Very very fecund. Think of rabbits, and then rabbits squared. This first one will self-gestate, probably soon. We need to sterilize it, or it and its self-replicating progeny will soon be eating up gardens, fruit stands, grocery stores, and farms. I'm exaggerating, but not by much.'

'I can't be part of this' said Razor. 'Why should we be the judges here. Let the thing live!'

'We can't,' said Miller. 'I mean, it'll live. But just it, just this one.' Miller picked the weaselmander up and fed it a small pellet from her bag. It slumped into a contented ball of sleeping fur.

'I can't believe this!' said Razor. 'You're disrupting things you can't comprehend. Things set in motion by entities outside our understanding. My dad would have assisted this beast, not operated on it, drugged it…'

He fidgeted with something in his pocket. 'I won't be part of your expedition. I wish you – all three of you – the worst possible fate. *Damn your eyes!'* He turned and hurried away, back into the deeps of the park.

The sisters watched, their breath held, in sorrow and some surprise.

'I'll walk this fellow – or this lady – back to Gamma,' said Miller. 'Meet you back where Biddle meets Tranquil. If you guys go to the Co-op, get me a sandwich or something.' She walked away.

'Razor's a rogue in the mix,' said Dragon. 'I feel bad for him. He's like, half and half. A bit like Lars but skewed, probably like his dad, in a way where the light and dark won't resolve without torment. I don't think he's inclined to evil, anyway.'

'I know,' said Boyd. 'He's twice had pieces of the Eden apple. Maybe seeds from it. A bit scary. He'll need support to come out of this. I don't think we're the ones to supply it. In fact, I believe he may have cast an eye on you, sister, in that particular *way*.'

'In that way?'

'Don't pretend. We're too over-knowing to start building false fronts,' said Boyd. 'Maybe this is because for the first time, we're not a trinity? Miller's away. Do you think?'

'Don't know. I'm not drawn to Razor, anyway. Just so you know. The stirring of puberty will probably rocket past us in a few weeks. Though right now wouldn't be so timely.'

'It would not,' said Boyd.

*   *   *

Miller brought the weaselmander home and into their house, where it awoke. Seren and Dippity were hospitable, slightly amused and a jot baffled. The nereBegat made itself at home.

'I'm heading back out. Fruit of life, wheelbone and nere-X. All we have to find,' said Miller.

Emma stopped her at the door. 'My mother's intuition is telling me not to worry. Logic is telling me all of you are in danger. So please – *be careful.*'

Miller looked at her, unable or unwilling to smile, and left the house.

*   *   *

The sky clouded over and rain was threatening. Razor had folded himself, as tightly as possible, into a small opening under a large fallen oak tree. He'd drawn blood on his fingertip from fondling the shears. He would wait here, until the sisters returned to the Nature Center, in the darkness, when the green glow of the nereBegat would reveal it. The sisters were too trusting, and too naive, to know their place. His father was crying out for retribution. His was the only sentience left which might provide it.

* * *

Miller had brought raincoats back for her sisters. It was spitting small beads which stung in an unusual way, harsh, for just a shower. Then the clouds opened and it poured. The Green sisters waited under a shelter in Fern Hollow. Though it was afternoon, it began to feel as though evening had arrived early. The rain finally slowed and they moved off up the Falls Ravine trail, towards the Nature Center build. The construction teams had left, the deluge shortening their afternoon. Boyd started up the X-Tector and its pulsing erupted: the nereBegat was at hand. A rocky prominence not far from the Nature Center site, where old timbers from the fire had been tossed, drew them. There was the glow, faint but present, in the afternoon's rainy gloom.

Boyd tucked away the X-Tector. The sisters bent over a tumble of rocks and began to lift each one, the glow brightening as they did. Then they saw it. A round, silver-grey, tubed ring, the size of a small plate, with a hole through its middle. Boyd lifted it and ran her finger around the inside hole. 'It's a perfect circle.'

'Is it a metal?' said Dragon.

'It's a bone,' she answered, in a low whisper.

'Why you whispering?' asked Miller.

'This is the one that brings new life. New kinds of life. The *wheelbone.*'

Boyd handed it to Dragon. They stared, and perhaps for the first time, the sisters joined the community of humanity in regarding the working miracle of existence itself. Boyd's eyes began to well up. Miller wrapped an arm around her younger sister's shoulders.

Whatever else became of them and their journey, after the bloom of the Square Miracles had moved far into the past, and been forgotten in the deeps of time, the sisters would have this moment in common, to share in remembering. The miracle that was the wheelbone seemed to authentic everything they felt, not just what the knew. A grace, a blessing, a now, and an end, all in one.

Dragon pulled her long hair back over her head – and suddenly felt pain, her hand gripped and pierced, as Razor Moss wrenched the wheelbone away from her.

'This is not yours to decide,' bellowed Razor, his forehead beaded in sweat, his dark eyes flush with anger. With one hand, he held the wheelbone out, the trophy he'd bagged. With the other, he brandished the garden shears.

'Razor…,' said Dragon, clutching her wounded hand, '…it's not meant for this world.'

'I'll decide that,' he said. 'You won't be part of its future.'

'We can't let you take it,' said Boyd. She reached out to take the wheelbone and Razor swung, striking her arm with it. Boyd tripped backwards, holding her forearm, grimacing. 'You hurt me.'

Razor held the wheelbone up to his face, looking with one crazed eye through the opening in its center. 'You analyze and you pontificate and you relish and you reside in your little haloed castle. While the rest of us – the *fallen* – crawl along in your wake. No more*!*'

He took out the vial, opened it, and swallowed the last apple seed.

'That's the third of your Eden magic I've had. And the tree, I won't say where it's planted, not to children who live inside their bubble of godliness and power. No! It will grow for the rest of us, for the –' He staggered back, fell, then raised himself.

'That seed – it's gotten hold of him,' said Miller. 'We need to take the wheelbone, now, sisters.'

She drew herself up in front of Razor, who sneered, and gathered himself to his full height, raising the shears over Miller.

'Razor,' said Miller. 'We'll call it *Gideon's Wheel,* in your father's honor. Please give it to me.'

Razor laughed, his eyes seemed to flicker green, he brought the shears down upon Miller, who blocked them with her glass rod, which shattered. Razor screamed, a scream of power, and pain. He turned, and like an athlete at the peak of his powers, charged off into the woods.

The sisters rose to give chase, Miller only pausing to gather her glass rod's broken shaft. The rain blitzed down again, the skies flashed a sickly yellow, and great booms echoed round.

'Can we catch him?' gasped Boyd as they leapt over a fallen trunk. 'He's like a cheetah. *That seed!'*

Dragon and Miller didn't respond: Razor was pulling away from them, the steam from the downpour and the dimness under the eaves assisting him. He careered out of their sight, racing away, down the trail towards the rain-drenched hollow, which he reached and flared right. Strange, regal admonishments were bellowing from his lungs, merging with the clash of thunder and wrack of battering water. And there, at the last, another figure appeared, his hair green – was it glowing – and Razor was knocked off his feet. A scuffle in the wet grass. A blur of fists and jabs, and thrashing. The green-haired male fell, a gleaming blade brandished above, glinting with water and blood, then the male retreated, tripping over onto his knees, scrambling through the wet weeds, frantic to crawl away.

Razor stumbled off, feet fighting for balance, disappearing into the whiplash of his roiling, unimpeded madness.

Time was suspended.

Miller was close enough: she pulled her arm back, then sent a long remnant of her glass spear flying. With a crack, it ran through the middle of the wheelbone, knocking it away from Razor. He froze – gawking, confused, unsure – and fled.

'I am he!' he shouted.

A last fading cry and they heard him no more.

From the wet mist a silhouette resolved to solid: Lars Patton, holding the glass fragment in one hand and the wheelbone in the other. His cheek was bruised, his green hair brown with mud, and his clothes sopping. He looked up at Miller.

'Hey,' he said.

'Lars,' said Miller, taking the glass from his hand. 'You Ok?'

'He's *strong*. Garden shears, for Christ sakes,' said Lars.

Boyd and Dragon caught up to their sister, panting and heaving for air.

'Lars,' said Dragon, between breaths. 'Timely intervention.'

Lars placed the wheelbone and glass on the ground and shook the mud from his hands. 'Dixon asked me to see if I could find his pocket-watch. Must have fallen out when the manta shrieked, last week. Thought I'd do him a favor. He's been a buddy. Never thought I'd see crazy Razor.' Lars lifted the wheelbone. 'I take it this is one of the thingy-wingys?'

'*Boneseed eleventh*,' said Boyd. 'Wheelbone. Engineers new forms of life right out of the gate. Built-in baby Genesis machine, kind of.'

Lars blew out a breath, shook some water from his green forelock. 'God help us. *Or*, God – help us.'

'You want to watch over it?' said Dragon. 'We have two nereBegats cloistered up at our place already. Razor may come looking. He's just re-seeded his physiology from the original apple.' She exhaled and shook her head. 'I hope we can reach him, help him. Anyway, if the wheelbone is not at our house, that would be good.'

'God, that kid. What he's been through,' said Lars. 'Sure, I'll keep it for a bit. Just don't let him know I have it.' He held it up near his face. 'Any special instructions?'

'Keep it away from water and soil,' said Boyd.

'I'll tell Mom not to use it in the kitchen.' He pulled his sopping jacket hood over his green head. 'I'm getting soaked. I'm going to do a quick check for Dixon's watch then get the heck out of here. See you guys!' He loped off.

The girls looked at each other, tears welling in their eyes. It was enough.

'Ok,' said Boyd, sniffing. 'That was a bit of a mess. Now what?'

'We sure Lars can guard that thing?' asked Miller. She retrieved a bandage wrap from her pack, and handed it to Dragon, who wrapped a compress around her bloodied wrist.

'I'd rather it wasn't at our house right now,' said Dragon, wiping at her eyes. 'Razor's a loose cannon, an unhappy loose cannon. Let's go home and talk to Mom and Dad.'

'And re-bandage your hand,' said Miller. She picked up the fragments of her glass rod.

'Can your glass be mended?' asked Boyd.

'I don't know. Might have to get back to the glass house and make another,' said Miller.

They moved off, continuing up the park access road towards Regent Square, til the road was bisected by the Braddock trail. Just short of the edge of the woods, a slightly-brighter-than-it-should-be green reflected near the roots of a small growth. Boyd cranked up the X-Tector, to clear pulses.

'It's the *fruit of life,*' whispered Boyd.

'Hey, listen,' said Miller. 'Blackhawks.'

*   *   *

'That's a storm and a half. Hope the girls are Ok,' said Abel.

'I think I hear helicopters. Do you?' asked Emma.

Abel stepped out on the porch and looked up. Two Army Blackhawk helicopters soared over, chopping the air with power and spray in the deluge. They rotored off and he came back inside.

'Well, we'll trust that wasn't a mission to locate unfallens,' said Abel.

'Not funny,' said Emma.

They heard the back door open. The girls were there, taking off rain slickers and removing muddy boots.

'You're all Ok!' said Emma. 'Oh, your hand, *Caroline…*'

'We're Ok,' said Rebecca, Caroline, and Maggie.

TWENTY FIVE

'Last seed, too much…'

Razor lay flat-out in the middle of his living room. His head was spinning. Gideon's Wheel was in his hands. Now not in his hands, though he swore he'd taken it, carried it home.

Someone had phoned about the Funeral Mass for his Dad. He'd told them he couldn't come, he was in shock. They'd get back. He cried. He laughed and spat at the vial that had held the last seed. He threw it.

'The undiscovered country from whose bourn no traveler returns. The wheel has come full circle…'

He found his phone, and called the reporter, Riley Cardle, who he'd threatened. A cold voice prefaced after the phone was answered: *'This phone call may be recorded.'*

'Don't hang up – it's Razor Moss.'

'Your call is being taped,' said Cardle, rubbing her eyes, squinting at Carmen and making an 'R' in the air with her finger.

'I won't burn you. I want you to write, tell the world…'

'Mr. Moss, I'm going to have to hang up. You don't sound well. Get help,' said Cardle.

'The Green daughters are witches. They're the Anti-Christs. They're from Hell. They're aliens: they've grown up in half a year, from infants to teenagers.' His voice grew in frenzy and pitch. 'You have to write this, get it out in the papers, get it on TV, on the web. Get it out into the world for all to hear about and understand. This is not some joke. Not some fantasy, or crazy conspiracy theory, or mind game I'm playing you for. They're aberrations, they control bizarre biological experiments – they have no ethics, no souls, no guile, no brains…! Are you listening to me?'

'I'm recording you,' she said. 'Now I'm going to hang up. Sorry to hear about your father. Goodbye.'

'Bastard. Bitch. Shrew,' he said to the dial tone, then hung up. He stood to wipe the glaze from his face, stumbled and crawled to the bottom of the stairs, where the small vial lay. He picked it up and put the opening against his eye socket. 'It'll be fine."

'So foul a day – I *have* seen. *I have seen….*'

*   *   *

Tuck was given a new slot on the network, and an evening show that began to reach a national audience through syndication. He polished the story, every now and then getting a new morsel from Fr. Jack. In the long run, his *Square Miracle* sermon became mixed in with the larger spiritual themes he cared about, and he could and would reference it as a booster to his talks.

Father Jack left the Roman Catholic Church, and joined the Eastern Orthodox Church, where the stricter, more literal canons could offset his relatively new struggles with sticking to the rules. His name was not forwarded by Bishop Garner as a problematic member of the clergy, to 'keep an eye out for', and so his journey of faith continued. He began writing a book, tentatively titled *The Only Prayer.*

Lars Patton brought the Gideon Wheel home. His mother took a fancy to it, and asked if she might hang it over the kitchen sink, as a kind of totem over her cooking. The idea of it hanging over water had Lars a little nervous. He kept his eye on it.

In the next year, he was invited to an early admission to Carnegie Mellon University's School of Biological Sciences, referred by Emma Green. A full scholarship was given for his "unprecedented abilities in combining chemistry and biology across a diverse portfolio of research and experimentation". His high school courteously accommodated his early graduation from the facility.

Sister Melanie Ignatius was named Principal of St. Anselm Catholic High School. Later in the year, she organized the commemoration of a new section of the school library; the Gideon Moss Theology section. A photo of Gideon was hung on the wall above a selection of titles, including the writings of St. Anselm, the school's patron saint and a Father of the Church. Gideon's personal copy of the Gideon International Bible was featured, secured under locked glass.

Razor Moss was admitted to Western Psychiatric Hospital, a mental wellness facility located in Oakland, not far from the Carnegie Mellon University campus.

The weaselmander was neutered, and given as a pet to be cared for by the Poor Clares Colettines of the Monastery of Our Lady of Guadalupe, their Motherhouse located in Roswell New Mexico. The sisters were asked to keep a careful eye out for unexpected pregnancies as the weaselmander lived out its expected five-hundred-years-plus lifetime. The black rose and the body of the banedagger were forwarded to an undisclosed academic institution, where a specially-selected science team was able to research potential energy opportunities from the rose's radioactive photo-synthesis, and explore whether the banedagger's anti-venom could serve against established poisonous species. Grey Cloud Roaringman had arranged for this research, but was not directly involved.

TWENTY SIX

The three Green sisters felt their main task and earthly responsibilities were complete. They bid their parents goodbye, as their accelerated physical development meant they'd be surpassing their parents' age in a few short years, which they deemed an untenable scenario to have to endure, for both parties, on a daily face-to-face basis. They had no qualms about visits, nor about regular communications with Abel and Emma.

They were welcomed to the Poor Clares Motherhouse in Roswell. A separate out-building was constructed for their use as living quarters. The fruit of life shrub was transported to be kept under their protection. Because it prolonged standard human life expectancies, it was considered a kind of fruited 'fountain of youth', and all in the know rightly guessed it would be sought after by the rich, powerful, greedy, and even by regular folks just looking for a fair opportunity to access its semi-miraculous potency. Boyd calculated that if the sisters themselves partook of its fruit, their own sped-up physiologies would not be slowed, but not reach terminal conditions as rapidly. The sisters agreed, consumed the first crop, and replanted the shrub deep in the wilds of New Mexico. Very few know of its whereabouts.

From the first, the sisters enjoyed visits from friends and family. Sister Ignatius saw them every other year, and they had enjoyable evenings recalling the Square Miracles, using plain language to relate the most un-plain of happenings. Ignatius occasionally added African drums to some of the musical numbers during what the Green sisters had termed, *First Friday Tunedowns,* a monthly sing-and-play-along gathering for Roswell locals and Poor Clares who wished to join in. They were careful to let life come to them versus impelling a future that, as unfallen, might have had its own unsuspecting traps. These they did not find or come to know. It seemed they were truly blessed, they truly understood it, and they remained truly thankful.

*   *   *

Abel finished writing up *The Banshee Patrol,* thinking it might serve as a disguised fictional version of the events he and Emma had witnessed, beginning on the day of her 29th birthday, that fateful October One. But he could never come to terms with publishing it. (Extracts from his writing are included or paraphrased in this text, courtesy of the Green family.) Tuck Gonferally's extrapolations were an agreeable diversion for him and Emma when they remembered to tune in to his show. He seemed a truly good guy.

Abel's work at CMU remained enjoyable and fulfilling, his seedy-advantage never quite disappearing. His life with Emma transformed; yet the mystery of her and of their life together, sans the children (though, thankfully, still with Seren and Dippity) remained a glorious, curious, ongoing comfort. A blessing, he would call it, with certainty.

*   *   *

A severe storm struck the Pittsburgh area less than two years after the events of the *Square Miracles,* sending torrents of flash-flood waters down the Falls Ravine trail, tearing out stoneworks, uprooting trees, and causing mud slides. The hidden Eden Tree may have been destroyed in this deluge. It's also possible it was covered in fresh slips of soil and clay.

The location of the tree remains unknown.

*   *   *

On October 2nd of the year following the events of the Square Miracles, just past four in the afternoon, Emma received a phone call.

Her husband had been killed, hit by a Tesla when walking across Beechwood Boulevard on his was back from CMU. He had died instantly.

The children were sad, but not inconsolable. They would travel back for the funeral.

She, herself, was launched into another orbit of shock and unreality. The days and nights merged into one grey field. Mind wander. Body shrink. Eyes close. Feet hurt. Heart. Heart. *Heart.*

She poured herself a gin and tonic, and sat down at the laptop to prepare some photos for the funeral booklet. *As you do.* But her eyes strayed to their home; the walls, the windows, the stairs he'd come down singing off-key on the cold mornings, grabbing her for a nice hug, telling her a dumb, useless fact and suggesting a movie for after supper.

There it was.

fiat lux finale

Hey. They're only letting me do one of these. Even a word limit, if you believe that. Anyway, all good here. Super seedy. You feel super-seeded. Get it? Gideon's here also. He's Ok. I love you. See you someday. Don't hurry. But don't be late. A.

p.s. - You will NOT be bored.

Her husband. A pun. From heaven.

She took another gulp of gin.

God... *this is not really fair.*

She lowered herself to her knees and said her first prayer.

'Hell with it. *I'm in.*'

ACKNOWLEDGMENTS

My upbringing in Swisshelm Park and affection for my hometown nudged this book into reality. Frick Park, just down and over the hill, was a wooded, unruly playground for my cousin Paul and I, throughout our unruly years as youths. Later, when Louetta and I lived in Regent Square, the Park loomed even more significantly, for us and our children, Luke and Rebecca. It offered its seasonal beauty, its diverse natural features, its shade, streams and trails, birds and animals, fellow walkers and wonderful interludes.

Louetta passed away on September 13, 2004. Her death sprung the theological trapdoor of what had been a foundational faith. And her life succored the journey forward, an attendant proof of the fine souls that earth has begotten. The middle road was dark and light. Inside this story, you can find both, just as I have. And inside this life, while both claim their position, the light always prevails.

*   *   *

Special thanks to Ben Wecht, Sarah Johnson,
Rebecca Anne Grace, Raglan Inkspillers Writers' Collective,
Dyana Wells, Matt Kennedy, and Ken Gormley.

A very special thanks to Alison Annals.

And a very special message of love to my son,
Lukas Joseph Elegius
words end ~ hope lives

MATTHEW KAMBIC

Matt Kambic hails originally from Pittsburgh, Pennsylvania.
He currently resides in Raglan, New Zealand.

His portfolio includes writing, art direction, music,
illustration, design, theater, and film.
Matt is cofounder of Chalk Hill Publishing,
along with his spouse, Alison Annals.

OTHER CREATIVE WORKS
WITH MATT KAMBIC AS SOLE AUTHOR
OR CONTRIBUTOR

Everest Rising

Last Voyage of the S.S. Panglossian

The Sherpa & the Beekeeper ~ Summit on Everest

The Walking Stick's Story

The Weapon

Fuzzyweeks

House of Doom

Ultraviolet Blackbody Catastrophe

Sir Cluck Press

Seasons in the Heart

Wrecked Interstellar Saucer Project
W.I.S.P.

a small bite out of Eternity ~
THE SQUARE MIRACLES

Book design and production by
kambicreative & Chalk Hill Publishing

www.ingramcontent.com/pod-product-compliance
Lightning Source LLC
Chambersburg PA
CBHW051604100726
47898CB00001B/227